WANDERING STAR

Stella Drexler

An imprint of Diogenes Club Press

Worldly, Whimsical, and Weird Books

www.diogenesclubpress.com

Dallas, TX

DC Dreams, an imprint of Diogenes Club Press
8619 Reva St. Dallas, TX 74227
www.diogenesclubpress.com

ISBN: 9781622010288

Library of Congress Control Number: 2015942418

Prologue

He was hot. Like s*mokin' heartthrob movie star* hot. Like *it doesn't even matter if he's the offbeat drummer in the crappy band because he's in a band* hot. Like *is this an alternate universe; why do I hear the theme to the Twilight Zone playing in the background all of a sudden?* hot. Like *why is he talking to me; does he think I'm rich or does he just want me to do his biology homework?* hot.

She blinked and pinched the soft skin just below her elbow.

Yep. The real thing. He was there, all right. In the flesh. And he was smiling at her. "Hey."

"Hey."

"You come here a lot?" Like *it doesn't matter if you have the worst pick up lines in the world because they are working* hot.

"Uh, sort of. I guess. Sometimes. I go to the University."

"Oh, yeah? What's your major?" Like *as if I don't hear that everyday, but it doesn't even matter that you ask stupid, boring, clique questions* hot.

"Organic Chemistry."

He laughed. It was a low, smooth chuckle. Like black velvet. Like something sinful and sweet. She didn't know if he was laughing at her. She really didn't care. She was used to being laughed at. At least he was still there. He hadn't gotten up and walked away yet. She didn't try to fool herself. He would eventually. She wasn't the *attract the attention of the hottest guy in the Northern Hemisphere* type of girl. She was the *oh, I didn't notice you there. I've been in class with you for how many years?* type of girl.

"Huh. I wouldn't have pegged you as a chemistry kind of girl. I thought maybe you'd study ancient dead languages or something."

She wasn't sure if he was teasing her. If he was teasing her, it was a weird kind of teasing. "What is that supposed to mean?"

"You just seem like the kind of girl no one would miss." Okay...maybe a little *I'm going to smile and pretend that wasn't creepy* hot. He laughed. His dark eyes crinkled at the corners. They had some blue in them. Like midnight. "I'm sorry. I was only teasing you. I think it went a little awry."

"Yeah, it did." But his smile was so genuine she relaxed. He was like *tall, dark and handsome with amazing eyes and such a sly, knowing smile that her heart was palpitating just looking at him* hot.

"You want another drink?" He was drinking something amber colored and sharp smelling. He didn't look as though he'd had very many. His dark, almond shaped eyes were clear and intense.

She looked down at her half-empty beer. She sighed. "I have class in the morning."

"Then what are you doing here?" He smiled. Her heart skipped a beat.

"I just..." She just couldn't face another night in her dorm room while her roommate and her roommate's boyfriend made out and listened to rap music at full volume. She and her roommate did not get along. "I just wanted to get out for a while."

"And here you are. You might as well make the most of it." He waved the bartender over and ordered her another round. He winked. "I don't think you have to worry about class tomorrow."

"Why?"

"Maybe we'll run away together."

She laughed. "Run away together? Where to?"

"How about...New York? We could join a traveling stage show."

"I don't think I'm cut out for theatre."

"We could sell seashells in Cape Cod."

"You have very unreasonable expectations for this evening."

This amused him. His eyes twinkled. "You think so?"

"You haven't even asked my name. How do you know I will run away with you?"

"Names aren't important. You'll come with me. You won't be able to resist."

"Do you know something I don't?

He chuckled low in his throat and peered for a moment at a point somewhere over her shoulder. She wanted to turn around and look at whatever it was. She wanted to make sure it wasn't another girl, a girl who actually deserved his attention. Then he looked back at her. "I expect I know a lot of things you don't."

This was a little insulting. She lifted her chin. "You don't know. I could know all sorts of things you don't."

"I'm sure you know many things I don't. But the question is, which one of us knows the most important things?"

She wasn't sure how to take this. She took a sip of her beer and studied him. He was a strange guy. But he was here, and he was talking to her. She couldn't even remember the last time a guy talked to her about something other than classes. And they certainly didn't buy her drinks or look at her with glittering, beautiful dark eyes. For a moment, she felt powerfully as though he wanted to devour her, to take every part of her and pick it apart until there was nothing left he hadn't touched. Her pulse raced. Heat surged through her.

She suspected the answer to his question was, *you do. Of course you do.* But she didn't say anything. She held his gaze until she had to lower her eyes. Her hand shook a little as she lifted her glass to her lips.

"Finish your drink," he said in a low, growling sort of voice that made her insides turn to liquid fire and color spread across her cheeks. "I'd like to show you the stars."

"The--" She took a deep breath because her voice came out as a squeak. "The stars?" She tried to sound cool and nonchalant, as though she wasn't on slow burn and so enthralled with him that she could barely catch her breath.

He grinned slyly. She wasn't fooling him at all. He was probably used to women reacting to him like this. "Yes. The stars."

"I have seen them, you know."

He hopped off his stool and held out his hand. "Not like this."

She stared at his hand a moment. She didn't even know his name. She had class in the morning. He said strange things that caused her to heat and cool so quickly, she felt as though there was a storm inside her belly. There were dozens of reasons she shouldn't go with him.

None of them mattered at all because she wanted to more than she'd ever wanted anything else in her life. She felt as though she might simply die of regret if she didn't.

She stood and took his hand. "Okay."

He drove silently. She didn't ask where he was taking her. She didn't want to spoil the mood. She didn't want him to suddenly look at her and change his mind. She stared at his profile. It belonged on the pages of a magazine, not in a small, black sedan. Not beside a girl like her.

She recognized the landscape streaking past her window. They were speeding toward the campus. She wondered if he was a student. He hadn't said. He hadn't said anything at all, not even his name. She felt a small thrill race down her spine. The mystery made the anticipation that much more poignant. He probably knew that. He did, in fact, know many things she did not.

Was he taking her to his dorm? Was she finally going to...if she was, it wasn't how she imagined it, but it certainly wasn't going to be a disappointment. He probably wouldn't even tell her his name afterward. He certainly wouldn't ask for her phone number. There would be no rose petals or champagne or bubble baths or any cuddling afterward. That was okay. She'd settle for this.

He didn't take the turn toward the campus. Instead, he steered the car onto a winding back road that led through a thick, green canopy of trees. It was so dark his headlights barely penetrated the inky blackness. She could hardly see the turn he took into a small parking area. He must have been there before. He probably took girls there all the time. She felt a tiny frisson of fear. She tamped it down. She had gone with him. She couldn't back out now. She didn't want to back out.

He glanced at her. His face was deep in shadow. He looked distinctly sinister. Her heart thumped wildly. He didn't speak to her as he stepped out of the driver's side door. She opened the passenger door. He was there, waiting to offer his hand to help her out. She didn't need help out of the car, but she took his hand. It was slender and strong. His fingers closed around hers. He didn't release her as he closed her car door and led her silently into the trees.

"You can't see the stars from here," she remarked in a quiet voice. The words were difficult to utter. She couldn't catch her breath.

He chuckled, but he did not reply. He tugged her further into the copse of trees. She could barely see his outline a few steps ahead of her. She stumbled on the roots and scattered branches underfoot, but he walked as confidently as though he could see through the heavy darkness. He paused. She bumped into the back of him. He spun around and caught her shoulders. She gasped as she felt his breath on her face.

"Do I scare you?" His voice was like a purr.

"A—a little," she admitted, and then she felt like an idiot. "I mean—no. I—I'm safe with you, aren't I?"

He didn't say anything for a moment. Then he chuckled again. His lips were so close to hers, she could smell the whiskey on his breath and feel the moist heat of his mouth. She wondered if he was going to kiss her. She wanted him to kiss her. She had never wanted anything as much she wanted him to kiss her. If he did, she felt she could die without any regrets, even if she never learned his name or saw him ever again. Even if the rest of her life was as mundane and disappointing as it had always been.

"Do you feel safe?"

"I—not safe, exactly."

"What do you feel?"

"I feel..." This was no time to be coy. "I feel excited."

He smiled. She could feel the movement against her lips. His arm slipped around her waist. He pulled her up against his long, lean chest. She could feel his flat muscles against her body. His other hand stroked so lightly across her cheek, it felt like a butterfly wing, like a whisper of breath. His fingers tangled into her hair.

"Do you want me to kiss you?"

His voice was like velvet, so seductive that heat surged through her entire body. He could probably feel it emanating from her. "Yes."

He didn't. Not right away. His hand flattened on her lower back. He pressed her closer to him as though he was afraid she would try to run away. She had no intention of running away. She wanted to lean forward, to press her mouth to his and break the unbearable anticipation. His hand tangled into her hair with a grip that warned her that he was completely in control. She would wait for him.

"Are you sure?"

Her voice shook. "I'm sure."

He smiled again, and then his mouth was on hers. His lips were soft and warm and full. She wasn't a good kisser. Well, she'd never kissed a boy, not for real, so she assumed she wasn't a good kisser. He was, though. His tongue dragged lazily across hers. An unfamiliar ache pulsed though her entire body. She couldn't catch her breath. He might have been drawing it out of her and into him. She was lightheaded and weak in the knees. If he hadn't been holding her up, she would have collapsed bonelessly to the forest floor. She didn't mind. As far as first kisses went, this one was epic.

She lifted her arms to wrap around his neck. He angled her head to deepen the kiss. Thoughts flickered through her mind and were gone so quickly they were like wisps of smoke on the wind. It seemed as though all the energy, the awareness of her body was rushing through her mouth and out into his. She reached up to stroke her hand down his cheek. He didn't change position, but she could feel his skin moving beneath her hands. Her eyes flew open. It was too dark to see his face.

Her body trembled. It wasn't with the thrill or excitement of his touch, of his kiss. The sense that her energy was rushing out of her intensified until she barely noticed the languid strokes of his tongue. He was sucking the breath out of her, sucking the life out of her. She pressed her palms to his shoulders and pushed, but he ignored her as though she were nothing more than a rag doll in his arms.

He wasn't kissing her anymore. It felt as though he was inhaling her. A sound like a whimper escaped her, but it was weak and breathless. She struggled against him. His grip was so strong and unbreakable he could have been made of stone. She beat on his arms with her fists. He shrugged them off.

She wanted to scream. She couldn't feel her legs or her arms anymore. She couldn't feel anything but the breathless fear and his mouth against hers. She could feel him devouring her, stealing the strength and energy from every sense and cell in her body. Her struggles grew feeble, and then she stopped struggling at all.

Suddenly, it felt as though she was floating, and there was no fear or pain. She would have sighed in gentle, unadulterated bliss but she had no body now, and she did not breath anymore. She forgot all about the boy in the forest, who staggered back in horror from the dried, shriveled body of the girl who had once been a plain, tiresome nobody that no one had ever really noticed and who nobody would even miss.

He dropped her on the forest floor and left her there, alone in the darkness. If he was lucky, it would be a while before they discovered the body.

They would remember her, though. After that night in the forest with the mysterious, handsome man with the dark, intense eyes and the face that shifted and swirled under her fingers, the first man who'd kissed her as though she was truly a woman, no one would ever forget her.

Her death would haunt them for a very long time.

Chapter One

A car horn honked outside. Aurora Geller jumped up from her seat at the small kitchen table. "That's Josie. I've got to go."

Her aunt Ruby waved a hand and sipped her coffee without even glancing up from her newspaper. "Have a nice day at school."

Aurora dumped the remnants of her eggs into the sink and slung her backpack over her shoulder. "See you later." She raced outside to the bright red Toyota idling in the driveway.

Josie Specter barely noticed Aurora as she slid into the passenger seat; she was peering at herself in the vanity mirror on the visor above her seat, straightening her chunky, overlong red bangs so they hung down into her thickly lined green eyes. She was dressed in a short, pleated black skirt, bright red sweater and striped, knee high socks today. She might have been headed to a seedy underground club where people did unspeakable things in dark corners with people whose names they didn't know, not the eleventh grade. Josie usually looked like that.

Aurora rolled her eyes. Josie snapped the visor back up. She grinned. "Happy Friday!"

"Yeah. Thanks." Aurora peered out the window in silence. It was a sunny day. The lawns and trees that sped past were turning green and lush with the onset of spring. Tiny, colorful flower buds blurred as Josie raced toward Diana Macy's house.

"Are you excited?"

Aurora wasn't excited. "It's just a party."

"What do you mean 'it's just a party?' It's going to be absolutely, positively the awesomest party of the entire year. There will be dancing and laughing and drinking and fun-having and mischief-making and Spin the Bottle for all."

"You know I don't drink. Anyway, it's bad enough dealing with our classmates when they're sober. How do you think it's going to be when they're drunk?"

"Oh, they aren't that bad."

"Can you imagine Sierra Drew in a tequila rage?"

Josie shuddered. "That does sound pretty horrible. But hardly a reason to miss out on potential Spin the Bottle kisses with Bryan Dymond."

"I don't want Spin the Bottle kisses from Bryan Dymond."

Josie laughed. "You might not, but there are other people in the world besides yourself. I am not letting you drag me down into your lack of enthusiasm."

"Okay, okay. When you put it that way..."

"You feel mighty guilty, don't you? We are going to this party, and we are going to enjoy ourselves."

"Just because you go doesn't mean I have to go."

Josie gave her a warning glare.

"Fine. I'll go. But if all hell breaks loose and the cops come, I am claiming no responsibility for your poor choices."

"No one in their right mind would blame you for my poor choices. I have proved myself quite capable of making my own bad decisions. Anyway, it's not going to get that crazy."

"Right. That's what you said about Greg Thompson's party at the cabin last year, and we all had to run into the woods in our bathing suits in the middle of winter to hide in the trees when his parents showed up unexpectedly for a romantic weekend getaway."

Josie laughed. "Yeah, that did turn out badly. But it won't be like that. Brayden's dad already knows about it. He's out of town with his new girlfriend or something."

"I doubt Brayden told him he was inviting the entire school and advertising it as the biggest rager of the year."

Josie waved her hand. "Oh, I suspect he won't mind too much. Bray says he's so wrapped up in his new girlfriend these days, he practically doesn't even remember he has a son. I also heard she's only about five years older than us. He met her at the University when he was giving a lecture."

"Gross. Sounds like a sleazy adult movie. Bray's dad's, like, fifty or something."

"Forty three. And he is kind of hot. For an older guy."

Aurora rolled her eyes. Josie steered toward the opulent Dinwiddie Hills neighborhood where Diana's parents and the other affluent families of the small, quiet town of New Coventry, Virginia lived in huge, colonial style houses nestled beneath a canopy of verdant green trees.

A wrought iron fence surrounded Diana's house. She was already waiting outside the large, white house with pale yellow latticework, leaning primly against the gate. Hers was one of the smaller houses in the neighborhood, but it was beautifully tended. The lawn was perfectly manicured with already thick, colorful flowerbeds and bushes shaped like perfect bulbs.

Diana was as well tended as her house. Her blonde hair was perfectly straight, cut into an old-fashioned bob. She didn't wear makeup, but she didn't need to. Her skin was clear and porcelain pale, and she had huge, dark eyes with thick lashes. Unlike Josie, she was a no-nonsense kind of girl. She was wearing jeans and a pale pink hoodie. She hadn't put any special effort into getting ready for the party that evening. She smiled at them with perfectly straight, gleaming white teeth as she opened the door and swung her backpack into the backseat ahead of her.

"Good morning."

"Happy Friday!" Josie repeated.

"Happy Friday to you." Diana was in high spirits. She leaned forward between Josie and Aurora's seats. "Are you looking forward to the party?"

Aurora groaned. "Not you, too."

"Aurora is not psyched about the party," Josie told Diana meaningfully.

"Are you afraid the Pops will drink too much and torment you?"

"Well, it did cross my mind. The last time we went to a party, Cami spent the whole time spreading rumors about how she caught me upstairs in Alec's parent's bedroom with Trent Hopper."

"Oh, no one believed her," Diana scoffed.

"That's because they all think I'm a total square."

"You are a total square, and that is coming from the girl who was voted Most Likely to Become the Hall Monitor at our middle school graduation."

"Hey, guys." Josie slowed the car in front of the huge house on the top of the hill. It was colonial white, surrounded by a tall, iron fence like many of the others, but the garden and trees were so overgrown, they were escaping from the gnarled confines of the rusty fence. It was usually perfectly silent, the gates closed tight and sealed with a huge padlock that prevented even the most resourceful vandal from getting inside the abandoned property. The windows were usually boarded and dirty. An unmistakable air of neglect hung around it like a dark storm cloud.

The house had once belonged to the Notts, a prominent New Coventry family, but they had all passed away many years ago under mysterious circumstances. The house had been for sale ever since. No one had even viewed it. The people in town regarded the house with a strange, silent sort of respect. Though no one ever spoke it out loud, the house bore an unexplainable stigma, as though it was jinxed or something. Aurora had always thought it was a terrible shame to allow such a beautiful historic home to fall into such disrepair, but she avoided the old place like everyone else in town.

It looked different today. The gate was open. A large moving truck was parked on the edge of the long, winding driveway. There were a couple men with hedge cutters moving around the property, attacking the stubborn, intrusive foliage. The boards were off the windows. The glass had been cleaned so they sparkled in the morning sun. Even the crumbling wood siding had been hosed off. It gleamed as it hadn't in many years.

"Someone bought the Nott house?" Diana said, leaning out the window to peer out at the old house. "That place has been empty as long as I've been born. I think it's been empty as long as my parents have been alive."

"I didn't think anyone was ever going to buy it." Josie glanced at her friends. "I heard no one wanted it because it's haunted."

"Oh, it isn't haunted." Diana rolled her eyes. "It's just old and neglected."

"Who do you think bought it?"

"Could be someone new in town, I guess," Aurora remarked. "Or maybe a house flipper or something."

"Maybe the bank sent someone in to clean it up so it might become appealing to buyers again," Diana said. Then she patted Josie's shoulder. "But we're going to be late for school, Jos."

"Right." Josie stamped on the accelerator. "I'm pretty sure the house is haunted."

"It's not haunted. There are no such things as ghosts."

"Yeah," Aurora echoed softly, peering at the old Nott house in the side mirror. "There are no such things as ghosts."

"Ghosts or not, who would want to buy a house where a kid killed his whole family and ended up in a mental institution?"

"Oh, Josie," Diana scolded. "You know that's not what happened."

"You don't know what happened. You said yourself you weren't even born."

"I'm sure someone knows what happened. It just happened so long ago, no one who remembers it is around anymore."

Josie cocked her head as she steered the car toward Henry Hudson High School. "Maybe it's a troupe of circus performers or something."

The other two girls looked at her incredulously. "What?"

"You know. The people who bought the house."

"Circus performers?" Diana said scornfully.

"Maybe they're witches," Aurora offered. She was warming up to the subject.

"Yeah!" Josie grinned. "Like a coven of evil witches who want to take over the town and are using the evil ghost powers in the house to magnify their witchcraft."

Diana rolled her eyes, but the corners of her mouth turned up in a reluctant smile. "Maybe it's one of the Notts distant relatives who inherited the house and has come to solve the mystery of their family's death."

"Maybe it's paranormal investigators who heard about the house and are shooting a documentary in there," Josie suggested.

"If that were true, I bet they wouldn't have cleaned up and tended the lawn," Diana argued.

Josie didn't let this deter her. "Or it could be a weird middle aged man and his mom and some of the townsfolk are going to start going mysteriously missing."

"It's not fun anymore when you say stuff like that," Aurora complained.

"Come on!" Josie said. "This town is so boring! Nothing ever happens. You don't think a serial killer would make life more interesting?"

"No. It would make it horrible and terrifying. It's only interesting in the movies. It wouldn't be so good in real life."

Josie sighed in disappointment. "Fine."

"How about a crazy cat lady who hangs out on her front porch and screams at people on the street," Diana put in.

"Yeah, who has a pet panther that eats people, so she's screaming at people to keep them away!"

They were still discussing the new owners of the old Nott house as Josie steered into the HHHS parking lot. It was jam packed with students arriving for class at the last minute. Josie cursed as she circled the lot for several moments before she found a spot wedged between a beat up robin's egg blue pick up truck pulled up into the spot in front of it so that it took up half of both spots and a gleaming red Mustang with the top down turned sideways to avoid door dings.

"God!" Josie complained as they struggled to get out of the car without getting wedged between the frames and doors. "Why do people have to park like such jerks?"

"It's high school. They do everything like jerks," Diana replied.

"This is why I don't like cars," Aurora put in. "There's never a place to park them."

Josie and Diana glanced at her, but they didn't say what she knew they were thinking. That wasn't the real reason she didn't like cars. They didn't mention it. They, at least, weren't jerks most of the time.

"Uh, oh, Aurora," Diana said quietly as they strode across the parking lot toward the long walkway though the courtyard to the main building.

She didn't even need to see to what Diana was referring; she already knew. Josie sighed dreamily, as they drew to a stop in front of Jesse Drake, who sat on his old, vintage Harley motorcycle as though he'd been waiting for them. He probably had been waiting for them. He waited most days. He wasn't wearing his helmet. His dark blonde, shoulder length hair blew slightly in the gentle early spring breeze. He smiled at Aurora.

He looked good. Jesse always looked good. Today, his face was scruffy as though he couldn't be bothered to shave this morning. His black leather jacket looked like he'd fallen off his bike in it. It was scuffed in interesting places. His jeans were practically glued to his legs. He flipped his hair from his startling blue eyes.

"Hi, Aurora." His mouth was full and sensual. It took an effort not to stare. He looked like a movie star or a model. He didn't look like he belonged in a high school parking lot; not in real life, anyway.

She paused in front of his bike. Josie smiled at him, but he didn't look at her or Diana. His beautiful blue eyes fixed on Aurora until she thought he might burn a hole straight through her. She shifted slightly in discomfort. "Hi, Jesse."

"You want to go for a ride?"

Beside her, Diana huffed in disapproval. Josie sighed that dreamy sigh, as though Jesse were some sort of teen idol or heartthrob instead of the same guy they'd known since kindergarten who'd followed Aurora around so relentlessly, she might have been the only woman in the world.

"Jesse, we have class in fifteen minutes."

"So? Some things are more important." He was so gorgeous, and he looked so appealing on that old, gleaming blue motorcycle that she almost relented.

She didn't. "I don't skip school. You shouldn't, either. You're in enough trouble with Mr. Warwick as it is."

Jesse scoffed. "I'm not afraid of the principal. This isn't elementary school. Come on, Aurora. Just this one time. I'll have you back by second period."

"No, thanks." She turned away from him and started back toward the school. Diana was right beside her, but she had to grab Josie's arm to drag her away from the handsome troublemaker.

Aurora didn't turn to look back at him. She knew what she would see. She'd seen the look of disappointment on his face so many times she was almost becoming immune to it.

"Aurora, wait!" He sounded almost shy.

Now she paused and turned to look at him. He looked very young. A lock of dark blonde hair fell into his eyes. Her stomach roiled a little. She hated having to tell him no everyday. She hated having to see his big, sad, blue puppy dog eyes when she refused another date.

"Yeah?" She hated the note of impatience she couldn't keep out of her voice.

"Are you going to Bray's party tonight?"

She didn't meet his eyes. "Maybe. I'm not sure yet."

He hopped off his bike and strode toward her. She took a step back from him. He was over a head taller than her. He looked large, broad-shouldered and strong. When he stared down at her like that, with that slight, shy smile, he made her very nervous. "Maybe I'll see you there, then."

"Yeah. Maybe. I have to get to class. See you later, Jesse."

Diana grabbed her arm and tugged her away.

"Bye, Aurora." His low, husky voice followed her as she hurried over the path toward the school with her friends.

Josie grabbed Aurora's arm. "You are going to the party, right? You were just trying to put him off? You aren't going to change your mind and ditch me at the last minute?"

"I wouldn't be ditching you. Diana's going."

"Yeah, but she's going with Zach!"

"That doesn't mean I'm going to be ensconced in some corner somewhere the entire night," Diana told her.

"Anyway, Aurora, you have to go. You promised you would go! You have to."

"Yeah, yeah. I'll go. I told you I'd go. I just...didn't want him to get his hopes up or anything."

Josie glanced back over her shoulder at Jesse. If he was still there, sitting forlorn and disappointed on his bike, she didn't mention it to Aurora. She heard his motorcycle whine to life, and then his tires squealed as he peeled out of the parking lot. Even his bike sounded bleak.

"Good riddance. I can't believe he still does this every other day," Diana said. "You'd think he'd get the hint by now. You are never going to go out with him."

"I feel a little bad for him," Aurora admitted.

"You should. He's been desperately in love with you for our whole lives, and you just keep breaking his heart over and over again, ruining him for those of us who would actually jump at the chance," Josie scolded.

"He brings it on himself," Diana said sharply as they strode inside. They

17

wove through the crowds of people hurrying to class or lingering in the halls talking to their friends or sharing sweet moments with their boyfriends and girlfriends before they had to separate and head to class. "He's the one who won't take no for an answer."

"I don't understand why you keep turning him down!" Josie said. "He worships the ground you walk on. He brings you presents and flowers and puts little sweet notes in your locker. He would do anything for you. He's a really good musician. He's all cool and soulful and sexy all the time. He drives a motorcycle, not to mention he's absolutely, positively the hottest guy in school, and the Pops totally want him and hate you because they can't have him."

"You say that like it's a good thing," Aurora muttered.

"That just shows how much you know about boys, Josie," Diana scoffed. "Don't be so shallow. Those are not the only things that are important. He's a delinquent."

"He's a troubled rebel," Josie defended.

"Troubled is right. He's always in trouble. He's flunking out of almost all his classes, and he doesn't even care. He's on the fast road to absolutely nowhere. He's not a good option."

"I disagree. I think he's redeemable. He's the redeemable bad boy. What girl doesn't want that? I think you should give him a chance, Aurora. He's not so bad. He's one of those tough on the outside and warm melty gooey lovey dovey soft on the inside guys."

"You should not give him a chance, Aurora. Don't listen to Josie. She doesn't know what she's talking about. He's bad news, and there's no changing that."

Aurora sighed. "He's isn't that bad, Di. He's just...lost. I think he's really good on the inside. He just hasn't found his way yet."

"His way is down. Straight down."

"He is a good musician," she said defensively.

"Well, sure he is, but that doesn't mean he doesn't need to go to school and be responsible with his life. He's never going to make it big as a rock star, not with those losers he plays with in their mothers' basements. He needs to get it together and start thinking realistically about his future."

"You're being very harsh, Di," Josie chided.

Diana relented. "Fine. Maybe I am. But I just don't want Aurora messing up her whole life by getting mixed up with him."

"I'm not getting mixed up with him," Aurora said. "I know I could never date him. We're not going in the same direction. But that doesn't mean I don't feel bad for him. I wish he would just move on and find someone else who he might have a chance of actually being happy with."

Josie leaned against her. "Yeah. Someone like me."

Aurora laughed. Diana scowled at Josie. "I don't think he's any better suited for you, Jos. You're way too susceptible to bad influences."

"I wouldn't mind letting him influence me. And I have you to scold me if I get out of control."

"Please. When have you ever listened to anything sensible anyone has to say?"

"Well, that's true. Anyway, I know I have no chance. There's no way he's ever going to get over Aurora or he would have after the first ten years of being turned down by her. He's not budging an inch."

Aurora frowned. "I really wish he would. It would sure make my life a lot easier."

The warning bell trilled through the halls. Josie gave a dramatic sigh.

"We'd better get to class," Diana said briskly. "See you guys at lunch."

"Bye!" Aurora called.

Josie leaned in to speak conspiratorially when Diana had gone. "Seriously, though, Aurora. He is hot. And dreamy."

"I know. He really is."

"It doesn't have to be serious. You could just…get a little experience. So you'll be prepared when you meet someone hot and respectable."

"That's not really my style, Josie. Besides, I think that would make things worse."

"You're probably right. You wouldn't mind if I got a little experience with him, would you? Maybe some Spin the Bottle smooches?"

"Sure. Go ahead. Knock yourself out."

"Great. Any ideas how to rig a bottle to hit the person you want?"

Aurora laughed and pushed her gently. "Get to class. You're going to be late."

"Yeah, yeah. You better get psyched for this party tonight!"

"I'll put all my energy into it. See you at lunch."

"Okay! Ask around about that bottle thing, will you?"

"Oh, absolutely. A whole week's gone by without anyone spreading nasty rumors about me. I was starting to think I'd never give them a reason to start another one."

* * *

The winter chill still hung stubbornly in the air despite the dazzling sun overhead. Nevertheless, students scattered on the campus lawn for their lunch period, wrapped in jackets, scarves and gloves. The stone tables were packed with people who shivered and pretended the sun warmed their faces and hands.

Aurora snuggled further into her red wool coat and sipped her cafeteria hot chocolate. Her peanut butter and jelly sandwich sat uneaten in front of her.

"Did you hear someone bought the Nott house?" Josie said, nibbling the edges off her ham sandwich.

Cera Coca lifted her eyebrows. She was a petite, dark-haired girl with dark, almond shaped eyes. They had known her since first grade. She was always interested in Josie's gossip. "The haunted house?"

"It's not haunted," Diana said exasperatedly. "There is no such thing as ghosts."

"You can be such a drag sometimes," Josie complained.

"I met them," Shane Hardy announced in such a mild, matter-of-fact voice that it took several moments before the girls realized what he'd said.

"You met them?" Cera demanded. "You didn't say anything about it. Who are they? What are they like?"

He shrugged. "Well, I met a couple of them. I think it's a whole family who moved in. They were in the hardware store the other day. They mentioned they had moved into the old Nott house and have been fixing it up. They were buying paint and tools."

20

"Well? Do you know anything about them?" Josie asked, leaning forward as though this were the biggest piece of gossip this year. It had been a slow year. Most years were slow in New Coventry.

"No. It's not like I asked their life's story. I just noticed them while they were checking out."

"Well, who were they?"

"A husband and wife. They said something about their sons helping them with the repairs."

"Their sons aren't enrolled in school," Cera remarked. Her mother worked in the school's administration office, and she always knew everything about everyone, including who was about to be suspended or expelled. She was as big a gossip as her daughter, so Cera always knew, too.

"They must be older or something," Diana said.

"What were they like?" Aurora asked Shane. "Did they seem nice?"

"Yeah, they seemed nice. They were friendly." His mouth turned up slightly. "The lady was hot."

The girls groaned in disgust. "Come on."

"What? Well, she was. I can appreciate older women."

Cera scoffed. "Don't even get him started. He's on a tear about older women these days. Apparently, high school girls aren't doing it for him anymore."

"Oh, that's not true. There are plenty of high school girls who do it for me."

Josie and Aurora exchanged a glance. They had always suspected that Shane and Cera liked each other, but they kept their relationship stubbornly plutonic.

Shane's eyes slid away. "I guess they're opening a home business, too."

"A home business?" Diana perked up. "What kind?"

"I don't know. I just overheard them talking to Mr. Reyes. He was all loopy and weird all day afterward."

"Loopy?" Aurora asked. "Loopy how?"

"I don't know. Just...sort of bubbly and happy. He even let me take a long lunch hour. I've never seen him like that before."

"Maybe he was on drugs," Cera suggested.

Shane laughed. "Yeah, right. I've never met anyone as serious and straight edge as Mr. Reyes. He's annoyed almost all the time."

"Maybe he thought the wife was hot, too," Josie remarked.

He grinned. "Yeah. Maybe."

"Oh, no." Aurora ducked further into her collar, but it didn't do any good.

"Oh, great." Josie's shoulders stiffened.

"Pops," Diana said in a low, disgusted voice. "What do they want?"

Aurora knew exactly what Sierra Drew and her entourage wanted. Sierra and the other Pops--the Larson twins, Cami and Callie, Sierra's best friend Brooke Hadley, and Claire Ames, a cheerleader who was only mean when she was with Sierra-- were all dressed in designer clothes and wore perfect makeup. They looked as though they belonged on the cover of a teen magazine.

Sierra had long, sleek black hair and huge, blue eyes. The twins were naturally blonde and petite and looked like everyone's dream of an all-American girl. Claire was tall and thin with long legs and long, wavy brown hair. Brooke wasn't like the other Pops; she was athletic and wore her caramel-colored hair in a short, curly bob. She wasn't mean, but she didn't stop Sierra or stand up for anyone, either, so she was almost just as bad.

The Pops hated Aurora. They'd hated Aurora since they were small kids.

The moment Sierra saw her, her expression shifted nastily. Her blue eyes gleamed. Aurora's stomach roiled. She knew what was coming. She stiffened and waited for it.

"Well, look at this," Sierra purred. She wore a short ice blue dress that matched her eyes. She didn't look like the cold was bothering her at all. She was probably cold-blooded like a snake. She looked like a model or a movie star. Her long, black hair shone in the sun. Her expression was ugly. "Are you planning to join the circus tonight, Jocelyn?"

Josie's lip curled. Sierra always called her by her real name. She hated it. Sierra knew it.

Sierra's smile was sharp as a razor. "You aren't planning on coming to Bray's party looking like that, are you?"

Josie glared at her.

"Leave us alone, Sierra," Diana ordered, scowling.

Sierra turned and smiled at her friends over her shoulder. The twins looked on with eager, hungry expressions. They couldn't wait to see the carnage their friend could unleash. Brooke always looked uncomfortable when Sierra got going, but she never said anything. Claire was looking around them so vaguely Aurora suspected she wasn't paying attention

"What do you think, girls? We have a clown, a bookworm, a mouse and— whatever those two are." She tilted her chin dismissively toward Cera and Shane. They had never been worth her notice. Cera looked offended. Aurora would have given anything to be beneath Sierra's notice.

Sierra wasn't done. She met Aurora's eyes and sneered. Aurora's stomach churned. She didn't say anything to Sierra. She never stood up to Sierra, no matter how much she wanted to.

"I wasn't aware this was a costume party," the black-haired girl added. "Were you?"

The twins grinned malevolently at each other and put their heads together to whisper in perfectly audible voices to each other. They didn't care about Josie and Diana. They only had eyes for Aurora.

"Can you believe she thinks she's going to go to this party like she's actually welcome?" Cami said.

"I know. Pathetic," Callie replied.

Josie lifted her chin. "Bray invited everyone. We are all welcome."

"I'm not sure about that," Sierra said. "Bray hates rodents. His father will have to hire an exterminator. You would be doing everyone a favor if you just stayed home, Aurora."

"Sierra," Brooke said so softly Sierra could pretend she didn't hear her.

Josie jumped to her feet to face Sierra. The black-haired girl was much taller. "Don't talk to her that way. You're just jealous because Jesse isn't interested in hopping into any of your evil little pants."

Sierra's eyes narrowed to slits. Cami and Callie glared murderously at Josie. Then all three girls glanced at each other and burst into laughter.

"Please," Cami said. "Jealous of her? What have we got to worry about from her? If any of us wanted Jesse, we would just take him."

Josie grinned. "Oh, really? It's been working so well for you so far. You've been after Jesse since middle school. He's been pretty clear that he isn't interested in having your claws in him."

Cami looked as though she wished she could kill Josie. Sierra tossed her hair.

"As if we'd be interested in a delinquent like Jesse Drake. He won't even graduate from high school."

Josie smirked. Aurora knew Josie thought she'd won the fight, but she was pretty sure it was her who was losing, not Josie or the Pops. She felt cold and miserable.

"Come on," Callie said. "We have better things to do than waste our time talking to nobodies. See you girls at the party."

The Pops grinned at each other. They lifted their noses in the air and started haughtily away. Sierra paused and looked back over her shoulder at Aurora. "You'd better be careful, Aurora. You don't want to get caught in any traps. Just don't eat any cheese."

Aurora stiffened and looked down at her sandwich as they stalked away. Callie flicked Aurora's hair as they passed, mussing up the long, strawberry blonde waves.

When they'd gone, Josie reached over and smoothed Aurora's hair. "Can't they come up with anything better than that? A mouse. Come on. You're not a mouse."

Aurora sighed deeply and wrapped her arms around her knees. "I feel like one sometimes."

"Don't let them do that to you, Aurora," Diana ordered. "Don't listen to them. They're just nasty and mean-spirited, and they aren't happy unless they're tormenting other people."

"I just don't know why they had to choose me. I never did anything to any of them."

Josie glared in the direction the girls had gone. Sierra stared down three sophomores until the younger girls jumped up to give up their table.

"They're just jealous because the hottest boy in school is interested in you and not them. Cami has been after Jesse since the sixth grade, and he won't even give her the time of day."

"Jealous? Of me?" Aurora asked doubtfully. "This is way beyond jealousy.

They hate me!"

"Well, they hate you because they're jealous," Diana told her.

"They shouldn't be. There's nothing about me to be jealous over. It's not like I'm going out with Jesse."

"What are you talking about?" Josie asked incredulously. "You're pretty, smart and a hell of a lot nicer than them. Not to mention Jesse is in love with you and always has been. He isn't interested in mean girls. It just burns them up they can't use those pretty faces and designer clothes to reel him in like the other boys in school."

Aurora sighed. "Maybe I shouldn't go to this party. I have enough trouble with them at school. I don't want to deal with them when they've had a few drinks and there are no principals or teachers around to keep them from ripping my hair out."

"Oh, no," Josie said, wagging her finger in the air. "You aren't letting those evil little bitches get in the way of our good time. Bray invited us, and we are going."

"And you're going to look so hot, they'll wish they could be you," Diana added.

Aurora laughed reluctantly. "I highly doubt that."

"Oh, they will when you show up looking like a rock star and Jesse can't keep his eyes off you."

"I don't think I want that. In fact, I know I don't. I've got enough problems."

Cera lifted her head—she knew better than to get involved when the Pops were on a tear, but now that they were gone, she rolled her eyes. "Yeah, it must be really hard to have the most popular boy in school interested in you. I wish I had problems like that."

Shane glanced at her as though she'd betrayed him.

"I promise you," Aurora told Cera. "You don't."

"I wouldn't mind having a chance to find out," Josie put in.

"I don't suppose you'd mind if I put myself in his way?" Cera asked.

Aurora huffed. "Why does everyone ask me that all the time?"

"Get in line," Josie told Cera dangerously.

Aurora laughed. She realized the girls were trying to cheer her up. She didn't feel any better, but they didn't need to know that. "Sure. You two can fight it out amongst yourselves. Just keep me out of it."

"Do I have anything to say about any of this?" Shane asked.

All four girls looked at him. "No."

* * *

The backdoor wasn't locked when Aurora got home. She slung her backpack over the back of a chair. "Hello?"

No one replied. Ruby was probably upstairs in her room getting ready for a date or something. Aurora opened the fridge and rummaged around for an apple. There weren't any left. She frowned. She was sure she had just bought a bag of them at the store last week. She sighed and grabbed a piece of string cheese instead. She would have to get ready for the party eventually, but she wanted to pretend for a little while that she could relax and just enjoy her solitude.

It was short-lived. There was a black messenger bag weighing down half the couch, stuffed with books and papers. Ruby's son, Christian, must have come home for the weekend. She strode to the closed door off the living room. "Chris? Are you here?"

For a moment, there was no reply. Then the door flew open and Christian stood framed in the doorway, grinning. He was holding a half-eaten apple. "Hey, Rory." She hated it when he called her Rory. He knew it, which was, naturally, exactly why he did it.

She lifted an eyebrow. "Do you have a date?"

He flipped his dark, carefully styled hair. It didn't move. It looked as though he'd spent half the afternoon tousling it into a perfect mess. He wore his nicest jeans—nicest meaning they had no holes in the knees—and a tee shirt with some band she'd never heard of on the front. It was his typical 'night out' look. It hadn't changed since they were in middle school. She couldn't believe he was so popular with girls. He looked like a ruffian, not a heartthrob. There was just no accounting for taste.

Christian was Ruby's only son. He'd never met his dad, and it was a general unspoken rule in the family to simply pretend he'd never existed. Christian was in his first year at Lynchburg College studying Chemistry. He lived on the campus and usually only came home when he needed to do laundry or was tired of the campus cafeteria.

"Maybe," he replied around a big bite of the apple she'd been intending to eat. "I was thinking of hitting Bray's party."

"What? I thought you were too old and too cool to come to high school parties."

He grinned. "Not when there are going to be hot high school girls there."

She snorted in disgust. "Oh, god. I don't think that's even legal anymore."

"I'm pretty sure a college freshman can go out with a high school girl."

"It sounds like you have one in mind."

His large, hazel eyes twinkled. "Maybe."

"Tell me it isn't Sierra Drew or one of the Lawson twins."

"Okay. I won't."

Her lip curled. "Of course."

"Are you planning on going to the party?" He stopped smiling abruptly and eyed her closely. "Are you still having a hard time?"

She sighed and turned away, but he followed her into the kitchen. "I don't want to talk about it."

"High school girls can be bitches sometimes."

She glanced over her shoulder at him. "And yet you still want to chase them around?"

Christian shrugged. "Those things aren't mutually exclusive."

Aurora scowled and crossed her arms over her chest. "I almost thought you were going to be a nice, supportive guy for once."

"Again, those things aren't mutually exclusive."

She rolled her eyes. "Whatever."

He perched on the stool at the bar across from her. "So what's new, little cousin-sister?"

She smiled. She liked it when he called her that. It usually meant he intended to be nice. "Nothing much. Oh, but there's a new family that moved into the old Nott house."

"The haunted house?"

"I guess they don't mind the ghosts."

"Huh. What are they like?"

"I don't know. I haven't seen them."

"If they are all pale and wear black all the time, I recommend you avoid them. I've seen films."

"I'll keep that incredibly helpful piece of advise in mind. I guess being in college has made you super smart."

"It sure has. I now know all the places in Lynchburg that let you in underage or barely glance at your fake ID."

"I'm sure your mother is proud she's paying all that money so you can find the drinking spots with the loosest law enforcement."

Christian laughed. "Come on. You know you're dad's paying for it all."

"That makes me feel better," she said brightly.

"It shouldn't," Mike Geller said from behind them. "There's no money left for your education, Rory. I hope you're either planning for a rewarding career in food service or you're making good enough grades to get a scholarship." His voice sounded wry, but his dark green eyes twinkled beneath his greasy Geller's Auto Repair hat. His face and over-long dark hair were streaked with dirt and grease. He still wore his shop coveralls.

Aurora wondered how long he'd been standing there listening. She smiled at him. "Great. I have to give up my future for a guy who'd only studying Chemistry because he thinks explosions are cool."

"Hey, I've been learning to mix drugs, too."

Mike rolled his eyes. "Don't make me change my mind about funding your education, Chris."

"Ah. Just kidding, Uncle Mike. Just...don't tell my mom I said that."

"Too late." Ruby had just walked into the backdoor, carrying a heavy computer case. She rolled her eyes at her son. "You've always been so bad at hiding things from your mother."

"Geez. Is this like some kind of intervention?" Christian demanded. "What are you two doing sneaking up on us from either side? Isn't there any peace in this house?"`

Mike laughed. "Your mother and I have had forty years of experience stealing any peace from everywhere we go." He strode into the kitchen to give his older sister a high five. He brought the smell of axel grease into the room.

Ruby smelled like flowers. Aurora's stomach clenched painfully. She remembered that poignant combination of smells so clearly she might have smelled it just yesterday. It was all wrong this time. She met her father's gaze. She wondered if he was thinking the same thing.

"What are you guys doing home so early on a Friday afternoon?" Christian asked.

Mike looked slightly embarrassed. Ruby smiled radiantly. They both replied at the same moment, "I have a date."

Aurora laughed. Christian rolled his eyes. He pretended he didn't want to hear about his mom's love life, but he liked to know she was happy.

"I don't want to know," he said. "You can tell Aurora. She likes all that romantic stuff."

"Hey!" Aurora called after him as he strode out of the kitchen. "What are you talking about? Since when do I like romantic stuff?"

He paused and stuck his head back into the room. "Just because you don't have first hand experience doesn't mean you aren't still a girl."

Aurora opened her mouth in outrage, but he slammed the door to his room before she could reply. She turned to her aunt and father. "Okay. I really do want to know. I do like all that romantic stuff."

Mike snorted and waved his hand. "You two can gossip about it all you want. I just want a beer and a shower." He ducked into the fridge and hurried out of the room as though he couldn't wait to get away from the girls.

"I'm going out with Blaine Daniels."

"Again? What is this, the second date?"

Ruby smiled. Her eyes slid away dreamily. "Third."

"When are we going to meet this guy?"

She lifted her shoulders. She looked prettier somehow than she had in a long time. She looked younger. Her long, red hair was tied back from her face. Her green eyes sparkled and flashed, and her cheeks were flushed and rosy. Maybe she was just happier than she'd been since Aurora could remember. "Oh, maybe one of these days. I'm not sure how it's going yet."

Aurora hadn't heard her aunt sound so excited in a long time. She smiled. "It sounds like it's going pretty well."

"I hope it is. I just don't want to jinx it this early."

"Well, good luck. I hope we get to meet him soon."

"But what about you? Are you going to this party, too?"

Mike strode back into the kitchen as though he'd been listening just beyond the door. He had probably been too anxious to drink his beer to bother with a shower first and didn't want to get grease on the couch. "Party?"

Aurora sighed. "I don't know. I guess I don't really want to."

"Why not?" Ruby asked. "You're in high school. Being at a party without adult supervision and lots of cute boys was pretty much what I lived for when I was your age."

"I'm not sure I like the sound of this." Mike didn't sound particularly stern. He never did.

"Oh, it will be fine, Mikey," Ruby told him, waving her hand. "How much trouble can she get into? She doesn't have a wicked bone in her body."

Aurora took exception to this. "Hey! I can be wicked."

Ruby and her brother snorted in amusement. Mike strode back toward the door. "I'm staying at Julia's tonight, so I won't be around to wait up." He turned back to look at his daughter with a smile. "Just make sure you're home at a reasonable hour, Rory."

"What is a reasonable hour?"

"I'm sure you'll know when it's stopped being reasonable. Just come home then."

Aurora rolled her eyes. "And don't wait up for me," Ruby said. "I don't know what time I'll be home...if I come home."

"Don't want to hear things like that about my sister!" Mike called from the other room.

Ruby ignored him and winked at Aurora. Christian poked his head back in the room. "Are you done talking to my mom about girl stuff?" he asked, as though he were utterly disgusted by the very idea.

His mother strode over and ruffled his hair. He swatted her hand away and grunted in irritation. Aurora sniggered. She suspected Ruby was perfectly aware of how long her son had spent on his hair. It just looked messy now.

"I suppose you won't be home, either?" Aurora asked him. She tried to keep the forlorn note out of her voice. She was used to being left at home alone by now.

Christian shrugged. "I thought I'd stay at Joey's."

"Let me guess," Ruby said wryly. "His dad's out of town and left the liquor cabinet open again?"

"Your lack of faith in me as a son is extremely troubling."

"Rory, how are you getting to the party?" Mike still hadn't gone into his room to shower. "Do you need to borrow a car?"

Her father was always offering her one of the many cars he kept at his shop in case a client needed to borrow one. She never drove them. She hated driving cars. "No. Josie is picking me up."

"Okay." He swallowed the last of his beer and slammed the empty bottle on the kitchen counter. "I'm off to get ready. See you tomorrow. Don't do anything I wouldn't do."

Aurora was sure parental figures should be more concerned about their seventeen year old daughters. "Now or when you were my age?"

He paused and poked his head back into the room. He was grinning. "Please, Rory. As if you'd do anything I did when I was your age."

She sighed. She didn't like this attitude. Christian sniggered at her.

Ruby smiled. "Well, I'm off to get ready, too. You two have fun tonight. Not too much fun, though. I don't want to be picking anyone up at the police station later."

Christian snorted and spun away. Aurora heard his bedroom door slam. He was probably going to spend the next hour putting his hair back into a more acceptable tangle. She trudged up the stairs to her bedroom. She opened her closet door unenthusiastically and stared for several moments at the clothes hanging there. She took a long time to select comfortable jeans and a jade green sweater the same color as her eyes.

It wasn't very daring, but she wasn't a very daring person. She looked into the mirror. She liked the thin, green sweater. It had been a gift from Ruby on her last birthday. It was tighter than most of her clothes, and Aurora suspected Ruby had been trying to get her niece to dress a little more provocatively. She wasn't sure that was such a good idea, but Josie would kill her if she didn't put in a little effort. She was tired of her old clothes, anyway. She was tired of the pale, delicate face in the mirror. She was tired of her long, strawberry blonde hair falling past her shoulders like a veil. She was tired of ducking her head and avoiding Jesse and the Pops. She was tired of never wanting to be noticed.

She lifted her chin and swept her hair back into a ponytail. She considered putting on some makeup, but she didn't want to look like she was trying too hard. She wasn't trying to attract anyone's attention, and the Pops would tear her apart. She preferred to be called a mouse. There were worse things, and at least they had the measure of her. She felt like a mouse, anyway. A small, scared and insignificant mouse. Sometimes she thought she would be a lot better off if she could just become invisible.

Aurora still hadn't fully convinced herself that going to this party was a good idea by the time she heard Josie's car horn blaring outside. She sighed and jumped to her feet to hurry downstairs.

"Bye!" she called on her way out, but there was no reply from any of the rooms in the house. Everyone else must have gone. They hadn't even said goodbye.

Josie was grinning widely when Aurora slipped into the passenger seat. She hadn't changed, but she'd touched up her makeup and teased up her red hair in the back so it looked wild and fun. Aurora wished she could be more like Josie. She never took anything too seriously, especially herself. She liked to have fun, and she knew how to do it.

"Hey! Ready?" Josie exclaimed.

"I guess. As ready as I will ever be."

"I think you need an attitude adjustment. Didn't I tell you to get psyched?"

She lifted her chin and smiled. "I did get psyched. As psyched as I can be, anyway. I'm in the car. Don't push it."

Josie laughed. "This is going to be the best night ever, Rora."

"Yeah. It sounds like it. The best night ever. It's been great so far."

Josie glanced at her with a sly smile. "What time do you have to be home?"

Aurora shrugged. "At a reasonable hour."

"What's reasonable?"

"Who knows? My dad says I'll know when it's become unreasonable." She glanced out the window. "It's not like anyone's going to be home to notice, anyway."

"You're so lucky. I have to be home at one."

"Yeah. I feel really lucky."

Chapter Two

Brayden's house was already so noisy when they arrived, they had to shout to hear each other over the music, laughter and chattering of their classmates around them. People were stumbling around as though they'd had too much to drink. There were a handful of kids grinding against each other in the middle of the living room. Bray had moved the furniture against the walls to give them more room, and the couches and chairs were already stuffed with couples making out as though they were the only people in the room. Others were sneaking up the stairs, giggling and groping at each other as they looked for private rooms to take things a step further.

Something about the scene made Aurora feel creepy. She didn't want to see her classmates so openly displaying their mutual affection. She wouldn't be able to meet anyone's eyes at school on Monday. Josie gripped her hand and dragged her further into the room, grinning as though there was nowhere in the world she'd rather be. Aurora hoped her friend wouldn't drink too much and end up with the other pairs on the couches.

It wasn't as bad as she expected, but she still felt intensely out of place. She didn't really belong at a party like this. Josie didn't agree. She craned her neck to search for their friends, dragging Aurora along behind her. Some of their classmates greeted them cheerfully, but they apparently weren't whom Josie was hoping to find. She didn't pause to talk to any of them.

"Aurora! Josie!" Cera called from a group of their classmates gathered in a circle against the wall in the dining room. They all had drinks in their hands, and at least a few of them were already drunk.

Josie steered Aurora over to them, though her green eyes continued to wander like she was looking out for someone in particular. "Hey, guys," Aurora greeted.

"You look nice, Aurora," Shane told her. "That sweater looks nice on you."

"Thanks."

Cera looked a little put out by this. She leaned against him. "You never tell me I look nice." Her voice was slightly slurred. She must have had more than one of whatever she was drinking out of a red plastic cup.

He smiled and wrapped an arm around her shoulders. "Oh, I tell you that all the time. You just don't pay any attention."

"Have you seen anyone interesting yet?" Josie asked.

By anyone, Josie meant 'boys', and by interesting she invariably meant 'cute.' "I saw Nick Shaw in the kitchen with Claire Ames," Cera said, lifting her hand to point vaguely over her shoulder.

"Ugh. And here I thought he wasn't a complete jerk," Josie complained. "Is Bryan Dymond here yet?"

"I haven't seen him," Shane replied. He knew Josie was boy crazy. Everyone knew Josie was boy crazy. He took it pretty well in stride, but Aurora suspected it was because he liked being with Cera, who was around Josie a lot.

Aurora wondered if they would finally admit their feelings for each other if they drank enough of whatever was in the red plastic cups. If they did, they probably wouldn't even remember it tomorrow and things would go right back to the way they'd always been.

Josie jerked her head. "Don't look now, Rora. Pops at ten o'clock."

Aurora did look. A circle of football players surrounded Sierra and the twins, who were laughing and tossing their heads like show ponies. They hadn't noticed her yet, and she hoped the boys could keep them busy enough that she could pass the whole night without having to talk to them. She doubted it. The twins, at least, seemed to possess an evil internal homing beacon that could find her anywhere she went.

Everyone else seemed happy to see her, though. They called to her and Josie as they passed by on their way from the kitchen to the main room. The Pops were horrible, but they weren't the only people in school. Aurora's spirits lifted a little. At least there were still more people who liked than hated her. It was just a shame that the ones who did hate her seemed to have so much bigger and more influential voices.

"You want to get a drink?" Josie asked.

"I don't know, Jos."

"It's okay, Rora," Shane said. He tipped his drink so she could see the contents. "There are sodas in there, too."

She smiled at him. "Yeah. Okay. Let's get a drink."

35

Josie threaded her arm through Aurora's and dragged her into the kitchen. She acted as though she was afraid Aurora was going to change her mind and bolt out of the house at any moment. She had considered it. When they had broken away from the group, Josie looked at her best friend closely. "Rora, are you okay today?"

Aurora looked back at her in surprise. "What?"

"It's just that...well, you seem a little more..." Josie paused as though she was looking for the right word. Aurora suspected it was a word that wouldn't hurt her feelings.

"Boring?"

"No! No. Not boring...just...square. More than usual." She glanced at Aurora sheepishly.

"You're right. I am." She lifted her chin. "Maybe I will have a drink. I could probably lighten up a bit, huh?"

Josie grinned. "That's my girl. Just let yourself have a little fun for once."

It wasn't the worst advice she'd ever received. At least she wasn't driving. And if something really bad happened, Shane was there and Christian would be there eventually. She was safe enough. She followed Josie into the kitchen. There was a group of girls from their class talking with their heads together over the bottles of liquor on the sticky counter.

"Oh, my god!" Mikayla Shultz exclaimed. "He was so hot. Like movie star hot. Like Calvin Klein underwear model hot. Like Jesse Drake hot."

Josie perked up. "Who are you guys talking about?"

"You heard some people moved into the old Nott house?" Mikayla asked.

"Sure," Aurora replied. "We saw some workers there this morning."

"Well, one of them is a super hot guy. One of the people who moved in. Not the workers."

"Yeah?" Josie asked. "How old is he? He isn't in school or anything. Where did you see him?"

"He was just walking around downtown. He didn't talk to anybody or anything. I think he's in his twenties. Definitely out of high school."

"What's he look like?" Rebecca Means demanded, leaning across the counter. She was wearing a pretty white sweater that looked expensive.

Aurora winced as the sticky red substance on the counter soaked through the other girl's sleeves. Rebecca cursed loudly and moved to the sink.

"He's tall, dark, handsome. The usual. He had these eyes like—like huge, dark stars or something."

"What's his name?" Aurora asked, pouring a tiny splash of vodka into her Sprite. She didn't drink often—she didn't really drink at all. She suspected she would regret it if she had any more; not to mention, if the cops did show up, she would prefer not to be one of the minors they took off to the drunk tank.

Mikayla shook her head. "I don't know. I didn't talk to him. He wasn't exactly approachable." She sighed dreamily. "He was so gorgeous. I probably wouldn't have been able to get up the nerve to talk to him, anyway."

"I would have," Josie said proudly.

Aurora rolled her eyes and smiled into her red plastic cup. Sure she would have. Josie liked to pretend she was brave, but she really wasn't. She could break the ice, but after that, she chickened out and ran away.

"I can't believe someone bought that creepy old house," Toni Grace put in. "It must be a huge mess in there by now. I heard the bank never even cleared out the furniture and trash that was left when the Notts died."

"I cannot wait to meet them," Josie said. She poured herself a beer from the keg on the side of the kitchen counter. Aurora wondered how Bray had gotten it. Perhaps his father had bought it for the party. Parents these days.

"Did you see Jane Alexander in gym class today?" Rebecca said suddenly, patting her arms with a paper towel.

"No. Why?"

"I think she might have dumped Paxton. She was hitting pretty hard on Matt Jenkins."

Josie lifted her eyes. "Really? Paxton was looking pretty rough in Spanish this morning. I wonder if he needs a shoulder to cry on."

"Oh, leave him alone, Josie," Aurora said. "Give him a chance before you swoop in."

The other girls laughed. "Anyway, no one thought it would last between Jane and Paxton," Mikayla put in. "He's too nice for her. She used to have a new boyfriend every week, until she started going out with him."

"I was kind of rooting for them," Aurora admitted. "She always seemed so...desperate for something more. I was hoping he would be it."

The other girls stared at her for a moment as though she'd said something completely insane. Then Josie grinned and grabbed her arm again. "Come on. Let's go check out the rest of the party. See you girls later."

"Bye!"

The house was packed almost to bursting. It was hard to spot Cera and Shane in the dining room. Josie didn't seem interested in hanging around in one place for very long though, and Aurora knew she was hoping to see Bryan Dymond, her latest crush. He was better than the last guy, who'd been a football player who only dated cheerleaders and girls like Sierra and the twins. Bryan, at least, seemed to be nice. He'd had the same girlfriend all through middle school and freshman year, and he hadn't gone out with anyone since they'd split up. Aurora hadn't told Josie, but she suspected he was still hung up on his first love.

"I wonder where Diana is," Josie remarked absently.

"She's probably with Zach somewhere."

Josie paused and glanced slyly over her shoulder at her. "Maybe they're up in one of the bedrooms."

"Oh, please. Even if they were doing that, they wouldn't be doing it at a party where anyone could walk in."

"That's true. Oh!" She nudged Aurora excitedly. "There's Bryan."

"Where?"

"He's over in the corner talking to Howie Keane."

Aurora craned her head to look over the heads of the crowd. Bryan leaned against a wall, looking cool. He had shortly cropped dark hair and big, amber eyes. Aurora could see why Josie liked him. He had a confidence about him that made him easy to talk to. He was cute, too, in a sort of baby-faced way. He wasn't really Josie's type—if she even had a type. She usually went for guys who were all good looks and wooden personalities.

"Are you going to talk to him?" Aurora asked.

Josie took a deep breath. "Do you think I should?"

"Yeah. Of course."

"In a bit. Maybe. How do I look?"

Aurora laughed. "You look great."

Josie smiled. "Thanks. You're always a good friend, even when you're being a square."

"I'll have you know, there is a whole teaspoon of vodka in my drink."

"Vodka?" Zach Carter repeated incredulously.

Josie and Aurora turned to him. Diana was beside him with her eyebrows raised in disapproval. The couple wasn't touching each other. They never touched each other when other people could see them. Aurora wondered if they touched each other when they were alone.

"Josie told me I needed to lighten up," she told them defensively.

Josie scowled at her. "I did not. You said that yourself."

"You're above peer pressure, Aurora," Diana scolded.

Aurora laughed. She felt more cheerful than she had all day. "Where have you two been?"

"Talking to Colter." Zach rolled his eyes. "He's having a hard time since Sherri broke up with him."

"That was three months ago," Josie said.

"Well, she's here with someone else tonight," Diana said. "And he's having a meltdown."

"That's too bad," Aurora said. "Keep him away from the alcohol. You remember the party we went to after Sherri dumped him."

"Yeah. I do." Zach shook his head. "He cried in a corner all night long and then threw up in the flower pot."

"See, drinking alcohol only leads to trouble," Diana told them imperiously. But then she laughed, and Aurora suspected there was something more than cola in her cup, despite her scolding. "Speaking of trouble, have you seen your cousin?"

Aurora frowned. "Not since this afternoon. Where is he?"

Diana's expression was stony. She lifted her hand to point toward the living room. Aurora groaned in disgust.

"What is he doing talking to Sierra?" Josie demanded, as though Christian had mortally offended them all.

Aurora's cousin was leaning over Sierra, smiling down at her as though she was the most interesting thing he'd ever seen. Sierra flirted right back. She tossed her hair and laughed and touched him arm as though she was actually interested in him. She'd never paid any attention to him before. In fact, she'd acted like he was some kind of creep.

Josie scowled. "I guess now that he's in college he's finally good enough to talk to."

Everyone knew that Sierra Drew only went out with older guys. She wouldn't even give high school boys the time of day, especially boys related to her mortal enemy.

"He's liked her since sophomore year," Aurora told them. "I guess I'm not really surprised. Most guys like Sierra."

"Not the sensible ones," Zach said. "She's bad news."

Diana smiled in satisfaction at this. "I don't think her interest is genuine. Nothing she ever does is genuine. She'll be giving him the cold shoulder again in no time."

"I would feel bad for him if he didn't already know what kind of girl she is," Aurora said.

"You're not going to say anything to him?" Josie asked.

"No. It wouldn't do any good. Anyway, he's old enough to take care of himself."

"That's not very nice. You know what she's going to do to him."

"So does he. I'm not going to get in the middle of that."

Josie wasn't paying attention to Aurora anymore. Bryan Dymond strode past them, probably on his way to the kitchen for another drink. "Hi, Bryan," she said, smiling.

Bryan paused and smiled back at her. Aurora glanced at Diana, and the two shared a grin. "Hey, Josie. You want to get a drink with me?"

Josie glanced back at Aurora.

"Go on. You don't have to babysit me."

Josie didn't need to be told twice. She waved at them and spun to walk with Bryan to the kitchen, chattering companionably. Aurora turned back to Diana and Zach. She didn't feel awkward being their third wheel. They weren't really the type of couple who minded when other people were around. They never had anything private or affectionate to say to each other, and they never seemed to want to sneak off to hold hands or smooch or even look sweetly into each other's eyes.

Aurora always wondered how they could be so unaffectionate toward each other, but it seemed to work for them. They had been going out since freshman year, and they seemed to genuinely like each other. Some couples were just different.

Aurora didn't know how she'd act in a relationship. She'd never had one. She was pretty sure she would expect more romance and affection than that. At least, if she were in love, she'd have a hard time hiding it like they did. She would probably be hanging all over the guy and shouting to the rooftops. She'd never been in love. She really had no idea.

With her luck, she'd fall in love with someone who didn't love her back and she'd be like Jesse, forever pursuing a lost cause.

"Aurora? Are you okay?' Diana asked, looking at her strangely.

Aurora smiled. "Yeah. Sorry. I just got lost in thought a moment. You guys don't have to worry about me. If you want to be alone, I'll be okay."

Zach and Diana glanced at each other as though this was a weird idea. Then Zach shrugged, and Aurora thought maybe he wasn't as cool and distant as he seemed.

"If you're sure you'll be okay," he said.

Diana looked at him in surprise then she looked at Aurora, who waved them away. "Go on. I'll just find Cera and Shane or spy on Josie and Bryan."

Diana laughed. "Okay. We'll check in on you in a bit."

Aurora found an empty spot on the wall to watch the party. It hadn't changed much since they'd arrived, except there were more people stumbling around, laughing loudly and doing things other people didn't really want to watch them do. She laughed to herself. It wasn't so bad. She was actually having a good time. She didn't spend much time with her classmates outside school, and it was kind of fun to see what sorts of things they all did when they thought no one was watching.

"I was hoping I'd see you, Aurora."

She sighed and glanced at Jesse. He looked the same as he had earlier,

41

but his hair was a little more wind-blown. Maybe it was the splash of vodka, but she didn't think he'd ever looked so good before. His smile was so shy and sweet, and his eyes were so large, so intense. He really did look like he belonged somewhere else, not this small town in Virginia at a party full of drunken high school kids groping each other clumsily on couches and chairs.

She supposed she should have expected him to show up eventually. He might have been watching her the entire time, waiting for the moment he could get her alone. His interest in her was flattering, but his intensity was scary. She'd considered giving into him more than once, but she was sure it would be a mistake. Diana was right; he was bad news, and she wasn't the sort of girl who took risks like going out with guys like Jesse.

Not for the first time, she wished she were. She wished she were cool and tough and confident. She wasn't. She was a goody-two-shoes who followed the rules and was scared of pretty much everything.

"Hi, Jesse."

"You want a drink?" He smiled, and there was something so appealing about that smile, that when she opened her mouth to say 'no,' "Okay," came out instead. His smile stretched wider and he offered her his hand.

She didn't take it, but she did follow him into the kitchen. He went for the keg and poured a beer. He offered it to her. She shook her head. "I think I just want some Sprite."

He lifted an eyebrow. "I meant a real drink."

"You know I don't really drink."

"You should. It's fun."

"It's illegal."

"So?"

This was exactly what was wrong with Jesse. He didn't care if it was against the rules. He didn't care if he was going to get in trouble. He only cared about how he felt right then and there and what he wanted to do. She didn't think he ever held himself back from anything. It might be an admirable trait sometimes, but not when it counted.

He seemed to sense what she was thinking. "Don't look like that, Aurora. You should lighten up. It's just life. It's just high school."

She wondered if he wasn't right about this, but she knew better than to agree with him. "Peer pressure is wrong, Jesse."

He laughed. "Okay. Okay. Have it your way. I didn't mean to pressure you." He glanced away sheepishly. "I just thought..." He didn't continue. She wasn't sure where he had intended to go with it, but she had a few ideas. He just thought she would like him better if she was drunk? He thought he could convince her to...No. He wasn't really that kind of guy. No matter what he was, he would never take advantage of her.

Aurora felt bad for him. He loved her. She could see it in his eyes. She had been able to see it in his eyes since they had been small children, before they even knew what love was. She doubted it was genuine love, though. He loved the idea of her; he loved her as an object to be won, but he didn't know who she really was, not really. She might be a totally different person than he thought she was.

She always wondered if he would change his mind if he got to know her.

He didn't have those concerns. He was looking at her with those glittering blue eyes again. "I just thought maybe we could talk."

"We are talking."

"No, I meant for real. Aurora..."

She looked away from him. She didn't know for sure what he was going to say, but she knew she didn't want him to say it. "Don't, Jesse."

He frowned. "You don't even know what I was going to say."

She did know what he was going to say. "I think you're a nice guy, but I can't go out with you. I'm sorry."

"Why not?"

"We're just...we're different, Jesse."

"Different?" He laughed wryly. "So? Yeah, we're different. You're different from anyone else I've ever met."

She wasn't sure if this was a compliment or not.

He held up his hands. "I meant that in a good way."

"Oh. Well...thanks. I guess."

"Am I not good enough for you, Aurora?"

"It's not like that. I don't..."

"You don't want to say it."

"It's just that I'm not...I'm not looking for that. For this."

"Then what are you looking for?"

She couldn't meet his gaze. "I don't know."

"Just not me, right?"

She didn't answer him. She didn't look back up at him. She felt his eyes on her for several long moments. Then he spun his back to her and walked away. His shoulders slumped. She sighed deeply. She wished he'd stop asking. If he'd just stop asking, she would be able to stop making him feel that way. She could stop feeling so guilty.

Suddenly, a wall of blonde hair and long, tanned legs stopped in front of her. She looked up at the Lawson twins, who were staring at her with identical sneers of disgust on their pretty faces. They didn't look real, even when they were looking at her that way. They had perfect skin and perfect hair, and their nails were always perfectly manicured. They should have been models, but instead they spent their free time tormenting her.

"It's just as well, Aurora," Cami said in a deceptively bracing voice. "I'm sure when Jesse realizes what you are—"

"An insignificant little mouse," Callie added helpfully.

"—he will leave you alone. You might as well get it over with now."

Aurora's face heated. She opened her mouth to retort, but nothing came out. She didn't have to say anything, though. Josie was beside her in a second.

"And what do you think will happen?" she growled at Cami. "He'll go after you? If he was going to fall for your batting eyelashes and designer clothes, he would have by now. Give it up. You're just jealous of Aurora because she doesn't have to do anything to get him to like her. Even after she turns him down for dates, he still won't go to you. Jesse will never like you. He doesn't like mean girls. He likes people for who they are. And you are just two girls who are so insecure, you attack the person you're jealous of so she'll be fooled and feel as bad about herself as you do."

Cami and her sister paled. Then Cami lifted her chin and curled her lip. "We're not jealous of her."

Callie's blue eyes narrowed and slid to Aurora. "Jesse always has liked broken things. Cars, motorcycles…girls who've lost their mothers."

Aurora's stomach sank. Josie fired back up. "Aurora is not broken. And you can't tear her down. She knows better than to listen to the two of you. All you have to offer anyone is hate."

Aurora didn't really want to hear how Cami and Callie would reply to this. She spun and walked away from them as quickly as she could go without attracting every eye in the room. She shouldered her way through the thick, noisy crowd toward the front door. Josie caught her arm before she made it. Her cheeks were still flushed, and her eyes gleamed.

"What are you doing, Aurora?" she demanded. "You were on a roll."

Aurora frowned. "No, I wasn't. You were. I didn't want anything to do with them."

"Well, you didn't deserve to be treated like that." She glared over her shoulder in the direction she'd left the twins. "You should just go out with Jesse. That would shut their conceited mouths."

"No, I really don't think it would. I don't think that's the solution at all. I'm pretty sure things would get a lot worse." She sighed. "I think I just want to go home."

"What?" Josie looked crestfallen. "But the party is just getting started. And you don't even have a curfew!"

"I know, but…I'm just really not having a good time. I tried, but I just want to go."

"I understand." Josie's eyes drifted past Aurora's shoulder. Her mouth tightened, and for a moment, it looked as though her eyes might spill over. Aurora turned to see what she was looking at. Bryan was dancing with a pretty girl with long, dark hair Aurora knew from class.

"Josie?"

She turned back to Aurora with a forced smile. "I'm not really having any fun, either. Let's go."

Aurora smiled. "You know, I think Bryan likes you."

"If he liked me, would he be dancing with Ella Nunez?"

"Yes. He's a boy. He'll dance with any pretty girl who'll have him. That doesn't mean she's suddenly become his choice."

"You really think so?"

"Yeah. He did come ask you to have a drink with him, didn't he?"

"Well, yeah."

"And how did that end?"

"Well, I...well, I came over to..."

"To defend me from the evil twins?"

Josie laughed. "Well, yeah. So?"

"So, if you weren't so dense, you would realize when a boy is actually trying to get to know you and you would stop running off before they have the chance to ask you out."

Josie blushed. "I don't do that!"

Aurora rolled her eyes and nudged her friend. "Please." She reached over and hugged Josie. "When you're ready, you won't run away. You'll know what to do."

Josie hugged her back fiercely. "Come on. I'll take you home. Diana's riding with Zach, anyway. We can send her a text. She won't mind. We can watch some chick flicks and eat junk food."

"Thanks, Jos, but no. You stay here. I know you want to. You're a good friend, though." She smiled. "I can walk. It's only a few blocks."

Josie chewed on her lip indecisively. "Are you sure?"

"Yeah. It's not too cold out, and I wouldn't mind the walk. It'll be nice."

Josie didn't looked as though she thought this was a good idea. "But—"

"Go on. The song's almost over. You should dance with Bryan."

"Okay. If you're sure."

"I am." She grabbed her coat from the hook near the door. "I'll call you tomorrow, okay?"

"Yeah. Okay. Talk to you tomorrow."

"Have fun."

Josie smiled. "I'll try." She gave Aurora one last hug and watched as she walked outside, turning her collar up against the slightly chilly air.

It was a nice night, even though the spring warmth had yet to fill the air.

It was nearly eleven. Only a few cars still zipped past on the streets. New Coventry was a quiet town. The sky was clear, and the stars glittered above. She looked up, and for the first time that day, she felt almost at peace.

She heard a strange sound, as though someone had jumped down onto the street from a tree branch or dropped something heavy on the sidewalk. She started and looked around. She thought for a moment that she saw a shadow move in the darkness just ahead. Her heart thumped.

"Hello?" she called. "Is someone there?"

No one replied. She paused and listened for a long moment. She didn't hear anything else. It might have been a cat, she supposed, startled to find her there in the streets. She relaxed. Yes, of course it had been a cat. Humans didn't leap from trees and streak into the darkness before she could make them out. She smiled a little at her silliness.

All the same, she quickened her step and did not pause to look back up at the stars.

* * *

"Hello?"

He crouched in the shadows. She was so close he could have reached out and touched her. He wanted to reach out and touch her. She looked so pretty, so small and alone in the street. So delicate...so fragile and human. His blood quickened. Heat pulsed through him. He took a step toward her, reached out a hand.

"Is someone there?"

She didn't sound afraid. She sounded strong and brave, but her jade green eyes were large and gleaming. He could practically feel her heart racing. His own heart thumped eagerly in his chest. He could sense her fear. It was as poignant as the scent of flowers that wafted around her. Hunger surged through him, but there was something else, too, something strange and hot that started in his chest and spread through his blood like a drug. He was so, so hungry.

She started walking. He watched her until she crossed to the next block, and then he streaked after her in the shadows. He could hear her footsteps echoing in his head. She was frightened, for her step was swift and light. She couldn't hear him, but perhaps she sensed him, watching her from the darkness.

For the briefest of moments, he considered stepping out of the shadows, considered revealing himself to her. He could look into her face. He could see her up close. Her breath quickened with her step. He was so, so hungry. If he touched her, it would be the end. He should turn around. He shouldn't follow her.

She paused in the street. She glanced around. "Hello?" Her voice was almost a whisper this time. He could hear the slight tremor in it. He backed away. Just a little. She relaxed again.

But she did sense him. She could feel him in her blood, in her bones as though there were an innate, instinctive part of her that had always known that there were truly things to fear in the darkness.

It wasn't just him who lurked there on the edges of human sight. There were other things, too. There were other things like him. He followed her. She sighed in relief and turned onto a walkway toward her house. He knew it was her house because the scent of her hung in the air all around it. Flowers. As though the place was filled with flowers.

She paused again on the front stoop as she fumbled her keys from her pocket. She looked around. She couldn't see him. If she sensed him, she was no longer afraid. It was as though standing on her own step had soothed her nerves, as though there were a protective shield around the entire place.

It wasn't so. He could have gotten to her there. He could have gotten to her anywhere.

She stepped inside, into the safer darkness of her house. He sighed. Lights flickered on through the house as she moved through it, as though she were turning them all on—just to be safe. It wouldn't have made any difference. If he'd wanted to, he could have been inside, in light or darkness. He could have moved so quickly she wouldn't have ever known he was coming.

He stared up at the house. She was alone. He could hear her moving around. A single set of footsteps. It wasn't safe to be alone, not looking so pretty and delicate and smelling of flowers. For the briefest moment, he considered staying there, outside her window. He didn't. He was so, so hungry.

He spun on his heel and strode quickly away.

* * *

Ruby hummed as she scooped eggs, bacon and French toast onto Christian's plate. Her cheeks were rosy, and she kept pausing to stare into space with a dreamy smile on her face. Christian didn't seem to notice. There was a smug gleam in his eyes this morning. The two of them had had a better evening than she had the night before.

"Are you sure you don't want any eggs, Aurora?" Ruby asked.

"No. Thanks. I'll just have toast." She barely touched it. Instead, she sipped her coffee and gave Christian a disgusted look as he tucked voraciously into the huge pile of food on his plate.

Mike tromped into the kitchen. "I'll take some eggs."

There was a slight smile on his face. He'd had a better evening than she had, too.

"How was the party?" Ruby asked Aurora.

She glanced at Christian. He smirked. "It was okay."

Mike eyed her closely. "You're quiet this morning. Are you hung over?"

Aurora laughed. "No. I didn't drink." Not much, anyway. She didn't think she needed to start an argument this early in the morning.

Mike lifted his eyebrows. He glanced at his nephew. "Is this true?"

Christian rolled his eyes. "You know Rory. She's a total square."

"I take that to mean you did drink," Ruby said in mock disapproval.

Now Aurora smirked at him. He held up his hands. "Hey, this isn't about me. And I am almost nineteen."

"Almost nineteen is not twenty-one, Chris," Mike told him.

"Leave him alone," Ruby ordered her brother. She was practically glowing. "I don't really want to know what he gets up to."

"How was your date?" Aurora asked abruptly.

Ruby sighed. "It was amazing. Blaine took me to the Lodge for dinner, and we got a room. We spent the night talking and laughing and--"

Christian held up his hands. "No. Nope. That's too much, Mom. I don't want to know all this stuff. I don't think my delicate constitution can handle it."

"Don't be so dramatic. I wasn't going to say anything inappropriate."

Mike eyed his sister. "You think this guy might be something special?"

49

Ruby smiled. "Yes."

"Do you know him, Dad?"

He shrugged. "I met him a couple times. He brought his car in for a tune up. He seems like a nice guy."

"He's the sweetest, most interesting, and romantic man I've ever met," Ruby added dreamily.

Aurora rose and dumped her uneaten toast into the trash. She wasn't sure she wanted to listen to Ruby gushing about her new boyfriend.

"What are you doing today, Aurora?" Mike asked. "Homework?"

"No. I already finished it. I thought I would go into do town and do some shopping. Maybe get some coffee or lunch."

"Is one of the girls going with you?" Ruby asked.

"I...haven't called them."

"You should," Mike said. "You shouldn't go out alone."

"I'll be fine. It's New Coventry."

"That's not what I'm worried about." Mike peered at her over the top of his coffee cup. "Are you okay, Rory?"

"What? Yeah. Of course." She smiled. It felt forced. "I'm going to get ready."

"Call Josie or Diana."

"Okay, Dad. I will." She suspected he knew she wasn't telling the truth, but he didn't make any remark as she climbed the stairs to her room. She stared at her closet for several moments. She wasn't really thinking about what to wear. She felt strange this morning. Everyone else in the house was aflutter with happiness. She wanted to feel happy for them. Instead she felt lonely and empty and sad. She wondered if she was that hard up for a date herself.

She glanced at the photo framed on her nightstand. Her mother Rosalyn smiled out at her. Her long, strawberry blonde hair was tied back in a long braid, and she wore a long, flowing green dress that matched her emerald green eyes. Flowers surrounded her. Flowers had always surrounded Rosalyn. It was as if they loved her and bloomed wherever she went just to be close to her. Since she'd died, the garden outside their house had shriveled and died with her.

Sometimes, Aurora thought something inside her had shriveled and died too.

She sighed and pulled on jeans and a black hooded sweatshirt. She peered out the window. It was a nice, sunny day. Small, green leaves were budding on the trees on the other side of the glass. It looked hopeful and cheerful. She glanced back at her mother's photo.

She smiled, but she didn't feel much like smiling. She would try anyway.

Ruby and Christian had finished their breakfast by the time she trudged back down to the kitchen. Ruby was probably daydreaming about her date with Blaine or getting ready for another. There wasn't any music blaring from Christian's bedroom. He could have been playing video games or meticulously styling his hair to take out Sierra later in the day. She didn't know if he'd actually asked her out, but she suspected he had or he wouldn't have been so smug this morning.

Aurora grimaced. Mike looked at her. He still sat at the kitchen table, sipping coffee and reading the morning paper. He smiled hesitantly, as though he wasn't sure what sort of mood she was in. She returned the smile, mostly to reassure him.

"Did you call Josie or Diana?"

"Yes. Diana is going to meet me later at Colletta's." It wasn't a total lie. Diana was usually at Colletta's with Zach on Saturdays.

He looked satisfied. "Good. Do you need to borrow a car?"

"No. It's okay. I can walk or ride my bike. It's a nice day, and I could use the exercise."

"Okay. See you later. I might be at the shop this afternoon, but you can call me if you need a ride home."

"Thanks, Dad." She kissed him on the cheek and stepped out into the backyard. There was a slight breeze, but it was warm enough. New Coventry was a small town, and they lived only a mile and a half from the city center. It was a pleasant walk. She remembered the previous night, when she'd felt as though someone was following her home. She'd probably been imagining it.

She shivered, despite the warmth of the day.

There were children playing outside in their lawns, chasing each other around, shouting and laughing. They waved at her as she passed them, and she smiled, waving back. As soon as she was out of their sight, her face fell. She had a strange feeling. Her stomach flipped, and she stopped in the street, spinning around. She expected to see someone behind her. She didn't.

She felt foolish. This was New Coventry. People didn't follow people around on the streets. People didn't creep around in the shadows.

Idly, she wondered about the new family in town. Would they be strange and secretive like the history of the house? New people moved to do town often enough. There had been the Landrys, who bought the Lodge and turned it into a quaint bed and breakfast. Ruby's new boyfriend, Blaine, hadn't been around long, as far as Aurora knew. It was a small town. Very little happened. New people were always interesting, especially if they had handsome sons.

The city center was crowded with people strolling along the noisy, cheerful high street, greeting each other and ducking in and out of the small shops and cafes. Outside Colletta's, the patio was packed with people enjoying the burgeoning spring weather. Her spirits lifted a little. What could be wrong on a day like this, when the entire town had come out to enjoy the beautiful Saturday morning?

People greeted her as she passed Colletta's. She smiled and waved at them. When her mother had been alive, she would have paused to speak to everyone who greeted her. Everyone had loved her mother, and they always had some piece of news or gossip to share with her. Aurora would have sighed and fidgeted and wished she would end the conversation so they could move along. Now she would have given anything to be bored by her mother.

She didn't see Josie, Diana or any of her friends, but they would find their way downtown eventually. She didn't go inside the cafe. She continued along the street toward the New Coventry Museum of History. There weren't any people outside; the museum was never a particularly popular attraction and certainly not on a warm, sunny day. People wanted to be outdoors, not wandering around the dim halls of the museum. They wanted new, shiny things, not old, musty things.

Aurora loved the museum. She loved old, musty things. As she stepped inside, it was as though she left the depressing, lonely feeling outside in the streets. Her spirits lifted. She went immediately to the American History wing. She never got tired of looking at the old, colonial furniture or the art on the walls. She even liked the old, moth-eaten clothes. She had seen the exhibit dozens of times, and it still filled her with a strange sense of peace.

There was a new exhibit in the World History wing. There were statues of Greek gods with placards describing their various powers and personalities. Bronze statues wore warrior's ancient armor and posed in frozen battle with strange, arcane weapons. She took her time studying the placards. She enjoyed Greek mythology: stories of heroes, wars and gods. She would have loved to go to Greece, to see the temples and monuments. She would have loved to be the one to discover the artifacts.

For a moment, she closed her eyes and imagined it. She imagined digging around the ancient ruins in fantastic foreign lands, searching for lost treasures and artifacts. She'd never told anyone her fantasies about being an adventurer or an archaeologist, not even her mother. Somehow, her mother had known. Her mother had always known what she was thinking and feeling.

"Aurora. How nice to see you."

Her eyes flew open, and she spun around to face Dr. Erickson, the museum curator. He was a tall, thin man with steel grey hair, sharp features and round, rimless glasses. He was wearing his usual dark blue suit. She smiled at him. "Hi, Dr. E."

She liked Dr. Erickson. He loved history, and he never tired of talking with her about the displays. "For a moment, I thought I was seeing your mother," he told her, smiling. "You are growing up to look so much like her." He sighed and glanced at a statue of an old, bearded god holding a trident up above his head. "Rosa used to come in here any time there was a new exhibit, but she really loved the planetarium. I used to let her hang around after hours and play with the star projector. Speaking of the planetarium, don't miss the show this week. It's right up your alley. It's about the Greek mythological origins of the constellations. It's pretty epic."

She laughed. "I won't. It sounds great."

He smiled. "I could teach you how to run the star projector some time, if you want?"

"Yeah. That would be awesome."

"Come back and see me in a couple weeks when the Ancient Greeks exhibit is closed. I'll have some time then."

She nodded enthusiastically. "I will."

When he'd gone to greet some of the other visitors, she examined the

Greek exhibit for a while. It wasn't the first she'd seen, but she enjoyed looking at the statues. She wondered how old they were, wondered where they'd been discovered.

Had they been preserved, passed from museum to museum since they'd been rendered? Or had they been discovered in some forgotten ruin somewhere? It would have been an impressive, exciting discovery. She entertained images of discovering a treasure trove of ancient artifacts of her own for a while, until a family joined her at the exhibit, and she felt compelled to give the excited little kids the chance to exclaim over the imposing bronze gods.

Aurora was happier when she left the museum than she had been in some time. She was still smiling when she stepped out into the sunny streets and nearly collided with someone standing outside the doors. She jumped back, and looked up, embarrassed. "Oh, I'm sorry--"

She cut off as she met his large, midnight blue eyes. He had dark hair swept carelessly across his forehead and thick eyelashes. She'd never seen him before. She would have remembered because he was gorgeous. Like drop-dead, take my breath away gorgeous. The air around her seemed to have gone suddenly out.

He looked back down at her with a tempestuous expression on his sculpted features. He didn't reply or apologize. She had the strange feeling that he had just been caught doing something he hadn't wanted her to see.

She opened her mouth to say something, to introduce herself or ask who he was, but he spun abruptly on his heel and strode away without a word. She stared after him in surprise. He disappeared around a corner so quickly he could have been running away from her. She paused a moment to catch her breath.

"Well," she muttered. "That was weird."

Her phone trilled in her pocket, startling her. She fumbled it out. Josie. It was as though her best friend had a sixth sense about things like mysterious boys appearing out of nowhere and behaving like jerks.

"Hey, Jos."

Josie groaned, as though she was stretching. Aurora suspected she'd just woken up. She always slept in on the weekends. She'd probably rolled right over and called Aurora the moment she'd opened her eyes. She didn't sound quite awake. "Hey."

"What's up? Did something interesting happen last night?" Aurora looked around the street for the dark-haired boy. She didn't see him anywhere; he'd disappeared as quickly as he'd appeared.

Josie sighed. "No."

"Did you chicken out?"

"Yeah."

Aurora laughed.

"You?"

She considered telling Josie about the weird feeling that someone had been watching her. "No. I just went home and went to bed. I think I saw one of the people who moved into the Nott house, though."

"What? Last night?"

"No. Just now."

"Really?" Now Josie sounded wide-awake. "Tell me about him."

"How do you know it was a guy?"

"Just something in your voice. What's he like?"

"I don't know anything about him. I just saw him—well, I almost ran into him outside the museum. I assume it was one of the new people. He sounded like the guy Mikayla was talking about. Tall, dark, handsome, the usual."

"Yeah? So he's hot?"

Aurora laughed. It was pretty much the only thing that mattered to Josie, at least in the beginning. Was he hot? Oh, yes. She thought of the way she'd nearly stopped breathing when she'd looked into his dark blue eyes, the way her heart still pounded just thinking about him.

"He was kind of weird. But he's hot, all right."

"Weird? How weird? Did you talk to him?"

"No. What would I say?"

"What do you mean, 'what would you say'? You could have introduced yourself. Asked his name and what those people are doing in that house."

"That would have been a little rude, don't you think?"

"No."

"Well, it's not exactly my style, anyway."

"No. I guess not. Where are you right now?"

"Outside the museum. I thought I'd head to Colletta's for a coffee."

"Wait for me. I'll meet you there."

Aurora hesitated. She didn't want company, but Josie wouldn't really understand.

"Yeah. Okay."

"Maybe we can catch a glimpse of the mystery guy again. I don't suppose you know where he went?"

Aurora glanced back down the street the way he'd gone.

"No. Of course not. I didn't follow him or anything."

"I would have."

"I know."

"I don't mind looking a little creepy when it comes to hot guys."

"I know."

"See you in a bit."

"Okay."

* * *

Colletta's Cafe was packed. It was a popular hang out, especially on a Saturday afternoon. The tables inside and on the patio were full. Aurora didn't mind. She would rather drink her coffee outside in the park or while walking around the tiny boutiques and shops along the main thoroughfare. She waited out on the street, her eyes intensely scanning the people who passed.

They smiled at her. They were odd smiles. She was being creepy.

If she was being honest with herself, she was looking for the boy from the museum steps. What had he been doing there? She wondered if he was embarrassed to have been caught going to a museum. That didn't make a lot of sense, considering she'd been coming out. Why had he run away like that, as though he'd been trying to escape her?

Maybe she'd been giving him an intense, creepy look, too. Maybe he'd just been trying to get away from her. Her cheeks flamed. Of course she'd make a total idiot of herself in front of the hot new guy in town. She didn't really know why she'd expect anything else. She wasn't exactly cool or confident or nonchalant. She'd never been good at hiding her emotions. He'd probably seen her reaction to him as soon as he'd met her eyes.

"Rora!"

She turned to see Josie hurrying toward her, dressed in a short, bright purple dress and leggings. She wasn't wearing as much makeup today. She looked prettier without it.

Aurora smiled. "Hey."

"Hey. So, any sign of him?"

"Is he all you've been thinking about since I talked to you?"

"Yes, pretty much. That and a blended orange mocha."

Aurora laughed. Josie thread an arm through hers to drag her inside.

"You are really not very helpful. Couldn't you have done something like take a picture or ask his name or just hang onto him until I could get here to check him out?"

"I could have done that...but I don't think those are the best ways to introduce myself."

Josie sulked. "I would have done it for you."

"I suppose you're a better friend than me. I just gaped at him in surprise and watched him walk away."

"Oh." Josie winced. "Gaped?"

"He crashed right into me outside the museum and didn't even say he was sorry."

"Maybe he was too astonished by your beauty to speak."

"Somehow, I don't think that's it."

The cafe was so noisy Aurora had to concentrate to hear Josie's retelling of the night before, during which she had spectacularly failed to secure a date with Bryan. It sounded like he was as awkwardly shy as Josie. It was going to be an uphill battle for them. Hopefully one of them would manage to get up the nerve to do something one day, or Aurora would be hearing about it for the next several months.

They ordered their coffees, waiting in the small group at the pick up counter. Aurora heard someone calling her name. She looked around for several moments before she saw Diana waving at them from a table in the corner. She was sitting with Zach. A pile of books and notebooks was spread between them. They'd probably been there since the cafe opened, studying and doing homework. Loving coffee and school were two things the couple had in common.

Aurora waved back. Diana looked extremely irritated.

"What's got Diana's bloomers in a bunch?" Josie demanded, affronted.

"I don't know. You know Di. It could be anything."

Josie snatched up their coffees as soon as they hit the counter and plowed through the crowd toward Diana and Zach's table.

"What, Di? Why are you giving us the stink eye?"

"I'm not giving you the stink eye," Diana replied haughtily. "I was giving the entire room the stink eye. Sit down. I can't even hear myself without shouting."

"It is crazy busy in here." Josie loved busy places. The busier, the better, even if it was inconvenient to everyone else. "Aurora, do you see him anywhere?"

"See who?" Diana demanded.

"One of the people who moved into the Nott house."

Diana rolled her eyes and grunted in irritation. "What is your problem?" Aurora asked.

"The Jaynes. They're all anyone can talk about."

"Who are the Jaynes?"

Diana looked at her as though she'd said something exceedingly stupid. "The people who moved into the Nott house."

"Oh." Josie sat up straighter in her seat. "Aurora met one of them today."

"You did? When?"

"Well, we assume it's one of them. It was a guy. About our age, I guess. Maybe older. I didn't talk to him or anything. I just saw him outside the museum."

"It figures." Diana's mouth pursed. "Anyway, we've been trying to study, but it's been so noisy. People are just going on and on like they're some

58

sort of miracle workers or something. The entire town has gone completely crazy."

"What are you talking about?" Aurora asked.

"They're doctors or something," Zach explained. "People are raving about them."

"They've seen them?"

"There's a little sign outside the house now," Diana added. "Homeopathic medicine or spiritual healing, psychotherapy or some other such nonsense."

"That was fast. It wasn't there yesterday."

"I know. Weird, huh? It's like it just went up. But some people have already been to see them. It's like the shop in Needful Things."

"I doubt it's like that."

Zach jerked his thumb over his shoulder at a table of people sitting and chattering loudly with their heads together. "If they have anything to say about it, it's a lot like that."

Josie leaned back in her chair to peer at the table next to them. "What are they saying?"

"I'm sure if you listen, you'll hear all about it," Diana said.

"How did they even get there so fast?"

"I guess they've been seeing people since Wednesday, but they weren't advertising or anything. They must have met a few people around town."

"I wonder when they got to do town?" Josie asked.

"I don't know. No one really seems to know for sure. No one really noticed when they showed up. They were just there."

"I think you're making it sound creepier than it is," Aurora said.

"I'm not trying to make it sound creepy. I'm just telling you what I heard."

"Hey, Lisel," Josie said, addressing one of the women at the table. She was a waitress at Archie's burger shop. The other people with her were friends of hers, a girl named Emily who worked at a local bar, Lisel's boyfriend, Rick, who sold cars at the Ford dealership, and Paul West, who Aurora had seen around town. He'd moved to New Coventry at the end of his senior year, when Aurora and her friends had been in middle school. She thought he worked from home in IT or something. He was nice, but he had a reputation around town for getting around. Emily was his latest conquest.

Lisel turned to Josie, grinning from ear to ear. "Hey, Josie. What's up?"

"I heard you met the people who moved into the Nott house."

Lisel was a pretty girl with platinum blonde hair cut in an A-line bob. She normally wore heavy dark eyeliner and thick, dark makeup to look tanned. Today, her face was bare. She looked young and radiant. "Yeah. Dr. Jayne. Mariah. She's amazing."

Her amber brown eyes were dreamy. "What kind of doctor is she?" Aurora asked.

Diana and Zach weren't interested in anything Lisel had to say. They ignored her. Diana looked annoyed that Aurora had even asked.

"She does all sorts of things. She can fix any problem. She's, like, a hypnotist."

"A hypnotist?"

"She helped me quit smoking," Emily put in eagerly. "I went to see her yesterday, and I haven't smoked a cigarette since."

"It's only been one day," Paul said in a low voice. He, too, had heard enough.

Emily looked annoyed. "Yes, but you remember I couldn't even go an hour without wanting one. After I left her office yesterday, I threw my pack away and haven't even thought about it."

"What did you see her for, Lisel?" Josie asked.

Lisel looked a little pink, but she smiled. "I just had some things I wanted to work out. I haven't felt this good since I was a kid. It's like...I'm ten years younger."

"Is it just her—Mariah?" asked Aurora.

Rick shook his head. "Her husband is a doctor, as well. I've been having back pain for weeks, and nothing was helping. Whatever he did, it's gone now."

"I think it's strange," Paul said. "None of those things should have been cured so easily."

Lisel shrugged. "I'm not going to complain about it just because it was quick."

"It's like a miracle," Emily said. "I swear. I never thought I could quit smoking."

"April Dupree went and saw Mariah," Lisel told Josie in a quiet voice, even though no one could really overhear them. The place was no noisy, and the more Aurora listened, everyone seemed to be saying the same words over and over: Jayne. Dr. Jayne. Mariah Jayne. Adam Jayne. Evelyn Jayne.

Lisel jerked her head toward the center of the room. A young, pretty women around Lisel's age with long, dark hair tied back in a braid sat, sipping coffee and smiling happily at her companions. Aurora blinked at her in surprise. "That's April?"

"Yeah."

Josie and Aurora exchanged a glance. Everyone in town knew April Dupree. She was the sort of girl who wore black all the time and hid her face behind a sheet of dark, greasy hair. Aurora had always felt bad for her. She'd seemed so alone, so dark and lonely. She worked at the local library, and it was as though there was an invisible bubble around the area she worked. No one ever asked her for help. No one ever went near her. She rarely spoke to anyone, but when she did corner someone, she made stark, uncomfortable remarks about their appearance or their personal lives.

April almost never smiled. When she did, it looked more like a leer. Aurora had never realized how pretty she was. She looked as though a shadow had lifted from her.

"Okay," Josie said, staring in open shock at the older girl. "Now that is weird."

"What did April see her about?" Aurora asked.

"Being a freak," Rick muttered.

"She wasn't a freak," Emily scolded. "She was just depressed. She's always been depressed, as long as we've known her."

"And she's better now?" Aurora asked doubtfully. She didn't think therapy was supposed to work that quickly. She didn't know much about hypnotism, though. She'd never really believed it worked.

Diana frowned. "I think there's something not right about it all. It just seems too easy."

It did seem too easy, but April looked so happy, so carefree...

61

"Aurora? Aurora!"

"Huh? What?"

Josie rolled her eyes. "I said, you want to go by the house later and check out the sign?"

"Yeah. I do."

"Well, count me out," Diana said. "I've seen it, and it's nothing special. Zach and I are going to go home and try to get some studying done."

"Boring." Josie waved her hand dismissively. "Don't you want to see what all the talk is about? Maybe we can get up a little closer and see people come out looking all moony eyed and hypnotized."

Diana scoffed. "There's nothing unusual about homeopathic medicine."

"What about hypnotism?" Aurora asked.

"Please. It's just a temporary fix. They'll all be back to their usual selves in a few days. It's not a miracle. It's just suggestible people falling for a scam."

"It doesn't look like a scam."

"Just wait. It will. You'll see. April will be pointing out that there probably isn't a Heaven for people who die in car crashes, and Emily will be smoking like a chimney every half hour, as usual."

"You are really not very optimistic," Josie scolded. "You don't even think it's interesting? We've never had a hypnotist in town before. They've got everyone all wound up and acting crazy."

Diana scowled. "It doesn't take much to get everyone in town all wound up and acting crazy. Anyway, we have a Calculus quiz on Monday. We need to study."

"Fine." Josie hopped up. "Come on, Aurora. Let's go snooping."

She didn't have to ask twice. "Call you later, Diana."

Chapter Three

Josie slowed to a crawl as they neared the Nott house. It looked bright and inviting now. It didn't look much like a haunted house. Aurora couldn't believe the change that it had undergone since they'd seen it yesterday. The gates hung open in an unspoken welcome. The pale green sign in the gateway wasn't large, but it was hand-lettered in a friendly script.

"What does it say?" Josie asked.

Aurora leaned out the window to read it. "It says Dr. Adam Jayne M.D. Homeopathic Medicine and Healing. Dr. Mariah Jayne P.H.D. Therapist."

"That's it?"

"There's some other stuff at the bottom. Hypnotism. Spiritual Cleansing. New Age Medicine. Palmistry. Free Consultations."

"Palmistry? That's weird."

"I know, right? What is New Age Medicine?"

"It's like chakras and chi and stuff." Josie's eyes lit up. "Maybe they do séances, too. Maybe they picked the old house because it's haunted."

"Well, it's not a coven of witches, but I suppose it's close enough."

"Close enough for New Coventry, anyway."

A black sedan barreled past them into the driveway. The young man behind the wheel slowed and scowled over at them. Aurora leaned back into the car, her cheeks hot. His dark hair swept across his forehead and his eyes were as dark as midnight. She recognized him. Even if he had not met her eyes, she would have recognized the set of his jaw and the imperial lift of his chin.

"That's him,"

"What?" Josie leaned across her to get a better look at him. "He is hot!"

He stamped on the accelerator and shot through the gates without looking back at them. "I know." Aurora waved her hand at Josie. "Go. Go. I don't want him to think we're stalking outside his house or something."

"Don't be lame. People have probably been stalking outside his house since they moved in. They're running a business out of their home. We have a right to look at the sign. That's what it's there for." She grinned at Aurora. "You want to go in?"

"What?"

"Come on. We could get one of those free consultations. Or a palm reading. We could get our fortunes told."

"No! We can't go in there."

"Why not? We could meet that guy, see what he's like."

"By getting our palms read? That seems like a lame excuse."

"There are lamer ones."

"I feel like a stalker."

"Oh, you aren't a stalker. We were here before he even got here. It's not like we were camping out waiting to get a look at him."

"Yes, we were!"

"But he doesn't know that. "

Aurora's cheeks felt hot. "Come on, let's just go home."

"You're never any fun. You're always so restrained."

"I don't think that's a bad thing."

"No?" Josie narrowed her eyes. "You won't be saying that when Sierra and the evil twins have met him first and sunk their evil bitch claws into him."

Aurora laughed. "I think I'll be all right if that happens. If he is the sort of guy who goes for girls like that, he probably isn't someone we want to hang around with, anyway."

Josie puffed out her cheeks in disappointment. "Fine. We can go. But just remember, you are a total drag, and I protest your lameness."

Aurora glanced up at the house. For a moment, she thought she saw a dark-haired boy move past a window upstairs, pausing to peer down at them. Her stomach flipped uneasily. "Maybe next time, Jos. After I work up the nerve."

"Yeah?"

"Yeah. Well, maybe."

* * *

Josie sighed around a mouthful of ham sandwich and looked around the courtyard with in disappointment. "Josie, what are you doing?" Diana asked.

"Just waiting for something interesting to happen."

"Like what?"

"Rora, how old do you think that new guy is?"

Aurora rolled her eyes. "Are you still on about him?"

"What guy?" Shane asked.

"The new guy. The one who moved into the old Nott house," Josie said. "The doctors' kid."

Aurora shrugged. "I don't know how old he was. He must be out of school. For all we know, he's Adam Jayne and Mariah is his wife."

"No, he isn't," Cera said. "Well, I mean, I don't know if you saw Adam Jayne, but he's not that young. He does have a son our age."

"You know something about them?" Josie asked eagerly. "What's his name?"

"I don't know. My mom didn't remember. She said it was something weird."

"Weird?"

"Like Gamble or something."

"Gamble? That's not a name."

Cera waved her hand. "She just said it sounded like that. That's what she remembered. Anyway, he's home-schooled. She said he's never been to a real school before."

"Where did they move here from?" Aurora asked, nibbling the crust off her sandwich.

"South Carolina, I think. I'm not sure exactly where they're from."

"How did she find out?"

"Oh, my mom went to see them. She's had a bad knee since she was in gymnastics in high school. Dr. Jayne cured her. She said she hasn't felt so good since she was a kid."

Diana looked doubtful. "Was she hypnotized?"

"No, she went to Adam. He did some kind of chiropractic stuff to it and gave her some supplements. She's said it's all better now."

"I'm sure it isn't all better. That sort of thing is not cured over night."

Zach patted the air above her arm. "Just leave it alone, Di. If they think it works, maybe it does. The mind is more powerful than the body sometimes."

"What are you two talking about?" Shane asked.

"Diana's in a huff about the Jaynes," Josie explained. "She doesn't believe they can do what everyone says they can."

"I don't know. I've heard a lot of people around town talking about them. They sound legit."

"Hypnotism is not legit," Diana argued.

"You don't know," Josie told her. "You've never been hypnotized. It could work. Lots of people believe in it. They have those people who do those seminars where they hypnotize everyone into losing weight and quitting smoking and stuff."

"That's just people being gullible."

"Does it matter?" Aurora asked. "Even if it is being gullible, if it works, what difference does it make whether it was the hypnotism or their own minds?"

"Actually, she's got a point, Di," Zach said.

Diana didn't look pleased. "Fine. Sure. If you say so."

"My mom says Mariah's sister lives there too," Cera added. "She's a psychic."

"A psychic?" Josie asked.

"She's probably the one who does the Palmistry and New Age Medicine," Aurora said. "She probably isn't really a psychic."

"Carmen Winkler thinks she's a witch," Zach added.

They all looked at him in surprise. "When did she say that?"

"Saturday. It sounded stupid, so I didn't say anything about it."

"She probably isn't a witch, either," Aurora put in. "We just aren't used to that sort of thing. We shouldn't call her a witch."

"Well, there is something weird about them," Josie said. "You have to be weird to move into a haunted house."

"Oh, the stupid house isn't haunted!" Diana snapped. "That's all just rumors. All of this is just rumors. They aren't miracle workers."

"Well, we would know if Aurora had just let me go up to the house."

"What would you have said?" Aurora asked. "You just wanted to check out that guy."

"Well, yeah, but that doesn't mean I don't have problems I could ask them about."

"You do have a lot of problems."

"Oh." Diana rolled her eyes. "You were stalking Gamble outside his house?"

"His name isn't Gamble," Cera said. "It's just what she remembered. My mom was a little loopy when she got home. She usually remembers stuff like that."

"We weren't stalking him. We were reading the sign. He just happened to pull up when we were there. I think he recognized Aurora."

Aurora lifted her eyebrows. "Why?"

Josie shrugged. "I don't know. He just looked at us weird. He did just see you outside the museum, right?"

"I hope he didn't recognize me. He probably thought we were creepers"

"I wouldn't mind seeing what all the fuss is about," Shane remarked. "Maybe they can cure my acne."

"Oh, maybe they can help me get a date!" Josie added.

"I don't think that's what they do," Cera told her. "They are doctors, not genies."

Josie stuck her tongue out at her. "I wish I really did have something I need to see a doctor about."

Diana gave her an incredulous look. "You don't think you have something you need to see a doctor about? I'm pretty sure you could use a good therapist."

Josie shoved her playfully, but Aurora didn't laugh with the others. She wasn't entirely sure she couldn't use a good therapist. If they really were miracle workers, maybe they could make the strange feelings in her stomach go away.

If they couldn't, she might see that guy again—maybe she really just needed a date, too.

* * *

"Aurora? Are you up here?"

"Yeah, Dad!"

"What are you doing? Can I come in?"

She closed her laptop cover with a snap and looked up as Mike poked his head into the room. "Yeah. Just doing some homework. What's up?"

He peered at her a moment as though he wasn't sure he believed her. "I was going to head over to Julia's…"

"Oh. Okay."

"I can stay if you want me to."

"No, that's okay. You go ahead. I'll just see you tomorrow."

"Okay. If you're sure."

"I'm sure. I'll be fine. Tell Julia I said hi."

"Sure." He smiled. "See you tomorrow. Good night."

"Good night, Dad." She waited until she heard his footsteps on the stairs and turned back to her computer.

Dr. Mariah Jayne, P.H.D. She didn't have her own website, which Aurora thought was a little strange in this day and age. Perhaps the Jaynes got enough work through word of mouth—it seemed as though everyone in town already knew about them and couldn't wait to see them about whatever real or imagined ailment they had. They were legitimate doctors, though; Dr. Adam Jayne was licensed in several states, and Mariah was a registered therapist. They didn't list hypnotism or New Age Medicine in their credentials, but at least they weren't frauds.

She wasn't sure if she expected to find out they were some sort of mysterious, unknown strangers who'd popped up out of nowhere with no history, but they weren't. In fact, they were as popular on the web as they were in town. Dozens of testimonials from past clients in different states raved about the miracles they'd performed.

"For years, I suffered with depression, but since I visited Dr. Mariah Jayne, I've felt as though a dark cloud has lifted. I've never been happier and felt more alive..." "Dr. Adam Jayne cured my chronic arthritis in one visit. I can play golf again..." "I didn't think anyone could help my agoraphobia. Dr. Jayne visited me at home, and I felt like a new person. I have a whole new life outside my home..."

They sounded just like the people in New Coventry. She wondered if Diana was right—could it all be a temporary fix? It did seem a little unlikely the doctors could cure such serious problems in a single visit. Even if it was temporary...

She sighed. Everyone was watching the Jaynes' house; everyone was talking about them and the things they could do. She didn't think she wanted anyone to know she was seeing a therapist. She had enough problems without the Pops finding out about it. She could just say she was trying to meet their son...that was worse. She'd rather be a nut than a creep.

The door banged open downstairs. She jumped and snapped her laptop shut. Her heart thumped.

A woman giggled. Aurora relaxed. Ruby was home. She heard another voice with her. It was deep and rumbling. She lifted her eyebrows and peeked down the stairs. "Ruby?"

Ruby giggled again. Aurora didn't think she'd ever heard her giggle like that. "Aurora Sky, come down here."

She descended hesitantly. Ruby stood at the foot of the stairs, grinning at her. "Hey. What's up?"

"I want you to meet Blaine."

"He's here?"

A tall, muscular man with curly, dark-blonde hair and a shortly cropped beard peered around the corner of the living room. He smiled at Aurora. He was handsome—he was really handsome, even for a man her dad's age. He looked as though he spent a lot of time working with his hands. They were large and callused. His jeans and plaid shirt were streaked slightly with a fine, white dust that looked as though it had been ground into the fabric.

"Hello, Aurora." His dark eyes twinkled. He looked nice. Aurora couldn't help smiling back.

"Hi."

"I've been looking forward to meeting you."

"I wasn't sure we were ever going to meet you. I thought Ruby was keeping you all to herself."

Blaine laughed. "Well, she would have liked to. I insisted it was time to meet the family."

Ruby's eyes shone. Aurora had never seen her look like that before. Aurora hurried down the rest of the stairs and shook the hand Blaine offered. "It's nice to meet you."

"And you."

"Is Mike with Julia?" asked Ruby.

"Apparently, I have to be approved by Ruby's baby brother," Blaine told Aurora, rolling his eyes good-naturedly.

"That is only proper," Aurora replied.

"Put in a good word, will you?"

"Sure."

"Blaine's just going to have a cup of coffee before he heads home," Ruby added. Aurora was relieved. She liked Blaine well enough, but she didn't really feel like spending all night making conversation.

Aurora smiled. "I've got some homework to do, so I'll leave you two alone. It was nice to meet you, Blaine."

"You, too, Aurora. I'm sure I'll be seeing you again soon."

"Yeah. Okay. Good night, guys."

"'Night!" Ruby caught Blaine's hand. "Come on. I'll make you some decaf."

Aurora waved and climbed back up the stairs. She lay back on her bed and stared at the ceiling. Ruby seemed really happy with Blaine. She didn't really blame her; he seemed really nice, and he seemed to really like her. She wondered what it would be like to be in a real relationship—one in which she liked the guy she was going out with as much as he liked her.

The memory of the gorgeous boy on the museum steps flashed in her mind. It didn't go away. She didn't know anything about him, other than where he lived, that his parents were doctors and he didn't go to school. It wasn't exactly a biography, but it would do. She climbed under her covers and snapped off the bedside lamp. His face didn't go away as she closed her eyes. It was the sort of face that could keep a girl busy for quite a long time.

If she was going to think about him this often, she probably ought to learn his name. It simply wouldn't do to fantasize about a boy she only knew as Gamble Jayne.

She was still smiling as she drifted to sleep.

He didn't go away, not even then. He didn't speak to her in her dreams, but he followed her silently, slipping from shadow to shadow, as she strode alone along the dark streets of New Coventry. She spun and tried to speak to him, to call out to him, but she didn't know his name. When she turned to confront him, he was behind her again. He stayed at her back no matter which direction she faced.

And then he stood in front of her. He didn't speak even then. He stared at her with that strange expression on his face, as though she'd caught him in something he shouldn't be doing. His eyes smoldered, even in the darkness around them. She moved toward him, but she couldn't get any closer, though he didn't seem to be moving at all.

"What is your name?"

He didn't answer her. He didn't even open his mouth. He turned away. She chased him, and this time she reached him. She lifted her hand to do touch his shoulder, but he spun back to face her so abruptly, she startled. Even in her dreams, her heart thumped and pounded. Her breath caught in her throat. She gasped for breath. He opened his mouth to speak.

Aurora jolted awake. It was dark in her bedroom. She sat up and glanced at the alarm clock. 4 a.m. Her heart thumped. She wondered if her dream version of him was going to tell her his name was Gamble. That simply wouldn't do, not even in a weird, almost frightening dream. She sighed and fell back onto her pillow. She hoped she'd see him again when she closed her eyes—it was the closest thing she'd had to a date for pretty much ever.

She really needed to get a life. Or at least find out his name.

* * *

When she got into Josie's car the next day, she tried to shake off the strange dreams from the night before. It was all right to fantasize about the new boy in town—Aurora was, after all, a healthy and curious seventeen-year-old girl—but she didn't want to admit she'd been doing it. She was pretty sure her best friend would see the evidence of her obsessive thoughts all over her face.

Josie had other things on her mind. "Have you heard?"

Aurora's stomach sunk, but then she realized Josie's eyes were sparkling in excitement. "What?"

"The Jaynes are having a party on Saturday."

"Really?"

"Yeah. I saw a flyer last night at Archie's."

"They're advertising a party with flyers?"

"Well, sure. How else? They don't have a website or anything. They don't even have a Facebook."

"How do you know?"

Josie shrugged. "I looked."

"Yeah. I looked, too. Do you have one of the flyers?"

"No, but I bet someone at school does. Or maybe it's on the sign outside their house."

Diana didn't seem as excited about the party. Aurora wasn't sure what sort of party a family of New Age doctors would have, but it was probably nothing like any party she'd ever been to. Would they display their impressive skills? Would they hypnotize the entire crowd and make them dance like chickens?

"A party?" Diana repeated. "What do they need to have a party for?"

"They probably just want to meet everybody," Josie said.

"Obviously, they're trying to drudge up business."

"Honestly, I'm not sure they need to have a party to do that," Aurora remarked. "There has been a lot of talk and rumors about them. They probably want to let everyone see what they're really like."

Josie grinned. "Or they intend to hypnotize the whole town and turn us on each other."

Diana rolled her eyes. "That seems reasonable."

"Anyway, it should be fun."

Josie slowed as they neared the Nott—the Jayne house. There was a little hand-lettered banner on the sign. It said: ?

LEASE JOIN US SATURDAY EVENING AT SEVEN FOR AN OPEN HOUSE AND BARBEQUE. EVERYONE WELCOME!

"Well, that doesn't sound very sinister," Aurora said. "It sounds pretty friendly to me."

Diana smiled reluctantly. "Actually, I wouldn't mind getting a look at the place."

"And the Jaynes?"

"And the Jaynes."

Josie didn't steer away. She looked as though she was considering stepping out and walking inside. "You think he's in there?" She didn't have to explain who he was. Aurora knew. She had been wondering the very same thing.

"Jos, we're going to be late for school," Aurora reminded her.

Josie sighed. "Yeah, yeah."

Everyone at school had heard about the party. Word spread quickly in a small town, especially when it had to do with a new family surrounded by mystery, rumor and controversy that hypnotized people and read palms.

"So...you guys are going to the party, right?" Josie asked as they stopped by her locker before class.

Diana didn't answer right away. "Do you think the house can hold everyone in town?"

Aurora shrugged. "Probably not, but you know a lot of people won't go. A lot of them are still creeped out by the idea of New Age Medicine and stuff."

"Yeah, but they might just want to get a look at them."

"You know some of the people around here," Diana said. "They get ideas in their heads, and they won't change them. They act like even being around a New Age doctor or palm reader or something would rub off on them."

"That's just stupid."

"This is Virginia. Anyway, it should be okay. The house is pretty big. I think it's about three or four stories, and the yard is huge."

"So you're going," Josie guessed.

"Yeah. I really do want to see what all the fuss is about, and I wouldn't mind getting a look at that mystery guy you keep going on about."

Josie squealed happily. "Aurora? You're going, too, right? You have to go."

"I don't know. I mean, I want to, but I'll have to ask my dad. He might not want me to go; I guess I don't know how he feels about the Jaynes. He usually doesn't go in for rumors and stuff like that, though. He might want to check them out, too."

"I wonder if we'll see some ghosts. Maybe they'll have a séance."

"I think you're getting a little carried away," Diana told her. "They aren't witches."

"They could be witches."

"They're doctors."

"Those two things are not mutually exclusive," Aurora remarked, thinking of Christian. "In fact, sometimes those things go together."

"Yeah. Like witch doctors. See, Di? Have an open mind."

Diana laughed. "Okay, okay. I'm sure they aren't witch doctors, but I'll concede that I am extremely curious to see what they're all about."

"Maybe they'll hypnotize you and make you more fun to be around."

"I am plenty fun to be around," Diana argued, but she grinned as Josie slammed her locker and started toward Aurora's homeroom.

"I can't wait until Saturday!" Josie pumped her fists in the air. "This is going to be the best. If nothing else, it'll be a cool party at a cool house, and we'll get to see people from town drinking and acting silly. And I bet they'll make their hot son meet everyone. Parents are always doing that to their kids."

Aurora smiled. At least she might learn his name. "I'm looking forward to it, too. It should be interesting. Hey, speaking of new people, I met Ruby's boyfriend, Blaine, last night."

"Yeah? What's he like?" Diana asked.

"He seems really nice. I didn't get a chance to talk to him much, but I liked him. He's really cute, too, for an older guy. I'm really just glad she met someone. He seems to like her a lot. I know she likes him."

"Maybe she'll marry him and move out," Josie said.

Aurora frowned. "I don't want her to move out. I like having her there."

"Well, maybe she'll move in with Blaine and you and your dad can move in with Dr. Fall. She's got that nice, big house in Dinwiddie Hills right by Diana."

"I don't really think I want to think about any of that right now. Anyway, I'm happy for Ruby. Blaine seems like a good guy. I just hope he turns out to be in the end. You know how most of her relationships turn out."

"Don't start talking like that now," Diana warned. "Negative words attract negative outcomes."

Aurora smiled. "I'd better get in. The warning bell is about to ring, and you two will be late."

"Yeah, yeah." Josie grinned. "What are you going to wear on Saturday?"

Diana rolled her eyes. "Oh, it's days away, Josie."

"So? That doesn't mean you can't plan ahead. In fact, don't you always like to point out that planning ahead is the only way to get anything done effectively?"

"Not when it comes to getting dressed. I'm sure there are much more significant things to be spending your time thinking about."

"Aurora?"

The girls cut off abruptly and spun to face Jesse. Aurora sighed inwardly. She hadn't forgotten about him, of course, but she had been hoping the conversation they'd had at Bray's party would have kept him away a little bit longer.

"Hi, Jesse," Josie greeted in a sing-song voice. She grabbed Diana's arm. "We've got to get to class. See you at lunch, Aurora."

Aurora would have liked them to stay for moral support. "Bye, guys." She tried to smile at Jesse in an 'I'm not mad at you, and I don't want to hurt your feelings, but I definitely don't want to encourage you either' sort of way. "Hi, Jesse."

"Hey." His blue eyes slid away. He lifted his hand to ruffle the back of his overlong blonde hair. He looked insecure.

She prayed the warning bell would ring. Any second now.

"I was wondering...I was kind of hoping..."

"What, Jesse? We're going to be late for class."

He looked back up at her. "I'm playing a show with my band on Saturday... nothing big, just a coffee shop in Lynchburg. I thought maybe...will you come see us? We can go together--"

"I'm sorry, Jesse. I already have plans on Saturday." She was glad she didn't have to lie for once.

His smile wavered. "You do? What plans?"

"There's an open house at the old Nott house—the new family is throwing it."

He looked a little confused about this. She wondered if he even knew there was a new family in town. He wasn't the sort of person to listen to gossip. "I would really like it if you could come, Aurora. I would like to see you out there in the crowd."

"I'm sorry, Jesse. I promised my dad I would go to the party with him."

He scuffed his foot. He wasn't prepared to let it go just yet. Aurora looked up at the bell, but it still didn't ring. "What about before the show? We could have coffee at Colletta's or something—"

"Jesse..."

"Just give me a chance, Aurora."

She sighed. "I'll...I'll think about it Jesse." The image of the dark haired boy with the midnight blue eyes swam into her head, but she reminded herself she'd made her decision about Jesse a long time ago. It had nothing to do with Gamble—or whatever his name was.

He knew she was lying. "No, you won't." He sighed and ruffled the back of his hair again. When he looked back at her, his eyes were bright. "I'll do whatever you want, Aurora."

"Jesse..."

"I can change. If that's what you want, I can do it."

"Jesse, this isn't fair to you. You should find a girl who will return your feelings."

He caught her arm abruptly. "I don't want another girl!"

Finally, mercifully, the bell rang. She sighed in relief and tugged her arm away from him. "I have to go. You should get to class, too. You can't afford another tardy."

He didn't step away. She backed up and hurried into her class before he could stop her. She heard him call her name. She didn't turn around.

She wished he would just find someone else and move on. It would save everyone a whole lot of trouble.

* * *

Aurora felt excited for the first time in a long time. Josie and Diana insisted they get ready for the Jaynes' party together, and the three girls squeezed into Aurora's small bedroom to share the full-length mirror behind her closet door.

"Rora, what are you going to wear?" Josie demanded.

Aurora looked down at her jeans and sweater. "I was going to wear this."

"Oh, no, Aurora," Diana said in disapproval. "This is not a high school keg party. This is a special occasion. You have to look fancy."

"What? Why?"

"Because when are you going to have another opportunity to put on a pretty dress and mingle with the town witches?" Josie asked.

Aurora laughed. "All right. What are you two wearing?"

"A dress," the both said in unison.

"I don't want to look like we all wore the same thing."

"We won't," said Josie. "See? My dress is black. And slinky. And short. And cool. Diana's dress is pink and boring."

"It not pink and boring. It's pink and demure."

"It's practically a June Cleaver dress. So if you wear—this dress, it will look nothing like our dresses."

Aurora took the pale green dress from Josie and held it up to her chest. It matched her eyes. It was a little too short for a party with her dad, but some leggings and boots would solve the problem. "Okay. I'll wear a dress."

"Yay!" Josie clapped her hands. "And makeup."

"Now, don't push it."

"Just a little mascara. And some lip gloss."

Josie acted like she was a doll. It was best to allow her to do whatever she was going to do. "Fine. Go to do town." When Josie had finished with her, she admired herself in the mirror.

"See?" Diana said. "Its perfect. How do I look?" She held out her arms to the sides to display the dress. It was pale pink with long sleeves and a skirt that twirled around her waist as she spun around.

"You want to borrow some bobby socks and penny loafers?" Josie asked.

Diana stuck her tongue out at her. "Whatever. Are you sure you don't want to stop by Hot Topic and pick up some plastic chains and body piercings to wear with that thing?"

Josie held up her fists as though she intended to fight her friend. "I look good."

"You both look good," Aurora interrupted. "You guys ready or what?"

"Yes!" Josie thread her arms through her friends'. "Oh, I am so excited. Are you excited? You should be excited."

Aurora didn't admit it to her friends, but the swarm of butterflies that had been living in her stomach since she had heard about the party was flying around as though they were trying to break out. "I'm excited," Diana answered.

"Oh, I hope Bryan Dymond is there."

"From the sound of it, everyone is going to be there," Aurora remarked. "Even if they haven't met the Jaynes yet, they've heard enough about them that they want to get a look at them."

"Rory!" Mike called from the bottom of the stairs. "Are you girls ready yet?"

"Yes, Dad! We're coming!"

Aurora was glad the girls had convinced her to dress up. Even Mike was wearing his nicest black slacks and a dark grey button up shirt. He'd even shaved his five o'clock shadow and combed his dark, slightly shaggy hair back from his face. "You look very handsome, Dad. Are you meeting Julia there?"

"As it happens, yes." He smiled. There was something in his dark green eyes when he talked about Julia. Aurora was glad. She knew her dad missed her mom, but it was time to move on. She wanted him to be happy. He deserved it. He always seemed a little sheepish about it, though. Perhaps he thought she expected him to stay faithful to his dead wife forever.

"Where's Ruby?" Josie asked. Aurora knew she really wanted to get a look at Blaine, but Josie and Ruby got along well. Sometimes Aurora thought they had a lot more in common with each other than she did with either of them.

"Blaine picked her up a few minutes ago." He seemed to like Blaine well enough. He was probably glad his sister had met someone nice for once.

"Are you interested in meeting the new people in town?" Diana asked.

Mike shrugged. "I don't know. I guess."

Josie shook her head as though he was being very silly. "Don't you want to see what they've got going on at that weird house with all the fortune telling and hypnotism and stuff?"

Mike snorted. "It's just a house, and I'm not superstitious. I don't think they're up to anything weird."

"You are really no fun."

"Sorry. If you want to go to this party, we'd better go before I change my mind." He yanked a little on his collar. "I hate this shirt, but it's Julia's favorite."

"It looks very nice. Aurora, are you coming with us?" Josie asked.

"I think I'm going to ride with Dad. See you guys there?"

Even Mike looked a little surprised. "Sure. See you in a bit."

"You're looking more and more like Rosa everyday," Mike remarked abruptly when they were seated in his black Charger.

"Thanks."

He was silent a long time. Finally he asked, "You don't usually want to ride with your old dad. Did you want to talk about something?"

He might be a guy, but he could be insightful sometimes. "I was wondering how you feel about therapy."

He lifted his eyebrows. "I don't go in much for that sort of thing; I'm a simple guy. Are you thinking I need something like that?"

Aurora laughed. "No. Not you."

"Oh." He was quiet a moment. "I suppose I haven't been very emotionally supportive. It's hard to be a single dad to a teenaged girl."

"That's not what I meant!"

"I know. But sometimes I worry I'm not so good at that sort of thing. If you feel like you want to talk to someone, I'll support you."

"I'm not really sure. I just wanted to see what you thought about it. I've been feeling a little...weird lately."

"Weird how?"

"I don't know. Kind of...empty. And kind of sad."

"I suppose I should be glad you're telling me instead of just keeping it all in, right? I'm not supposed to freak out, right? I'm supposed to just listen and say whatever you want?"

Aurora patted his arm. "I'm not suicidal or anything. I just don't feel quite right. Maybe talking to someone would help."

"Maybe you should, then. I don't think I'm equipped to handle that sort of thing. I wish I was."

"It's okay, Dad. You can't do everything."

"Am I a bad father because I can't handle that sort of thing?"

"Of course not. You're a good father. You do your best. Sometimes you just need to go to someone who does that sort of thing. That's what they have professionals for."

"Are you bringing this up now because we're going to see those doctors?"

"It crossed my mind."

"Maybe we'll have a chance to talk to them about it."

She smiled. "Maybe not at the party."

"You're probably right. We could check them out, anyway. If you don't like them, we can find someone else. We could find someone we know already and trust. I don't want just anyone picking around inside my daughter's head."

Aurora didn't want just anyone picking around in her head, either. She didn't even know if she wanted the Jaynes to do it. "Sure, Dad. We'll see what we think about them."

Dinwiddie Hills was jam packed with cars. Mike had to park a block away from the old Nott house, but Aurora didn't mind. It was a nice night.

"Why you didn't come with Julia tonight?" she asked her dad as they walked side by side along the sidewalk toward the brilliantly lit house. There were people all over the place, lingering outside the gates, greeting each

80

other and walking up the winding pathway toward the front door.

"I thought I have been spending a lot of time with her lately and not enough time with my daughter. I suppose I should have done it sooner."

"No. I'm not feeling off because of you. I don't think there's anything anyone could have done. I have lots of people around who love me. I think it's just part of being a teenager." And losing her mother, she thought, but neither of them said it. "You know, Dad, I really like Julia."

This change of subject threw him off his stride. "Yeah?"

"Of course. She's nice. And I'm glad you're happy. I haven't really seen you this happy since...well, Mom."

He exhaled heavily. "Yeah. I still miss her everyday, Aurora."

"I know. Me, too. But it's no reason to put your whole life on hold. She's gone. We miss her, and we remember her, but you shouldn't have to be alone forever. She wouldn't have wanted that. You know her."

"Yeah. I do. And you're probably right."

"If you want to get married again—to Julia or whoever—"

He held up his hands. "Whoa. Hey. We're not talking about marriage here. Why are you talking about marriage all of a sudden?"

Aurora laughed. "I'm just saying. You've been with her a long time. If you guys are taking things slow for my sake, I just want you to know it's okay with me."

"I appreciate that, but Julia and I like the way things are."

"Okay, but if you decide you—."

"I get it, Rory. Thanks."

They walked through the friendly open gates. "Wow. They really did fix this place up."

The overgrown trees were trimmed back and carefully manicured. They formed a canopy over the thick, bright green grass of the lawn. Flowers bloomed in colorful beds, and bushes shaped like light bulbs lined the winding pathway toward the house. The pathway opened into a roundabout where several cars were parked around a gleaming stone fountain. Aurora remembered peeking into the gates with Diana and Josie when they were children. The fountain had been covered in moss. Now it quietly spurted water into the air and flowed into the small pool beneath.

The house had been given a new coat of paint. It wasn't yellowed and crumbling anymore. They'd stripped the old, peeling paint from the wood and stained it a pleasant, rustic mahogany. The front door was electric blue. There was a large lion's head knocker in the very center.

"They did this in a week?" Mike looked impressed.

"I know, right? They must have sent some people ahead."

"I wonder what they did on the inside." He grinned at his daughter and offered his arm. "Shall we?"

"Yes. I can't wait to see what they're like." She took his arm and they followed the procession up to the front steps.

"Is everyone in town here?"

"Yeah. Haven't you heard all the rumors? People can't wait to get a look at them and decide if they're witches or circus acts or something."

Mike laughed. "Shh. Someone could hear you."

She rolled her eyes but she snapped her mouth shut as they reached the front door. A woman with long, wavy dark hair stood in the doorway. She wore a short, midnight blue party dress. It matched her eyes. She was dazzlingly pretty. She reminded Aurora of the boy she'd seen in front of the museum. She wondered if she was Dr. Mariah Jayne. She looked a little young to have a teenaged son.

She smiled radiantly. She practically glowed. "Hello. Welcome to our home. I'm Evelyn Jayne." She stuck out her hand to Mike.

He shook it. Aurora smiled. He looked a bit dazed. There weren't women this pretty in New Coventry—at least, there hadn't been. Then he realized his behavior and inclined his head to Evelyn politely. "Thank you. I'm Mike Geller. This is my daughter, Aurora."

Evelyn's eyes lingered on Aurora. She smiled at her. "Hello, Aurora."

"Hi."

"Please, come inside and make yourselves at home. There are drinks in the parlor, and Father is barbequing on the patio outside. I hope you enjoy the party."

"Thanks." Mike tugged on Aurora's arm, and they left Evelyn to greet the other guests waiting outside. "Well, what do you think about this?"

"Very fancy. I guess they must be rich, huh?"

The entrance hall was huge with ceilings four stories high and stairs on either side of the room leading to the upper levels. There was a very simple chandelier hanging above their heads. The room was very pleasant. It felt soothing and serene. It didn't look overly opulent or ostentatious. The Jaynes obviously had money, or they would not have been able to afford so many changes to the house so quickly. It looked like they didn't want to make a big deal out of it.

The probably had offices somewhere further into the house. There was a large opened door to the left that led to what Evelyn had called the parlor, which was really just a large living room with a bar on one side where a local guy was serving drinks. The room was furnished with minimal decoration: some thick, leather sofas and chairs and some bookshelves. There were a few paintings hanging on the walls. Many of the citizens of New Coventry were inside. Everyone seemed to be having a good time.

Her eyes anxiously swept the rooms, but she didn't see any of the other Jaynes—if she was honest, there was really only one for whom she was looking. She didn't see him anywhere.

Mike was looking for someone, too, but there was no mystery there.

"Dad, go find Julia." She shoved him gently away.

He looked at her, embarrassed. "It's okay—"

"Go on. You know you want to. I'll wait for Josie and Diana. They'll be here any second, and I'm sure they'll be dragging me off anyway."

"Okay. He leaned down and kissed her on the cheek. "Have fun. I'll meet you in a while."

"Bye, Dad."

When he'd gone, she wandered through the parlor, hoping she didn't look too obvious. Some of the townspeople she knew greeted her and complimented her dress. Everyone looked dressed up. It wasn't every day the whole town turned out to meet one family. She didn't see anyone in jeans. She was glad she'd let the girls fix her up. She didn't feel quite so out of place.

Josie and Diana weren't in the parlor. Neither was the mysterious Jayne who made her heart race and her breath catch. She felt suddenly as though she was doing something deceitful, stalking around his house under false pretenses to get closer to him. She wasn't the kind of girl to scheme or sneak around to get a boy's attention or even like a boy enough to try. She didn't know what she felt about the mysterious new boy, but there was something different about him, something exciting and new. She'd never felt anything like this before. She wasn't sure she wanted to.

A strange sensation crept along her spine. She spun around, expecting to find someone directly behind her, breathing down her neck. There was no one there, but the people around her glanced at her curiously. Her cheeks colored. She smiled at them and started out toward the patio. Her friends had to be here by now.

The sensation of eyes pursuing her didn't fade as she moved through the parlor. She felt hunted and helpless. She looked around. She couldn't see anyone paying any particular attention to her. Her belly filled with ice. Her spine tingled.

"Aurora!"

She practically jumped out of her skin as Josie and Diana bounded up to her in the entrance hall. She breathed a sigh of relief. "What's wrong with you?" Diana demanded.

Aurora laughed. The sensation lifted as though it had never been there at all. "Nothing. Sorry. Just got a little carried away."

Josie looked around them with huge eyes. "Can you believe this place? It's amazing!"

Diana smiled. "It is pretty impressive. How did they manage to do all this so quickly?"

"I guess this is what money can buy you." Josie gave Aurora a sly look. "So, have you seen any ghosts?"

Aurora laughed uncomfortably. "No. No yet." What had she felt moments ago? It was like a breath of cold air, like there was something stalking her behind the shadows, in the spaces just beyond her vision. If there were ghosts, they probably felt a lot like that. She tried to suppress a shiver.

The girls weren't paying attention. They watched Evelyn greet the guests, smiling tirelessly. Aurora wondered how long she was expected to perform the duty. She wondered if her Jayne would have to take over. If he did, she knew Josie would sneak out the back and come right back in just to get a chance to meet him. Aurora would probably chicken out and just ask for the details later.

"So that's the older sister," Josie said. "She's really pretty. And nice. I wonder what the other ones are like. Have you seen any of them yet?"

"No. I just got in. I was waiting for you before I started creeping around trying to get a look at them. Evelyn said they were out on the patio."

Josie threaded an arm through theirs. "Well, let's go find them. I cannot wait to see what all the fuss is about."

The Jayne's backyard was massive. The patio extended far past the house, shaded with a wide awning that twinkled in the twilight with festive colored lights. Chairs, tables and patio loungers were spread around so the revelers could sit and chat with each other around the crackling, pot-bellied chimineas that glowed in the descending darkness. Townspeople stood around in small groups, greeting each other gaily as though it had been ages since they'd spoken.

Everyone was in high spirits. They drank out of plastic flutes and swayed to the soft, lively music that played in the background, insinuating itself into their moods. People lined up to pile their plates high from a table loaded with appetizers, salads and barbequed meat. Beside the table, a young man in a tee shirt and black slacks served drinks from a makeshift bar.

The Jaynes were easy to spot in the assemblage. They stuck out of the crowd, the only strange faces in a herd of familiar ones. It wasn't their strangeness that attracted Aurora. A subtle, diffuse glow spread out around them, bathing those nearby in a faint sheen. They were good-looking—extremely good-looking, like Evelyn and their son—but it wasn't their looks that drew the guests to their sides. Even at a distance, Aurora could feel the magnetism of their presence.

She wasn't the only one affected by their charisma. She and her friends could barely get close enough to catch their words or admire their faces. The guests clustered around them like groupies at a rock concert, exclaiming over the house, the party, the food, the lights, the yard and the amazing ways in which the Jaynes had changed their lives.

Mariah, the therapist, was a tall, slender woman with long, wavy, hair like her daughter, but hers was much lighter, a stunning gold. She looked like Evelyn, with huge, midnight blue eyes. She looked her age—likely in her mid-forties—but she was still very beautiful in a natural, confident sort of way. She wore a pale pink pants suit that looked very expensive.

Her husband, Adam, looked almost exactly like her mysterious Jayne, but he was much older. He was tall and lean with dark hair swept back from his forehead. His eyes were dark, almost black, and lined with lashes so thick, he could have been wearing eyeliner. His face was lined and strong. His eyes crinkled as he smiled, which he did often. He kept a hand on his wife's back or on her arm as though he couldn't bear to be separated from her. When he looked at her, his dark eyes twinkled.

Aurora couldn't help but smile. They made her feel oddly content. Just being close to them was like being bathed in warm, glittering sunlight after a long, hard winter. She glanced at her friends beside her. They, too, were smiling.

Josie sighed dreamily. "Look at them. They look so happy together."

Even Diana was affected. "They seem really nice, don't they?"

"I wish someone would look at me the way he looks at her," Josie agreed. "Do you think we'll get a chance to meet them?"

"That's the general idea," Aurora replied. "But I'm not sure we'll be able to get through the crowd."

"Everyone will calm down soon enough," said Diana. "They're not celebrities or anything. They're just new."

Aurora wasn't so sure. Perhaps she was allowing the atmosphere and the soft, subtle music to go to her head. Looking at them, she felt better than she had in some time. She felt hopeful. The closer they came to the doctors, the lighter her spirits became. They could help her. They could make all her worries fade away as though they'd never been there at all. She knew it, and she hadn't even spoken to either of them yet.

"You want to get something to eat?" Josie's smile practically split her face.

"Definitely," Diana replied. They tugged Aurora toward the table and filled their plates.

Aurora hoped the crowd around the Jaynes would thin so she could get closer to them, but no one moved away. The girls found a few empty deck chairs and sat down to eat.

Josie nudged Aurora. "Is that him?"

She swallowed a mouthful of food and looked around. Her pulse leapt. She didn't see him immediately; there were so many people, but Josie could always spot a cute boy in a crowd. When Aurora saw him, she knew something was wrong.

He was tall and handsome, but his dark hair was shorter and slightly disheveled. There was an edge to his smile. He looked almost exactly like her Jayne.

"It's not him. I think it must be his brother."

"Brother?" Josie perked up. "There's two of them?"

"Yeah, but..." Aurora cocked her head to study him. He looked older than them, probably in his early twenties. He was smiling, but there was something in his smile that made the hairs on the back of her neck prickle nervously. He had the same subtle magnetism about him as his parents and sister, but there was something cold and strange about him, too. It was probably her imagination—she couldn't possibly tell that from so far away without ever having spoken to him.

"It looks like the Pops have already met him," Diana remarked dryly.

Aurora hadn't even noticed Sierra, Claire and the Lawson twins surrounding the older Jayne boy. Sierra stood close to him and was smiled her most predatory smile. She laid a possessive hand on his arm. Even from a distance, Aurora could see Sierra's shiny red fingernails. They looked like talons. Sierra sure didn't look as though she remembered behaving the very same way with Christian a week ago.

She hoped Christian hadn't taken Sierra too seriously. He should have known better, but boys could be stupid sometimes. If he'd thought Sierra's interest was sincere, he deserved to get his feelings hurt. All the same, she didn't think she would mention anything to him.

"He's hot, but he sure has bad taste," Josie said. "When are boys going to stop being so dumb about girls like them? They're all just nastiness and pretty faces."

"Boys only care about the pretty faces part. That's never going to change," Aurora muttered.

"Maybe they'll let up on you, though," Diana said. "Maybe with this new guy around, they'll stop caring about Jesse and leave you alone."

"I doubt it. I think our feud has gone on too long and runs a little too deep for them to just move on."

"Well, it's something to hope for anyway."

"Or you could just fight back and make them regret picking on you," Josie scolded. "He is cute, though, isn't he? I might think of moving my interest to him."

Diana laughed. "Move your interest? I just thought you spread it around all over the place."

"Well, I do have plenty of interest to go around."

Aurora frowned. "He is cute, but something about him doesn't seem quite right."

They girls looked at her in surprise. "What are you talking about?" Diana asked.

"He looks fine to me," Josie said.

He didn't look fine, not really. There was something almost frightening about him. He was as good-looking as his brother, but her heart didn't flutter when she looked at him. A strange, creeping sensation shivered down her spine. She looked away from him and into the crowd. Her Jayne was around somewhere, but she couldn't find him. Perhaps he was like most other teenaged boys. He was probably hiding out in his room or where he thought his parents might not catch him shirking his hosting responsibilities.

Or, perhaps, she couldn't see him because of the girls surrounding him, fawning over him like they were fawning over his brother. She didn't know anything about him—not even his name. For all she knew, he could be ensconced in a corner somewhere with some girl. He might have a girlfriend or be the sort of guy who had a different girl every week.

He could be the male version of Sierra. She shuddered.

Beside her, Josie and Diana gossiped about the guests and the hosts, classes and their parents. Aurora interjected when they asked her a question, but her mind wandered around the party. She watched the older Jaynes as they spoke to their guests. She wanted to meet them, but she didn't think she wanted anyone to get any ideas. She knew it was stupid, but she'd had enough experience with the Pops to know better than to give them any weakness to exploit.

Zach joined them, balancing a huge plate of food on one hand. Diana smiled, but she didn't jump up to greet him or lean over to give him a kiss. Josie and Aurora exchanged a secretive eye roll. They liked Zach. He was a good boyfriend to Diana, but they didn't really have anything in common with him. He wasn't that much fun at parties. He didn't gossip or enjoy silliness. He usually talked about classes or other boring things like current events and criminal trials. He didn't have a lot of imagination.

Diana didn't mind. She listened to him go on about an essay for Government class without even a hint of boredom. She must really like him, even if they did act distant toward each other most of the time. Diana never really talked about it, but Aurora was glad she had somebody that made her happy.

Josie tried to look glad, too, but her eyes glazed over. Suddenly, she lit up. "There's Bryan."

Zach paused in mid-sentence and turned his head to look at her. Aurora jumped in quickly. "Go on and talk to him, Jos. We don't mind."

Diana smiled. "Yeah, go on. We're all right here."

Josie took a deep breath and squared her shoulders as though she was planning to storm into war. "Okay. I'm going. Wish me luck."

Aurora watched her go. Bryan stood by the food table, looking around the party. Aurora hoped it was Josie he was looking for. Boys could be funny sometimes. They didn't always behave the way she expected them to. He looked happy when Josie approached him. He probably wasn't enjoying the party much and was looking for a friendly face.

She spotted Ruby and Blaine in the crowd, holding hands and sipping bottles of beer. They were laughing with a group of Ruby's old friends from high school. Ruby looked up at Blaine with wide, shining eyes. Aurora's aunt had been looking for someone like him for a long time—pretty much forever. Christian's dad had been her first love, but he'd left when he found out Ruby was pregnant right after high school. He'd come back eventually, but by then it had been too late. Christian talked to him sometimes. Ruby never did.

"Aurora? Aurora."

She started and looked around at Diana. "Huh?"

Diana frowned. "Are you okay?"

"Yeah. Of course. Just...distracted, I guess. I was thinking about Ruby." Zach stood beside the lawn chairs, looking expectantly at the two girls. "Oh. It's okay. You two go on if you want some time alone. I'll be fine."

Diana looked as though she wasn't sure it was a good idea to leave her friend alone. "Are you sure you'll be okay?"

Aurora smiled. "Of course. I'm sure Josie will be back with her tail between her legs in a few minutes, and I can go talk to Ruby and Blaine if she isn't. Go on."

Zach smiled and turned to walk away without waiting to see that Diana was following him. Diana gave Aurora a guilty smile and hurried after him. Aurora sighed deeply. It had been one thing to let her eyes and mind wander when she was with her friends. It was entirely another when she was standing alone with a stack of empty plates, looking like a dope. If the Pops saw her, she would never hear the end of it.

She considered joining Ruby and Blaine, but she felt silly. They were having a good time; a high school kid hanging around would probably put a crimp on things. She strode past them, toward the edge of the patio. Beyond the twinkling lights of the awning was the deep darkness of the courtyard beneath its canopy of trees. The soft, moody music from the speakers on the patio barely penetrated the heavy stillness of the night.

She stepped off the tiled patio and strode toward the small clearing of trees on the edge of the lawn. The stars glittered overhead. They seemed closer than they did in the city. They were clear and bright and so numerous, they had taken over the sky here. Behind her, the noise of the party faded away. She sighed and wrapped her arms around herself.

She felt peaceful there, alone in the darkness.

She wasn't alone. After several long, quiet moments, the shadows beside her moved. The grass rustled so softly, she thought she might have imagined it. And then she felt the air shift. She spun toward the noise. "Who's there?"

The moving shadow didn't say anything. Finally, a low, sardonic voice replied, "I could ask you the same thing. This is my house."

Her pulse leapt. She knew it was him before he stepped into the pale glow from the party lights behind them. The shadows across his face made him look sinister. He met her eyes, and her breath caught.

"Well?"

She realized he was waiting for her to say something. "What?"

"Who are you?"

"I'm Aurora. Aurora Geller."

"What are you doing out here?"

She couldn't tell if he was angry, but his voice was cold and hard. She felt as though she was someplace she shouldn't be, invading his privacy and his space. "I just...wanted some fresh air." Her voice was steady, but her heart thumped in her chest.

"We're outside."

"I just...wanted to look at the stars." Even as she said it, it sounded extremely lame. She blushed in the darkness.

He didn't say anything for a long time. He didn't move. Then, "Me, too."

She turned toward him in surprise. There was something different in his voice now, something strange and soft. He sounded almost lost. Her stomach wrenched. She was lost, too.

She expected him to shoo her away. He didn't. She didn't say anything to disturb the quiet between them. She peered up at the sky, but she wasn't really seeing it. She was so focused on him, on his closeness and the sound of his quiet breath, she might have forgotten she was even there beside him, as though she had simply became a part of him.

"That one is Draco." She lifted her hand to point at the long, slender constellation in the sky. As soon as the words left her mouth, she winced. Her voice was like feedback in the silence.

He turned his head to her. She could barely see his eyes in the shadows. They were so dark, so expressionless. "I know what it is."

Her stomach sank. "Sorry." She felt rooted to the spot. If she left now, she might never have another chance to speak to him. He didn't seem to want her there.

He spoke again, and his voice was gentler than before. "Do you know them all?"

"Some of them. A lot of them, I guess."

"How about that one?"

She stepped slightly closer to him to see the formation he indicated. "That's Hercules."

"Oh." There wasn't any expression on his face. "Do you spend a lot of time looking at the stars?"

She wasn't sure if he was teasing her. "Yes."

She wanted to ask to his name, but her cheeks were hot. She wasn't sure she could get the words out without embarrassing herself.

He spoke out of the shadows as if he'd read her mind. "I'm Sable."

Sable. "Oh. Uh...hi."

He laughed so softly she almost didn't realize he'd done it. She turned to look at him. His face was turned up to the moonlight. It was sculpted and still like a statue. He was so gorgeous he might have been made of stone instead of flesh.

"Your house is really pretty," she said, casting about for something to say.

He shrugged. "It's my parent's house. I just live here."

She opened and closed her mouth to say something, but no words came out. As the silence stretched on, she felt stupid. Then it was too late. She heard him shift again beside her. When she turned to look at him, he was directly in front of her, looking down into her face with a strange expression that sent a ripple of trepidation down her spine.

"What are you even doing here, anyway?"

"What? I...I was invited."

He scowled. "You should stay away from here."

"What? I don't—but I--" She snapped her mouth shut in confusion.

"Don't come back."

He spun abruptly and strode away from her, disappearing into the crowd. She took a deep breath to steady her nerves, but it didn't do much to soothe her hurt feelings. She'd thought things were going well. Clearly, they weren't. She didn't know what he meant, but she knew one thing quite certainly.

She wanted to go back now more than ever.

Chapter Four

Aurora didn't see Sable again the night of the party, but she hadn't stopped thinking about him since their strange conversation under the stars. She thought of him as she lay in bed at night, unable to sleep. She wondered what he'd meant when he told her to never come back. Even now, his words—the tone of his voice, the look in his eyes—haunted her. A trickle of fear shivered down her spine.

More than anything, she wanted to see him again. She could hardly think of anything else.

She hadn't seen him around town or in any of the places she and her friends hung out on the weekends or after school. She didn't see him downtown near the museum. She passed by his house everyday on the way to pick up and drop off Diana from school, but he was never outside the house when they passed. She could go in, she could get a consultation with his mother—she wanted to, anyway—but she didn't have the nerve.

You shouldn't be here. Don't come back.

She never mentioned to Josie and Diana that she'd met him that night in the backyard. She couldn't explain what happened. She didn't even know. She didn't want to admit that she hadn't been able to think of anything else since. They would probably think she was crazy. Maybe she was. She'd never been so infatuated with anyone—not even when she'd had a crush on Will Ranier in eighth grade and had followed him around like a lonely puppy until he'd started going out with Erica Snow, who was in ninth grade and starred in the school musical.

Stay away. She didn't care what he said. If she wanted to see his mother—if she wanted to see him—she was going to do it. The decision made her stomach flutter. She took special care getting ready for school. She didn't know exactly for whom she was wearing her favorite emerald green dress, but it made her feel more confident than she had in a long time.

She felt like she could storm into Sable Jayne's house. He could stare her down and warn her away all he wanted. He wasn't the boss of her.

Josie looked surprised when Aurora climbed into her car. "Hey. Nice dress. What's the special occasion?"

"I just felt like looking nice."

"Is there something you haven't told me?"

"Like what?"

"I don't know. Like...is there someone special you haven't told us about?"

"Someone special?" She thought of Sable, but she wasn't ready to talk about him yet. Anyway, she hadn't seen him since the party. She doubted today would be any different.

"You know, like a boy? Did you meet someone at the party or something?"

"No. I didn't meet anyone." Her cheeks pinked, but Josie didn't notice.

"Well, I like it."

"Thanks."

Diana gave Aurora a long look as she slid into the car. "You look nice."

"Thanks." She looked up as they passed the Jayne house. She didn't see Sable or his black car. She thought, for a moment, she saw someone pass by the window on the top floor, but when she blinked, there was no one there. Wishful thinking.

She was still thinking of Sable when they pulled into the school parking lot. Jesse was waiting by his bike for her. He smiled, but he looked oddly downtrodden. She wished she could pass without saying anything, but he rose to block her path. "Hey, Jesse."

"Hi, Aurora." He ruffled the back of his shaggy dark blonde hair.

She felt awkward. "How...was the show?"

He smiled crookedly. "It was good. We had a lot of people show up. The girls seemed to like us."

She knew girls liked him. If they didn't, she probably wouldn't have so many problems with Sierra and her gang of she-devils. Maybe he'd finally discovered that there were other girls in the world. "Oh. Well. Good...I guess. I'm glad it went well."

"Aurora, we have to get to class," Diana told her.

"Yeah. We'd better go. Bye, Jesse."

He caught her arm as they started away. She gestured Josie and Diana to go on ahead. They didn't go very far. Instead, they waited for her, looking nosy and annoyed respectively.

"Aurora, I–I just..." He let go of her arm. "Sorry."

She felt bad for him. "You should get to class too, Jesse."

"If I did better in school, would it make a difference?"

She considered this very seriously for a moment. "Yes. Maybe it would."

"Okay." He stepped away from her abruptly and strode away.

"What was that about?" Josie asked.

"I don't know. I just don't get boys."

The rest of school didn't go much better. She hesitated outside the door to her English class. She hadn't run into the Pops yet today. It had been really nice, but she couldn't avoid them any longer. By a stroke of incredible bad luck, Sierra, Claire and the Lawson twins were all in the same class. They generally took the opportunity to do torment her whenever their teacher, Mrs. Lima, wasn't paying attention, which was most of the time.

The warning bell trilled. She sighed and stepped inside. A frigid chill emanated from the Pops' side of the room. Aurora lifted her chin and ignored their glares, taking a seat in the middle of the room where she could duck her head behind her book. She could feel the twins' and Sierra's eyes on her as though they were poking her with tiny, hateful little needles.

Josie and Diana were wrong. Even if the Pops had turned their attention to Sable's older brother, they still had enough reason to dislike her. Jesse. She didn't really know what had happened that morning, but it wasn't the first time she'd considered what would happen if he did change. What if he did start doing well in school, stopped getting into trouble, and started to think about his future for once? Jesse was a troublemaker, but he was a nice guy, and he loved her. She wondered if anyone would ever love her like he did. Was she turning down her only chance to have someone who felt like that about her?

She thought of Sable Jayne. She had known Jesse since they were just kids. Even when he was professing his love and showering her with gifts, she'd never felt such breathless, heart thumping attraction. Sure, Jesse was hot and he adored her, but he didn't make her insides flutter like Sable had in just a few minutes of strange, almost hostile conversation. She hadn't seen him since, though, and Jesse was here. Wonderfully, reliably, irrevocably here.

She could see him any time she liked.

Still, she couldn't shake her thoughts of Sable. He was there, in the back of her mind, even when she was trying not to think about him.

All around her, a low, urgent buzzing sound filled the room. She looked up from her book in interest and met Sable's midnight blue eyes. She blinked, wondering if she was imagining him standing there, if her obsessive thoughts of him had brought on a full-blown hallucination.

But, no. She wasn't the only one who saw him. He was there, standing just inside the classroom in jeans and a black hoodie, almost as if he was supposed to be there. And he was looking right back at her, as though there was no one else in the classroom. She felt the air go out of the room, felt time stop as she looked back at him. He was as handsome in the bright, florescent lights of the classroom as he had been in the sinister shadows of the courtyard. He might be there looking like he belonged, but he didn't. Not really.

And then the bell rang, and the spell was broken. It might have only been a second, but it had seemed as though his eyes had pierced straight through her, turned her insides to butterflies and stolen any chance that Jesse or anyone else would ever make her feel like he did. He didn't even noticed. He snapped his eyes away from her and scanned the classroom in complete indifference.

Sierra and the twins snapped to attention. They tossed their hair, batted their eyelashes and looked as appealing as they were capable of looking–which, Aurora thought with a sinking feeling–was pretty appealing. Sable didn't notice them, either. He walked right past without a second glance at them and took a seat a few desks away from Aurora.

The teacher rose to greet the class. Aurora wasn't paying attention to her. Though she couldn't see him, she could feel Sable behind her as if he were the center of the entire world. Hot tingles raced along her spine. She turned her head just slightly to the left. He was closer than she'd realized. He looked right back at her. She turned her eyes away, ducking her head to hide her flaming cheeks behind her long, strawberry blonde waves.

Mrs. Lima rose from her desk. "Okay, class." She might not even have noticed the new student or the stir he was causing through her classroom. "Let's all open our books and begin reading Chapter Thirteen."

Aurora opened her book gratefully. She could still feel the tingle of

Sable's eyes on her back. It was probably just her imagination or a phantom echo of his intense stare. She took a deep breath and tried to focus on the pages before her.

Romantic Poetry. Terrific.

* * *

"Oh, my god, did you hear?" Josie asked.

"Hear what?"

"Sable Jayne."

"Yeah." Her eyes scanned the parking lot, hoping to catch a glimpse of him again. He hadn't spoken to her in class—he hadn't spoken at all in class—and he'd left without acknowledging her at all. He might not remember her or realize it he had met her in the courtyard the night of the party. That, or he just didn't care. "He's in my English class."

"Really? I wish he was in one of my classes. Or all of my classes. I haven't even gotten to see him yet."

"I'm sure you'll get your chance."

"I wonder why he came to school all of a sudden."

"I don't know. Maybe his parents made him."

"Maybe." Her face suddenly lit up. "Is that him?"

Aurora turned in the direction of her gaze. Sable strode toward a black sedan parked a few spaces away. He turned his head toward them as though he felt their scrutiny. His eyes met hers again, and she felt the same curious sensation of being turned inside out. She turned away immediately. "That's him."

"He is so hot."

"I know." She waited for Josie to get into her car, but her friend waited to watch Sable until he climbed into the black sedan and peeled away. "He isn't that nice, though."

"How do you know? I heard he didn't say a word in class."

Aurora hesitated. "I met him. Before class."

"What? You didn't even mention it! Tell me everything."

"There's not much to tell. I just ran into him at the party. He was hanging out in the dark."

"In the dark?"

"In the yard. I went out to get a couple minutes alone and there he was."

"What did he say? What is he like?"

"He hardly said anything." *Stay away. Don't come back.* Josie would have enjoyed the drama, but Aurora still didn't understand it herself. She wasn't entirely sure he hadn't simply been rejecting her. "He said he wanted to be left alone."

"So you went?"

"Well, yeah. Of course. I'm not going to hang around where I'm not wanted. It would have been awkward and rude."

"I would have stayed."

"I know."

"I don't mind being awkward and rude." She sighed dreamily. "He is so gorgeous. Definitely as good-looking as Jesse, which means I have no chance. Speaking of Jesse, what was that all about earlier?"

"I don't know. I just wish he would find someone else and move on."

"Do you really? You don't think it's fun to have some gorgeous guy all the girls want pining all over you?"

"It sounds like it would be, but it isn't. It's kind of horrible. He seems so... well, I just feel bad. I wish I didn't have to hurt his feelings."

"Oh, he'll get over it."

"I'm not sure he will." Aurora was silent a moment. "He asked if I would give him a chance if he did better in school."

Josie lifted her eyebrows. "What did you say?"

"I said maybe."

"Did you mean it?"

"No. Honestly, not really. He's already done too much damage. It's too late. Even if he did change and start to make something of himself...it's just too little too late."

"It should never be too late. You could change him. You could turn him into a decent guy."

98

"That's not for me to do. It's not good for me to be the reason. He has to decide to do it on his own."

But that wasn't really it, was it? She had considered it, for a split second. For more than a second. And then Sable had walked into her classroom.

"He does anything you want," Josie said. "Maybe you could just send him along my way?"

"Next time I talk to him, I will give the order."

"You're a very good friend."

* * *

She heard the soft hum of the television in the living room. She dropped her backpack on the kitchen table. "Hello? Is someone home?"

She wasn't expecting anyone; she usually came home to an empty house after school. She wasn't in the mood to spend another night alone in front of the television, her homework or her computer. Maybe Christian had driven home for the night. Even if he were here to see Sierra or go out with his friends, it would be nice to have someone to talk to, at least for a little while. She would even put up with his snarky comments. She might even listen to him talk about Sierra for a while

It wasn't Christian who strode into the kitchen. The scent of flowers preceded Ruby. Aurora perked up.

"Hey, Ruby. I didn't know you were home. Shouldn't you be at the shop?"

"No. I thought I would leave early. I can let Marisa handle it for a few hours. It hasn't been that busy lately, anyway."

Aurora eyed her suspiciously. "Are you meeting Blaine?"

"No. His business partner just flew into do town, so he's meeting with him tonight." Her mouth turned down just slightly at the corners as she leaned against the kitchen counter.

"I didn't know he had a business partner."

"Well, in truth, neither did I." She walked to the refrigerator and rooted around for a diet soda. "We never really talked about it. They've been partners from the beginning, though. Apparently Troy's the one with the cash, and Blaine's the one who does the work. Troy comes around every now and again to check up on Blaine and his investments. I think Blaine was excited to see him. He said they've been friends since they were teenagers."

"There are worse reasons to be put off for an evening."

"It isn't so bad. I have been neglecting things. I need to catch up on my DVR and plan to eat something very bad for me."

"You have been seeing a lot of Blaine lately."

Ruby sighed happily. "Yeah. He's great."

"You really like him?"

"How could I not? He's gorgeous, fit, well-off, sweet, strong, handy with... his hands."

Aurora rolled her eyes. "Yeah, yeah. In other words, he's the perfect man?"

Ruby laughed. "Well, he's not perfect, but he is everything I've been looking for. For the most part. He does have an unfortunate obsession with 80's rock ballads."

"He seems like a really nice guy. And he's totally cute."

"Yeah. He's so cute." Her eyes shone. "When he kisses me..."

Aurora lifted her hand. "Okay. Okay. I don't need to know about that kind of stuff. We're friends, but not like that."

Ruby laughed, and then her expression became suddenly very serious.

"Uh, oh. What's going on? I should have known something was up. You never leave the shop early."

Her aunt looked perfectly innocent. "Sure I do."

"Did Dad put you up to this?"

"Well..." Ruby looked sheepish. "He just thought maybe you needed someone to talk to. I offered my services as your aunt and someone who's been a teenaged girl."

Ruby was better than Josie or Diana, anyway. "Okay."

"So, what's going on?"

"I've just been...feeling weird lately."

"It sounds like we need to have a girl's night. Your Dad will be conspicuously gone all night. How about we bake some cookies and talk about it? We can skip dinner and go right to the sweets. And then we can order pizza later if we aren't miserably full of cookies. Even if we are."

Aurora grinned. "That sounds good."

Ruby bustled around the kitchen, pulling out supplies from the cabinets for the cookies. "So, weird how?"

She perched on a stool beside the counter island. "I don't know. I'm not sure. Just sort of..."

"Unhappy?"

"No. I'm not unhappy. I'm just feeling sort of...empty. Like something is missing."

Ruby looked at her sympathetically. "Like your mom?"

"Maybe. I used to think so."

"Now?"

"Maybe I just need to meet someone like Blaine."

Ruby laughed as she tossed ingredients into a huge red bowl. "Well, as much as I love dating and meeting a good man, I am an expert when it comes to thinking a man will make things better. They won't. If there is something missing inside you, you're the only one who can find it."

"I know. I was thinking maybe I could go talk to Dr. Jayne. Everyone seems to think they can work miracles."

"I don't know if I believe that. There is no such thing as a quick fix, but it wouldn't hurt to talk to someone. You lost your mother when you were really young. I'm amazed we didn't think to send you to someone sooner."

"I've been feeling all right. It's just been different lately. I guess I just feel lost."

"We all feel that way sometimes. It might not mean there's something wrong with you."

Aurora leaned over to scoop up a handful of chocolate chips. "I don't think there is anything wrong with me. I feel the same as always. I feel like me. I just feel like there is more to all of this—to life—that I am missing out on."

Ruby smiled. "Yeah. I know exactly how that feels. I know that feeling a little too well." She was silent as she scooped cookie dough onto a baking sheet. Finally she looked back up at Aurora. "Have you thought about what you want to do when you get out of school?"

Aurora hesitated. "Yes."

"Really? What?" Ruby looked at her in surprise, her wooden spoon poised in mid-air.

She'd never spoken it out loud, not even to Dr. Erickson. "I want to study archaeology or anthropology in college."

There was a moment of silence. "Well...that's great. What do you want to do with that?"

This was why she didn't tell people; most of them didn't understand. "I want to work for a museum like Dr. Erickson. Or maybe go searching around the world for historical artifacts for museums." It sounded a little silly when she said it aloud, but she lifted her chin and committed.

Ruby thought about it for a while before she smiled. "That sounds fun, Aurora. I know how much you love the museum. Why haven't you told your dad about this?"

"I just...wasn't sure what he'd think about it. It isn't...well, it isn't like being a doctor or a lawyer."

"Honey, your dad is a mechanic. He doesn't expect you to do anything you don't want to do. I think he'd appreciate finding out his daughter wants to be the next Indiana Jones."

Aurora laughed. "Well...maybe not quite like that. Dr. Erickson says he spends most of his time digging through boxes in a dusty backroom."

"It sounds like you've got things figured out, Aurora." She winked as she stuck the baking sheet into the oven. "I think you're going to be just fine."

Aurora smiled wanly. She didn't think it was going to be that easy, but her aunt looked pleased, and she didn't want to burst her bubble—not when she was baking Aurora cookies and trying to help.

"So how about dating?" Now Ruby's eyes twinkled a little as she sat beside Aurora at the island. "Are you seeing anyone?"

Aurora rolled her eyes. "Come on. I think you would know. I'm not good at hiding stuff like that."

"I wouldn't know; you could have been hiding a secret boyfriend for the last several years and I wouldn't have any idea."

"Well, I'm not."

"Well? So? Any prospects?"

"Dating prospects?"

"Yeah."

"Well…"

"Well? Anyone you like?"

"Well…" Sable hadn't been far from her thoughts. He came again, and her cheeks heated. "Yes. There's someone I like…I think. I don't know him well. I don't really know much about him at all."

"Who is he?" When Aurora didn't reply, she smiled. "Okay, okay. You don't have to tell me. Fine."

"I just…he doesn't like me back. I don't think he even knows who I am."

"Well, you should let him know. Have you talked to him?"

"Yes, but not on purpose."

"Maybe you should talk to him. Any guy would be lucky to go out with you. Maybe he just needs to get to know you."

Aurora sighed.

"I know. I know. It's a lot more dramatic when you're in high school. When you get to be my age, you just go for what you want. You run out of time to wait in agony for them to notice you. You just go up and make them notice."

"I wish I could be more like that."

"It's okay. You have time. You have all the time in the world. It was getting too late for me. I had to just take my chances with Blaine and hope for the best. If I didn't, I might have missed out on him."

"I might not have all the time in the world. He might be gone as soon as he came."

"If you like someone, Aurora, sometimes you just have to put yourself out there and risk getting hurt." The oven timer beeped urgently. Ruby rose to pull the steaming cookies out of the oven. She scooped one onto a napkin and handed it to Aurora. "It's hot."

Aurora didn't care. She picked it up and bit into it without waiting for it to cool. It burned her tongue. She fanned her mouth. "Oh, I shouldn't have done that."

Ruby laughed. "You never could wait for it to cool. It used to drive your mother crazy." She picked up another cookie and placed it on a plate in front of her.

"What about a boy who...there's a boy who likes me."

Ruby smiled knowingly. "Jesse Drake?"

"You know about that?"

"Everyone knows about that. He's been in love with you since you were little kids. I remember Rosa telling me about him following you around preschool, talking about how many kids you were going to have when you grew up."

"He's well...I just don't know, Ruby. He's just trouble."

"Yes, I've heard all about him. The town juvenile delinquent, right? But that's high school stuff. That's not all he is. Don't you like him?"

"I'm not sure. Sometimes I think I do or I could, but then..."

"So he's not the boy you like."

"No. Just the only one who might actually want to date me."

"I don't think that's true. Maybe you just need to make yourself known."

"I think I'm pretty well-known."

"Well, maybe boys are too afraid to approach you."

"Why would they be afraid?"

"Well, you are beautiful, just like your mom. Boys are always a little scared of pretty girls. And you're sweet and funny and smart."

Aurora frowned. "That makes me too scary to date?"

"Well, that and you have the town bad boy hanging around you, probably scaring everyone else away."

"I've never actually thought about it. You think he might be scaring other boys away?"

"Maybe not on purpose. But how many guys do you know would go after Jesse Drake's girl?"

Aurora dropped her head in her hands. "None. None at all. Well, that... that's just unfair!"

"You just have to find a guy who isn't afraid of him is all. Do you think the boy you like can handle him?"

"I'm not sure. I don't know much about him. I guess he seems like the kind of guy who isn't afraid of anything."

"Aurora Sky, if I know anything about men, it's that they are all afraid of something."

Chapter Five

Aurora lifted her chin and squared her shoulders as she yanked open Mrs. Lima's door. The Pops weren't going to ruin her day. She wasn't going to let them, not today. She hitched her backpack over her shoulder and smoothed the front of her favorite green sweater. She ignored Sierra and the Lawson twins as she strode past them to her usual seat near the back of the classroom. She felt their eyes upon her, heard their voices like the hisses of snakes, but she didn't turn in their direction.

Her eyes swept the back of the room. She let out a breath she hadn't realized she'd been holding. He wasn't there. Her stomach sank in disappointment. Had he stayed home? Her gaze locked on the door. She tried to force it back down to her desk, tried to focus on drawing her books and pens from her backpack.

If the Pops noticed her watching for him, they would guess what she was thinking, and they would tear her apart. She would rather he didn't notice her than see her shrink and flush and stutter stupidly under Sierra's and the Lawson twins' stinging barbs.

It didn't matter anyway. He hadn't acknowledged her since the party at his house. If he remembered her, he didn't seem to want anything to do with her. She should just forget him; let this silly unrequited crush go before the Pops noticed and leapt upon another excuse to make her life a living hell. She should forget about it before he noticed her attention and turned that cold, indifferent expression on her.

But...she would prefer he hated her than not thought about her at all.

When Sable walked into the room, she knew it was hopeless. Even if he never looked at her, never noticed her or acknowledged her, even if the Pops discovered her crush and teased her ruthlessly, it wasn't just going to go away. When he walked into the room, she felt as though he had just stolen her breath. Let it go? Yeah, right.

His eyes flicked over the room. He caught her looking at him. She didn't drop her gaze. She could feel the top of her head prickle, and she felt a blush coming on. She caught her breath. No. She wasn't a deer caught in headlights. She was a girl, and he was more afraid of her than she was of him—at least, that's what Ruby said, anyway, and Ruby knew a lot more about boys than Aurora did.

She lifted her chin and gave him a tiny smile. He blinked.

"Hi, Sable," Cami Lawson purred. Her smile wasn't shy or tiny at all. It was predatory.

Sable glanced at Cami. His expression was so cold he could have chilled the air around him.

"Will you sit by us?" Callie added, draping her arm across the empty desk beside her.

Aurora tried to look away, to duck her head and ignore the Pops trying to sink their claws into Sable. She couldn't. She held her breath. If he went for it, she promised herself, he wasn't worth all the nights she'd laid awake, analyzing every inch of him so obsessively. She didn't think she could have a crush on someone who fell for the twins' batting eyelashes and perfect makeup.

He didn't fall for it. His eyes slid back to Aurora. His cold expression hadn't warmed even a degree. She sat up straighter in her seat as he strode toward her. Her pulse raced.

He walked right past her to a desk a few seat away and slunk down into it, crossing his arms over his chest and staring out the window as though it were more interesting than anything in the room. From across the room, Callie glared at Aurora, as though she was to blame for Sable's cold treatment. At least they couldn't hate her any more than they already did. It wasn't much comfort.

Mrs. Lima walked into the room with a dour expression. She didn't speak. She didn't even sit down at her desk. She hovered awkwardly near the doorway, as though she was considering fleeing at any moment. She startled when the doorway filled inexplicably with an expansive, balding man in a blue uniform, though she seemed to have been expecting it.

The classroom buzzed noisily at the appearance of the New Coventry police chief, Reggie Gray. He was normally a jovial, smiling man drinking coffee at Colletta's on his breaks or good-naturedly hassling teenagers making out in their cars. Aurora had never seen him look so serious, even when he was pulling Jesse over on his bike or investigating the Dinwiddie Hills break-ins a few years ago. Today, his mouth was a tight, grim line. He looked older without his smile. His eyes were weary.

"Jane Anders," he said in a quiet voice. "I need to speak with you outside the classroom, please."

The tall, thin, dark-haired girl froze. Her narrow, pretty features paled. She glanced around the classroom as though someone might know what was happening. No one did. They all stared back at her blankly.

What had happened? Was someone hurt? Jane's mother, Susan, was notoriously wild. She spent most of her nights out at the bar with her friend, Ellen Horne, drinking until they could barely stand up. If the rumors were true, they were often seen leaving in the company of whomever was desperate enough to take them.

Had there been an accident? Had Susan been hurt?

Jane must have been thinking the same thing. She rose slowly and walked toward Chief Gray like a person walking to her execution. His expression softened in sympathy. Jane's step faltered. Her hands shook. The chief extended an arm to draw her out into the hall in a sort of paternal half-hug. He shut the door behind them.

The classroom exploded instantly. Mrs. Lima tried to call for order. Her voice could barely be heard above the students' loud speculation. They ignored her. Finally, she dropped back behind her desk.

"Do you think she's in trouble?"

"Her mom is the town drunk. She's probably wrapped herself around a pole or something."

"I heard her dad's been in and out of prison. Maybe he's done something again."

"I don't even think her dad's around anymore. He left before she was born."

Aurora's stomach roiled. They sounded so gleeful. New Coventry was a small town, and not much happened. A police officer had never shown up at school to pull someone out of the classroom—not even Jesse, and he was getting called to the principal's office to answer for some infraction everyday.

She turned her head in the confusion. She expected to find Sable still peering disinterestedly out the window. He wasn't. He sat straight up in his chair with his ear turned toward the closed door as though he might catch a word of the conversation in the hall. His brow furrowed as though he heard something he didn't like.

Jane didn't return. Mrs. Lima gave up trying to reign in the classroom.

She wrote an assignment on the board, but Aurora didn't think anyone had actually noticed it. She tried to focus on her textbook, but her eyes drifted to the closed door as though it might yield answers.

When she lost her struggle to control herself, she caught Sable doing the same thing. When the bell rang, he jumped out of his seat and darted out of the room. She watched him go in surprise and rose to pack her bags. She felt the skin prickle on the back of her neck and looked up into Cami's cold, hateful eyes. She sighed.

At least she'd gotten through most of the day before it had turned miserable.

Jane Anders was the only thing anyone talked about the rest of the day. The speculation about what had caused Chief Gray's unprecedented visit to the school had grown increasingly more outrageous. People speculated that her father was the leader of a drug-dealing ring. They suggested Jane might be living a double life. They thought maybe she knew something about a young teacher having an affair with a student.

Mostly, they talked about her mother. Aurora didn't want to be involved in the gossip. It seemed mean-spirited. She suspected Susan had simply been in an accident. She hoped it wasn't too serious. She hoped Jane's mother was going to be all right. She knew what it felt like to lose your mother. It was the worst feeling in the world. She wouldn't wish it on anyone, especially not just to have something interesting to talk about.

Josie and Diana whispered with their heads together on the front steps outside the school. Josie spun to Aurora as soon as she emerged into the sunlight. "Aurora."

Josie looked different. Her eyes weren't gleaming at all, despite the drama around them. She and Jane Anders had grown up in the same neighborhood. They'd played together as children. Josie knew Susan. She even liked her, despite the awful rumors about her.

"What's going on?"

Josie gripped her wrist. "Did you hear about Jane?"

"No. Not exactly. Chief Gray came and got her out of Mrs. Lima's English class, but she never came back. I don't know what happened."

"It's Susan," Diana said grimly.

"What happened to her? Was she in an accident?"

"No. No, nothing like that—well, they don't know, actually."

"What do you mean?"

"She's missing," Josie said. "Jane doesn't see her a lot—she works a lot at the warehouse, you know. She's not as bad as she seems. She gets out of hand, but she always goes to work. So when she didn't show up the last couple days, Ray Boggs called the police and had them check her house. She wasn't there, and it didn't look like she'd been home for a while."

"Is that unusual?"

"I don't know. I guess sometimes she's gone for a night, but never this long, especially not without calling. I know she's wild, but...she tries not to worry Jane. Still, knowing what she's like...well, I think maybe they're expecting to find her car wrapped around a pole somewhere."

The color drained from Aurora's face.

"Oh, Rora," Diana said softly. "I'm so sorry. We didn't mean to—"

Aurora swallowed thickly. "It's okay. So they're looking for her?"

"And Ellen," Josie added. "She's missing, too."

"It doesn't sound good, does it? You think something bad really happened to them?"

"Maybe." Josie sighed. "Maybe they've just...run off together like a drunken Thelma and Louise." She didn't sound amused. "It's as likely as anything else, anyway."

"That isn't very optimistic, Josie," Diana scolded.

"It's better than thinking they've been in an accident. Poor Jane. She must be so worried."

"What did you say, Aurora?"

He'd come upon them so suddenly and so silently they hadn't even noticed him until he spoke. Josie goggled at Sable as he appeared beside Aurora with a strange crease between his brows. Diana lifted her eyebrows. Aurora opened and closed her mouth in surprise. So he did remember her from that night under the stars.

She'd been silent too long. Sable lifted his eyebrows expectantly. "Oh...we were just talking about Jane Anders. She was the one—"

"Yeah. I remember. I was there."

"Her mother's missing."

"Missing."

"Yes. She and her friend, Ellen Horne. They never showed up for work the last few days and no one's seen them."

He frowned. "No one has any idea what happened to them?"

"No, not really. I mean...they probably have some ideas. They're a little... well, they're a little wild."

"What do you mean 'wild'?"

"Well, they...they drink a lot, I guess. They might have...been in an accident."

The crease between his brows deepened as he considered this. "I have to go."

They stared open-mouthed after him as he spun on his heel, hurrying away from them with long, agitated strides. Josie didn't turn back to the other girls until Sable had disappeared between the cars in the parking lot. "He is so mysterious."

"He's mysterious, all right," Aurora replied. "He seems really upset about Susan and Ellen."

"Maybe they're his parents' patients," Diana suggested. "Maybe he knows them."

Josie shook her head. "I don't know. From the sound of it, if they were the Jaynes' patients, they wouldn't be in this mess. I've been hearing a lot more about the Jaynes since the party, and they are some serious miracle workers."

"I think I'm going to walk over to my dad's shop," Aurora said suddenly.

Josie looked around at her in surprise. "Okay. I could drop you off if you want. We could swing by the Jayne house first, maybe catch another glimpse of Sable?"

"No, that's okay, Josie. You and Diana go ahead. I could use the fresh air. I'll call you later, okay?"

Josie glanced at Diana, but the blonde girl didn't seem to think there was anything unusual about this. "Okay," Josie said finally. "Sure. Yeah. See you tomorrow."

Aurora waved at them and strode away. She turned her head to peer around the parking lot, but she didn't see Sable anywhere. Of course he'd already gone. She turned onto the high street toward her father's mechanic shop.

It was a cool afternoon, but spring was in the air, and the walk was short. The town square was already filling up with high school kids getting out of class and meeting for a snack at Archie's or coffee at Colletta's. Some younger kids played in the small, green park in the center of the square despite the chill breeze while their mothers sat around on park benches, sipping warm drinks and gossiping comfortably about their neighbors or the townspeople who passed by.

Geller's Auto Repair was noisy with the sounds of screeching metal, clanging wrenches and the mechanics shouting back and forth at each other from underneath the cars and trucks parked in the open garage. Aurora ducked inside, smelling gasoline and motor oil, the scents her father brought home each night. They were comforting, these smells. They reminded her of being a small child, waiting excitedly for her daddy to come home from work and watch television with her or read her a bedtime story.

She recognized her dad's oil-stained boots underneath a battered grey Volvo and bent down to peer at him. "Hey, Dad."

Mike dropped his wrench and swore. "Aurora?" He rolled out from under the car and peered up at her in surprise. "What are you doing here?"

"I just wanted to talk to you."

"Is something wrong? Did something happen?"

"No. Not to me."

"Why don't you come into my office? You want a soda?"

"Sure."

His office was a mess. Stacks of paper spread across the desk, weighted down by tools or greasy car parts waiting to be installed. Pictures of cars and women in bikinis lined the walls. Aurora knew her mother had been amused by the photos; her father always said it wasn't so much his own love of women in bikinis that inspired his decorating—though he did, he insisted, love women in bikinis—it was that his customers and employees expected a man in his profession to enjoy that sort of thing. They made Aurora slightly uncomfortable. She wondered what Julia thought about them.

Mike opened the mini fridge beside his desk and handed Aurora a Coke.

"So what's up?"

Aurora stared down at the can for a moment. "I want to go see Mariah Jayne."

He blinked, but his expression didn't change. "Okay." He wrapped his hands around the thermos sitting among the rubble on the desk as though to warm them. "Did Ruby talk to you?"

"Yeah. She did, and it was really nice of you to suggest it. I know you are trying to help, but I just...think I need to talk to someone who isn't part of the family. Someone who I haven't known my whole life, who doesn't know anything about me."

Mike nodded slowly. "Okay. If you want, I will call for an appointment right away. I'll take you."

"No, it's okay. I can go myself. I think I need to do it by myself."

He opened the thermos and peered inside, at a loss for words. Finally, he looked back up at her. "All right, Aurora. If this is what you want, I'll support you."

"Thanks, Dad." She leaned back in her chair and watched him pour some of the dark liquid from the thermos into an old, chipped coffee cup with *Geller's Auto Repair* emblazoned across the side.

After a long, silent moment, he lifted his eyebrows at her. "Is something else bothering you?"

"It's just...you heard about Susan Anders?"

"Yes. I heard. What about her?"

"Her daughter, Jane, is in my English class. Chief Gray came and got her out of class to tell her. Jane didn't even notice she'd been gone a couple days. She almost never even got to see her. She must be so upset." Aurora twisted her hands in her lap. "I just...wanted to spend time with you, I guess."

He lifted an eyebrow. "In case I disappear too?"

Aurora smiled. "Something like that, I guess. Things happen unexpectedly sometimes. You know that. I just wanted to see you."

Mike stood abruptly and rounded the corner of his desk. He leaned down to lay a kiss on the top of her head. He smiled a little awkwardly. "How about we have dinner tonight. Just the two of us? Ruby will be out with Blaine, and I'll just tell Julia I need to spend some time with my kid. We can go to

Constantine."

She grinned at him. "Sure, Dad. That sounds good."

"Okay. I have to get back to that Chevy, but I will meet you at the house, okay? I'll come right home when it's done. Want me to have one of the boys take you home?"

"No. It's okay. I'll walk."

"Sure."

She kissed his cheek on her way out. "See you at home." She felt better as she stepped back out onto the sunlit street. Her smile slipped as she saw a flash of dark hair disappear into the short alley between the shop and a hardware store next door. Her stomach fluttered. *Sable?* He had a way of appearing at the strangest moments.

She hesitated. It was stupid, she knew. He would probably think she was some sort of stalker or something—maybe she was starting to think so herself. But if she could just see him, maybe even talk to him...Her feet were already moving before she'd fully made up her mind to follow him.

If he caught her, she could just say she was using a shortcut home from her dad's shop. He wouldn't know the difference. It's not like he knew where she lived. She was surprised he even remembered her name.

He was moving slowly, aimlessly through the alley. There was something different about him today. Maybe he looked broader or taller or...older. Not Sable. She realized she'd opened her mouth to call his name, but she snapped it shut.

No, it wasn't Sable. Something about the hitch of his shoulders, the slouching, prowling way he moved was all wrong. It was the other one. The older brother she'd spotted at the party. Her stomach sank.

She took a step backward, intending to go back the way she came, but he spun suddenly as though he'd heard her quiet footfalls on the concrete. He stared at her with eyes so intensely dark blue she wondered how she had ever mistaken him for Sable. Their features were similar—almost identical—but his eyes were colder, much more dangerous. There was something about him that made the small hairs on the back of her neck prickle in alarm.

She wanted to back away, to run, but he was already striding toward her, smiling an oddly warm smile that clashed horribly with her idea of him, with the almost predatory look in his eyes. She felt rooted to the spot, pinned by his unbroken stare.

"Hello." His voice was low and husky but it carried through the alley as though he'd spoken against her ear.

He was suddenly in front of her, peering down at her with those eyes so like and so different from Sable's. She opened and closed her mouth. She felt heat flood her cheeks. "Hi."

His smile stretched wider at her obvious unease. "I'm Van. Who are you?"

"Aurora." For some reason, she hadn't wanted to tell him, but she was unable to stop herself. "Aurora Geller."

"Aurora." His voice was a caress. It was as though he'd reached out and stroked a hand down her back. "Such a pretty name. You are very pretty, Aurora."

"Um...thanks."

He took a step closer to her. She could see his eyes darkening, the pupils dilating, turning them to black. Her breath caught in her throat. She felt strange, frightened and excited in the same instant. She wanted to run, and she wanted to step closer to him.

"There's something about you...you're so fragile."

Her brow furrowed irritably. "I'm not fragile."

"Yes. You are. You all are."

There was a coldness in his voice that sent a chill down her spine. She wondered if he was on some kind of drugs. His eyes still looked weird; the pupils were growing larger and larger as he stared intently down at her. Her feet finally obeyed her. She took a step away from him.

"I have to go."

His hand shot out so suddenly, she had no time to react. He caught her wrist in long fingers so hot, they were almost searing.

"Don't go." The purring quality was back in his voice. "We're just getting to know each other."

She tried to pull out of his grasp, but it was like a vice. Her heart thumped. "Let me go."

His fingers only tightened on her wrist. His mouth turned up into a dangerous smile. He tugged her toward him. He opened his mouth as though he intended to lean down and press it against hers. She struggled, but he was so, so strong.

"What the hell is going on?"

Her heart fluttered in relief. "Jesse!"

Jesse strode toward them with a thunderous expression. His hair looked windblown. He had probably been passing by on his bike when he'd seen her there in the alley, struggling to free herself from Van Jayne. When his eyes fell on Van, he looked surprised. He, too, must have mistaken him for Sable at first glance. His eyes narrowed at Van, who smiled back at him. He didn't let Aurora go.

"Is this your boyfriend, Aurora?"

"No."

"Let go of her," Jesse barked.

"Are you going to make me?"

Jesse looked fully capable of taking on the slimmer man, but something about Van made Aurora's pulse race in alarm. Jesse's jaw clenched.

"Yes. I am." He took a step closer to them, so close she was sure Van could feel his breath on the side of his neck.

Van released Aurora delicately and turned to face Jesse. "Are you?" He was still smiling, and it was such a feral, dangerous smile, Aurora wondered how Jesse could face him so fearlessly.

"Jesse, don't do this," she pleaded, clenching her fingers on his arm. "Let's just go." The two men didn't move. They stared at each other, waiting for the other to strike the first blow. She pushed between them, pressing a hand to Jesse's chest. "Jesse!"

He wavered, peering down into her worried eyes. "Aurora…"

"What, are you backing down?" Van's voice sounded like the crack of a whip. He looked amused. "I thought you wanted a fight."

Jesse's eyes snapped back to him. He reached out a hand to shove Aurora out of the middle of the fray. She stumbled backward with the unexpected force, but Jesse didn't notice. He only had eyes for Van. He stepped closer to him.

Aurora felt hands on her arms, steadying her. She jumped in alarm, spinning around to find Sable looking down at her with those midnight blue eyes—Van's eyes, though now that she saw them, she realized what was different about them. Van's eyes looked hungry and crazed. Sable's just looked...well, they looked concerned, but there such was a dark, terrible anger behind them that she worried he might suddenly snap at any moment.

"Aurora, are you all right?" His hands felt hot on her arms, just like Van's, but they were gentle as he drew her toward him, away from Jesse and his brother.

Her heart fluttered again. She nodded dumbly. She couldn't find breath to speak when he was staring down at her with those beautiful, intense eyes and while his hands were gripping her with such care, her stomach almost ached.

Then, just as suddenly as he'd appeared, he released her and stepped toward his brother.

"What the hell are you doing, Van?" His voice shook slightly with that anger Aurora had seen hiding behind the tenderness in his eyes.

Van's eyes rolled to him. They glinted in amusement. "Well, if it isn't my little brother. And what are you doing here, Sable?"

"Van, let's go."

"Oh, no. We were just starting to have fun."

"Aurora, go." He didn't even look at her. His eyes fixed on his brother.

Aurora hesitated. There was something about the way he'd looked at her before.

When she didn't move, Sable glanced at her, and that swift, fierce glance sent a jolt through her entire body. He looked angry, yes, but now there was something else in his eyes that scared her.

Was it fear? Not of Van. She could tell he was not afraid of his brother. The disdain with which he looked at Van convinced her he disliked him more than he feared him. But it was fear, and now Aurora felt it, too. She had to get Jesse away from Van.

She caught Jesse's arm and tugged on his wrist. "Jesse, come on."

"Don't go, Aurora." Van didn't look at her, either, directing the words at his brother.

Sable's eyes narrowed. "Aurora, go! You shouldn't be here."

Van laughed. "Are you trying to protect her, little brother? That's sweet. Since when did you care about a h--"

Sable moved quickly, slamming his brother back against the wall of the hardware store. He pressed his forearm pressed against Van's windpipe, cutting off whatever he had intended to say. Van didn't lift a hand to defend himself. His eyes glittered with cold, mean amusement.

Sable turned his head to Aurora. His eyes blazed. "Aurora!"

She didn't need to be told once more. She seized Jesse's arm and dragged him out to the street. He didn't resist. He looked down at her in confusion, as though she might understand what had happened back there. She didn't understand it at all. Her legs were shaky, and she thought she might burst into tears.

Something wasn't right with Van—more importantly, something wasn't right with Sable. What had that been about? What had he been afraid of? What had he stopped his brother from saying?

"What was that, Aurora?" Jesse still looked angry. He looked ready to dart back into the alley and finish what he started with Van. "What the hell?"

Her entire body trembled. "I don't know, Jesse."

"What were you doing with that guy?"

"I wasn't doing anything! He walked up to me." Well, sort of. "If you hadn't shown up..." She took a hitching breath.

Jesse's expression softened. He stepped forward and wrapped her in a hug. His arms felt warm and reassuring, and she leaned into him, thankful for the security of his familiar, reliable strength. His body felt powerful, and he smelled of cedar and a bit like exhaust. It felt good, pressed against him, comfortable and safe, but it wasn't his face she was seeing as she closed her eyes. She was seeing Sable's intense, tender eyes as he held her, as he looked at her with that odd, frightening alarm. She sighed and pulled away from Jesse.

A flash of dark hair and a black hoodie drew her eye. Sable. This time it was Sable, striding swiftly along the high street toward his back sedan. Van wasn't with him. Aurora hoped, wherever Van was, he wouldn't bother them again. Sable didn't turn to look at them. He got into his car and peeled out.

"Do you think you could take me home, Jesse?"

"Of course." For a moment he hesitated. "Do you want to stop and get coffee on the way?"

"I just really want to get home. I'm kind of...freaked out."

"Okay. Sure. Of course. Come on." His motorcycle was parked on the street nearby. He only had one helmet. He placed it gently on Aurora's head before climbing onto the bike. He smiled. "It's safe, Aurora. I'll drive slow."

She breathed a sigh of relief. "Thanks." She'd never been on Jesse's motorcycle. She'd never been on any motorcycle, though her dad had owned one, years ago. After her mother's car accident, he'd gotten rid of it, though it hadn't really had anything to do with it. Perhaps he'd simply become suddenly, terribly aware of how fragile life could be sometimes.

She climbed onto the small seat behind Jesse. There wasn't a handle or even a seat back, and she envisioned herself tumbling backward off the bike. She wrapped her arms tightly around Jesse's waist. Jesse chuckled and loosened her arms.

"You don't have to hold on that tight. I'm not going to be going more than twenty five miles an hour, and if you cut off my circulation, we're going to crash for sure."

She let out a breath. "Okay. Sorry. I'm ready."

"Are you sure?"

"Yes."

He didn't wait for her to change her mind. She clutched his waist as he flipped the bike in gear and peeled out. Despite the suddenness of the move, he was true to his word. He drove slowly through town, and she relaxed, holding loosely to his waist. After the first, terrifying minute, she began to enjoy the ride. A light, chilly breeze lifted her hair behind her. She could feel Jesse's blonde hair tickling her cheek. She leaned against his back, watching the familiar streets pass. It was different than walking or driving in a car. Everything looked different.

When the ride ended, she was disappointed. It would have been so nice to keep riding, keep on until they had circled New Coventry and she had seen everything for the hundredth time as though it was the first. Jesse would have taken her if only she'd ask. For a moment, she considered it. Then she leaned back and climbed off the bike. Jesse rose to lift the helmet gently off her head.

She tried to smile at him. "Thanks for the ride, Jesse."

"Sure. Anytime." He kept looking at her. She braced herself. She shouldn't have encouraged him. She shouldn't have wrapped her arms so tightly around him. She shouldn't have enjoyed doing it so much. He reached out and smoothed her long, strawberry blonde waves. "I'm always here if you need me, Aurora."

With that, he placed the helmet on his head and sped away without waiting for her to reply. She watched after him, but she remembered her plans with Mike in a couple hours. Her knees still felt a little wobbly. Whatever had happened in that alley with Sable and Van, she didn't want her dad to know anything about it. She wasn't sure what he would do, but she was sure he wouldn't approve of her going anywhere near the brothers or their parents again.

She wasn't going to let him stop her.

* * *

Aurora heard the door slam downstairs. She jumped to her feet and checked herself in the mirror. She looked normal. She looked like she always looked, dressed in jeans and a tee shirt. She was sure her father wouldn't notice the questions swirling around in her mind, the memory of Van's searing fingers or Sable's gentle hands. She swept her hair back into a ponytail and hurried down the stairs to meet him.

His cheeks were streaked with grease, but he smiled when he saw her. "Hey, Rory. Just let me get cleaned up, and we'll get out of here."

"Sure, Dad."

She watched him go, relieved that he hadn't noticed anything strange about her. She could keep it together. She just had to do it for a couple hours, and then she could hide out in her room and think about the Jaynes all she wanted. She was happy, at least, to spend some time with her dad. It had been a long time since they'd done anything like have dinner together, just the two of them. There were always friends, aunts, cousins and girlfriends hanging around.

She started as several sharp, rapid knocks sounded at the door. Aurora hesitated. She looked toward her dad's room and heard him turn on the shower. She peered cautiously through the peephole and sighed in relief as she spotted Blaine standing on the stoop. She opened the door.

"Hi, Blaine."

Blaine darted past her without waiting to be let in. He looked agitatedly around then realized Aurora was the only one there. He spun to face her.

120

His features looked normal, but there was something odd in his eyes. He looked...freaked out.

"Oh. Hi, Aurora."

"Hi, Blaine. I wasn't expecting you."

"Yes. I'm supposed to be meeting Ruby tonight." His words were jumbled, as though he were anxious to get them out and over with.

"She isn't home yet."

"Oh." He looked down at the watch on his right wrist, then back up at her. Then he looked back down at his watch. A furrow crossed his brow. "I must have mixed up the time."

Aurora stared at him. There was something strange about his skin. It was tanned and golden. It seemed to glow in the pale sunlight filtering in from the living room curtains.

He looked relieved. Had he been nervous about meeting Ruby? She smiled. Perhaps he was nervous. Perhaps he was planning something big for the evening. Perhaps he wanted to ask Ruby something. He certainly looked like a man afraid of something. If she knew him better, she might have asked him.

"My dad and I are going out for dinner in a few minutes, but you can wait for her if you want."

"No. No. I just got mixed up. She must have said eight, and I thought she said six. Sorry." He spun and started toward the door. "I should go."

"Okay, if you're sure, but if you want to wait--"

"No, I should go." He bobbed his head in a strange, jerky nod. "Goodbye."

Mike emerged from his bedroom, buttoning a plaid shirt over his bare chest. "Was someone at the door?"

"Yeah. It was Blaine. He was here to pick up Ruby, but he was early."

"Oh. He didn't want to just wait?"

Aurora glanced toward the door through which Blaine had just left. "No." She shook herself and smiled at her dad.

"Well, are you ready?"

"Yeah."

Mike grinned and offered her an arm. "Let's go, then."

* * *

Sable slammed the front door behind him as he strode inside the enormous old house. His mother and her client, a middle-aged woman in a crisp navy pants suit, stared at him in surprise from the entrance hall, where Mariah was bidding the smiling woman goodbye.

"Don't mind Sable," Mariah said, smiling serenely.

The woman's eyes were slightly unfocused as she looked at him. "Teenagers are always so dramatic," she murmured dreamily.

Mariah laid a gentle hand on her shoulder. "Come back and see me next week, Rhonda. We can finish our conversation then."

Rhonda nodded happily. "Sure. See you then." She turned her radiant smile on Sable as she past him. "Goodbye, Sable."

He dipped his head in a perfunctory nod. As soon as the door closed behind her patient, Mariah turned to him with a frown.

"What is wrong with you? We're running a business here."

"Van."

Mariah's face changed instantly. Her mouth thinned to a fine line. She turned and strode to the closed double doors to the west of the large, winding staircase in the center of the hall. "Adam."

Sable's father yanked open the doors. There were no patients in his office, but stacks of unfinished paperwork spread across his desk.

"What is it?" He did not like being interrupted.

"Van."

Adam peered out into the hall, as though someone else might be with his wife and youngest son. He gestured them inside the room. "We shouldn't talk out here. Someone might come in."

His office had once been a library. Rows and rows of bookshelves lined the room, filled with Adam and Mariah's textbooks, manuals and treatises. A large, leather sofa sat near the center of the room. Adam's worktables and equipment littered the remaining floor space so the room looked almost cluttered, despite his meticulous, minimal decorations and furniture.

Adam did not sit behind his desk, nor did Mariah or Sable take the couch or one of the leather wing-backed armchairs in front of it.

"Where is he?" Mariah demanded.

"He's still in town. He wouldn't say where he was staying," Sable explained.

"You saw him and you let him go?"

Sable scowled. "I didn't have a lot of choice. He didn't give me the chance to put him down. I think he almost attacked a girl in town in broad daylight."

"What?" Adam crossed his arms over his chest.

"What do you mean attacked?" Mariah gasped.

"What do you think I mean? He had ahold of her, and he looked ready to turn right there in the street."

"Did he?"

"No, of course not. If he had, we would have people banging down our door with pitchforks."

Mariah and Adam exchanged a look. Sable didn't even try to interpret it.

"Is the girl all right?" Mariah asked softly. "Does she have any idea what happened?"

"No. A friend of hers came to the rescue. I don't think either of them understood what was happening. She got out of there before it got too bad."

Mariah sighed. "Do you have any idea where he could be now?"

"No. He got away from me. He could be anywhere now." Sable scowled.

"What is it?" Adam asked.

"I just...I don't know if he is going to go back for her."

"What do you mean 'go back'?" Mariah demanded. "Why would he?"

"I don't know. It's just this feeling I got when he was with her. I should check on her. Just in case."

Adam nodded slowly. "That's not a terrible idea."

"Just until we know where he is," Mariah added. "Until we're sure he isn't planning something."

Sable didn't leave the room.

"Is there something else?" Adam asked.

"Yeah. There's...two women from town who went missing."

"Missing?"

"No one knows what happened to them. They just disappeared. No one's seen them for a couple days."

Mariah's face went curiously blank, but Adam looked grim. "No one has any idea what's happened to them?"

"No. The rumor around town is they're the local drunks. They were drinking at a bar and left together. No one's seen them since."

His parents shared a long look.

"You should check on the girl," Adam said finally. "We will see what we can learn about the missing women. It's probably nothing to worry about."

"It isn't exactly..." Mariah trailed off.

"I know. It isn't exactly Van's style. He's usually not so subtle."

"That is not what I meant."

Sable strode toward the door. "Yeah, well, I'm tired of this. I'm tired of running. He's your son. Don't you think it's time to do something about him?"

He threw open the door. He waited a heartbeat, but they did not call him back. He slammed the front door and climbed into his car. If they wouldn't do anything, he could make sure Aurora was safe.

If he had to lurk outside her house all night, she would be safe.

* * *

There was a burst of laughter from the living room as they opened the door. Mike and Aurora exchanged a glance and strode together to peek into the room. Ruby sat beside Blaine on the sofa. Across from them, a man Aurora didn't know sipped a beer and smiled rakishly. He was not a tall man, but his figure was thick and strong looking. He wasn't particularly handsome, either, but his dark eyes danced merrily, and he had a nice smile.

As they entered the room, Blaine shot guiltily to his feet. The strange man across from him lifted his eyebrows in amusement.

"Oh, hello, Mike," Blaine said quickly. "Sorry. We had planned to be gone by the time you got home."

"Why? You think I'm Ruby's dad? I'll have you know she's older."

Blaine laughed as Ruby drew him back down to sit beside her.

"Did you two have a nice time on your daddy-daughter date?" Ruby's cheeks were flushed in happiness.

"Yeah. It was nice," Aurora replied, trying to catch a glimpse of her aunt's fingers. Ruby wasn't wearing a new ring.

"Mike, Aurora, this is Troy Hallow," Ruby said, gesturing toward the stranger, who rose to shake their hands politely. "Blaine's business partner."

"Nice to meet you both." Troy smiled broadly. His grip was warm and firm. He inclined his head gallantly to Aurora. "Sorry to intrude. Ruby invited us over for dinner, and we lost track of time."

Aurora found herself smiling back at him almost unconsciously.

"Actually," Blaine said, grinning at his partner, "Ruby invited me, but Troy gave me his big puppy dog eyes, and I got him an invite, too."

Ruby and Troy laughed at this. Aurora wasn't sure Blaine was teasing.

"That's not true," Ruby protested. "I hoped to meet this mysterious business partner of Blaine's who's been taking up all his time lately."

"Now, I don't want to be held responsible for that," Troy complained. "I certainly didn't mean to seem selfish." He bent in an exaggerated bow. "On that note, I'd better go. I trust my best friend is in good hands, and I have an early morning at City Hall. Thanks for dinner, Ruby. It was great." He bent down to kiss her cheek.

Ruby beamed at him. "Of course. Anytime."

"Mike, Aurora, it was nice meeting you." He reached out to shake Mike's hand again and gave Aurora a smile. "Blaine, don't forget our meeting with the inspector tomorrow morning."

Blaine smirked. "If I'm a little late, just get started without me."

Troy rolled his eyes. He waved as he passed them to step outside into the cool evening air.

"Well," Mike said. "I think I would prefer not to think about what that means, Blaine. I'm off to bed. Night, Rubes. Night, Rory. Blaine."

Aurora smiled. "Good night, Dad." When he'd gone, she peered at Blaine and Ruby. She had the distinct impression they wanted to be alone. "I guess I'd better go up and get some homework done. See you guys later."

"Good night, Aurora," Blaine said.

"Night, honey," Ruby added.

Once she was alone, Aurora couldn't focus on her History paper. Dinner with her father had been nice. It had been a long time since they'd spent time alone together. He hadn't seemed to notice her distraction, and if he suspected something strange had happened earlier, he didn't ask her about it. He didn't really ask her about anything except school and her friends. She didn't think he really wanted to talk with her about boys or why she thought she needed a therapist, which she appreciated. They talked about classes and Julia and gossiped about Ruby and Christian and people they knew from town.

She hadn't mentioned Sable or his frightening brother. She hadn't mentioned that she was as anxious to see Sable again as she was to learn the truth about the Jaynes and their rumored abilities to solve problems overnight. She hadn't mentioned that her mind had been somewhere else all night. Mike was good about stuff like that. If he wasn't totally clueless about what was going on with his teenage daughter, he was pretty good at pretending he was.

She snapped her laptop shut. She paced the room. She tried not to think of the strange scene in the alley that afternoon, but she couldn't think of anything else, especially not the fall of the Roman Empire. What had Van meant to do? What would he have done to her if Jesse hadn't shown up?

She shuddered. She didn't want to know. Jesse had shown up. And then Sable had rescued her...actually, Jesse had rescued her first, but he'd seemed more interested in fighting it out with Van than worrying about her safety.

She sighed and paced to the window. She pushed aside the curtains to peer up at the sky. It was cloudy, and there were only a few stars twinkling overhead. Full dark had not yet descended. She considered waiting there until the clouds moved aside and revealed the stars to her.

In the shadows below her window, something moved.

Her heart raced. She leaned against the cool glass. The shadows seemed thicker tonight, filled with secrets and hidden things. She pushed the window open and leaned out to stare down at the front lawn.

There was nothing there. There was no sound or movement in the darkness.

She felt like an idiot. It must have been a trick of the light or a neighborhood cat streaking across the lawn. It hadn't looked like a cat, though. It had been larger...as large as a person. She shook her head. Of course it had simply been her imagination. There was no one there. She would have seen them in the meager streetlight across the street.

She rolled her eyes and flipped her computer open. Clearly, she was still freaked out from earlier. She tried to focus on her History paper, but her mind wouldn't cooperate. It kept replaying the moment Sable had pushed his brother into the wall. It kept trying to remember the way Sable's hands felt on her skin, the way he'd looked at her when he'd told her to go...

She rose abruptly and stuck her head out the window. Nothing had changed. The night was silent. She shook her head to clear it, but she couldn't shake the feeling that something was not quite right down there in the thickening darkness. After several moments, she had to admit she must have been imagining things.

She pushed the windowpane back down and locked it with a decisive click. She spun away from the window and climbed into bed. There was nothing for it. She wasn't going to get any work done tonight. She wasn't even sure she would get any sleep.

She picked up the book on her bedside table. It was a mystery, but she couldn't remember what crime the hero was trying to solve. She couldn't figure out why all the characters suddenly seemed to be young, dark-haired boys in black hoodies. She was asleep before she'd even realized she'd closed her eyes, and all the characters in her dreams looked just like the characters in her book.

Chapter Six

Aurora took a deep breath. Her heart thumped nervously in her chest. The old Nott house looked huge and grand and intimidating in the late afternoon sun. She considered getting back into her dad's car and driving back home. This was a stupid idea. If the Pops or anyone else in town found out she was seeing a therapist, she would never hear the end of it.

Don't come back here.

He might have been standing behind her, whispering in her ear. Had he been trying to warn her? Had he been afraid of what Van would do?

This was a terrible idea. She didn't know what might have happened if Sable hadn't arrived that day in the alley. She hadn't been able to make any sense of it. If there were something wrong with Van, wouldn't someone know? He'd never done anything odd or dangerous before. Maybe she had misinterpreted what had happened.

Aurora, go!

She squared her shoulders. She would be perfectly safe. There were rumors about the strange things the Jaynes could do, but none of them suggested Van had ever hurt anyone. If Sable had been trying to keep her away, he would just have to deal with it.

And she wanted to see him. She wanted to see him so badly her chest ached. She hadn't seen him in school since the day he'd rescued her from his brother. She didn't know if he was avoiding her. Maybe he didn't want to have to answer her questions. Maybe he just didn't want to see her. Maybe it had absolutely nothing to do with her.

She wasn't the sort to force herself on someone who didn't want her, yet here she was, standing outside his house. A half smile turned up her lips. It was too late now. She'd come too far to turn back. If he didn't want to see her, that was his problem. She had a right to be there. She had an appointment and everything. Not even his harsh words or his creepy brother were going to keep her from that house.

She checked her watch. If she didn't stop arguing with herself on his doorstep like an idiot, she was going to miss that appointment. She didn't think Mariah would wait. Half the town was visiting her these days. Aurora had been surprised the doctor had even managed to fit her in.

She steeled her nerves and strode up to the electric blue front door. She lifted her hand to strike the lion's head doorknocker before she could change her mind. Before she reached it, the door flew open. She reared back in surprise.

Sable stared at her for several seconds. Her pulse leapt, and she felt heat rising to her cheeks. He scowled. "What are you doing here?"

She wanted to turn and run from those cold midnight eyes, but she reminded herself she was supposed to be there. He didn't get to dictate where she could and could not go, even if it was his own house. She lifted her chin defiantly.

"I have an appointment."

"Why?"

"None of your business."

"You shouldn't be here."

His words stung. Then she felt a surge of irritation. Did he treat all his parents' clients this way?

"I have every right to be here. I have an appointment. You can't just decide who can and can't come here just because you don't like me."

He looked as surprised at her heated words as she was. "It has nothing to do with you. It isn't about that."

"What is it about, then? Your brother? What happened the other day?"

He looked torn. It was the first time Aurora had seen him look anything but cold and confident. The expression was gone in seconds. His jaw stiffened, and he stared at her silently.

"Are you going to let me in or not?"

He didn't move, and he didn't seem to intend to anytime soon. They stared at each other so long she began to wonder how to explain to her father why she'd failed to make her appointment.

He stepped back. "Go ahead." His voice felt like an arctic chill.

She lifted her chin and strode past him into the large, elegant entrance hall. She could not hear his footsteps on the marble floor, but she felt him on her heels. She stopped beneath the large, glittering gold chandelier hanging in the center of the vaulted ceiling.

Sable collided with her and swore quietly as he rebounded away from her. She spun around to face him.

He scowled. "What did you do that for?"

"Why are you following me?"

"I'm not following you. I'm just walking."

"Well, walk somewhere else."

"This is my house. I can walk wherever I want. It wouldn't be a problem if you weren't stopping in the middle of the room for no reason."

She gave him an incredulous look. "It's a really big room. You didn't have to be right behind me. There is plenty of space."

The light click of heels on the marble floor broke their glower. Sable looked over Aurora's head. She spun to see Dr. Mariah Jayne striding toward them with a smile. Her long, wavy golden hair was unbound, and it looked oddly incongruent with her sleek black dress. She wasn't much taller than Aurora. She was shorter than her son, but there was something so powerful about her presence, she seemed to do tower over them both.

Her smile was sweet and welcoming. "Ah. You must be Aurora." Her voice was a low, soothing purr, and Aurora felt the excited race of her heart suddenly calm. Even Sable couldn't shatter the serenity that suddenly overwhelmed her senses. She couldn't help but smile back.

"Yes."

"I'm Dr. Jayne. I see you know my son, Sable." Her smile didn't waver, but her eyes were sharp as she glanced up at her son.

"We're in class together." Aurora forced her eyes forward, forced herself not to turn back and meet Sable's gaze. It felt like ice on her back.

Dr. Jayne's eyes lingered on her a long moment. Aurora felt as though the woman could read her every thought, every feeling. She felt sure she could sense the intense urge to spin around, to catch one more glimpse of Sable, whose presence was like a magnetic field behind her. Then the moment passed, and the doctor's smile seemed warm as ever.

"Please come in, Aurora. Thank you for bringing her this far, Sable."

There was something austere in her tone, but Sable hesitated. His mother's eyes narrowed at him. Aurora heard him sigh irritably. He spun on his heel and strode toward the stairs without turning back. Aurora watched him go, but Dr. Jayne reached out a hand to lead her toward a set of French doors.

The room was large and inviting. The walls were pale, bright beige, and lovely, serene landscapes in blues and greens and brilliant yellows decorated the walls. It looked a bit like an art gallery, for there was only a single, plush mint green couch in the center of the room, across from which was a comfortable leather chair and small table. Dr. Jayne's desk was rich, shining black wood, but she did not move toward it. She gestured toward the couch.

"Please made yourself at home, Aurora." She smiled as Aurora peered doubtfully at the couch. "You don't have to lie down, but I do like my patients to be as comfortable as possible."

"Thanks." Aurora perched on the edge of the sofa and felt like a fool. She leaned back against the cushions.

"Would you like something to drink?"

"No, thank you."

"All right. Let me know if you change your mind." She sat across from Aurora in the leather wing-backed chair. "You can take a moment to get comfortable, if you like."

Something in the doctor's eyes was so gentle, so friendly Aurora felt she could tell the woman anything at all. "I'm okay. I'm comfortable."

"Well, then, why don't you tell me what brought you here to see me today?"

"I'm not sure how to explain it."

"Just do your best. There's no pressure to get it right the first time. We can work through it together. Just take it slow."

"I'm been feeling sort of...strange lately."

"Strange how?"

"Sort of...like there's something missing."

"I understand you lost your mother several years ago."

Aurora hadn't realized Dr. Jayne already knew this much about her. "Yes. I was eleven. She was in an accident."

"I am very sorry to hear that. Do you believe this is affecting how you are feeling now?"

"Yes, of course. I miss her all the time. I'm sure part of what I am feeling is missing my mom. I feel like...like I've been cheated."

"Out of having a mother?"

"Dad's sister, Ruby, moved in to help out after she died, but she's more like an older sister than a mother."

"Does that bother you? Do you wish she was more like a mother to you?"

"No. It's nice to have someone like her. It's just...it's a not a substitute."

"I understand. You said it was only part of what you are feeling. Tell me more about what you think might be causing you to feel like something is missing."

"I don't know. I sometimes...most of the time, I feel like there is this empty void inside me. Like what's supposed to be there to fill it up is missing."

"Have you always felt this way?"

Aurora had to think about this. "I must have. I don't feel like it's suddenly happened, like something I had has gone away or anything. It feels like nothing was ever there at all."

"Did you feel like this before your mother passed away?"

"I don't know. I don't think so. At least, if I did, I didn't notice." Suddenly, Aurora felt foolish. "Is that...is that just a normal part of being a teenager?"

Dr. Jayne smiled. "It's hard to say. No teenager or person is the same. What is normal for one person is not necessarily normal for another. Do you feel as though this feeling you have is normal?"

"Compared to my friends...I guess not. They don't seem to be feeling this way."

"How can you be sure? Have you talked with them about it?"

Aurora laughed wryly. She imagined talking about something like this with no-nonsense Diana or carefree Josie. "No. I haven't really told anyone about it except my Dad and my aunt. I didn't want to sound like the tragic girl who lost her mom."

"You don't. But I can see why you would hesitate to share these feelings with your friends. It is quite normal. So, do you have any ideas what you think might be missing? Is it something inside you or something in your life?"

Suddenly, unbidden and mortifyingly, she pictured Sable's face. She forced down a blush. She couldn't possibly tell Dr. Jayne about having a crush on her son. Anyway, it would be ridiculous and immature to think a boyfriend could fill the missing pieces inside her. She suspected it would take a lot more work than getting a date.

Unless it was getting a date with Sable. She felt as though she could do just about anything more easily than she could do that.

"I don't know."

"Okay." Dr. Jayne smiled. "I suppose if you did, you wouldn't need to talk to me. You would just be able to go out and get it on your own."

Aurora doubted it would be so easy, even if she did know, but she liked the idea that Dr. Jayne thought she could.

"Tell me a little about your life," Dr. Jayne said.

"Like what?"

"Why don't we start with your home life?"

"Well, I live with my dad and my Aunt Ruby."

"What is your dad like?"

It seemed like a difficult question to answer. "He's nice. We get along really well."

"Do you spend much time together?"

"Not as much as we used to."

"Why is that?"

"It's just...school. Work. Friends. Dating. They all get in the way, I guess."

"Are you dating?"

"No. Not me. Dad."

"Do you wish you saw more of him?"

"Sometimes, but I think he doesn't really know how to deal with me now."

"What do you mean?"

Aurora sighed. "Since I turned sixteen he just seems to be a little confused about his role."

"And how do you think he is dealing with that?"

"He's...well, he's pretty cool."

"Cool how?"

"He kind of lets me do whatever I want."

"And how do you deal with that?" Dr. Jayne wasn't taking notes, but Aurora suspected she would remember everything she said.

"I don't."

"Do you mean you take advantage?"

"No. I'm not really...that type. He trusts me to act responsibly."

"And do you?"

"Yes." She felt almost embarrassed admitting it. She would rather have had some reason for being troubled, would rather she were forced to come to a therapist for being reckless and out of control. Instead, her life was tragic and empty and...boring.

"Do you feel your father is supportive of you?"

"Yes. I mean, I know he's always here for me if I need him."

"Is he emotionally supportive?"

Aurora wasn't sure exactly what that meant. "I think he would be, if I gave him the chance."

"You don't think you give him the chance?"

"I don't talk to him much about stuff."

"Why is that?"

"Well...he's a single dad. He doesn't know how to handle teenaged girls."

The doctor smiled. "So how does he deal with that?"

Aurora smiled back. "He sends Ruby."

"Does that help?"

"A lot of the time it does, but it isn't the same as having a mom."

"Does your father punish you?"

"I don't even remember the last time I was punished."

"Do you remember the last time you deserved to be punished?"

She felt her cheeks heat. "No. I'm pretty sure he would punish me if I deserved it, but..."

"But what?"

"I'm not exactly...well, most people would think I'm a goody-two-shoes or something."

Dr. Jayne smiled again. "And how do you feel about that?"

"I suppose it's positive when I'm not in trouble at home or at school, but sometimes I wish...I wish I was less afraid of breaking rules. I think I would have a lot more fun in life."

"Do you believe letting go of that fear would help you? Do you think letting loose is something you've been missing?"

She'd never thought about it before. "Maybe. Not being afraid to have fun is definitely something I've been missing. I'm not sure if it would improve my life or the way I feel about it, though."

Finally, Dr. Jayne picked up her notepad and scribbled a few notes. "How about your aunt? What is your relationship like?"

"We're close."

"You talk with her about the things that are happening in your life?"

Aurora laughed. "Not much does, but yeah. I mean, more than I talk to my dad, anyway."

"Why?"

"Well, she's a girl. She understands things. And she's...she's not judgmental."

"And you like that about her?"

"Yeah. She's made a lot of mistakes in her life, so she doesn't judge other people's mistakes. She's got a lot of wisdom. She thinks mistakes are a way to learn something important."

Dr. Jayne tapped the tip of her pen against her lips. "But you don't feel like you can talk to her about this feeling you have?"

"I tried, but...I don't think she really understood. She's very empowered."

"What do you mean by that?"

"She likes to think we are all responsible for our own happiness and our own decisions."

"Do you disagree?"

"No. I agree. I like the idea that we're in control of what happens to us. But I guess I feel like sometimes people need help."

"Is that why you came to see me?"

"Yes."

"Do you have any brothers or sisters?"

"No. I have a cousin. Ruby's son. He's a year older. He's in college so he isn't around much."

"Are you close with him?"

"Yeah. We're like brother and sister."

"Do you talk to him about what is happening in your life?"

"Sometimes. Not about boys and emotions and stuff. He's not that kind of guy."

"What kind of guy is he?"

"He's the kind of guy who likes to have fun, go out with a bunch of girls, mess around with his friends."

"So he's not very serious?"

"Well, he did well in school and he's doing well in college, but he doesn't take anything very seriously."

"Do you consider this to be a good or a bad quality?"

"I think it gets him in trouble sometimes because he doesn't think the consequences of his actions through all the way, but I think it's mostly a good quality."

"Why?"

"He's just...he's not worried about stuff all the time."

"And you are?"

Aurora sighed. "Often. Most of the time."

"What sorts of things do you worry about?"

"A lot of things. I worry about grades and my future and stuff like that."

"Do you feel you worry more than you should?"

"I don't know how much I should worry. But I worry more than I like."

"Is the worry taking over your thoughts?"

Aurora was silent a long moment. Dr. Jayne smiled patiently and sat back to await her response. "No. Not really. I mean—I guess worrying about the consequences of things holds me back a little."

"So you believe you are holding yourself back."

"Yeah. I guess I do."

"Do you feel you would be happier if you took more chances?"

"Yes. Probably. I'm not sure. I don't take chances very often, so I wouldn't really know."

"You took a chance coming here."

Aurora smiled. "Yeah. I guess I did."

"Do you feel better now than before you came?"

"I'm feeling...a little more hopeful."

"Were you feeling hopeless before?"

"Not hopeless. It wasn't that bad. I just felt like nothing was happening."

"Is there anything else you want to talk about today?"

Aurora was surprised. She'd expected therapy to be a lot harder. She'd expected Dr. Jayne to bombard her with pointed, sensitive questions and give stern orders. She hadn't done either of those things. It felt almost like chatting with an old friend. The question popped out before she even realized she was going to ask it. "How do you stop a boy liking you when you don't like him back?"

Dr. Jayne laughed loudly. "I'm not sure I can help with that problem, Aurora. I could probably spend some time with him to find out what is causing him to pursue a girl who doesn't return his feelings, but I suspect that would not solve your immediate problem. If you want advice like that, you should talk to my sister, Elise. She is the life adviser in the family."

Aurora sighed in disappointment. "I was beginning to think you could solve any problem."

"I do my best to solve the ones I can. Other problems take time and more effort than people are willing to give."

"Do you think you can solve mine?"

"I think we need to discover what it is before we can solve it."

"I need to come back?"

Dr. Jayne smiled. "You can't do it all in one day, Aurora. It takes time to take control of your feelings and emotions. If you are willing to take the time, I think I can help you."

"Okay."

The doctor sat forward in her seat and reached for Aurora's hands. "Now I would like to try something, if you are willing."

She hesitated. She had heard the stories of hypnotism. She was so comfortable she'd almost forgotten the rumors about the Jaynes. Dr. Jayne's expression was so encouraging she finally nodded. "Okay."

"Close your eyes."

The doctor's hands were cool and soft. Aurora's unease ebbed. She closed her eyes, and instantly, a strange, eerie peace overcame her senses.

"Now, Aurora, I want you to picture yourself in your favorite place. It doesn't have to be a real place. It could be where you go when you're dreaming or daydreaming."

"Okay." Her voice sounded far away.

"You don't have to talk. Just picture it and listen."

Aurora thought she heard a faint noise, like the tinkling of bells in the distance. She hadn't seen any bells in Dr. Jayne's office when she'd arrived. She tried to ignore the bells, to picture her favorite place. She didn't know where it was, not at first, and then she was in the very same house, in the backyard under the stars with Sable.

In her daydream, though, he was different. He looked the same, but his eyes were warm and gentle. He talked to her, took her hand and confessed he felt the same as she, that he'd been watching her, admiring her from afar, that she was all he thought about. They stared up at the stars. He turned her to face him in the starlight, and then he leaned closer and closer until his eyes blotted out the stars with their glittering intensity--

"Wake up, Aurora."

She came slowly back to herself. Heat surged across her cheeks as she realized where she was...and whose son she was thinking about. Her eyes fluttered open. Dr. Jayne sat directly in front of her, smiling serenely.

"Did you have a nice dream, Aurora?"

For a moment, she wondered if the doctor had somehow sensed her thoughts, but there was nothing sly or condemning in the older woman's eyes. The embarrassment over dreaming of the woman's son faded as quickly as it had come. A gentle contentment stole through her entire body. Heat was filling the empty spot inside her, spreading out into every inch of her. She sighed dreamily.

Dr. Jayne rose to her feet. Aurora blinked in surprise then stood to face her.

"Is it done?"

"Yes."

"But I've only been here a few minutes--" She glanced at the clock. It was already five o'clock. Her time was up. "Did I fall asleep?"

Dr. Jayne smiled. She laid a hand on Aurora's shoulder. Her touch so soothing, Aurora suddenly didn't mind. If she had fallen asleep, it was as it should be. She hadn't felt so calm and content in so long she couldn't remember the last time.

"You were just in a trance."

"Is that normal?"

"It is part of the process. How do you feel?"

"I feel...good. Like a weight has lifted."

"It is not a traditional treatment, but it is very effective for many people."

"So I hear." Her voice was dreamy. She understood now. She understood what everyone had been talking about.

"I would like to see you again next week."

Yes. Of course she would come back next week. She would come back every day if she could feel like this again.

"Have your dad set up another appointment."

"Okay."

Dr. Jayne turned her gently toward the door. "I can help you, Aurora, if you are willing to take the time. There is nothing more important than being in control of your mind and emotions."

"Okay." Even to herself, she sounded far away.

Dr. Jayne opened the door for her. "See you next week."

She was still smiling as she stepped out into the hall. When she saw Sable leaning against the wall nearby, she stopped abruptly. He scowled at her.

Something surged inside her, but it wasn't fear or insecurity. She smiled. "Hello, Sable. Were you listening in?"

"What? No!"

He strode toward her until he was standing so close to her, she had to drop her head back to meet his gaze. She held his eyes as he stared down at her with such intensity, she felt as though he was turning her inside out. She didn't flinch or blush or turn away.

He stepped back just as suddenly. She turned and started away from him toward the door.

She waved at him over her shoulder. "See you in class tomorrow."

For a moment, he didn't move. Then he hurried after her. "Are you okay?"

She turned back to face him. "What?"

"I mean...are you feeling okay?"

She lifted an eyebrow in amusement. "Why? Are you hoping I won't come back?"

He opened and closed his mouth. He looked at her for a moment as though he'd never seen her before. "No. It's just...I wanted to be sure you're okay."

"Well, that's very nice of you. I am fine. And I will be coming back, so you'd better get used to the idea. Bye, Sable. See you in class."

He didn't look happy. "Yeah. Sure. See you in class."

* * *

She didn't even glance back at him as the door closed behind her. Sable

140

spun and stormed into his mother's office without bothering to knock. "What did you do to her?"

"I beg your pardon?"

"Aurora. What did you do to her?"

"Aurora is a patient, Sable. I can't discuss her session with you."

"You know what I mean!"

"She came to me for help. I am helping her."

"Don't change her."

She regarded his serious face for several moments. "I'm not changing her, Sable. I'm taking away the pieces of her that she doesn't want. The parts of herself that make her unhappy."

Sable scowled. "You're feeding on her."

"We do what we have to do to survive. It doesn't mean we can't be humane about it. We can help them."

"Leave her alone."

"I'm not going to hurt Aurora. She's a very sweet girl. I would never hurt her, but there are things about herself she wants to let go of, and I am helping her with that."

"She doesn't need to change anything. Just leave her alone!"

Mariah's face was deadly serious. "Is there something going on between you and that girl, Sable?"

He blanched. "What? No! She's just a classmate. She's not even my friend."

"Sable."

He couldn't hold her eyes.

"You know it is dangerous for you to be involved with a human girl."

"I'm not involved with her! I barely know her."

"Keep it that way, Sable. You don't need to worry about Aurora. She is perfectly safe."

"She's different. Already she's different."

Mariah's mouth turned up in a small smile. "She is becoming who she truly is without the unnecessary encumbrances."

"She was fine the way she was!"

"She does not feel that way. She is allowed to make her own choices."

"She did not choose for you to feed on her!"

"You know it is the only way I can help her. You know I would never do anything to hurt a human. We have to feed to survive, but we can give them something in return. I am giving her what she needs."

Sable pushed his hands through his dark hair so it stuck up from his forehead.

Mariah rose and laid a hand on his shoulder. "I promise you, darling, I will not hurt her. I would never even dream of it. I will only help her."

"Just...be careful with her, Mom."

"You do the same, Sable. Do you understand me?"

He nodded wearily.

She relaxed and stepped away from him. "Have you found your brother?"

"No. He's still in town, but he's staying hidden."

"That is bad."

"Yeah. I haven't been able to find out anything more about the missing women. They still haven't turned up."

"Then it may simply be as it seems."

"It might."

"Let us hope that it is."

"Do you really believe it?"

"I am choosing to. They haven't found the women; it is not like the others. It's not the same, Sable."

"You're still protecting him, even after everything he's done."

"He is my son. And he is your brother. Families protect each other. We have to or we will not survive."

Sable's lip curled in disgust. He spun away from her and strode toward the door.

"Sable." He half turned back to her. "Remember that. We have to protect each other. Find your brother. Bring him home."

His shoulders slumped. "I will, Mom."

* * *

"Bye! I'm going to school!" Aurora called as she scooped up her backpack and headed out the door. She didn't pause to wait for a reply, but she heard her father grumble something as she stepped out onto the front porch. She smiled to herself and hurried to Josie's car idling in the driveway.

Josie didn't throw the car into reverse and squeal out of the driveway. She stared at Aurora, open-mouthed.

"What, Josie?"

"There's something different about you."

"What are you talking about?"

"What is it?"

"I don't know what you mean."

"Did you change your hair?"

Aurora smoothed the long, strawberry blonde waves back over her shoulders. "No. It's the same as always."

"Are you wearing makeup?"

"No."

Josie gasped. "Oh, my god, you had sex! Who was it? Was it Jesse?"

"Josie! Of course I didn't. You're being ridiculous."

"Well, you look different. You look...happy."

"I went to see Dr. Jayne last night.

"What? Seriously?"

"Yeah."

Josie was hurt. "You didn't even tell me." She held up her hand. "Wait. Don't tell me anything. Wait until we get Diana."

Aurora rolled her eyes. "There isn't much to tell."

Josie frowned as she backed quickly out of the driveway and steered toward Diana's house. "What are you talking about? You didn't tell your best friends you were going to see a shrink and now you're all weird. I think that necessitates discussion."

"Fine. Whatever you want, Josie. I won't say a word until Diana's here."

"Good. Let's talk about something innocuous until she's here. Have you heard anything about Susan?"

"That's not innocuous. Anyway no. I though you would have heard something if there was anything to know. You're closer to them."

"No one's heard anything from them since they went missing. Jane's been putting up flyers all over town. Have you seen them?"

"No. Do you think someone will answer them?"

"This is New Coventry. It's small enough everyone knows everyone else— if someone's seen her, they would have said already. It's not like a lost dog."

"I guess there isn't anything else she can do," Aurora peered out the window as they approached Dinwiddie Hills. There was no sign of Sable heading toward school.

"I called Jane last night," Josie said.

"How is she doing?"

"Not well. She's really worried. Susan hasn't answered her phone. She's never been gone this long before."

"Where is Jane staying?"

"Her aunt flew in from Vermont to stay with her while they look for Susan. If she doesn't come home...Jane might go with her when she goes back home."

"She's going to leave?"

"She's never really liked it here that much. Her mom's reputation never made it easy in school. I think I would want to leave, too, if my mom just disappeared. Bad memories."

"Yeah. Did she say what she thinks happened to her mom?"

"Well, she knows her mom can get wild sometimes, but she's never disappeared for this long before. She doesn't think she would just get in her car and leave. Eventually she would have sobered up and called home. She's not perfect, but she'd never just leave Jane all alone with no one to take care of her."

"It would be so terrible if something has happened to them. You'd think if

144

they were in some kind of accident, they would have found them by now."

"Yeah. I think Jane is thinking the same thing." Josie sighed. "I feel so bad for her."

"Me, too. I know what it's like to lose your mom. At least I knew what happened to her...not knowing for sure must be awful."

Josie glanced cautiously at Aurora as though she expected her to crumple or burst into tears, but, for once, Aurora didn't feel the barely healed wound ripping open in her belly. There was only a low, dull ache where the memory of her mother was. She smiled reassuringly.

Josie slowed as they passed the Jayne house. There was no sign of life in the house. Josie looked disappointed as she steered toward Diana's house. Aurora wondered if she would see Sable in class today.

Diana was already waiting on the curb. She gave a perfunctory wave as she climbed into the backseat. Then she frowned. "What's wrong with you, Aurora?"

She rolled her eyes. "There is nothing wrong with me."

"I know, right?" Josie said. "There is something different about her."

"What is it?" Diana demanded.

"I went to see Dr. Jayne yesterday."

"And she made you weird?"

"I'm not weird. I'm fine."

"Well, what happened?" Josie asked. "Tell us everything."

"I just talked to her."

"What about?"

"I don't really think that's any of our business, Jos," Diana said reproachfully. "Anyway, why do you think?"

"It wasn't about my mom," Aurora told her. "Not completely, anyway. I've just been feeling like...I need someone to talk to."

"A shrink?" Josie's said sharply, and Aurora suspected her feelings were hurt.

"Well, I guess. Yeah."

"You are the most level-headed person I know. You don't need a shrink."

"There is nothing wrong with talking to someone," Diana put in.

"Yeah, but we're her friends. You could have talked to us, Rora."

"Sometimes it's good to be able to talk to someone who doesn't have any investment in your life," Diana replied. "Even though I am not sure I approve of the Jaynes."

"What is she like?" Josie asked. "You saw Mariah, right?"

"Yes. She's really...nice."

"Nice? What did she say?"

"Not much. She just asked me questions the whole time."

"About what? About us?"

"No. Not about you. We didn't get that far. I just talked about my family."

"It wasn't weird?"

"No. It wasn't weird."

Diana leaned between the seats. "Well, it seems to have done some good. You aren't acting all crazy like everyone else, but you seem...happier. Did you talk about your mom?"

"No. Not really. Not yet."

"She didn't do any weird stuff to you?" Josie sounded disappointed.

"Weird stuff?" Diana asked scornfully.

"She didn't do weird stuff."

"People are coming out of there like she is some sort of miracle worker or witch or something."

"She's not a witch. She's not a miracle worker, either. I don't feel like I've changed or anything. I just feel...kind of better."

"Did she do mystical stuff to you? Read your fortune?"

"Come on, Josie," Diana snapped.

"She just seems like a normal doctor."

"It doesn't sound like it when you hear other people talk about it," Josie said sulkily. "It's like she's hypnotized them or something."

"Actually, she might have."

"What?" Josie had to jerk the wheel back to avoid swerving into the wrong lane.

"Well, she did some kind of relaxation treatment with me. She didn't wave a spinning pendulum in front of my eyes or anything. She just talked to me. I kind of went into a sort of daydream. I might have fallen asleep. When I woke up again, I felt all relaxed and happy."

"Weird," Josie said. "If she really is hypnotizing people, it's probably how she's is curing all those addictions and other things. I have heard that really works."

Diana didn't look convinced. "You aren't going to start quacking like a duck if someone says the word tater tot or something, are you?"

Aurora laughed. "No, I don't think so. She's not that kind of hypnotist. It was more like meditating. As far as I know, she didn't tell me to do anything while I was out."

"Well, you wouldn't know, would you?"

"I guess not."

"We'll be paying close attention in case you do," Josie promised.

"Thanks."

"Don't listen to Josie, Aurora. I am glad you went to see Dr. Jayne. Even though I am not sure how I feel about this hypnotism thing, and I am sure it won't last, it could be really good just to talk to someone. Even if you feel fine, losing a parent so young can really do things to your mind you don't even notice until it's too late."

"Thanks, Diana. I think it could be really good. It's kind of nice talking to someone who doesn't know everything about me."

"Are you going to keep seeing her?" Josie asked.

"Yeah. I think so. I'm going back next week."

"Did you see Sable?"

"Yes. He was there. It's his house."

"Did you talk to him?"

Aurora thought about telling them everything he had said, but she hadn't told them about the afternoon in the alley. There was a lot she hadn't been telling them lately.

"Not really. He just answered the door and took me to his mom's office."

Josie was disappointed. "Oh. Well, he's probably used to that sort of thing."

"I don't know. He didn't seem used to it at all. I probably just happened to show up as he was leaving or something." But he hadn't left, had he? He'd been there the entire time. She'd thought he'd been waiting at his mother's door for her to come out.

"He's so mysterious and lofty. And sexy. I would take any excuse to run into him."

"He doesn't seem that nice," Diana told her. "You know him best, Aurora. What do you think?"

"I hardly know him at all. He's just kind of...weird."

"Weird?"

"Just kind of different. I can't really figure him out."

"Maybe he's shy," Josie suggested.

"Yeah. Maybe."

"He probably just needs to get to know all of us. I would be happy to show him around, introduce him to all the important people in town."

The girls laughed. "I'm sure you would," Diana said.

"I think the Lawson twins are looking to do the same thing," Aurora added.

"Well, that could be good for you, right?" Josie asked. "If they move their wicked little attentions to Sable, they might not care about Jesse anymore."

Aurora scoffed. "Even if that did happen, I think they would still hate me."

"They're just jealous," Josie said for the hundredth time.

"I know. I don't care what they have to say. They're just mean girls who like to put people down."

Diana smiled. "It sounds like seeing Dr. Jayne is working for you."

Aurora grinned as Josie steered the car into the school parking lot. "Yeah. I think things are going to be different from now on." She craned her neck as she spotted Sable's tall, dark-hooded figure staring resignedly up at the school. Her pulse leapt. "At least I hope they're going to be."

148

Chapter Seven

"You're so lucky, Aurora," Josie said, staring dreamily after Sable as he strode swiftly up the steps to the school. As though she were equipped with some sort of hot boy homing beacon, she'd spotted him as soon as she'd parked the car and dragged her two friends after him as if there was even a remote chance they might catch him. "You have him in your English class, and now you get to see him at his own house."

Aurora watched him disappear around the corner. "I'm not sure how lucky I am. It's not like he pays any attention to me." And when he did, it was so strange she didn't know if he hated her or was worried something terrible might happen to her.

"I'm thinking about going to see the doc myself," Josie added. "Lord knows I've got issues."

Diana smirked. "I would not outright discourage you from that action, Jos."

"Oh, my god!" Josie's focus switched so quickly, Aurora started and looked around in surprise, half expecting to see Sable streaking toward them in his underwear.

"What is the matter with you?" Diana demanded.

"The Spring Formal. I had almost forgotten about it." Josie pointed toward the flyer tacked to the glass front doors.

"It's just a few weeks away," Diana remarked. "Can you believe it? We'll be done with junior year and be seniors soon."

"Are you going to the dance with Zach?" Josie asked her.

"Naturally."

"Who are you going with, Aurora?"

"Oh, come on. How would I know? I just found out about it. Anyway, you'd probably know before me if I did have a date. I doubt I'll go with anyone."

"Why not? If no one asks you, you could always ask them," Diana told her. "There aren't many dances left before graduation. You should make the most of it."

Josie grinned. "You know Jesse will ask you. You could always say yes."

"Yes, he'll probably ask me. Ruby thinks he might be scaring off other guys who might want to ask me out."

Diana lifted her eyebrows. "Well, yeah. He could be. I don't know many guys who would want to go up against him if it came down to it."

As she processed this, Josie looked crestfallen. "I never thought about it. There are worse things, though, you know, Rora. Maybe you could just go to the dance with him and see how it goes."

"Come off it, Josie," Diana scolded.

"Why don't you go with him?" Aurora suggested.

Josie scoffed. "I would if he asked me. We all know he won't, though."

"What about you? Who are you hoping to go with? Bryan Dymond?"

"Oh, Bryan, sure. But I'd settle for Eric Hayes or John Hawthorne...or Trent Meyers. Or anyone who asked me, really."

"Even if it was Dylan Springer?"

Josie pretended to gag. "Well, maybe not Dylan Springer."

The girls laughed as they pushed open the doors. They stopped abruptly as they ran right into Sable, who stood in the hall holding a book and looking as though he'd been watching the closed doors with a frown.

Aurora's stomach flipped. She heard Josie suck in a surprised breath beside her. "Hi, Sable." She was pleased that she didn't stammer.

Sable didn't say anything in response. He stepped toward Aurora and stared down at her with that weird, intense scrutiny with which he had looked at her outside his mother's office.

"What?" Aurora demanded. "Why do you keep looking at me like that?"

"It's nothing."

"Then quit frowning at me like I've done something you don't like."

Sable's frown deepened. "It isn't you."

She opened her mouth to reply, but he spun on his heel and strode quickly away.

"See?" Aurora said, rolling her eyes. "He's weird."

"What was that about?" Josie demanded.

"I have no idea." Aurora tossed her hair and started toward her classroom. "He's been acting really weird lately. I can't figure him out. Sometimes I think he's nice, and other times he acts like that."

Josie hurried to block Aurora's path. "There's something going on there, Aurora. I think he might like you."

"Why would you think that? He doesn't act like he likes me at all."

"Well," Diana said thoughtfully, "I've never actually seen him talk to anyone else. I've seen him talk to you twice."

"More than twice," Josie added.

Aurora paused in the hall outside her classroom. "There's something I have to tell you guys."

Their eyes widened as she told them about meeting Van in the alley, about Jesse arriving to defend her and Sable's interference.

"Aurora!" Josie exclaimed when she'd finished.

"I can't believe you didn't tell us," Diana said.

"He saved you?"

"Actually," Aurora said, gesturing Josie to keep her voice down. "Jesse did."

"This is the craziest thing that's ever happened to any of us," Josie hissed. "Why didn't you tell us? What do you think it means?"

"I don't know what it means. It might not mean anything. I didn't tell you guys about it because I still don't really get what was going on."

"Still, we're your friends," Diana scolded. "You should have mentioned it."

"It wasn't as dramatic as it sounds."

"What do you think Van was planning to do?"

"I don't know. I think he was probably just drunk and messing around with me. He looked kind of weird. I don't think he really would have done anything to me, not right outside my dad's shop in broad daylight."

She'd almost convinced herself of it. Except Van hadn't seemed drunk

151

at all. She hadn't smelled alcohol on him. And if he'd just been drunk and messing around, if it had not really been any big deal, why had Sable reacted the way he had, as though he'd stopped Van doing something really, really terrible? Something...well, something he'd probably done before. She pushed the thoughts away.

"You've been acting kind of weird yourself lately," Diana told her. "Keeping things like this from us."

Aurora waved her hand dismissively. "He's probably just a creep. I didn't think it was a big deal."

"It sounds like Sable thought it was, though."

"Or maybe he just overreacted because he's so into you," Josie suggested.

"If he was so into me, I doubt he would have let me leave with Jesse."

"So how did that go?" Diana asked dryly.

"Actually, he was really good about it. He was kind of...sweet. I'm glad he was there."

"When did your life get so interesting?" Josie asked enviously. "A few weeks ago, you were this quiet, unassuming and uninteresting girl, and now you're living in some drama."

"Uninteresting?" Aurora was outraged.

"I think you're exaggerating, Josie," Diana put in.

"I don't know about that," Josie said. "Ever since the Jaynes came, she's started seeing a therapist, been hypnotized, pursued by one of the hottest boys in school, and now she's being attacked in any alley by another creepy— but hot—guy and then rescued from him by two hot boys."

"If you hadn't added the 'hot' part each time, it would not have sounded so stupid," Diana told her. "And she was being pursued by Jesse before the Jaynes came."

Josie glared at her. "You always try to ruin everything."

"Anyway, you make it sound very romantic, but it isn't," Aurora told her.

"Why not? Why can't it be?" Josie nudged her. "Just enjoy it, Rora." She ignored the warning bell. "Maybe Sable will ask you to the dance."

"I doubt it. Even if he was into me—which I am sure he isn't—he doesn't seem like the dancing type. And he really doesn't seem like the tuxedo type."

"You never know. It could be like one of those teen romance movies where the star-crossed boy and girl finally meet up and confess their mutual smoochy fantasies."

"Come on, Josie," Diana said.

"What?"

"Life isn't like the movies."

"Rora's is beginning to sound like one."

"I promise you, it isn't," Aurora insisted. "It probably won't end like one, either. It'll be just as boring and uninteresting as anything else that's ever happened to me."

"Well, I think we should be the ones to decide that. We're the ones living vicariously through you. And don't keep anymore interesting stuff from us!"

Aurora laughed. "Okay. I promise I won't keep anything you would want to exaggerate and romanticize from you from now on."

Josie stuck her little finger out toward Aurora. "Pinky swear?"

Aurora rolled her eyes and wrapped her pinky around Josie's. "Yeah. Okay. I pinky swear."

* * *

"Are you coming, Aurora?" Josie asked as the girls strode toward the parking lot after school.

"No. I think I'm going to go by the museum."

"The museum? Why?"

She shrugged. "I like to go there."

Diana lifted her eyebrows. "Since when?"

"Since always."

"Something else you haven't told us?"

She smiled at them. "Yes."

"You sure have a lot of secrets these days." Josie hitched her hands onto her hips in consternation. "I'm beginning to think we don't know you at all."

"Of course you do. It's just...something I like to do by myself sometimes. I like to go see the new exhibits and the star shows in the planetarium."

"Okay." Josie didn't look especially appeased. "If anything else happens along the way, you had better call and tell us about it this time."

"I will. I promise."

"Good. And if you run into Sable or his creepy brother, you put us on speaker phone so we can listen in."

"Josie," Diana scolded.

"Okay, okay. Maybe that's going a little too far. But call us as soon as you can. Right after."

"I'm sure it will be uneventful, Jos. I'm not going looking for any trouble today."

"That doesn't mean you aren't going to find it, so keep me on speed dial."

Aurora smiled. "You always are. See you guys tomorrow."

"Bye, Aurora!"

She waved and strode away from them. Her eyes swept the parking lot, searching for Sable's car. She didn't see him. He was probably long gone by now. He certainly wasn't hanging around hoping some foolish, infatuated girl would come along to pester him.

It was almost warm today, and Aurora paused to stuff her pink windbreaker into her backpack. A strange, creeping sensation shivered down her spine. She felt eyes on the back of her neck. The hair on her arms stood up in alarm. She took a sharp breath and lifted her head slowly to look around.

There was no one around.

She shook her head, feeling foolish, and slung her backpack over her shoulder. The breeze was light and pleasant. Leaves had sprouted on the trees almost overnight. The small buds would soon bloom into large, bright flowers. The branches had been mostly bare just weeks ago.

She heard a soft, almost inaudible footfall behind her.

Aurora stopped and spun around. There was no one there.

This was getting ridiculous. "Is someone there?"

No one answered. She needed to get a grip. No one was following her. She was probably still just a little freaked out by the last time she'd been downtown.

She wasn't going to chase anyone resembling Sable into any alleys today.

154

She was heading straight to the museum and then right home. No getting herself into weird situations and needing rescuing today.

Her mind drifted back to Sable. Okay, maybe she would go chasing after him if she caught sight of him, but only if she was sure it wasn't Van. She wondered, for the hundredth time that day, about that look he'd given her this morning. He hadn't spoken to her in English. He hadn't even acknowledged her existence, and she hadn't been brave enough to confront him about it. Instead, she'd spent the entire day obsessing about it.

He knew she'd gone to see his mother. Was he trying to figure out what was wrong with her? He probably had a pretty good idea if he had been listening in on her session. This didn't bother her as much as it should. If he'd been trying to hear what she said to his mother that meant he actually cared. Maybe. It wasn't exactly the sort of attention she'd hoped to receive from him.

There was something about his expression this morning, though, something about the strange things he had said. He didn't want her to see his mother. She was certain he'd been trying to warn her away.

She didn't think she'd ever understand Sable. It was half the reason she liked him.

She looked for him as she strolled toward the museum, enjoying the warm spring day. The pleasant weather had drawn out most of the town. She saw several of her classmates pulling into the last few parking spots, heading for coffee dates or after-school burgers at Archie's. She stride right past them, not caring if they thought it was strange that she was heading to the museum on such a beautiful day.

The museum was practically empty. It was stuffy and dim compared to the breezy, brilliantly sunlit day outside. The Ancient Greeks exhibit had been cleared out and replaced by the usual world history artifacts that filled the space when Dr. Erickson didn't have anything special to show. They looked almost boring compared to the shining bronze statues and displays that had decorated the room weeks ago.

"Aurora! It is so nice to see you." Dr. Erickson appeared beside her so quietly she hadn't noticed him. He looked crisp and polished as ever in his blue curator jacket. The light from a statue of an ancient Hindi god reflected off his round glasses so she couldn't see his eyes, but he was smiling as though she was the highlight of his day.

She grinned. "It's probably nice to see anyone today."

"It has been rather quiet around here. It always slows down this time of year. It's just too nice outside to be hanging around a stuffy old museum. It will get a little busier in a couple months when everyone remembers we have air conditioning."

"No one ever appreciates history."

Dr. Erickson cocked his head to the side and studied her. "You seem different today. Did something happen?"

"No."

"Are you sure?" His smile was kindly. "You look like someone in love."

Her cheeks heated. "No. I'm not in love."

"Well, something is different about you."

"Maybe I am just starting to feel more like myself."

"Well, you seem happy, anyway."

"I think I might be getting there."

"Are you here to see anything particular today or have you decided to take me up on my offer to learn the star ball?"

"Yes. I would like that."

"Great. Come with me. I think we've got a little time. Anyone who comes in today will be all right on their own for a while." He led her through the display rooms toward the dark hallway near the back of the museum. The wall was decorated with thousands of tiny, glittering metal stars. "I've never met a high school girl who was so interested in the museum. It takes a lot of effort to force most girls your age to come in, let alone actually want to learn about history."

Aurora smiled. The planetarium's white dome ceiling was dark, and the rows of seats, set in a large circle beneath the dome, were empty. "It's my favorite thing. I want to be an archaeologist."

Dr. Erickson turned to look at her in surprise. "Is that so? I thought you wanted to be an astronomer."

"Well, I love looking up at the stars, but there's no adventure in it. I want to see the world. I want to experience it myself instead of just through the objects left behind." As soon as the words were out of her mouth and out in the world, it seemed so intensely, poignantly possible that she caught her breath.

Dr. Erickson's eyes slid away as he smiled wistfully. "I wanted to do the same thing myself. I studied Anthropology, but I spend most of my time in dusty backrooms with the remnants of ancient civilizations."

"You could still have adventures."

"Oh, no. I'm too old now. Too settled. But you are still young enough to do anything you want. Have you picked a college yet?"

"No. I've been looking a little. The truth is, I always wanted to do it but I never told anyone." Aurora smiled sheepishly. "I sort of assumed I wouldn't ever actually go through with it."

He looked aghast. "If it's your dream, you have to give it a chance. You might find it isn't for you, or you might find it's your life's work." He looked around the dark, empty room and grinned conspiratorially. "Come on."

She watched him in surprise as he darted back toward the door. "Where are we going?"

"You can learn the planetarium any time. It's just a bunch of buttons and a joystick. Do you want to see the newest exhibit?"

"Where is it?"

"In the backroom. I haven't put it out yet. It just came in a few days ago, and I have been cataloguing and going through it all. You want to see it?"

"Yeah!"

Dr. Erickson led her through the Ancient Egyptian display, past gold statues of gods with the heads of cats, jackals, cows, hawks and snakes. The discreet door marked Employees Only was half hidden behind a tapestry depicting hieroglyphic writing, and the old curator pushed the tapestry aside to unlock the door, gesturing her inside almost grandly. The door had always seemed mysterious, as though some magical, clandestine world of wonder and history waited breathlessly in the room behind it.

Aurora felt a thrill shoot down her spine. She had only imagined what was in the room. Now, she would finally see it.

It was dark when she walked inside. Dr. Erickson flipped on a florescent light beside the door, flooding the room with stark light. The room was filled mostly with boxes, some of which were still closed and others that had packing popcorn spread on the floor around them. Shelves lined the walls, housing dusty artifacts that had once been interesting but had been replaced by the more exciting exhibits outside. A large table in the center of the room was strewn with stacks of papers and pencils. It seemed to be Dr. Erickson's desk.

"Have you thought about working in a museum when you're done traveling the world and hunting for interesting treasures?"

"Yeah, I have." She could see the exciting edges of new artifacts protruding from the open boxes. She had an urge to rush forward and dig them out, to do touch what had once belonged to someone so long ago, it was unlikely anyone remembered their name. "I would love that."

"Well, now you can see what it is all about. It isn't as exciting as adventuring, but I enjoy it. I enjoy discovering new civilizations through the objects they leave behind. It is fascinating work. You know, I often assist the universities and occasionally the Smithsonian with translating ancient scrolls and texts."

"I didn't know that."

"I am something of an expert in ancient languages."

"That sounds interesting. But what are you doing working here?"

He laughed. "Well, I could work at the Smithsonian with the other anthropologists, but I prefer to have my own place where I can choose my own exhibits and run things the way I like. It is far more rewarding than being a cog in the genius wheel over there. I bet you could work for them someday, if that is something you are considering. You would have to work hard."

"That would be amazing. I love the Smithsonian. Still, I can see why you would want your own place." She stepped up to the desk, fluttering her fingers over the old, chipped pottery and tarnished knives spread out on the surface next to the inventory sheet. She itched to do touch them, but she didn't dare in case the objects turned to dust beneath her fingers.

Dr. Erickson gestured toward the stack of crates beside the desk. He reached into one of them and gently lifted out an old flute and a drum that looked as though it would scarcely make a sound anymore. "Well, here it is. The vestiges of the ancient Assyrian society. Some of them, anyway. We're still discovering pieces of their civilization in what used to be Mesopotamia. This is one of the biggest collections on the museum circuit. It just shipped here from Maine."

"It's so old."

"Yes, it is old. And just recently discovered, in fact. In Turkey. It was quite difficult to get the items out of the country, I understand, but they are here now."

Aurora bent down to admire the intricately carved flute. "That must have been really exciting, searching for buried treasure."

"Yes, well, I expect when you are doing the same thing, you will send me frequent emails."

"I will." She hovered over a beautiful, carved gold necklace with small, green jewels that Dr. Erickson lifted from inside one of the crates on a velvet pad.

"Go ahead. You can touch it. If it has survived this long, you won't be able to break it."

She picked up the necklace, examining the small animals carved into the gold. It had been recently polished, but it still looked old and well worn. "It's so pretty."

He glanced down at his paperwork. "It once belonged to a princess named Shamiram. She wore it on her wedding day to a prince of neighboring land. Sadly, Shamiram died in childbirth thereafter."

"Wow. It is so amazing to hold pieces of the past like this. Sometimes I wonder what someone will be holding to remember me someday."

He smiled. "I often wonder the same thing. It's part of the job, I believe."

A loud bell trilled through the room, startling them both.

"Oh, my goodness," Dr. Erickson said. "I was so wrapped up in our conversation, I forgot I had a class coming in for a planetarium presentation." He looked deeply abashed. "I apologize for having to cut it short. I don't suppose you want to stick around and see how it all works?"

"I would really like to, but I think I should probably get home. I didn't tell my dad I wouldn't be home for dinner."

Dr. Erickson bustled her out of the room. "Of course. Come by anytime, Aurora. It is always nice to have someone to talk to. There aren't many people who are interested in listening to an old man drone on and on about ancient cultures and languages."

"I will. Thanks for letting me see all this."

"I am always happy to share the past with someone, especially when they are as keen as I am."

The small group of bored junior high kids loitered in the lobby as though approaching any of the displays around them might rub off and make them old and boring. Aurora waved to Dr. Erickson on her way out.

After the dusky, stuffy backroom filled with old, dusty artifacts, the sun was brilliant. She blinked for a few seconds on the front steps, blinded. She waited for her eyes to adjust and hurried down the stairs. She thought about visiting Ruby's flower shop, but it was already nearly five o'clock, and her aunt would be heading home by now or on her way to meet Blaine. Mike would be home in less than an hour. She might as well just head home, though it was such a beautiful day, she knew she ought to be out enjoying the weather like everyone else lingering in the square and chatting in the streets.

She turned down the road to her house. The warm breeze lifted her long hair. She sighed contentedly. Out of the corner of her eye, she caught a flash of dark hair. She spun toward it, her heart hammering in her chest.

There was no one there. Had she imagined him? Had she only wished so badly to see him, even her eyes were playing tricks on her? She took a step toward the corner around which she thought he might have disappeared. Her step faltered.

If it was Van, following him was a tremendously bad idea. But if it was Sable, if she could just see him...

She squared her shoulders and went after him.

Then she stopped. What was she doing? She'd already promised herself she wouldn't do this. She wasn't the sort of girl who chased after boys, especially when they'd made it clear they didn't want her anywhere near him.

If her therapy had urged her to follow him after everything that had happened in that alley last time, perhaps it really was changing her. Maybe not for the better.

* * *

Ruby sat at the kitchen table, sipping a steaming cup of tea. Aurora was surprised to see her. "Hey, Ruby. What are you doing home so early? More girl talk?"

Her aunt smiled. "No, not tonight. Unless you think you need it. Then I can cancel our plans."

"No, no. I'm feeling great."

"Hot chocolate?" Ruby hopped up to pour hot water into a mug. "So Dr. Jayne is helping, huh?"

Helping, maybe. She felt better, anyway, but there was something alarming about how recklessly she'd nearly chased after Sable or Van or some other dark-haired person earlier. Still, it was better than before, when there had been nothing but empty, hollow longing.

"Yeah. I think so, anyway. I feel like things are getting better."

"Good." Ruby handed her the steaming mug. "I thought you would be home sooner. Where have you been? With Josie and Diana?"

"The museum, actually." She didn't wait for her hot chocolate to cool, and she coughed as it burned down her throat. Ruby rolled her eyes.

"The museum? What for?"

"Dr. Erickson showed me the new Assyrian exhibit he just got in from Maine. It was a civilization that was around in Mesopotamia a really long time ago. It was really interesting. There were old pieces of pottery and stuff they used back then. There was a necklace that used to belong to a princess who died in childbirth. He let me hold it."

"Sounds like you had a nice time. I had no idea how much you really do like that stuff."

"I love it. I love history and just seeing the evidence of people who lived a really long time ago."

"Have you told Mike about your plans after school yet?"

"No. Not yet. I'm not sure I'm ready to tell him."

"Well, I am sure he will be very happy to hear about it. Give him a chance to be. He'll be happy to know you're planning to pursue something you love."

Aurora smiled at her aunt over the top of her mug.

"Speaking of that, Blaine's just got the last inspection approved on the house he's been flipping. He's invited us all over for dinner."

"We're having dinner at Blaine's?"

"Sure."

"All of us?"

Ruby laughed. "Yes, all of us. You, your dad and me. Christian has an exam in the morning, so I told him to stay at school, but Troy will be there, too. It'll be a little celebration for finishing another house. They've already got a buyer lined up. So how about it? I know it might not sound like the best night ever for a teenager, but it could be fun."

"Sure. It sounds like fun."

"Great." She hopped up, dumping her tea out in the sink. "I have to go up and get ready. I smell like flowers."

"Is that bad?"

"It could be worse. I could smell like axle grease. Tell your dad when he gets home, will you?"

"Sure. He'll probably be happy to have someone other than us make dinner for him. I think he's getting sick of our limited repertoire."

Ruby grinned. "I suppose a man can only live on mac and cheese and tomato soup for so long. I'll just be a minute."

"Should I change?"

"Oh, you always look beautiful. You're fine the way you are."

Aurora rolled her eyes and marched up the stairs after her aunt. She only took a moment to glance in the mirror, and she was surprised by what she saw. She did look different. Her long, strawberry blonde hair was the same. Her small, delicate features hadn't changed at all, but there was something almost...pretty about them. There was something in her eyes that startled her, something fierce and glittering.

What had Dr. Jayne done to her?

She rolled her eyes at the idea. Of course the doctor hadn't done anything. Aurora might feel different, but she was still herself. She couldn't change her, not like that.

The front door slammed downstairs. Aurora spun away from the mirror, embarrassed at the thought of bring caught admiring herself in the mirror, though she knew her father would never walk into her room without knocking—in fact, she could hardly remember the last time he'd walked in there at all.

She could hear Ruby humming down the hall. Aurora sighed, wishing she knew what it felt like to get dressed up for someone—someone who actually cared that she'd gone through the trouble. She pushed the thoughts aside and hurried downstairs to meet her father.

Mike was hanging up his jacket in the hall. His face was streaked with grease. "You look nice, Rory. Do you have plans tonight?"

"We all do."

"Oh?"

"Blaine invited us over for dinner at his house tonight."

Mike sighed. He looked tired. "Tonight?"

"He finished the house and wants to show it off before he sells it, I guess."

"I suppose Ruby would not accept no for an answer."

"I think we both know the answer to that."

"All right, all right." Aurora suspected he secretly liked the idea of spending the evening drinking beer and talking about manly things with Blaine and Troy. "I'd better get cleaned up." His eyes drifted toward the stairs.

"She's getting ready to see Blaine. It might be awhile."

He laughed and strode over to kiss her on her forehead. "Maybe I'll have a beer first."

* * *

Blaine's house was in the hills, set back from the street and surrounded by tall, lush overhanging trees. A tall, metal fence lined the property, barely containing the verdant flora. The gate hung open, and lights flickered merrily in the large house beyond. It was so brilliant white, it practically glittered in the starlight. An elegant wooden widows-walk wrapped around the third story.

Mike lifted his eyebrows. "Wow. Blaine does good work. This place used to be a dump."

"How long has he been working on it?" Aurora asked.

"About six months, I think," Ruby told her. "Amazing, isn't he?"

"He did it all by himself?"

"He had a little help sometimes: day laborers and some contractors. He redid most of the rooms, put in a new kitchen and did the bathrooms. He put in all new floors and repainted all the walls. You'll see when you get inside. He wants to show it off."

Mike pulled up into the wraparound driveway in front of the house. A large, elegant black Cadillac was already parked outside. They stepped up onto the wide porch, which was decorated with potted flowers and trees which gave the impression of an overgrown garden. Ruby was anxious to see Blaine, though she'd probably seen him every day for the last several days. She hurried up to the door and knocked.

Troy opened the door, grinning. "Hey, guys. Welcome to our place. Come on in."

Ruby smiled. "Hello, Troy. Where's Blaine?"

"He's just working on dinner. He sent me to greet you like a proper little butler." He gestured them inside with a flourish. He stuck out a hand to Mike. "Mike. Nice to see you again."

Mike grinned, shaking his hand. "You, too, man. The place looks great."

"I know, right? Whatever I might say about my best friend, he does good work." His grin stretched wider as he caught sight of Aurora. "Aurora, glad you could make it. We thought you might have some much more exciting teenager stuff to do tonight."

"I don't know when you were last a teenager, but we don't really have exciting teenager stuff. At least none that I am involved in."

He laughed. "Well, we're happy you could come."

"I didn't have anything better to do," she teased. "It's free dinner, anyway."

Mike rolled his eyes. "Charming. I didn't realize you have a sense of humor, Rory."

"Oh, please," Ruby said. "I'm surprised she isn't snarkier, considering her father."

"And her aunt."

Aurora smiled at Troy. "Thanks for inviting me. I am looking forward to seeing the work Blaine's done in the house."

"And that would be her mother coming out."

Troy swept his hand toward the living room. "Come on in to the living room and have a seat. It's the best room in the house."

The living room was beautiful. The cathedral ceiling was high and bright with a swinging crystal chandelier. The walls were a soft, textured sand color, though there were few pieces of art hanging upon them. Instead, potted plants and tarnished metal abstract sculptures decorated the tall, wide empty spaces. Beige leather sofas and thick armchairs were widely spread around the room, emphasizing the large, bright space. A bay window overlooked the manicured trees outside.

"What do you think of it?" Troy asked, smiling as he gestured them to take a seat on the sofas.

"It's really pretty," Aurora told him. She liked the pale, neutral colors and the abstract sculptures.

"Not bad," Mike said. "I heard you've already got a buyer."

"Yes. We had interest right away. This is a prime property, but it needed a lot of work. There was some water damage in the basement, and the electrical had to be completely re-wired. Most of the people who were looking at the place weren't interested in taking on such a big project. These old colonial houses are our bread and butter. People are willing to pay a lot of money to have a house like this, especially after it's been totally re-vamped. That's where we come in. We buy up these great properties that need a lot of work, Blaine fixes them up and we make a hefty profit."

"How long have you two been doing this?" Mike asked.

"Almost twenty years. We started with the house Blaine and I bought together right out of college. It was a dump. We were a couple single kids who wanted a place to bring home girls." He winked at Ruby. "The year or so we lived there, Blaine fixed it up, and when we found out how much we could profit, we realized it wasn't a bad way to make money. Better than working at an office, anyway. We've been all over the country, mostly along the east coast. They have the best old houses here. We've been to New Hampshire, Maine, Connecticut, Massachusetts, Delaware, New York."

"Do you ever help?" Aurora asked.

"No, not me. I'm the idea man, really. Blaine has always been the handy one. He's like an artist with his tools."

"I can see that," Mike remarked.

"Are you talking about me?" Blaine poked his head into the room.

"Blaine!" Ruby exclaimed, jumping up to greet him with a kiss. "Nice apron, sweetie."

He snorted. "I'll have you know, there's nothing wrong with a man wearing an apron."

Troy waved his hand. "There's nothing right about it, either. Anyway, we've only been saying good things. You know I would never throw my best friend under the bus."

Blaine rolled his eyes. "Since when?"

"Well, I didn't want to start turning these people against you. It seems like you have a good thing going here." He winked at Ruby again, and she flushed with pleasure. "I was telling them about some of the work you did on the house."

"We can take a tour later, and I'll tell you all about it. You guys ready for dinner?"

Mike surged to his feet. "I know I am."

"Blaine's been working on dinner all day," Troy said as they followed Blaine to the kitchen. "He had to start over a couple times because he kept burning everything."

"Please," said Blaine. "You know I make the best damn roast you've ever had."

"It's true, but to be fair, my mother was the worst cook in the world. Compared to that, anything this guy cooks is gourmet."

Blaine rolled his eyes, wrapping Ruby's hand in his. "I hope you like roast beef and mashed potatoes."

"Who doesn't?" Mike asked happily.

Blaine grinned, gesturing them into the kitchen.

"I hope you all know, dinner was really just an excuse to show off the new kitchen and dining room," Troy said with a smirk.

"This guy just can't stop giving me a hard time," Blaine said. "Anyway, he's right. Check it out."

The kitchen was a soft, pale blue with polished sandstone countertops. Dark, rich wood accented the light, pastel colors, and copper pots and pans hung over the wide island in the center of the room. It smelled strongly of roasted meat, and it was warm and toasty.

"It's amazing," Ruby told him.

"The new owners picked the colors. It's not what I would have chosen. I prefer something a bit darker."

"I like it," Aurora remarked. "It looks nice. Kind of like a beach on a sunny day."

Blaine looked around the room with pride. "You're right. It is nice."

"So it's already sold for sure?" Ruby sounded somewhat disappointed. "I'll be sorry to see it go."

"That would be the first rule of house-flipping," Troy told her. "Don't get attached. It's just about settled. We're in final negotiations. It's a matter of paperwork at this point."

"That's where Troy comes in," Blaine explained. "I hate paperwork."

The dining room was not large, but the ceiling was high, and a crystal chandelier hung over the round, polished mahogany table that was set for dinner. A large roast sat on a silver platter, and bowls of steaming vegetables and potatoes surrounded it. Mike was anxious to eat. He took the first seat, set with a bowl of red soup and a wine goblet. Blaine and Troy waited for Ruby and Aurora to take their seats before sitting down.

"This is the fanciest spread I've seen since Easter," Mike was barely able to contain himself, waiting for his hosts to indicate it was time to eat.

"I like to make a big deal out of things," Blaine said. "I don't get to do it very often. Anyway, I'm glad you could all come."

"He would have been heartbroken if you hadn't. You just dig in there, Mike," Troy said. "We aren't formal around here, as much as Blaine is trying to impress everyone."

Mike didn't need to be told twice. He tucked into his dinner with gusto while Blaine made a face at Troy. No one said anything for a moment as they piled their plates high with the food. "So what's your next move, Blaine?" Mike asked after he'd swallowed enough food to be capable of civilized conversation. "Are you going to move on to a new project?"

"I have to. I can't keep living here." Blaine smiled.

"We're thinking of buying a house on Dinwiddie Lane," Troy put in.

"The big one with the old latticework?" Mike asked.

"That's the one," Blaine agreed. "It's been on the market a long time. Troy thinks we could buy it up for a pretty good price. I think we could flip it and sell it for a good profit."

"I've talked to the listing agent about it, and they are going to the owners with an offer next week. We should hear about it in a few days."

"Are you going to hang around and oversee the project?" Ruby asked.

Troy waved his hand. "Nah. I have some business contacts in Maryland I need to visit. Blaine isn't the only one who works on the houses. We've got a couple guys who do work for us when Blaine can't be there. I typically scout around the country looking for promising new projects and the guys do the work."

"Sounds like a pretty nice life," Aurora commented.

He laughed. "Well, I do a lot more talking than working, that's for sure. It's not a bad way to make a living. I get to see a lot of different places, and I get a lot of time to enjoy myself."

"If he wasn't my best friend, I would kick him to the curb," Blaine said. "He thinks he runs the place."

"Well, I like to let myself think I do now and again. I'm hoping to get this guy to work on a house in Connecticut for me. It's a great old mansion, but he doesn't seem to want to leave anytime soon."

Blaine smiled at Ruby. "Lucky for me, he doesn't actually run the place. We can still take the house. We'll just get one of the other guys to do the work."

"It just don't be the same. Blaine is the best. That's why I started this thing with him to begin with."

"It is a rather convenient partnership. I'd rather be in the trenches under a stack of drywall than schmoozing realtors and negotiating deals, and he'd rather be traipsing around the country having business lunches."

"And you get to stay here, in scenic New Coventry." Troy gave him a pointed look.

Blaine pretended not to notice. He smiled at Ruby. Aurora smiled at the sight of them. He seemed to really like her aunt. She hoped he would stick around. Ruby deserved to be happy.

"So, enough about us. How's the shop going, Mike?" Blaine asked suddenly.

Mike shrugged and swallowed a mouthful of roast beef. "Same as ever. A new busted radiator or dropped transmission everyday. There's always something to do around that place."

"I have heard around town you're the only man to talk to if you have car problems," Troy said.

Mike grinned. "I've heard the same thing." He leaned forward to refill his wine goblet.

"How about you, Aurora? What are your plans after high school? Ruby tells us you're a junior this year."

She'd been half-hoping to get out of too much dinner conversation, but she liked Troy, and she didn't mind answering him. "Yeah."

"Are you planning to go to college when you graduate next year?"

She glanced at Ruby. Her aunt gave her an encouraging smile. "Yes. I definitely plan to go to college."

"Do you know what you're going to study?"

"Well…" She looked at Mike. He leaned back in his chair and looked mildly interested in her response. They hadn't talked about it before. "I really want to study archaeology."

Her father looked surprised. "You do?"

Troy grinned. "It sounds like your girl wants to be an adventurer, Mike."

"Well, maybe a little. I like history. I want to study past cultures and discover new places."

"I didn't know that," Mike said. "Ruby, did you know about this?"

"I might have heard Aurora Sky say something like that once."

Aurora's pulse leapt. "Is that okay?"

Mike grinned and reached over to ruffle her hair. "I'm just happy you want to go to college. And if you want to be the next Indiana Jones, that's fine with me."

"Well, I'd probably spend most of my time in dusty old backrooms in museums. Dr. Erickson at the museum said he would teach me about the planetarium, too."

"It sounds like you have a good plan," Troy said.

"Well, it's an idea, anyway. I don't know how easy it is to get a job in that field."

"Well, it sounds like you have an in with the curator around here," Blaine said, smiling encouragingly. "Maybe you can take his place someday."

"Maybe I'd like that after I've seen the world. I love New Coventry, but I would like to see what else is out there first."

"Ah, a sense of adventure."

"I didn't know you had it in you, Rory."

She smiled at her dad. "Well, I'm not sure I even knew it, not until recently."

"I bet you love these old houses, then," Blaine added. "There's a lot of history in them."

"Oh, yes. I really like the history around Virginia. American history is exciting, but I especially love ancient civilizations. The really old ones no one can even remember anymore."

Ruby grinned. "Maybe you'll be the one to finally discover the lost city of Atlantis, Aurora Sky."

"That would be awesome, but I'm not sure I believe it exists."

"What? What sort of adventurer are you?" Troy demanded. "They're digging up old sunken cities all the time."

"Yes, so it seems as though they would have found Atlantis by now."

"But don't you want to obsessively chase down mythical treasures and die alone in a hut somewhere lamenting the lost dreams of your youth?"

He sounded so dismayed by the idea that this was not her dream that she laughed out loud. "I'm not sure what sort of dreams you had when you were a kid, but I am not sure that is the dream I'm going for. Though I suppose it does sound about right."

"Well, what do you think about this grand dream of Aurora's, Mike?" Troy asked.

"It sounds fine to me. I'm just happy she has something she cares about. A lot of teenagers don't even want to think that far ahead. If dying in a hut somewhere is what Aurora wants, that's good enough for me. As long as it isn't anytime soon."

Troy rose as they cleaned their plates. "We'll let Blaine clear this up later. Why don't we let him show us all the hard work he's done?"

"I would love to see it all finished," Ruby said.

"It's settled, then." Troy brandished the bottle of wine. "Shall we freshen our drinks?"

Mike extended his glass. "Sounds good to me."

"I never turn down good wine," Ruby added.

Troy waggled his eyebrows. "How about you, Aurora?" He grinned around at the adults. "What do you say we get the kid drunk?"

Blaine snorted. Troy's eyes twinkled merrily. "I'm pretty sure that isn't appropriate," Aurora told Troy. "Someone will probably have to drive these guys home tonight."

Troy shook his head sadly. "Whoever heard of a responsible teenager?"

"Aurora Sky is as responsible as it gets. She makes me feel ashamed of my behavior most of the time," Ruby laughed.

Mike scoffed. "Don't start encouraging her to misbehave before it's even her idea."

Troy held up his hands. "I was only joking. You people are sensitive. How about a frosty root beer, Aurora?"

"Sure. That sounds good. You got any ice cream?"

"Have I got any ice cream?" Troy grinned and looked to Blaine, who shook his head. Troy's face fell. "No. No, I don't have any ice cream. Sorry."

"Come on," said Blaine. "I'll show you guys the house."

"Before it's gone forever," Troy added. "That's business, though. You have to say goodbye to a lot of houses like this that you love." His eyes twinkled. "Still, it's a shame. I'm starting to like New Coventry. It's not half bad."

* * *

Mike stared out the window at Blaine's house as Aurora steered out of the driveway. "He's a little weird," he said suddenly.

"Who?"

"I'm not sure about that Troy guy."

"What do you mean?"

"He just seems a little...off."

"What's off? What's that even mean?"

"I'm not sure."

"He seems like a really nice guy."

"Yeah, I know." Mike frowned. "Those business guys, though. You can just never be sure if the charm is real or not."

"Huh. I thought he seemed totally okay."

He turned to study her seriously. "So, you really want to be an archaeologist?"

"Yeah."

"How long has this been going on?"

"Forever, I guess. I mean, I've always liked it."

"I always thought you would be like your mom. Take over the flower shop."

"Mom always wanted to be an astronomer."

"Yeah, she did, but then we got married and she didn't want to leave for school. She did really well with the shop. She loved it."

"Yeah, but that isn't my dream."

"What about astronomy?"

"I think it's interesting. I want to study it a little, but a lot of my interest has always come from the stories behind it, the names of the constellations and their histories and stuff. I think I'm mostly interested in the history of the people who first looked at the stars and gave them names."

He considered this as she steered them slowly through the quiet streets. "Okay. Why didn't you tell me about this sooner, Rory?"

"I guess...well, maybe I was a little scared."

"Huh. Scared to tell me about it?"

"I wasn't sure how you would react." They were quiet a moment. "I think Dr. Jayne is really helping me."

172

"Already? You've only seen her the one time."

"I know. Maybe it's just beginner's luck. But I haven't felt this...good and normal since Mom died."

He breathed a deep sigh.

"I'm starting to feel like things are going to be okay." She couldn't read the expression in his eyes. "I guess what they say is true, huh? Maybe they can work miracles."

His smile looked forced. "Then I suppose it's a good idea you keep seeing her."

"Yeah. I think it is."

"I'm glad you're feeling better."

"It's not your fault, Dad."

"What?"

"It's not your fault I felt bad. You did the best you could. It's just...I guess it does something to you to lose a parent. I mean, of course it does. There wasn't anything you could have done better."

"Teenaged girls are a mystery to me. They always have been. I always thought Rosa would be here to help me out." He stared thoughtfully out the window. "Seeing as it's working so well for you, maybe I should think about talking to Dr. Jayne."

"It wouldn't be a terrible idea. We're both a bit messed up. Anyway, it's totally fashionable to see a therapist these days."

"I'm not sure I'll tell Jules about it, though. She probably wouldn't like the idea of me seeing another doctor, especially a good-looking lady doctor."

She snorted. "I won't tell anyone about it."

"I would appreciate that. I don't think it's very manly to see a therapist. Even if it is fashionable."

Chapter Eight

There was no sign of Van, but Sable hadn't expected to find his brother so easily. If Van was still in town, he knew how to hide. Van was good at hiding when he didn't want to be found. If Sable was lucky, he'd show himself one night at the bar. By then it might be too late.

When Van was drinking, it was already too late.

The streets were quiet and dark. No one was out wandering this late at night, though full dark had only descended about an hour ago. It was the sort of town where people stayed in for dinner and watched television with their families. It wasn't the sort of town where people prowled the streets at night in search of trouble.

That was good. The people of New Coventry were safer indoors when Van was the one out prowling.

Sable didn't pay attention to where he was driving. He wove slowly in and out of the neighborhoods, alert for any glimpse of moving shadow or darting figures.

"Where the hell are you, Van? What have you done this time?"

Up ahead in the darkness, something moved.

Sable slammed on the brakes. He turned off his headlights, squinting through the moonlight to make out the figure strolling unhurriedly along the sidewalk.

He realized where he was. He'd been in the neighborhood nearly every night since he'd began his search for Van. He didn't know if he really expected to find his brother there, but if he did come, if he planned to do something—

The door barely made a click as he climbed out of the car. The figure ahead was not moving with any haste or direction. His strides were longer, more purposeful, and he caught up to the moving shadow in seconds.

She stepped into a pool of streetlight that burnished her hair a glowing rose gold. He froze. What was she doing out here, wandering alone in the dark? Didn't she understand the danger she was in, with Van loose in the streets? If Van got it into his head to finish what he started that day--

He moved before he even thought about it, and she collided with him, rebounding off his chest with a soft grunt. He caught her shoulders to steady her.

She blinked at him in shock. "Sable? What are you doing?"

He released her quickly, as though her skin could burn him. "Keeping you from falling down. Why don't you watch where you're going?"

"I was watching where I was going. You weren't there a moment ago."

"Why are you walking around in the dark?"

"Why are you?"

He hesitated, staring out into the shadows. "I'm looking for my brother."

"And you think he might be in my neighborhood?" If this frightened her, it didn't show in her eyes. They glowed pale, translucent green in the moonlight.

"No, I–" He stopped abruptly. "Why are you out here wandering around?"

"I'm just taking a walk."

"It's a little late for a walk."

"It's only nine-thirty. I like to walk at night."

"You shouldn't be out here. It's not safe."

She smiled. "You haven't been here long. I promise you, nothing ever happens in New Coventry. Besides, there's a nice park down the street. I go there on clear nights sometimes to see the stars. Why are you looking for your brother in my neighborhood? Where's he gone?"

"I didn't know I was in your neighborhood," he said defensively.

"Okay. Is he missing?"

"He takes off sometimes. He gets drunk for a few days and wanders around. I usually get stuck looking for him and convincing him to come home."

"What should I do if I see him?"

There was no humor or irony in his voice. "Stay away from him."

She didn't question this. "Okay."

"You shouldn't be out here. You should be at home where someone can look after you."

She drew herself up to her full height. "I can look after myself."

"Don't you have parents?"

"Just my dad."

"Is he worried about where you are right now?"

"He isn't home. I was alone. I wanted to get out of the house."

"You shouldn't be walking around alone at night."

"What are you talking about? Why are you being so weird? I've been walking around here for years. No one's ever bothered me before you came along tonight."

"I'm not–" He sighed. "At least let me walk you home."

She tilted her head to study him. "What?"

"You need to go home. I'll walk you there."

Something flashed in her eyes. She hesitated as though she might refuse. "Okay."

He didn't meet her curious gaze. Instead, he turned toward her house and started walking. When she didn't follow, he spun to look at her. "Are you coming?"

"Do you even know where we're going?"

"I, uh–No," he lied.

She fell into step beside him. "You were going the right way."

They walked in silence. She wasn't in a hurry, and he didn't rush her. She paused often to peer up at the stars, but she did not tell him about the constellations. She didn't say anything to him. He caught her studying his profile out of the corner of his eye.

Her voice startled him. "How come you came here?"

"What?" He glanced at her face, searching for any sign of suspicion in her eyes.

"I'm sorry. I meant how come your family decided to move to New Coventry?"

"It's just...what we do."

"What do you mean?"

"We move around a lot." He couldn't keep the bitterness from his voice. He tried. "Start new lives."

"Why?"

"It's just something we've always done."

Aurora looked disappointed. She slowed her step. He turned back to her. She tilted her head back to gaze into the sky, but she did not seem to be studying the stars. Instead, she looked troubled.

When she dropped her head to look at him again, he was directly in front of her. "It must be difficult," she murmured.

She winced, as if she expected him to snap or snarl in response. He studied her. She looked all right, but she seemed unable to decide if she was angry or frightened of him. Her eyes glittered in the moonlight.

He shrugged uncomfortably. "It's all right."

"Come on. You don't have to be so cool all the time."

"All right. It's hard. It sucks. I never get to settle down, never get to make any friends."

Her eyes riveted to his, and his discomfort increased. She was far too close. He forced himself not to move. "Is that why you came to school?"

"What?"

"I heard you were home-schooled before."

"You people seem to know a lot about me."

"Well, it is a small town. People talk. A lot. They find things out." She smiled uncertainly. "Don't worry. I'm not stalking you or anything."

His snort sounded uneasy. "That's a relief. We hardly know each other."

She smiled, but there was something strange in the expression.

"You spend a lot of time at the museum," he blurted and then felt like smacking his palm on his forehead.

"How do you know?"

He lifted a hand to muss the shaggy dark hair at the nape of his neck.

"People talk about stuff. You said so."

She looked suspicious. He wondered if he was the only one who had noticed. He held his breath. "Yeah...I uh...I like it there. I kind of want to study archaeology in school."

"Really?"

"Yeah."

"Like Indiana Jones?"

"Is that the only archaeologist anyone's ever heard of?"

"Well, do you know any others?"

She opened her mouth to retort then shut it again. "Well, no. I just like the history. I'd like to learn about new cultures and see places I've never seen before."

His eyes lifted to the sky. "Like the stars?"

She followed his gaze. "I guess I've never thought about it before. That's not really what I had in mind. You?"

"Well, what little boy hasn't wanted to explore space?"

"You aren't a little boy."

He smiled wryly. "Sometimes I still feel like one. Sometimes I still want what I wanted then."

She was quiet for a moment. "So you want to be an astronaut?"

"Maybe not so much."

"Well, what do you want to be, then?"

He took a step back. "Is this a date, or am I just walking you home?"

Her cheeks colored. "I was just asking. You don't have to be rude."

"I'm not trying to be rude. I was just making a joke. Don't be so sensitive."

She was already walking away. He recognized her street. She stopped in front of her house and looked up at him. Her eyes weren't glittering anymore. They were guarded.

"How can your parents just leave you at home alone? You aren't even a grown up." It came out gruffer than he intended.

She drew herself up to face him. "I'm old enough to look after myself for the night."

"Are you alone a lot? Where are your parents?"

"My dad is with his girlfriend. My mom...well, she's dead."

He shifted uneasily. "Sorry. I don't know what that would be like."

She smiled sadly. "I wish I didn't. I live with my dad and his sister. They spend a lot of time with their girlfriend and boyfriend these days. They think I'm old enough to take care of myself."

"Do you?"

There was an insolent look in her eyes. "Well, I haven't been in any trouble, so I must be."

"I'm not sure that's really an answer."

Aurora turned away from him and started up the walk to her house. He hurried to catch up to her. She didn't say anything to him as she fumbled her keys from her jacket pocket. She paused with her hand midway to the door. "Thank you for walking me home."

He stared at her until she grew uneasy. "You should be more careful, Aurora. Don't go out alone at night anymore. Not until--"

When he didn't say anything more, she tilted her head expectantly. "Until what?"

"Just don't. Not alone. Promise me."

Her brow furrowed. "I promise."

He nodded curtly and spun away from her.

"Sable."

He stopped in his tracks and turned back to face her.

She looked as though she was about to say something. Then something changed in her eyes, and she lowered her head. "Just—thanks. See you."

"Yeah."

* * *

Sable was so exhausted it took him several moments to realize his brother, sitting casually on a stool at the bar in the Boundary Stone pub, wasn't a hallucination. He hadn't been there two hours ago. Now Van leaned against the wooden counter, smiling lazily at the pretty, blonde girl beside him.

Sable could see the haze of alcohol in his brother's dark eyes, and the glint of something else—something black and dangerous.

Sable strode toward him and gripped his arm. "Van."

Van lifted his eyebrows insolently. His mouth twisted in a sneer. "What the hell are you doing here, Sable?"

"I think we both know." Sable barely spared the blonde girl a glance. "Get out of here."

She was very pretty, and she was very drunk. She didn't like his tone. She lifted her chin defiantly. "You don't tell me what do. We're having a nice time."

"You don't want to know what could happen to you if you don't get lost."

Something in his eyes convinced her. She glared at him, but she hopped off the stool and scurried away. Van curled his lip. "What the hell'd you do that for?"

"I'm not going to answer that. Not here. It's time to go home."

Van threw off his grip and turned back to the bar. "Get off me. What the hell, man?"

"Van, what are you doing here?"

"Since when did you become my keeper? Or are you just here to hassle me and take away my prey?"

Sable glanced around, but no one was willing to come close enough to overhear. "That is not what we do, Van. It's not the way. If you slip again, it will be the end of us here."

"So?" Van swallowed the contents of his glass in one shot. "What do I care about this place?"

"Mom and Dad want you to come home."

"I'm old enough to take care of myself. I don't have to stay with my parents."

"You need to come home." He lowered his voice. "They have summoned you. You can't ignore them."

Van snorted, but it was half-hearted. "Oh, no?"

"We need to stick together, Van. Something isn't right. They think it was you."

Van's dark eyes flared in anger. "They think I had something to do with those women?"

"It wouldn't be the first time."

"I didn't have anything to do with it."

"Then you have to answer for it. If it wasn't you, you have nothing to worry about. But you know what will happen if you don't come home. They sent me to find you, and it's your only chance. They won't give you another one." His eyes darted around. A couple girls were eyeing them across the bar. Sable bent toward Van's ear. "You know what will happen if Dad's the one who has to hunt you down this time."

Van scowled. "Fine. But I'm not promising I'll stick around."

"I don't care what you do afterward. It's your problem. Come on."

His brother grumbled, but he slid off the stool, wobbling unsteadily for a moment before he yanked his arm out of Sable's grip. "I can walk on my own."

They didn't speak on the way home. Van had been so close to blowing everything again. He could see it in his eyes. And that day in the alley with Aurora...if Sable hadn't been there--

His knuckles turned white as they tightened on the steering wheel.

Van glanced at him out of the corner of his eye. There was something unnervingly perceptive in his gaze. A frisson of dread raced down Sable's spine.

A single light burned in Adam's study when Sable pulled up into the driveway. Van climbed out of the car, slamming the door as he strode with his chin up toward the house. Sable hurried to follow him, half expecting Van to spin on his heel and make a run for it.

Van didn't even hesitate as he yanked open the door.

Their parents waited for them in the foyer. Adam's cold features belied no emotion. Mariah hurried forward to greet her sons. "Sable, you found him. Van, where have you been?"

Van barely spared her a glance. His eyes darted to his father. "You summoned me."

Adam's inclined his head. "I did, and you did not answer me. I had to send your brother to hunt you down. Well done, Sable."

181

Van glared at Sable over his shoulder. "Well, what do you want?" he growled.

Adam's cold expression did not change. "I want to know if you are responsible for the missing women."

"You're always blaming me."

"You're usually to blame," Sable hissed.

"Shut up, Sable. I didn't have anything to do with those missing women. I've been hearing things around town. We don't even know they haven't actually just run off and disappeared. They were like that. It wasn't my kill. We don't know if it was anyone's kill."

"Perhaps it is time to consider moving on," Mariah said quietly.

"What are you talking about?" Sable burst out. "No! We can't just go. Nothing's even happened. It's got nothing to do with us."

Van glared at his mother. "I didn't do anything."

"Van didn't do anything. There's no reason to go. Nothing happened. We can stay."

There was a wicked glint in Van's eyes. "You got some reason you're so attached to this town, Sable?"

Sable glared at him. "I don't want to move again. We've done this too many times. I just want to settle somewhere, for once. I don't want to keep doing this. For the first time I feel like we can have a normal life here."

"You're fooling yourself." said Van harshly. "We can never have a normal life. We aren't normal. We aren't even human. You think you can live among humans? Pretend to be one of them? Date them?"

"You don't know anything about what I want, Van. I just want to try not having to run for once. And I don't want you screwing it up like you always do."

Van chuckled derisively. "I haven't done anything. I told you. Calm down."

Mariah caught Van around the collar and tugged him to face her. Her amber eyes were very serious. "Show me."

"Wh—what?"

Van struggled to break free of her, but she held tightly to him. "Show me."

182

"Mom, no--"

"Stop acting like a child," Adam snapped. "Show your mother."

Sable took a step away from them. Van looked like he would refuse. Then he relaxed and opened his mouth. Mariah leaned toward him as though she intended to kiss him. The air swirled around them. Van stiffened as his mother drew his breath, his memories, thoughts and his fears.

It was only a moment, but when she pulled away, Van sagged as though the energy had been completely drained from his body. Sable's mouth tightened into a thin line.

Mariah looked at her husband. "He did not do anything. He knows nothing of the missing women. I think he's...genuinely trying."

"Mom!" Van's hiss sounded strained. He glared balefully at the floor.

"All right," said Adam. "We aren't leaving. Not yet, anyway. We've only just started building a life here; it would be a shame to allow it all to go to waste. Sable, Van, go to your rooms. It's late. Sable has school in the morning. And Van...I think it's time you started trying to do something with your life."

"What's the point?" Van asked sulkily. "I'm not human. I shouldn't have to live like one."

"Yes, you do. It's the only way we can survive. I want you to start acting like you have something to live for."

Van scowled. "I don't."

"Then pretend. I am not going to watch you ruin your life and ours over and over again. We've let this go on for too long. If you don't start acting like a responsible adult, I will have to force you."

Van reared back as though his father had slapped him. "You wouldn't."

"Perhaps I wouldn't have in the past. But now I am afraid I might not have any choice. It's been long enough."

"Mom!" Van turned horrified eyes to his mother.

There was genuine sadness in her voice. "I am sorry, Van. It is for your father to decide. He is the head of this house, and he has been lenient. If he decides now it is necessary, we will all submit to him."

All the fight went out of Van. He avoided his family's gazes as he slunk up the stairs to his room.

Sable's eyes followed him. "I don't know why you haven't done it already," he muttered coldly. "He's dangerous. He can't control himself."

Adam's eyes narrowed. "That is not the sort of man I am, Sable. I do not wish to force my children to do anything. But you are not wrong. It has gone on long enough." He jerked his head toward the stairs. "Go on up to your room. You have school in the morning. Thank you for bringing your brother home."

Sable scowled, but his father was in no mood for argument. He spun and marched up the stairs, slamming the door to his room. It wasn't anything special. It was big, but all his rooms had been big. He had the same band posters on the walls and the same stacks of disorderly books. It was different here. He liked it here. He didn't want to leave it all behind, not again. He liked...

Luminous jade green eyes and long, strawberry blonde hair...

New Coventry. He liked New Coventry. It was a nice little town. He even liked school. It wasn't so bad. He wasn't ready to leave. For the first time, he almost felt normal.

Except that I spent the last few days skipping school to hunt down my brother so my mother could suck out his memories to make sure he hasn't killed anyone lately...

He threw himself down on the dark grey covers and flipped off the bedside lamp. He wasn't that normal. He wasn't normal at all.

* * *

"Finally!" Josie exclaimed, leaning back to warm her face in the sun. "Sundress weather!"

Josie wasn't the only student taking advantage of the warm morning in the courtyard before class. Several groups of students, most of them boys leering around at the girls in sundresses, lounged around on the grass. Aurora's eyes swept the courtyard, but Sable didn't seem much like the sunbathing type.

"I love springtime," Josie said happily. "It's an excuse to wear short skirts and tank tops. Boys love short skirts and tank tops."

"Speaking of short skirts," Diana said without opening her eyes. "Has anyone asked you to the formal yet?"

Josie grinned. "Yeah."

"What?" Aurora asked. "Who?"

"Oh, just Charlie Bower."

"Aw. I thought he'd given up asking you out after sophomore year."

Josie rolled her eyes. "I thought he had, too. Apparently, I am just too amazing to get over so easily."

"Did you say yes?" Diana demanded.

"What? To Charlie Bower? No. Of course I didn't."

"Why not? He's not a bad guy. He's always been nice."

"Since last year he's changed a lot," Aurora added. "He's grown about a foot, and he's finally got those braces off. He's not bad looking these days."

"I heard he was going out with Mandy Barnes," Diana said.

Josie shrugged. "I guess they broke up. Anyway, yeah, he's changed, but I can't get the image of that nerdy kid out of my head. Remember when the seniors used to dump him in a trash can? It's hard to take a man seriously when you've seen him completely robbed of his dignity."

"Oh, you're being too picky. Charlie's a nice guy. You should have said yes."

This did not move Josie. "Well, it's a week away. There's still time for Bryan to ask me."

"Has it occurred to you to just ask him?" asked Aurora. "I don't think he has a date yet."

"He doesn't. I've been keeping tabs."

"So, why don't you just do it?"

"Sure, I've thought about it, but..."

"You're too afraid?"

"Well, yeah."

"What about you, Rora?" Diana asked suddenly. "Has anything interesting happened lately?"

Aurora hesitated. Josie narrowed her eyes. "Well? Something has, hasn't it? Tell us! You promised!"

"I did see Sable the other night."

"What? When? How?"

"I was just taking a walk in the neighborhood. He was, too. We ran into each other."

"What happened?" Josie squealed.

"It was so weird. He made it sound like New Coventry is some dangerous place you can't go walking around at night."

"Since when?"

"I know, right? Anyway, he walked me home."

Josie gripped her arm. "He walked you home? That's so—so sweet! Did anything happen?"

"Like what?"

"Well, did he hold your hand or kiss you or anything?"

"Josie," Diana scolded.

Aurora rolled her eyes. "No, Josie. Of course he didn't. He just walked me home and left."

"But what was he doing in your neighborhood?"

"I don't know. He said he was looking for his brother."

"Just out in the streets?"

"I guess."

"Well, that's just weird," Diana remarked. "I wonder what his brother would have been doing out in your neighborhood."

"He probably wasn't. Maybe he just took off, and Sable was looking everywhere. Maybe Van goes out and acts like a jerk all the time."

The girls laughed at this, but Aurora wasn't sure how funny it really was. Van seemed like someone to take quite seriously, especially if he caught you alone in the dark.

"So, I mean, is there something going on between you two?"

"I told you there isn't. I promised I would tell you if there was."

"What about the dance?"

Aurora gave her an exasperated look. "What about it? I mean, I like

186

dancing as well as the next person, but not the school dance kind. It's all uncomfortable clothes and having to turn down boys for dances or—worse—ending up in awkward slow dances with them while they try to cop a feel with sweaty hands."

"What?" Josie looked utterly dismayed. "Aw, come on! The awkward slow dancing is the best."

"When was the last time you had to do it?"

"I'm hoping for a first time."

"I never dance. You don't have to dance, Aurora," Diana told her.

"That's easy for you to say. Zach never wants to, so he never makes you."

Diana shrugged. "That's why we're so perfect for each other."

Aurora smiled reluctantly. "It is a little fun to see all the boys looking nervous and terrified. They always do before a big dance."

"And the girls are eyeing them like cows to a slaughter," Josie added, giggling.

The warning bell rang through the courtyard. "Time to go," Diana said. The girls scooped up their backpacks and headed toward the school with the other grumbling students.

"I wish it was summer already," Josie groaned. "It is so hard to go to class when it's so nice outside."

Aurora's eyes flicked over the crowd of students heading to class. She didn't see Sable's dark hair. Perhaps he'd ditch again today to spend the day searching for his brother.

"Has Jesse asked you to the dance yet?" asked Josie.

"No. Not yet, but I am not getting my hopes up. He will. He always does."

"So? Have you thought about it? Will you say yes this time?"

"No."

"Is there someone you do want to ask you?" Josie could be uncannily perceptive sometimes.

Aurora didn't blush or stammer. She shrugged. She was proud of her composure. "Maybe."

"What?" Josie's eyes lit up. "Have you been harboring some crush you haven't told us about yet?"

"No." Her voice sounded perfectly even.

"Yeah, right." Josie rolled her eyes. "What high school girl isn't harboring some crush? Besides, we know you well enough to know when you're distracted. Di and I are in perfect agreement that it must be a boy."

"I'm not ready to talk about it."

Josie's eyes widened. "Oh, my god! Is it Alex Cahill?"

"What? No."

"Mark Shaw?"

"No. He's cute, but no. Come on. I told you I don't want to talk about it."

"Is it Sable?"

"I am not going to talk about it, Jos. Just let it go."

"It is, isn't it! Of course it is. We know you too well for you to lie about it. It is Sable!"

Diana came to her rescue. "You heard her, Jos. Let it go. If she doesn't want to talk about it, she doesn't have to."

Aurora smiled at her. "Thanks, Di."

Josie looked hurt. "Fine. But I don't understand why you won't tell us. We're your best friends!"

"Josie," Diana warned.

"You never tell us anything."

"I'm sorry, Josie. I'm just not ready to talk about it. When I am, I'll tell you everything."

"All right, all right. But I won't forget this, Aurora. I will remember forever. I have a very good memory. I will be waiting to hear all about it over ice cream and old 80's horror flicks."

Aurora laughed. "All right."

They rounded the corner and Aurora groaned as she spotted Jesse, leaning against her locker and looking very cool in a white tee shirt that showed off his thick arms and broad shoulders. When he lifted his head and caught sight of her, he started forward. "Aurora."

"It's okay, guys," she whispered to her friends. "I'll see you later."

Josie didn't seem to want to go, but Diana caught her arm, dragging her through the throng of students digging out their books for first period.

"Hi, Jesse. What's up?"

He was so gorgeous when he smiled, for the briefest moment, she wondered why she didn't feel anything toward him. He ruffled the long, blonde hair at the nape of his neck. "The Spring Formal is coming up."

"Yes. I know."

"You know I want to ask you."

"Yes. I know."

"Will you go with me?"

She held his beautiful blue eyes for a moment. "No, Jesse. I'm sorry."

"Why not? Why do you really keep turning me down, Aurora? Do you like someone else or something?"

Her eyes slid away. "No."

Something in her tone betrayed her. His eyes narrowed. "Who is it?"

"I didn't say there was anyone else."

"Then go with me."

"Jesse, no. I can't--"

"Why not?" There was an edge to his voice.

"Because I don't..." She cut off.

Sable rounded the corner on his way to class. His midnight eyes, so cold and so different from Jesse's warm, hopeful ones, met hers. He stopped abruptly in the hall and spun toward them. Her breath caught. She darted a glance at Jesse.

Jesse whirled around. His eyes narrowed as he caught sight of Sable striding toward them. Sable did not meet his gaze. His eyes held Aurora's as he drew up beside her. "Hi, Aurora."

She was relieved her voice didn't waver. The dozens of butterflies in her belly tried to fight their way out through her throat. "Hi, Sable."

"You're going to be late for class." With that, he turned and walked casually back the way he'd come.

When Aurora looked back at Jesse, he scowled. "I see."

Her cheeks heated. "What?"

"Just forget it." He stepped past her and stormed down the hall without looking back at her.

She stomped her foot. "Stupid dance."

Things just got worse from there. Sierra and the Pops suddenly rounded the corner around which Jesse had just disappeared. They hadn't failed to see him. Aurora groaned under her breath. They hadn't bothered her in so long, she'd almost forgotten the feeling of dread that surged through her at the very sight of them, especially when they caught her alone in an empty hallway.

Sierra's mouth turned up in a nasty smile as she strode directly toward Aurora. Her friends formed a wall behind her, glaring at Aurora as though she'd already insulted them. "What's the matter, Aurora?" Sierra's voice was a sneering purr. "Has Jesse finally realized what kind of girl you are?"

Aurora's teeth clenched. "And what sort of girl, exactly, do you think I am?"

The Pops were surprised by Aurora's defiance, but they would only enjoy crushing her all the more if she fought back a little beforehand.

"We think you're nothing," Cami said, curling her lip as though Aurora was something foul she'd found on the sole of her shoe.

Aurora lifted her eyebrows. "Is that really true? Or are you just trying to put me down because you can't stand it that I can have something you don't?"

The Pops stared at her in stunned silence. Then Cami's eyes narrowed in a murderous glare. "You have nothing we want that we couldn't get."

"Really? Then how come you don't have Jesse? I know you like him. Everyone knows."

This was something new. Sierra laughed derisively. "You think you're something special all of a sudden?"

"No. I think I'm the same as I've always been. And that's what you hate so much about me. You can't do anything to me. You can't even hurt my feelings because I know what all this is really about."

Sierra's mouth tightened into an angry line. "And what is that?"

"You're jealous. You're jealous of me. I don't have to be mean and nasty and put people down for a boy you like to like me instead if you. Maybe if you tried to be a decent person for once, you might get what you want. You wouldn't have to try to take it from someone who actually deserves it."

The tardy bell clanged through the hall. Aurora didn't wait for Sierra's response. She pushed past them toward her classroom. She would probably regret what she'd said to them. They were capable of reaching heights of such meanness she couldn't even comprehend them. It still felt good to finally stand up to them.

Aurora nearly collided with Sable, who lounged against the wall right around the corner. He straightened when he saw her and stared hard into her eyes. She blinked at him in surprise. He didn't speak or smile.

Had he heard everything?

She didn't have a chance to ask him. He spun around and walked away without a second glance back at her. She rolled her eyes. "What happened to 'hi, Aurora'?"

It was turning out to be another really bad day.

Chapter Nine

Aurora's stomach fluttered as she drew closer to the Jayne house. It was silly to read too much into what had happened with Sable that morning. Saying hello and then staring at her as though she had proclaimed a burning desire to run off with a troupe of drunken circus performers was hardly a profession of love or even a mild interest in being friends. He was so hot and cold, it was impossible to know what to expect from him from one moment to the next.

What was he was thinking when he was looking at her with such intense scrutiny? What was he looking for? Why had he rescued her from the embarrassing scene with Jesse? And why he had walked her home the other night? And then there was the alley with Van...

There she went, reading too much into things again.

Sable had spent most of his life moving around and home schooling. He probably didn't know how to behave appropriately with people his own age. Even if he did want to be friends or...something more, she doubted he would even know how to go about it. Maybe he didn't think there was any point, if he was just going to leave again so soon.

There was no sense getting worked up over someone who might be gone in the blink of an eye. He probably wouldn't even say goodbye.

She still wanted to see him. She always wanted to see him.

He didn't answer the door when she knocked lightly. She knew she didn't need to knock. She had an appointment, and it was a place of business. She'd been hoping...well, she'd been hoping he would be there to greet her like last time, even if the encounter had turned very strange very quickly. She'd been hoping he might...well, that he might actually want to see her, too.

That was stupid. He probably didn't even know she was coming. If he did, he was obviously avoiding her.

Aurora hurried to Dr. Jayne's office. She tapped lightly on the doorframe, though the door stood open and the doctor was already waiting for her in her chair, poised to take notes. "Dr. Jayne?"

Dr. Jayne rose to greet her with a sweet smile. Warmth spread through Aurora. The woman's smiles were like a soothing balm. She smiled back without even realizing it. "Good afternoon, Aurora. I am happy to see you again."

"You, too."

"Please, have a seat." She gestured toward the couch and waited for Aurora to sit before resuming her own seat. "How are you this afternoon?"

"I'm...good. I think."

"You think?"

"It's been a weird day."

"I see. Would you like to talk about it?"

Aurora leaned back against the couch cushions. "I've been feeling different since I saw you last."

"Different how?"

"Just...better. More confident, I guess. I actually stood up to the popular girls today."

"You stood up to them? Why would you need to?"

"They're always horrible to me. They pick on me. They have since we were little."

"Why is that?"

"I always thought...well, it doesn't matter. It's because they're jealous, really. That's all. A boy they like likes me and always has."

"Is that so?"

She could feel the surge of assurance she had felt earlier that day coming back to her. She nodded. "And for the first time, I actually had the nerve to tell them so. Before I would never...well, I would have just tried to escape without breaking down into tears and curse myself about it later."

"Not today, though."

"No, not today. Today, I actually understood them. I know it won't help matters that I said the things I did, but it felt good to say them. And I feel like maybe next time I will be able to stand up to them again. Now that I have."

"That is wonderful progress, Aurora. You should never feel less than anyone. You have the right to stand up for yourself, especially against girls who try to make you feel bad about yourself to make up for their own failings."

"I know that now."

"So what else have you noticed since we last met?"

"I guess I just feel more like myself."

"Have you continued to experience the feeling you mentioned last time?"

"It's not totally gone. It's still there sometimes, the emptiness. Sometimes it hits me so hard, I feel like I'm going to suffocate." She smiled wryly. "Like you said, therapy isn't a miracle or anything. It's only been a week. But I haven't felt so—well, free—in a long time. Everything just seems a lot easier to take and to do. Like speaking my mind. I used to be so afraid and now it's like I wonder how I could ever have been scared."

"It sounds as though you have experienced some positive results. You are taking control of your thoughts and feelings."

"So far. It might just be beginner's luck. Like a placebo. I know it's all inside me, inside my head."

"That is what therapy is about, Aurora. Learning to take control of what's inside you to make positive and healthy choices about how to express it. Sometimes just letting out your feelings and your fears helps." She glanced down at her notebook. Aurora sensed it was her way of changing the subject. "Why don't we start today by talking about your mother?"

Aurora hesitated. "Already?"

Dr. Jayne's laugh sounded like the tinkle of bells. "Well, that's where people normally start."

"I suppose there are lots of people with mommy issues."

"It does seem to be the most prominent affliction amongst patients. Funny how that works, isn't it?"

"My mom was wonderful. If she hadn't died…I probably wouldn't have issues at all. At least not any more than any other teenaged girl."

"But she did die."

"Yes. And I guess I'm as messed up as everyone else."

Dr. Jayne smiled gently. "I think you will be fine, Aurora. You are stronger than you allow yourself to be. You just need someone to guide you."

She was grateful for this. "My mom…I don't even know where to start."

* * *

"What was she like?"

His mother's voice drifted up to him from under the door. Sable leaned against the wall, his heart hammering. He shouldn't be listening in. He half rose, but then her voice, soft and wistful, pierced through his good intentions.

"She was amazing. She was sweet and kind to everyone. Everyone liked her. She taught me how to be a good person. She always stood up for people who needed it. She taught me about the stars. She always smelled like flowers."

"How did she make you feel?"

"Safe and loved. Always. How a mother should, I guess. I always wanted to see her. I couldn't wait for her to get home from the shop every night or tell her about what had happened at school, even if it was that I'd been picked on again. She always made it better. If she'd been around, maybe I wouldn't have put up with them for so long. Now I come home and sometimes my aunt comes in, and she smells just like flowers, and for a moment I think it's her and I start to rush downstairs to tell her about what happened to me at school..."

She faltered. Sable could hear nothing. There were no sobs. Aurora didn't sniffle or weep. When she spoke again, her voice was almost inaudible.

"I miss her. Everyday. All the time. I just wish she were still here. I'm sorry. That wasn't what you asked."

"This is a safe place, Aurora. You may say whatever you wish here."

Sable scowled. It wasn't a safe place. Not for Aurora. She didn't know what his mother would take from her. She didn't know that part of her was already gone. Even if she didn't miss it, even if she hadn't wanted it, it was still gone, and she wasn't the same anymore. She would never be the same.

He waited for her to speak again. It wasn't right, listening in like this to her most private thoughts. She probably wouldn't want him to hear all of those things. He should get up and walk away.

He didn't move. He tried not to listen to her words when she continued. He closed his eyes and listened to the gentle murmur of her voice. For a moment, he could almost pretend she was speaking to him. He could pretend she was saying something else, something meant for him, not something she'd be horrified to discover he'd overheard.

"Last time I saw her...she was just going out for a walk. She always did that. Every night. She said it was to look at the stars. She asked if I wanted to go with her...I said I was reading a good book. I said no. If I had gone, we would have been together when she died. A drunk driver hit her while she was walking. But if I had been with her...maybe I could have warned her or pushed her out of the way or...or maybe I would have died, too. Or I would have been hurt very badly. Maybe I wouldn't have, and maybe I would have been with her in the end. Instead...she just died there all alone, and they didn't find her until the next day. The driver didn't even know he'd hit her."

After a long moment of silence, Mariah asked, *"Do you feel guilty you did not go with her?"*

"Guilty? No. Not guilty so much. Just regretful that she had to die alone like that. I didn't have one of those last moments where I was rude or mean to her or anything. She told me she loved me. She always said that. She never forgot. And I always told her back because I did. I loved her so much. But that doesn't mean I don't still wish I'd had more time or a chance to say goodbye. I just want...more time with her. I would give anything for that. But I will never have it."

Sable sighed deeply. So that was why he'd found her wandering the streets. Was she continuing her mother's tradition, or did she have some unhealthy fascination with the place her mother had died? Perhaps she just wanted to do something to remember her mother, something they had once done together.

He surged to his feet. He knew what came next. He didn't need to hang around. His mother would take away the parts of Aurora that made her hurt. She would take away the parts that made her her. He couldn't stand to look at her eyes as she came out, to see the dreamy look that meant she wasn't the same anymore.

Van lounged on the stairs above him. He smirked at Sable. "What have you been doing, little brother? Spying?"

Sable ignored him and tried to pass him on the stairs. "Just leave me alone."

Van stepped into his path. "Do you listen in on all Mom's patients or just this particular one?"

Sable glared.

196

"Does that human girl mean something to you, Sable? She is...very pretty." Van's voice was a feral purr. "She smells like flowers."

"Stay away from her," Sable snarled.

"Don't worry, little brother. She's not my type."

"She was your type that day in the alley."

Van laughed. "Are you still angry about that? I was just having a little fun. So, is she the reason you don't want to leave this shit hole town?"

Sable pushed past him, colliding roughly with his shoulder.

Van caught his arm in a grip that could have bruised. "She is, isn't she?"

"No."

"Don't lie to me. I've been in love before. I know what it looks like. And I know how it ends." Van's eyes burned into Sable's. "You think I would be who I am if Alexia hadn't left?"

"What you are is a monster, Van."

"You think I would be if not for her?"

"Yes. You made the decision to be what you are. You could have been anything you want."

"Don't fool yourself. You think you would be any better? You think if she breaks your heart you will still be the pure, righteous monster you are now? You wouldn't. And she will break you heart. She's human."

"You don't know anything about it."

"Don't I?"

"Alexia wasn't human."

"No. She was one of us. But she was a woman. And she did what women do."

"Is that why you kill them?"

"I feed to survive, Sable. I'm not the kind of monster you think I am."

"I feed to survive, and I don't kill!"

"But you haven't always been such a saint, have you? You have blood on your hands, too, little brother, so don't play perfect with me. If you aren't careful, it will be her blood. Just wait and see." With that, Van tossed his arm away and stomped up the stairs, slamming the door to his bedroom. Sable could feel it reverberate through the house.

He heard Aurora's soft murmur move closer, and then she stepped out into the hall. He ducked behind the bannister, but she didn't even turn her eyes up to him. She wore a small, contented smile.

Mariah was glowing as she led Aurora to the front door. "You have made a lot of progress today, Aurora. I look forward to seeing you next week."

Sable leaned around the corner. Aurora's eyes glinted in the soft chandelier light. They were hazy and unfocused. "Thank you, Dr. Jayne. I'll see you next week."

"Good evening, Aurora." She closed the door behind the young woman and was startled to find Sable standing in the foyer behind her. "Sable. What are you doing down here?"

"Nothing." His eyes strayed toward the door through which Aurora had just disappeared. "What are you taking from her?"

"Her fear."

"Her fear?"

"Yes. It is the only thing holding her back." Mariah's eyes slid away thoughtfully. "There is something about that human that interests me."

He frowned. "Why?"

"There is something in her spirit. She is special." Her gazed focused on him. "You think so, too, don't you? You see it."

Sable shifted uncomfortably. "I don't know what you mean."

"Yes, you do. It's why you're always hanging around whenever she comes over. Do you have some interest in her?"

"I told you I don't."

"Remember what I said, Sable. You know what could happen if you get carried away."

"I know, Mom."

"Remember what happened the last time."

"I know, Mom!"

"Stay away from her, Sable."

"I haven't gone near her. She's just a human. She's just someone I know. It's nothing." He spun towards the stairs and raced up to his room, slamming the door behind him. He threw himself down on the bed, pressing the heels of his hands to his eyes.

"She's nothing."

* * *

The night of the school dance had finally arrived. Aurora sat on her bed, watching Josie and Diana primp for the event. Ruby and her father were downstairs with Blaine and Troy, drinking beer and waiting for the girls to descend in their formal finery; Ruby was, anyway. The men were just drinking beer.

"Ruby's boyfriend is so hot," Josie remarked, applying a thick black line of kohl to her eyes.

Diana looked at her incredulously. "Hot? He's so old!"

"He's not old! He's in his thirties. He's just...distinguished. Like Brad Pitt or something."

"He doesn't look like Brad Pitt."

"Well, they're both old and hot."

Aurora rolled her eyes. "Josie, do you ever think about anything but boys?"

"Yes, but not on a night like this. This night is all about thinking about boys." She swiveled her gaze from her own face to Diana's. "Diana, why doesn't Zach pick you up like a normal boyfriend?"

Diana shrugged. "You know how he is. We're just meeting there. And I wanted to get ready with my friends." She pushed a rhinestone headband through her blonde chignon and rose to spin before them. She looked pretty and prim in a knee-length, cream-colored satin dress.

Josie was wearing a short, crimson red dress, and she'd twisted her choppy red and black hair at the nape of her neck. She looked pretty, but Aurora secretly thought she would look better without all the black makeup on her eyes. Nevertheless, she was glowed with excitement. She jumped up and spun on Aurora, who wore a light, jade green crepe dress she and Ruby had picked out at the local boutique at the very last minute. They'd been lucky to find anything at all, let alone such a pretty dress that matched her eyes so perfectly.

"Oh, Aurora, let me do your hair!" Josie squealed.

Aurora held up her hands, suddenly facing her two best friends, who looked uncannily like two vultures. She reared back. "Oh, I don't know. I was just going to leave it down—"

Josie rolled her eyes at Aurora's complete lack of understanding. "Oh, come on. It's a dance! You have to be fancy."

Aurora sighed. Josie wouldn't give up, and if Diana took her side, they would be unstoppable. "All right, but nothing crazy. You know I don't like crazy."

Josie scoffed. "It won't be crazy. That's my thing, not yours. I know that."

Aurora sighed, but she sat at the vanity mirror while Josie braided her long, strawberry blonde hair into a plait and twisted it around at the nape of her neck. A few stray wisps of hair framed her face. When Josie stepped back, Aurora admired the affect. It looked pretty. The dress complemented her green eyes. She smiled slowly at herself.

"Thanks, Jos."

"Don't sound so surprised. I can do a few things, you know. You look really pretty."

"So you do, Josie." She rose and hugged her friend. "And you, too, Diana."

"Well?" Diana asked. "Are we ready?"

"There's nothing like going to a dance with your two best friends," Josie said wryly. "And no boys."

They laughed together. "Well, I'm sure there will be plenty of boys there," said Aurora. "You should actually ask one of them to dance."

"Seal the deal for once," Diana added.

Josie ignored them and led the way downstairs. Ruby heard them coming and flew out of the living room with a beer bottle in her hand. "Here they come!" She whipped a camera out of her pocket.

"Oh, no," Aurora sighed. "Pictures? Really?"

"Of course! Come on. I'm a mom! I need this. Chris never let me take pictures, and I never even got to see his date to the Spring Formal."

"That's because she was a total tramp," Josie muttered. Aurora elbowed her.

Ruby laughed. "That sounds like my son. Come on. Please? Just one. All three of you together."

The men leaned around the doorway as the girls posed for the picture. "You ladies look nice," Blaine told them. Ruby smiled over her shoulder at him.

"Thanks, Blaine."

"Remember to behave yourselves tonight," Mike said, but the stern tone was belied by the small smile on his face as he tilted his beer to his lips.

"Please, Mr. Geller," Josie said, her hands on her hips. "When does Aurora ever not behave herself?"

Troy smiled from behind his best friend. "I don't remember the girls in my school looking so pretty. I guess when you get old you forget things like that. The boys at your school are lucky."

Mike wagged a finger at them. "Make sure they aren't too lucky."

Aurora rolled her eyes. "Come on, Dad. You know me." She ignored Ruby's sly wink.

"Will you be out late?"

"I don't know. Probably just midnight or one."

"Do you need some money?" He reached behind him to pull out his wallet and handed her a twenty-dollar bill.

"Thanks, Dad." She hurried forward to kiss him on the cheek. "See you later."

"We won't wait up," Ruby said gaily.

"Be home at a reasonable hour, anyway," Mike added.

"We will. Good night!"

Josie bounced in the driver's seat of her car. "This is going to be so great. I love school dances!"

"It will be fun," Aurora said with forced cheerfulness.

"Oh, Aurora, you're going to have the time of your life. You'll be the belle of the ball. You just have to let yourself have fun for once," Diana said, smiling.

The other girls looked at her archly. "You're one to talk," Josie remarked.

Diana did not deign to respond.

"Do you think Jesse will still be there, even though you turned him down?" Josie asked Aurora.

"Yes. He knows I'm going. He'll be there."

"Will you dance with him?"

"I don't know."

"Really? You might?"

Aurora lifted a shoulder. "Well, he's not so bad, I guess. He's actually kind of sweet."

"And hot."

"Yes, he's very hot. It's just that...I don't know. Maybe it's just too easy. I know how he feels about me."

"Everyone knows how he feels about you. We've known since we were little kids," Diana said dryly.

"Exactly. There's no mystery. We've known him forever. We pretty much know everything about him. Maybe I just want someone who's a little harder to get."

"I get it," said Josie. "A little mystery, some mind games and some agonizing make things a lot more interesting."

"Is that why you always avoid actually going out with guys?" Aurora asked, amused. "You prefer the chase to actually being with them?"

Josie snorted. "Well, yeah. Maybe. Mostly. I wouldn't really know, would I? I only ever kissed Joey Jenkins in the eighth grade."

"Anyway, maybe if he didn't chase me so persistently and single-mindedly, I might actually feel a little differently about Jesse."

"I think you should give him a chance, Aurora. It's at least worth finding out what it would be like. It might be awesome."

"Maybe. I suppose." She didn't mean it. She didn't say anything more as Josie flew toward the school, gossiping with Diana about their classmates, most of whom had spontaneously coupled for the dance.

Aurora didn't really care about any of that. She stared out the window, her mind drifting as she watched the streets fly by. She wondered if Sable would show up at the dance. He didn't seem like the dance type of guy, but she realized she didn't really know anything more about him than what he'd told her the night he'd walked her home.

She'd taken special care to look nice that evening. She had a sinking feeling it was all for nothing. Of course Sable wouldn't show up at the school dance. She'd heard a few girls had even asked him to go with them, but he'd coldly shut them down. She'd probably end up spending the night running away from Jesse. Even if he was angry with her, he wasn't one to be kept down long.

Of course it was flattering to have one of the hottest guys in school relentlessly chasing her, but after a while it was just exhausting. She wished she felt something for him. It would be so much easier than these uncertain feelings for Sable. It would be nice to be with someone who loved her completely, not made her feel strange and confused all the time.

But she didn't want Jesse. She didn't want unconditional devotion, not like that. She wanted excitement and mystery and someone who made her heart race just by looking at her. Jesse didn't make her feel any of those things.

Sable did.

Josie swerved into a parking spot. Aurora snapped out of her maudlin mood. Their classmates were walking toward the school, dressed in suits and dresses, holding hands or looking awkward when they accidentally brushed arms. The music from the auditorium was so loud, the school vibrated.

"This is going to be so great!" Josie squealed, linking her arms through her friends'.

The auditorium was decorated with huge, brightly colored paper flowers. The Pops, of course, were part of the dance committee, but even Aurora could admit the place looked amazing, like a life-sized spring garden. They reminded her of the talking flowers in Alice in Wonderland. These flowers didn't talk, but the soft pink lighting added to the surreal mood. It made everyone look soft and hazy around the edges.

Zach materialized around a purple paper begonia that looked as though it could open its mouth and swallow his head. He smiled as Diana stepped forward to meet him and presented her with a small, sweet-smelling rose corsage, which looked dwarfed amongst the gigantic paper flowers. "Oh, Zach, I love it!" Diana told him, but she did not lean forward to kiss him or even squeeze his hand. Instead, she held out her arm, and he slipped it on her wrist.

He smiled at Josie and Aurora, but he didn't hold their gazes long. Josie glanced at Aurora with arched eyebrows. Aurora knew exactly what she was thinking. Zach wasn't the flower-giving type. Perhaps this was a special night for them, and Diana hadn't said anything. If something special did happen between them, Diana would never tell.

Aurora's eyes swept the gym as they moved further into the crowd, most of whom were gathering in small groups or sitting around at tables. A few people had already begun dancing. Sable wasn't there, or at least she couldn't see him. He had a way of skulking around in the shadows. If he was there, she wouldn't see him until he wanted her to.

Josie maneuvered Aurora to a table near the dance floor where Shane and Cera sat with a couple people Aurora thought she recognized from some classes but had never really talked to. She realized immediately the tall, skinny dark-haired boy was Cera's date. He leaned in close to talk to her. Shane clenched his teeth. Aurora was surprised. She'd expected them to arrive together, but it became clear the girl sitting beside Shane, looking bored, was with him.

The music was good. Jonny Granger, a very popular senior to whom Aurora had never even spoken was disk jockeying. He bounced to the music behind a big speaker box on the makeshift stage. He grinned at the girls gathered around him. Aurora could see him shaking his head at them, as though they were trying to convince him to dance.

Aurora liked watching her classmates like this. Some of them looked forlorn and lonely. Others shot mooneyes toward their crushes but were too afraid to ask them to dance. She understood their fear. She doubted she could ever approach Sable and ask him for a dance. Of course, he was much scarier than Luke Lester or Emma Spencer, both of whom were oblivious to the longing gazes their classmates gave them.

She caught sight of Jesse. Her stomach sank. He cleaned up very well. His blonde, shoulder-length hair was down, but he'd shaved, and he looked very good in a black suit. She ducked her head, but then she realized it was ridiculous. He could see her if he turned his head in her direction, and she doubted anyone would mistake her strawberry blonde hair, even in the soft light.

His blue eyes met hers across the floor. His jaw tightened, and he turned away. Aurora was relieved. She felt bad for hurting him, but it was better than having to fend him off so early in the night, probably ruining her mood completely. It wasn't her fault he was angry with her; she had never given him false hope. She had been perfectly clear about her feelings, and he'd chosen to pursue her anyway. She wasn't responsible for his hurt feelings.

She glanced away from him and put him out of her mind.

She saw Cami and Callie sitting with a couple senior football players, who looked uncomfortable in their suits. She knew the boys, but she avoided them. They were both good-looking and popular and horrible. They were bigger bullies than Sierra, and they were probably perfect for the twins. Aurora just hoped no one would get hurt—especially her.

The twins, despite the gleefully nasty expressions on their faces as they pointed around at their classmates, looked beautiful. Their hair, makeup and nails were professionally done, and their dresses had probably cost a fortune. Being pretty didn't make them any nicer.

Claire Ames and Brooke Hadley sat at the same table with their dates, but they weren't talking to the twins. Claire giggled at her date, a boy from their class who just looked happy to be there with her. Brooke and her long-time boyfriend, Nick Dempsey, the football captain, murmured softly to each other, looking as sweet and in love as ever.

Aurora didn't understand why Brooke, who had never done anything nasty to anyone, hung around them. She'd been best friends with Sierra since they had been in diapers, but Aurora would have expected the pretty, athletic girl to dump Sierra when her true colors had shown. She never had, though. Aurora didn't dislike her, but she couldn't like her, either. She never even tried to stand up to Sierra.

Sierra. Where was Sierra? She was almost always with the other Pops. She was their evil queen bee. Aurora looked around, but she couldn't see the beautiful, black-haired witch anywhere in the gym. Surely she was coming. She'd spent the better part of the last two months putting together the dance. There was no way she would give up the chance to see all her hard work in action.

Unfortunately.

Josie nudged her. "Oh, there's Bryan."

Aurora craned her neck to see the tall, sandy-haired boy standing on the edge of the crowd. "Is he here with anyone?"

205

Josie squealed. "No. He's alone." But a pretty blonde girl in a pale yellow, floor length dress strode up to Bryan, and he smiled down at her. Josie deflated. "Maybe not."

"Who is that? Is that Amanda Price? He's not going out with her. Just because he's talking to her doesn't mean they came together."

This didn't cheer Josie up. Her shoulders slumped.

"Come on. It's your own fault. You could have asked him. You could be with him right now."

Josie crossed her arms sulkily. "You aren't as nice as you used to be."

"Oh, I'm nice enough to tell you the truth. You can't very well be upset if Bryan is with another girl when we both know he would have said yes if you had just asked him yourself."

Josie scowled at her, but then Amanda Price waved at Bryan and hurried away to take the arm of a boy in Aurora's Physics class. Josie instantly perked up. "Well, I...well, maybe you're right, Aurora. It would be my own fault if he came with Amanda, but he didn't."

Indeed, it seemed as though Bryan had come alone. He joined a group of his friends, who gathered near the dance floor, checking out the girls. Every now and again, one of them would dart out of the safety of the group and ask one of the girls to dance.

This lifted Josie's spirits. Her face lit up again, and Aurora tried not to let her friend see her eye roll. Josie didn't move from her seat to approach him, though. She watched him avidly from across the room as though attempting to psychically lure him over. It wasn't working. Bryan didn't even glance their way.

She didn't understand Josie's fear. Bryan liked her; it was obvious, and Josie knew it. If Aurora had a chance to be with Sable, she would take it. She sighed and glanced around the room. Not that she would ever get the chance, and maybe Josie did have a point—even the new Aurora would want a sure thing before she threw herself on the mercy of some incomprehensible boy.

And on that, a jolt shot through her entire boy. Sable wore a suit like he was born into it. She wasn't sure if it was her love goggles or that he really did look as comfortable as he did in jeans, Converse sneakers and a black hoodie. The other boys in the auditorium certainly weren't so graceful, so mysteriously confident. He stood near the refreshment table, glancing around at the room from under his long, dark eyelashes.

206

Her breath caught. She turned her eyes from him before he caught her staring.

Josie had spotted him, too. She jerked her chin in his direction. "I did not expect to see Sable here. He doesn't seem like the type, huh?"

"I was thinking the same thing," Aurora admitted. "Maybe he's never been to a school dance before. Maybe he just wanted to see what it's like."

Josie looked skeptical. "I don't know any guys who admit to liking school dances. From what I understand, they do it for the girls. So, the question is— which girl?"

She shrugged as though the question meant absolutely nothing to her.

"He does look good in a suit, though," said Josie. "Really good."

So it wasn't just the love goggles. That was encouraging.

They watched him for a moment. Aurora, despite what Josie said, could not figure out what he could possibly be doing there. He didn't speak to anyone unless they spoke to him first, and then his reticence sent them shuffling away immediately in disappointment. Mostly, they were girls. Aurora felt a small thrill of pleasure seeing him turn them away. At least she wasn't the only one he treated like she had some sort of communicable disease.

Josie grinned slyly at Aurora. "Why don't we get some punch?"

Aurora rolled her eyes. "I know what you are getting at, Jos. I doubt we'll have any better luck than anyone else."

"Oh, I just want to see what will happen."

She couldn't find a good reason to refuse. Sable was, after all, standing in the highest traffic area in the room. If he didn't want anyone to approach him, he should go stand in a dark corner. "All right. I am feeling a little thirsty."

Josie linked her arm through Aurora's to drag her toward the refreshment table. Sable appeared not to notice them, but he shoulders suddenly tensed. He glared down at the floor.

Then Andy Kennewick, a boy from their class, appeared out of nowhere, stopping in front of Josie. "Hey, Josie. Want to dance?"

Josie's eyes flicked involuntarily to Bryan, but he didn't notice her plight. She took Andy's offered hand. He was cute, but there was something a little mean and dangerous about him. Aurora would never, ever be alone with him, but he probably wouldn't do anything untoward as long as Josie didn't leave with him or let him talk her into finding a quiet corner somewhere.

Josie looked at Aurora apologetically. Aurora waved, watching Andy lead her away. She turned back to the punch table. She could see Sable's long, dark figure looming close by out of the corner of her eye. Her heart thumped. She thought about turning around and retreating to her table, but she would look foolish. She'd obviously been on her way to the refreshments.

As she neared him, she turned her head to acknowledge him, but he was looking the other way. He didn't seem to have noticed her at all. Well, two could play at that game. If he wanted to pretend he didn't see her, that he hadn't confessed that he sometimes felt like a little boy and all the other strange things he'd ever said to her, she could be just as cool.

She lifted her chin and strode forward, ignoring him completely.

"Aurora."

It wasn't the voice she wanted to hear. She turned to Jesse with a sigh. He stood so close she reared back. He caught her arm to hold her in place. His eyes glittered intensely down at her. "Jesse—"

"I'm sorry I got angry with you, Aurora."

She tensed and tugged her arm out of his grasp. He let her go, but he didn't step away.

"I just...I can't stand not being with you."

"I'm sorry, Jesse."

His body was close. She tried to step back, but he caught her wrist again. "You know how I feel about you, Aurora."

"Yes. I know. You have made it clear."

"Then just dance with me, okay? One dance."

She looked up into his eyes. They were so earnest, so open. She relented. "All right. Just one dance, Jesse. Don't make it more than it is."

He ignored this, smiling as he slid his hand from her wrist to wrap around her fingers. Josie grinned at her over the shoulder of her dance partner as she and Jesse neared them. Aurora tried to smile back.

A slow song was playing. Jesse pulled Aurora close against his body. He didn't speak. He stared down at her with such naked devotion she blushed.

208

His large hands cradled her into his chest, and his touch was so gentle, he might have been afraid she might break in his arms. Perhaps he was simply afraid she would bolt.

She wrapped her arms around his neck. She had expected the slow dancing to be awkward, but somehow, with Jesse, it wasn't. She didn't think Josie, who kept repositioning her partner's hands to more appropriate locations, felt the same way. For several long moments, Aurora allowed Jesse to sway her silently to the music.

Then he dipped his head, and his voice was a low purr against her ear. "Aurora."

"Hm?"

"You feel so good in my arms. It feels right."

For a moment, it was as though the rest of the world didn't exist. He brushed his fingers over the ends of her hair. She shivered voluntarily. He felt her reaction and leaned back to look at her with a smile.

"This is right, Aurora. This is how it should be."

The contentment she'd felt moments before slid away as she stiffened in his embrace. "No, Jesse. It isn't."

"I'm not giving up on you. I will find a way to convince you. We belong together, Aurora."

"No, we don't." She took a step back, but his hands clenched around her waist, reminding her that his fingers could be as strong as they had been gentle moments ago. Her heart raced.

"Don't do this. Don't keep running. I would be everything you want. I would give you everything."

"Jesse--" He wasn't hurting her—Jesse would never, ever hurt her; she knew that—but his hands clenched around her waist, trapping her against him. She pressed her palms to his chest to shove him away. "Let me go."

And then there were different hands, cold, unfamiliar hands on her shoulders. She stopped struggling abruptly, turning her head to look up at Sable in utter shock. His expression was mild, but his midnight eyes glittered with an intensity that startled her. She couldn't read the emotion in them, but her pulse quickened in alarm.

"Do you need help, Aurora?" His voice was so toneless it sent a chill down

Aurora's spine.

Jesse did not take Sable seriously. He did not notice that something about him was very frightening, despite the casual tone of his voice. Aurora could feel the tension of his body through his fingers, which practically vibrated against her bare skin, as though he might clench them around her and drag her away from Jesse.

"She doesn't need help," Jesse growled. "She's fine. It has nothing to do with you, Jayne. We're having a conversation."

"I wasn't asking you. I was asking her."

Aurora turned to meet Jesse's eyes. He scowled, but there was such hope in his eyes, she knew what she would say next would seal their fate. "Let me go, Jesse."

Anger flared in his eyes. His gaze darted to Sable's hands, which tightened on Aurora's shoulders. She knew Sable wouldn't let go. He would hold onto her until Jesse went away and never came back. "Aurora..."

"Please."

For a moment, he did not release her, but then his hands loosened. He took a step away. "Fine. If that's what you want." There was anger in his voice, but there was something pitiable and pleading, too. "But you're making a mistake."

"I don't think she is," Sable told him coldly.

Jesse glared at him. It looked as though he might say something, but then he spun on his heel and stalked away. Aurora let out a breath she hadn't realized she'd been holding. She turned her head to Sable, expecting him to walk away, as he always did. This time, he spun her around to face him. His eyes still glittered with that angry intensity.

"Thanks for—well, for that."

"You looked like you needed help."

"I guess I did." She sighed. "This has been going on forever. He's just never been so...well, forceful."

His brow furrowed thoughtfully, and then, so naturally he might not have even known he'd done it, his hands slipped down to her waist. He swayed her slowly to the music. "Is he your boyfriend?"

"What? My boyfriend?"

210

"Well, you went off with him that day...in the alley. And he's always around you. I just assumed."

"No. No, he's not my boyfriend."

"He wants to be."

"Yes. He does. He really always has. Ever since we were kids."

"Why isn't he?"

"What?" She narrowed her eyes at him. "Are you on his side now, or something?"

His mouth twitched almost imperceptibly. "No. Definitely not. I'm just curious. I guess I...don't really understand girls. I thought girls liked guys like him."

She snorted. "Yeah. A lot of them do."

"But not you."

"I guess I just never felt that way about him."

"Well, what kind of guys do you like, then?"

"I, uh..." She flushed. "I'm not sure, I guess."

He lifted an eyebrow. "You've never liked a guy before?"

"Oh, I have." She tilted her head back to meet his gaze. "Usually I... suppose I like the guys I can't have."

"Why can't you have them?"

"They...don't like me back."

They stared at each other silently. "How do you know they don't?" he asked finally.

Her blush deepened. "Well, they never show any interest in me."

"Maybe you just don't realize they are."

"What are you even talking about right now?"

To her surprise, he laughed. "Nothing. It just seems like maybe that guy scares off other guys."

"Are you suggesting he's scary?"

Sable's grin stretched wider. "It depends on who you ask. I'm sure he scares a lot of people."

"What if I ask you?"

"No. He doesn't scare me. It takes a lot to scare me." His voice was low and deadly serious. She believed him.

He lapsed into silence, and she cast around for something to say. It came out very bluntly. "What are you even doing here?" She winced at her own rudeness.

"What?"

"I'm sorry. That's not what I meant. I just wouldn't have thought you were the sort of guy who goes to school dances."

"I'm not. Well, I guess I wouldn't really know. I've never been to one before. They don't have dances when you're home-schooled. There's no one to dance with. I wanted to see what it was like."

"Has it met your expectations?"

He lifted his shoulders in a shrug and glanced around the auditorium. "I have seen films. It's pretty much like I expected except no one is as attractive as on TV."

Aurora lifted her eyebrows.

"Well, most of them aren't. Also, they look a lot younger than they do on television."

She rolled her eyes. "You don't strike me as the kind of guy to be fooled by what you see on television."

Sable laughed, and it was an oddly warm sound, so unlike the chilly tone of his voice. It was nice. His smile suddenly slipped. "Do you think I might have caused you trouble stepping in on Drake like that?"

She hadn't even though about it. "I don't...I don't know. I've never seen Jesse like that before. He's always been harmless. I don't think he would do anything to hurt me. We might have just...hurt his feelings. You might have caused trouble for yourself, actually. I don't really know what he'll do."

"I'm not worried about that." He stared down at her. "If he does anything to you or makes you uncomfortable like that again, will you tell me?"

"I--"

"I mean it, Aurora. If I did something that put you in any kind of danger, I want to know."

212

Her heart thumped. She became aware of how cool his hands felt on her waist compared to the heat that seemed to be spreading over her entire body. There was something going on behind the chill in his eyes, but she couldn't name it. "Um...I'm sure I will be fine. But if I'm not...you'll be the first to know."

"Good." For a long moment, he didn't say anything. He didn't meet her eyes when he spoke again. "Aurora..."

He stiffened suddenly, startling her. His mouth snapped shut, and his hands clenched around her waist. He was remarkably strong, and the pressure was almost painful. A muscle worked in his jaw as he caught sight of something over her shoulder.

"Sable? What is it?" His fingers tightened until she was afraid they might bruise her. "Sable, you're hurting me."

His head jerked slightly as he snapped back to attention, looking down at her as though he'd forgotten she was there. His grip loosened. He took a step back from her like he'd been caught doing something he shouldn't have been. His eyes flicked back over her shoulder.

"What's going on?" She turned her head to follow his scowling gaze.

He was looking at Sierra. The tall, beautiful, black-haired girl looked stunning in a tight, emerald-green sheath. Her face lit up as she grinned around at her classmates, and the pale pink light made her glow. Actually, Aurora realized, he wasn't looking at Sierra. He was looking at her date, who stood beside her with an arm wrapped around her waist.

Aurora opened her mouth in surprise. "Is that...?"

Sable's teeth were clenched. "My brother. Yes."

Van spotted his little brother and smiled. There was a glint of something dark, something mysterious in his eyes, eyes so like Sable's it was uncanny. Without taking his eyes off Sable, he murmured in Sierra's ear, steering her toward his brother and Aurora.

"Aurora, go."

She didn't like this. Was he embarrassed for Sierra and his brother to see them together? If he was, he was going to have to deal with it; he'd been the one to interfere. He'd been the one to pull her into a dance. She ignored him as they watched Sierra and Van approach.

It was too late for her to escape, anyway. Sierra was already swooping down on her. "Aurora!" There was something strange in her voice. Her smile stretched across her entire face. There wasn't a hint of malice in her eyes. "I'm so surprised to see you here. I thought you didn't have a date."

Perhaps Aurora had been wrong about the malice part. She fought a flush and shrugged. It was safer not to say anything.

Sable didn't even look at the black-haired girl. He narrowed his eyes at his brother. "What are you doing here, Van?"

Van smiled. "Dancing. Or I will be." He eyed his brother up and down. "Look at you in your suit, little brother. You look good." His gaze flicked to Aurora. "And who is this? Aurora, isn't it? We've met before. Remember?"

Of course she did. Sable hadn't forgotten the incident, either. He subtly angled his body until he was standing between her and his brother.

"I remember." She was relieved her voice sounded perfectly level. She felt more confident with Sable in front of her. She reached out instinctively, her fingertips barely touching Sable's right shoulder. His muscles were tense. If he noticed her touch, he ignored it.

"I'm sure you know my date, Sierra." Van drew Sierra closer to his side.

Sierra looked very smug. "Hello, Aurora."

Aurora waited for the taunts to come.

Sierra looked between she and Sable. "Are you two here together?" Aurora couldn't read the tone of her voice or the expression in her eyes.

Van's smile was rapier sharp. "I didn't know you had a date, little brother." The way he said little brother was hard and laced with something unidentifiably chilling. "Though I shouldn't be surprised to see you here with her."

The tension in Sable's shoulders didn't ease. "We are not together."

"Oh? It looks as though you are." There was a mean glint in Van's eyes.

"We were just dancing." Sable spoke through clenched teeth.

"Sure you were." Van turned that sharp smile on Aurora. She fought the compulsion to flinch away. There was something creepy about Van, something that was somehow worse because, even looking wicked and mean and dangerous, he was uncannily gorgeous.

"You shouldn't be here," Sable told him. "You aren't even a student."

"I was invited by one. Isn't that right, Sierra?" He smiled down at his date, who squeezed closer to his side.

Aurora looked at Sierra. "How do you two know each other?" She was pleased that she sounded almost as though this was a perfectly normal situation, not something bordering on surreal and unfathomably dangerous.

Sierra's eyes glittered. "We met the night of the party, of course. But we ran into each other again the other night at--"

She cut off suddenly and looked up into Van's eyes. They shared a secret smile that struck Aurora for all its artlessness. She suspected they had met somewhere Sierra ought not to have been. She'd heard enough rumors about the things Sierra did—drinking underage, sneaking out to Lynchburg to go to frat parties, joyriding. She didn't know how much of it was true, but it didn't surprise Aurora that Sierra had come across Van somewhere.

"Oh, just around," Sierra finished.

Van smiled down at her. Aurora wondered if there was something sinister and insincere about the simpering look on his face. Sierra didn't seem to notice anything amiss.

"Well, we can't stand around here chatting with the riff raff all night," Sierra said suddenly, tossing her long, black hair. "Come on, Van."

Aurora stared after them in bemusement as Sierra led Van into the crowd.

"I have to go," Sable said abruptly.

She opened and closed her mouth in confusion. "What? Why?" She wanted to add, now? She had been sure there was something he'd meant to say before his brother had arrived on Sierra's arm. The way he'd said her name, so uncertainly, so determinedly...

He was scowling when he glanced at her, but he wasn't scowling at her. In fact, she thought he was hardly seeing her at all. Then his eyes focused on her. "Just stay away from my brother, Aurora. He's trouble."

Before she could form a reply to this, he spun on his heel and made a beeline for the exit. She gaped at him in surprise, then snapped her mouth shut when she realized that she was attracting attention. Her face flushed. She lifted her chin and turned toward the table at which she'd left Cera, Shane and their dates before the night had taken a turn for the bizarre.

Josie and Diana looked fit to burst when she arrived, but, for some reason, they didn't jump up to drag her back to the table to demand a detailed description of the weird encounter. When she caught their eyes, she noticed that everyone at the neighboring tables was staring at her, whispering behind their hands.

What was worse, the Lawson twins were glaring daggers at her from their table. Terrific. Jesse had cornered her, Sierra had insulted her, Van had—well, he'd just given her that creepy looking-her-inside-out look—and then Sable had unceremoniously ditched her in front of the entire junior and senior class.

And yet, all she could think about were those few moments when Sable had been smiling at her, really smiling, and talking to her as though he was a normal high school boy who didn't turn hot and cold and behave in incomprehensible ways. But he wasn't. There was nothing normal about him or his brother. There probably wasn't anything normal about his family at all.

"What?" she asked her friends uneasily as she sat back down. She tried to sound cool and defiant, but she just sounded embarrassed. "Why are you looking at me like that?"

"What do you mean 'what'?" Josie hissed back. "Would you care to explain all that?"

Her cheeks were on fire. "I wish I could." Her eyes wandered to Sierra and Van, who joined the other Pops at the twins' table. At least the girls' attention was mercifully elsewhere. "I wonder what Sierra is doing with Van. He is so creepy."

"Then they deserve each other," said Diana coldly. "She probably doesn't have any idea what he's really like."

"Or vice versa," Aurora muttered.

"That is not what I was talking about!" Josie said. "You said there is nothing going on between you and Sable. But it looked to me like something was going on just now! Spill."

"There's nothing going on!" Aurora protested. "Nothing I know about, anyway."

Diana almost never took Josie's side, but she did this time. "It looked a lot like there was, Aurora."

"He was all over you!"

Aurora rolled her eyes. "He wasn't all over me. He was trying to protect me from Jesse."

216

"From Jesse?" Even Diana looked surprised by this. Cera, Shane and their dates were pretending not to listen, but Aurora knew they could hear every word. The whole story would probably be all over the school on Monday, if it hadn't already ended up in the local newspaper by tomorrow morning.

"But Jesse would never hurt you!" Josie burst out indignantly.

"I know that, Josie. Sable didn't know that. He just misread the situation. Well, he didn't misread it, exactly. He just—made more out of it than he needed to. It's nothing." Her voice trailed away as her eyes swept the room. She ignored her classmates, who had turned their attention back to their friends or their dates now that whatever had been going on was over. She didn't see Jesse or Sable anywhere.

What she did see was Sierra leading Van around like a show pony, intent that everyone at the dance saw them together and knew exactly who he was. Van didn't seem troubled in the least by this. He played along. Aurora could see the mysterious, dark glint in his eyes even as he smiled. Perhaps it was just how he smiled.

Her gaze found the twins once more. Cami watched Sierra with an irritated twist on her lips, but Callie looked genuinely upset. Had she even met Van before? Ah, yes—the party. She remembered it now, remembered the way Callie's eyes had shone as she looked at Van. Well, it wouldn't be the first time Sierra had taken something someone else had wanted. She probably wouldn't even want it if someone else hadn't seen it first, whatever—or whomever—it was.

"Callie doesn't seem too happy about Sierra bringing Van as her date," she remarked.

"So?" Josie snarled. "Good. She deserves it for being a raging jerk. What do you care how Callie feels?"

"I don't. I just noticed. I didn't realize Callie liked him."

"I didn't even know they knew each other."

"They met at the Jaynes' party, not that it matters. Everyone in town is watching the Jaynes like they're some sort of reality TV stars or something," Diana scoffed.

"Well, it's just like Sierra to steal Callie's crush," Josie added. "She's been doing it since sixth grade. She's never stopped at tormenting her enemies. I think she likes tormenting her friends even more. The Pops deserve each other."

"Sable wasn't happy Van was here." She was speaking to herself. She winced. She really didn't want to talk about Sable.

"Why would he care?" Josie asked. "Does he like Sierra?"

"What?" Aurora was so surprised she snapped her head around to look at Josie. It hadn't occurred to her. Sable had behaved as though Sierra wasn't even there. He'd never paid her a shred of attention, but...but it was Sierra, and almost every boy liked Sierra. The very idea made Aurora sick to her stomach.

"Come on," Diana cut in. "Of course he doesn't. Obviously, he likes Aurora."

"What?" She was sure she was going to give herself whiplash.

Josie squealed. "You're so lucky, Aurora! First Jesse Drake; now Sable Jayne. You're a hot broody boy magnet."

"I don't think Sable likes me. You're making more out of it than there is." But her pulse leapt at the idea. "If he does, he has a funny way of showing it. He ditched me as soon as his brother got here."

"Those brothers," Josie murmured, watching Van as he passed by with Sierra. Van caught Aurora's eye, and she thought he winked, but it was over so quickly, she must have imagined it. "They sure are weird."

"Yeah. They're weird, all right," Aurora muttered. *Just stay away from my brother, Aurora...*

Josie sighed dreamily. "But I wouldn't mind taking all the time in the world to figure them out. Up close and personal."

Aurora's reply was deadly serious. "Something tells me that's not such a good idea, Jos."

Chapter Ten

Nothing else had happened the night of the dance. It was as though Aurora had suddenly contracted a deadly disease. After the scene with Jesse and Sable, the rest of the boys gave her a very wide berth. If she'd even approached the punch bowl when they'd been standing there, they'd bolted as though she had been wielding some sort of weapon toward their heads.

The girls weren't much better, but at least they kept their gossip behind their hands. Everyone was talking about her. She'd spent the evening trying to ignore them and watching everyone--mostly Sierra and Van, who made a striking but very unnerving couple--dance. The Lawson twins spent their evening glaring between Aurora and Sierra as though they were suddenly partners in crime.

She didn't care. She was used to being gossiped about by now, especially with the Pops' determination to do torment her in every possible way. She was used to people talking about her mother's tragic death or Jesse's not-so-secret obsession with her. She wondered now why it had ever bothered her. If her classmates had nothing better to do than talk about her, it wasn't her that had the problem.

What bothered her was Sable. He hadn't come back, and, though she'd spent the weekend wandering around downtown in hopes of running into him again, she hadn't even caught a glimpse of dark hair. By Sunday, she would have been happy just to see Van, even if she wouldn't have approached him if her life depended on it. But if she did, Sable might appear again to rescue her...

Stay away from my brother.

He really needn't have worried. Van made her extremely uncomfortable. She wasn't that reckless.

By Monday morning, she still hadn't forced Sable out of her thoughts. For the smallest moment as they were dancing she'd looked into his eyes, and she had seen something. Something like what she saw in Jesse's eyes when he looked at her. Then he was gone. She didn't understand him at all.

Her pulse quickened as she heard Josie's car pull up to the house. She'd never been excited to go to school. Sierra and the Pops made it a point to hunt her down and insult her at least once a day. Jesse made it a point to seek her out and ask her out most days, and everyone else just tried to pretend she wasn't the tragic girl who lost her mother. School was, for the most part, a nightmare.

But now...now things were different. She wasn't afraid of Sierra and the evil twins anymore. She didn't care if people talked behind her back. She didn't even care that she would probably have to face a very hurt and irate Jesse.

Because Sable would be there. Well, maybe.

Josie looked as chipper as ever this morning. She'd woven red feathers into her choppy bob, and she was taking advantage of the warmer weather in a short black sundress. "Hey, Rora."

"Hi, Jos." She braced herself.

It took about two minutes before Josie finally broke the loaded silence. "So...have you heard from Sable?"

"Why would I have heard from Sable?"

"I just thought maybe after the dance on Friday, he would have called you."

"Come on. It wasn't like that. It was just..." She cut off. "Well, I'm not sure what it was. I think he was just taking pity on me or something."

"Why would he do anything like that if he didn't like you?"

"Don't make more out of it than it is. I don't think he likes me. I think you like to make drama out of things when there isn't any."

This didn't offend her friend. "No. I just have a keen eye for spotting it when it is there. And there is definitely drama here." She scowled at Aurora as she steered into Dinwiddie Hills. "And you, quite rudely and for no reason, are keeping it from your two best friends."

"Please, Josie. I'm just...I'm not sure what to think of the whole thing. Just give me a little time to figure it out, okay?"

Josie sighed. "Fine. Sure. If that's what you need." She looked downtrodden as she swung into the Macy's driveway.

Diana did not ask Aurora about Sable, but she did eye her friend a little more closely than usual that morning. They all turned to peer at the Jayne house as they passed. The gate was open, but they couldn't see any of the

Jaynes. Aurora wondered if Sable had already left for school—or wasn't coming at all.

"I wonder what is going on with Sierra and Van," she said abruptly.

Josie snorted indelicately. "Oh, the usual, probably. Sierra wants an older trophy boyfriend to parade around and make people jealous. She always has to show off."

"I wonder what Van is thinking, though."

Diana shrugged. "Who knows? Maybe he just likes her."

"He's probably just thinking about sex," Josie said meanly. "You know Sierra."

"Yeah. Well, no, not really," said Aurora thoughtfully. "I've just heard rumors."

"Everyone's heard rumors," Diana dismissed. "And you know how often those are actually true."

Aurora did know. She knew very well.

"I wonder how old he is," Josie said. "Aurora, do you know?"

"No. It's not like he and I have ever had a conversation."

"But you've had conversations with his brother."

"He's never mentioned Van." *Just stay away from my brother.* "Not really."

"I bet it's not even legal," Diana said.

Josie rolled her eyes. "Sierra is almost eighteen, and her parents pretty much let her do whatever she wants. They probably don't even know about Van. If they did, they wouldn't do anything about it, anyway."

"They deserve each other," Aurora said ruthlessly. "They're both horrible."

"For once, I actually feel a little bad for Callie," Josie admitted.

"What? How could you possibly?"

"Well, her best friend did steal the guy she likes. If one of the guys I liked became one of your romantic casualties, I would probably feel pretty bad."

"Romantic casualties?" Aurora demanded. "What are you talking about?"

"Well, you do seem to have an awful lot of guys interested in you these days, Rora," Diana put in.

"What? I do not! Well, just Jesse, but that's never changed."

"Come on. There is definitely something going on between you and Sable, Aurora," Josie's voice brooked no argument.

Aurora argued all the same. "No, there isn't, Josie. Stop reading so much into one stupid dance."

"I think if you aren't going to read into things, there's not a lot of point being involved in them," Josie replied. Aurora laughed. "Come on. Just admit it. You like him. It's obvious. And why wouldn't you? He's hot, mysterious, new in town and he's always coming to your rescue."

"I wouldn't say he is always coming to my rescue. Okay, he has come to my rescue a couple times. But Jesse has, too."

"Aurora, that is not a very good argument," Diana told her gently. "Jesse is in love with you. Why is it so hard to believe Sable would be, too?"

"Because guys like Sable don't like girls like me."

"And why, exactly, not? What's wrong with you? You're beautiful and smart, and you aren't nasty like the Pops," Josie told her. "If a guy like Jesse can be in love with you, so could Sable."

Aurora stammered. "Well, I—he doesn't act like—he's just so confusing."

"Well, I haven't seen him so much as talk to anyone more than a couple times, and most of the time he looks like he's ready to bolt when he does. You have to admit, he's different with you."

She had noticed this, but she had always thought she was just always in the right place at the right time. Sable hadn't had much of a choice but to talk to her or come to her rescue those times. "I don't know, Jos."

"Tell the truth. You like him."

"All right, all right. Yes. I suppose I like him."

"Finally! She admits it!"

"Was that so hard?" Diana asked, patting her shoulder gently. "We are your best friends."

"I just didn't..." Aurora smiled wryly. "I wasn't sure. He is so weird sometimes, and I just didn't want to feel like an idiot for liking some guy I could never have."

"I like guys I can't have all the time," said Josie. "It's half the fun."

"It just seems stupid to like him."

"Why?"

"Because everyone likes him! And he doesn't seem to like anyone."

"Except you."

Aurora ignored this. "And I told you—I'm not the kind of girl guys like him like."

"How do you even know what kind of girls he likes? Can you see him with someone like the Pops or something?" Diana demanded.

"Well, maybe. I mean, they're popular and pretty and--"

"Total bitches!"

Josie and Aurora looked at Diana in shock. She cleared her throat primly.

"What I mean to say is, he doesn't strike me as the kind of guy who goes for mean girls. He's never given a single one of them the time of day since he got here."

"At least they have experience with guys," Aurora muttered. "They would know how to act around him. I probably wouldn't even know what do with him if I had him."

"It's not hard to figure out along the way," Diana told her.

"And you would try if he asked, right?" Josie asked.

"Well...maybe. Yes. Probably."

"That's good enough then." Josie grinned. "I have to know there might be at least a chance I can live vicariously through you."

Aurora rolled her eyes. "You wouldn't have to if you would just take a chance once in a while instead of chickening out every time."

"I am coming around to it. I did dance with Bryan Friday night, and he kind of mentioned he would be going to Colletta's on Saturday."

Aurora looked at her in surprise. "What? When did this happen?"

"Oh, while you were all wrapped up in whatever was going on with Jesse and Sable and Van."

"Did he invite you to go with him?"

"No, not exactly, but I sort of...dropped by and ran into him and had coffee with him."

"What? You had a date? Diana, did you know about this?"

"Yes, of course I knew about it. Josie told me when you wouldn't answer your phone. Where were you all weekend, by the way?"

"Just...around. Hanging out with Dad and Ruby." It wasn't entirely a lie. She had spent some time with her aunt and father; she'd just spent most of her time wandering around ignoring phone calls or lurking in the museum.

"Anyway, it wasn't a date," Josie said glumly. "Turns out he just wanted to borrow my Geology notes. But he could have asked a lot of girls. And I'm not even the best in class."

"Far from it," Diana put in.

"I can't believe you've been going on and on about some nonexistent thing between me and Sable when you were out having coffee with an actual boy on Saturday."

"It was nothing special. We were just studying."

"But you were studying with the boy you like. And having coffee. That is something."

"Well, he didn't exactly ask me out again or anything. He sort of...well, the truth is I thought maybe he wanted to—we were having a really nice time—but he couldn't get up the nerve."

Aurora shook her head as Josie steered into the school parking lot, nabbing the first available space in the back of the lot. "Why didn't you just ask him? You had the perfect chance."

"Come on, Aurora, telling me to do it over and over isn't going to suddenly change my personality."

Aurora laughed. "Seriously, Jos. I think you need to go see Dr. Jayne. She's really good at that sort of thing."

"What sort of thing?"

"Taking away your fear."

Jesse was leaning against the wall when they reached Aurora's locker. When he spotted her, he scowled and stormed off the other way. It wouldn't last, but it was nice to start the day without a fight for once.

Aurora smiled and added as though nothing had interrupted her train of thought, "It changes everything."

* * *

Sable stared in confusion at the front door as though no one had ever knocked on it before. Someone was knocking on it now, and they didn't seem to be going away. He pulled the door open, quickly smoothing his irritated scowl into a neutral expression.

The man on the front porch looked familiar, but Sable couldn't quite place him. He had dark hair combed back from a lined, rugged face. He didn't think his mother had any appointments this afternoon.

"Can I help you?" He was proud that his voice sounded perfectly polite.

"Hello. I'm Mike Geller."

Geller. "Uh–hi."

"I'm here to see Dr. Jayne."

"Male or female?"

Mike looked a little uncomfortable, as though he was doing something he ought not to be. "Female."

"Sure. This way." Sable turned to lead him to his mother's office. He knocked lightly on the door.

"Yes?"

He poked his head in. "Mom, there's someone here to see you."

His mother smiled as though this was the most pleasant thing in the world. "Oh. I didn't have any appointments set up today. Are they here for a consultation?"

"It's Aurora's dad." He didn't sound quite so normal this time. When he glanced back at Mike Geller, the man looked at him a little strangely.

Mariah pretended not to notice. "Ah, lovely. Come in, Mr. Geller."

She rose to greet him, closing the door behind them with a pointed look at Sable. He ignored it. He didn't go far. He slid down the wall to listen through the crack under the door.

"What can I do for you, Mr. Geller?"

"Call me Mike."

"Are you here for a session?"

"No. I just wanted to talk about Aurora."

"Ah, I see. Please, come sit. I'm afraid I can't tell you what your daughter says in her sessions. Many parents have a problem with that, but there is an expectation of privacy when one comes into this room."

Mike chuckled. "I don't want to know. I'm sure I wouldn't like it, and I would stop sleeping at night. Anyway, I think you're the one who would know what to do about it. I'm no good at emotions. I just wanted to..."

"Make sure she is in good hands?"

Aurora's father laughed again. It wasn't like her laugh. It was low and gruff. Her laugh was soft and tinkling.

"I assure you, she is. I have much experience working with girls her age."

"She lost her mother several years ago. I probably should have sent her to someone sooner."

"For a teenaged girl who lost her mother, she is remarkably well-adjusted."

"Does that mean she won't need any more sessions?"

Mariah's voice was gentle. "It's up to her to decide how she feels. It is not a miracle therapy."

"Some people seem to think it is."

"Many people who have never had anyone to talk to experience unusually strong results in the beginning. It usually takes a lot more work before they're ready to cope on their own. But I assure you, your daughter is going to be fine. It always helps to have someone to talk to who won't judge you."

"I don't judge my daughter." He sounded affronted.

"I was not referring to you. I understand that. But you know her quite well, and there are many things a teenaged girl has trouble telling her father—even her mother most times."

For a moment, there was silence. Then Mike asked, hesitantly, "She's not crazy?"

Mariah laughed. "No. She's not crazy. Far from it. Just because someone seeks therapy does not mean they are crazy. Sometimes it just means they

226

have things to work out, and they have exhausted what they are able to do on their own. They need a second opinion."

"You're not giving her pills or anything, are you?"

"No, no. That's not my sort of medicine. I am unable to prescribe medication to a minor without parental consent, besides."

"But you're doing that...holistic stuff? Acupuncture or something?"

"That is a specialty of my daughter, Evelyn's, but Aurora has not sought such treatment. If she does feel she requires further treatment, as though she wants to do more than simply talk, I will be sure to seek your permission first."

"Good. That's good." He sighed. "Maybe I should set up an appointment myself. I lost my wife, too. Maybe I could use someone to talk to."

"Certainly. Is there something in particular bothering you?"

"Same as any other single dad with a teenaged daughter, I suppose. I'm always worrying I'm making mistakes, that I'm not emotionally supportive enough."

"I think I can help with that. I would like to try something that might ease your worries."

He sounded skeptical. "What is it?"

"A simple relaxation technique I like to do with some of my patients."

There was a pause. Finally Mike replied, "Okay."

Sable cursed under his breath. He knew what his mother was doing. For a long moment, he couldn't hear anything from behind the door. He turned and cracked it a fraction of an inch to peer inside. His mother's human mask had slipped. He could see the livid swirls outlined in her red skin. It looked as though she and Aurora's father were locked in a heated kiss, but faint puffs of what looked like smoke flowed from his mouth to hers.

He ducked out of the room before she sensed him. Aurora's father would emerge from the room, bleary-eyed and content, and any concerns he had regarding Aurora's treatment would be long gone. Damn. He considered urging the man to keep Aurora as far from his mother as possible, but it would be no use. He belonged to Mariah now. There was nothing Sable could do.

He heard his mother speak again. Her voice was thicker, huskier than before. "I have an appointment available on Wednesday."

Mike sounded dreamy. "Yes. Wednesday sounds good."

"Is there anything else you wanted to speak to me about, Mike? I don't wish to be rude, but I do have some paperwork I must finish."

"No. Of course. Thank you for seeing me."

"I will see you again on Wednesday."

"Yes. Great."

Sable could hear them moving toward the door. He scurried toward the stairs. When his mother and Mike emerged into the hall, she spotted him. "Sable, can you walk Mr. Geller to the door, please?"

He glared at her. "This way, Mr. Geller." The man looked as though he hadn't any idea which way to turn and was perfectly content to just stand there all day.

He would snap out of it in a few moments. Sable hoped he'd be all right to drive himself home. If he wasn't...Aurora would be all alone again. He followed her father outside, though the man smiled serenely and didn't seem to notice.

He cursed under his breath and hurried to his car to trail the man home. He couldn't stop his mother from feeding on the man, but at least he could keep him from running off the road. She shouldn't have to lose another parent just because his could not manage to control herself.

* * *

Aurora closed her eyes as she lay back on her bed. The glowing green stars her mother had placed on her ceiling had nearly lost their incandescence, but she'd never taken them down. She couldn't, not when her mother had spent so much time placing them into perfect constellations. It made her sad to look at them, but sometimes they were soothing. She could close her eyes and picture her mother propped up in the bed beside her, pointing out the Big Dipper, Orion, Draco, Cassiopeia and Scorpio.

Tonight, she didn't want to look at them, even as their glow faded into the shadows. She was disappointed. She didn't know what she had expected, but Sable hadn't been in school that day. She wondered how he got away with only showing up to class about half the time, how long it would take before he got himself kicked out and back into home-school.

She wasn't really worried about his academic career. She just wanted to see him, to talk to him or just know he was there. She wanted some sort of confirmation that she hadn't just imagined what had happened the night of the dance. She wanted to know if something had changed between them, even if she knew it was stupid to hope it had. Mostly, she wanted to know what the hell was going on with him.

School had been horrible. She'd even been optimistic when the day began, but it had only gotten progressively worse. Sierra spent the entire English class period telling Brooke how amazing Van was. The twins spent half their time glaring at her and the other talking about Aurora just loudly enough for her to hear every single nasty word. They might have been too terrified of their ring leader to talk badly about her, but they had found Aurora a suitable alternative upon which to take it out.

As though she didn't have enough to worry about, Cami had taken a shine to Sable, and his attention to Aurora at the dance had stoked the fire of their hatred. She tried to ignore them.

It would have been nice if Sable had been there to come to her rescue or put the rumors about them to rest. At the very least, he could keep the twins from talking so loudly.

The door banged open downstairs, startling her from her reverie. It was only four in the afternoon, and apart from not wanting to be caught brooding in her room with the curtains drawn and the lights off, she was surprised anyone was home this early. She hopped up from the bed and hurried down the stairs.

Ruby looked more flustered than Aurora had seen her in some time. "Oh, Aurora," She sighed in relief as she pressed a hand to her chest. "There you are. Where is your dad?"

"It's only four o'clock. I'm sure he's still at the shop."

"Right. Of course."

"What are you doing home so early?"

Her aunt was distressed. "You haven't heard?"

"Heard? Heard what?" Alarm roiled in her belly.

"The Kessells were found in their house this morning."

"The Kessells?" Aurora's brow furrowed in confusion.

"They were customers of mine.

"What do you mean they were found in their house?"

"Dead. They were found dead, Aurora."

"Oh, no. What happened to them?"

"No one really knows. I heard they were sort of all dried up. Like...like they'd been dehydrated or mummified or something. It sounds horrible."

"What? How could that happen?"

"I don't know. I haven't ever heard of anything like it. They were just asleep in their beds when it happened."

"But were they sick or something?"

"I don't know. No one knows. I heard about it this afternoon from one of their neighbors. They think maybe they had some sort of flu or something."

"But what did the police say?"

"Nothing yet. They haven't released any statements or anything. It's very unusual. They weren't very old. They were in their sixties, retired, and used to be very active. Lately they spent most of their time at home and only came into do town about once a week. They usually stopped in and said hello when they were downtown. They sent flowers for all their friends' birthdays."

"It's very strange."

"Yes. It reminds you how fragile we can be, doesn't it? Your mom...the missing women. Us."

"So you...do you think the same thing happened to Mrs. Anders and Mrs. Horne? They got sick, too?"

"There's no evidence of that, but I suppose anything is possible. They had nothing in common with the Kessells, as far as I know. It's more likely they're in a ditch somewhere—" Ruby looked suddenly ashamed. "That was awful of me. I shouldn't have said that."

"You aren't the only one in town who's said it," Aurora said quietly.

"It's still horrible. I'm sorry. It's just...I don't know what's going on in this town anymore."

"What do you mean?"

"It just feels...different these days somehow. Don't you feel it, too?"

"Yeah. It does feel different." She felt different. "I'm not sure it's such a bad thing."

"I'm not sure it's a good thing, either. Something just seems…off in this place."

"You're unusually reflective today, Ruby. Did something happen?"

"What? No."

"Something with Blaine?"

Ruby waved her hand dismissively. "No, no. He's great. It's just…I don't know. I guess New Coventry doesn't feel quite like home anymore. Not like it used to. I can't really put my finger on it." She smiled sadly. Her eyes slid away. "Maybe…well, maybe it's felt like that since Rosa passed."

Aurora sighed. "Yeah. I guess I feel that way sometimes, too."

Ruby shook off whatever melancholy had seized her. She did this a lot. She'd had a difficult life, practically growing up a single mother, but she never let anything bother her for long. Her entire countenance changed. Suddenly she was smiling. "How about I order some pizza? You can tell me all about the dance on Friday without your dad listening in."

Aurora was surprised it hadn't already gotten around town. She rolled her eyes. "It was just a dance. Nothing special."

Ruby didn't let this deter her. "Then I can tell you all about my last date with Blaine." The stars in her eyes glittered. "I think I might be in love."

Aurora grinned. "Really?"

"Yeah. I think this might be the real thing this time, Aurora. I just hope… well, I just hope he sticks around."

"You think he might not?"

"Well, there seem to be too many people disappearing lately. I just don't want him to be one of them."

"Yeah. I understand better than I would like to."

Ruby hadn't heard her. She was already punching in a number on her phone. "Pepperoni?"

"Yeah. That sounds good."

* * *

Sable slammed the front door, hurrying toward his father's office. He knew better than to ignore an urgent text from his mother to return home immediately, though he would have preferred to spend the evening wandering alone under the stars, trying to figure out exactly what the hell it was he thought he was doing thinking of human girls. There was no time for that tonight. He would have to sort out his problems on his own time.

His parents sat with his sister Evelyn and Aunt Elise. None of them were spoke. They were tense and worried. He'd seen that look before. Van's absence from the room spoke volumes that he wished to never have to hear again.

"What's going on?" he asked tiredly, though he had been in this very meeting dozens of times. He could guess. His head pounded. Not again.

"Where is your brother?" Mariah demanded.

"I don't know. I thought he would be here."

"Where have you been?" Adam asked in a deceptively calm voice.

"What? I was just out."

"Doing what?"

"Just driving around. I got some coffee. What's going on?"

"We need to find your brother," Mariah replied.

"Why?"

"Either he has killed again or there are more of us in town."

This was unexpected. "What?"

Mariah handed him the evening edition of the paper detailing the discovery of the Kessells. He needed only a split second to understand. The color drained from his face. "Someone has fed on these people."

"Obviously."

"And you think it was Van? This isn't really his style. When has he ever gone after people in their beds? He's more of an opportunist."

Van strode unexpectedly into the room. "I suppose you're all blaming me for this."

"Mom, I don't think it was him." Sable's vehement words surprised them all.

"I didn't do it. It wasn't me." Van hesitated. "If you don't believe me, I will show you."

Adam's voice was very quiet in the tense room. "Then this is far more troubling."

"You think there could be more of us in town?" Evelyn whispered.

"I have never come across another Jivina since...since we left Azil." As Adam said the name of his home village, there was something sad and bitter in his voice. "But if we can live here among humans, anyone can."

"It is certainly possible that we are not alone in this town," Mariah agreed gravely. Her eyes strayed uneasily toward her daughter then snapped guiltily away. "And if we are not, if there are more of us here, we must discover who they are."

Sable glanced at his brother, who frowned thoughtfully. Then Van looked at Evelyn, his face lighting up. In the same moment, everyone turned to her. Evelyn's eyes flared with anger. She drew herself up to her full height and glared around at them. "I still think it might be Van."

"You always think it was me," Van growled. "It wasn't."

"Let me see."

He rolled his eyes, for his sister's commands meant nothing to him.

Mariah gave Evelyn a stern look. "I believe him, Evie. He was not responsible for these deaths."

Van and Evelyn glared at each other. "I don't think it was Van," Sable repeated. His brother looked smug, but Evie glared at him as though he'd mortally offended her. "It's just not his style. Not to mention, he prefers them much younger."

Van did not display appreciation for his brother's support. "What's that suppose to mean?"

"You know what I mean."

His mouth twisted maliciously. "I'm not the one chasing human girls."

"I'm not chasing anyone!"

Mariah frowned. "Sable, is this true?"

"No!"

"It's the Geller girl, isn't it? I told you to stay away from her."

Sable clenched his teeth. "I have not gone near her."

"That's not how it looked to me at the dance," Van put in ruthlessly.

"You were at the school dance?" Adam's calm exterior cracked for the briefest instant. His eyes flared at Van. "What were you doing at a high school dance?"

Sable couldn't resist the urge to lash back at his brother. "He had a date."

"A date? What is going on in this house? My sons are dating high school girls? *Human* high school girls?"

"No," Sable replied vehemently. "I'm not dating anyone."

Van snorted derisively. "I was just playing around. She asked me, and I thought it might be a laugh. It didn't mean anything."

Mariah peered meaningfully at her husband. "Maybe it is time to go. We have gotten too wrapped up in life here."

"No!" Sable hissed. "Isn't that the point? What was the point of leaving the village, trying to live among humans, if we aren't even going to try to be normal? We didn't kill those people. If there is another Jivina in town, it is their problem; not ours."

"It is our problem," Adam snapped. "If someone begins to suspect we are anything other than we seem we could be exposed."

"But why would anyone suspect us of anything? We haven't done anything. They don't have any idea what we are or what killed those people. Even if they did know, there is no way they could trace it back to us. We didn't do anything!"

"It isn't safe, Sable. You know that," Mariah told him. "We have to be careful. If any humans find out what we are, there will be no life for us anymore. They would hunt us down and kill us without giving us a chance to explain we weren't responsible."

"Not to mention, they probably wouldn't be happy to learn how you are accomplishing all that miracle therapy," Van said.

They all ignored him. "So what are we going to do?" Evelyn asked. "I can't just pick up and leave again. I'm starting to like it here."

"We find them." They all looked at Elise in surprise.

"Find them?" Adam repeated, lifting his eyebrows.

"We find the other Jivina and put them down." Elise's pale blue eyes flashed. "They are endangering us all. They might not care about living a normal life amongst the humans, but they aren't going to take ours away. The authorities know nothing. The police have no leads, and the medical examiner has not pinpointed the cause of death. They think it is some sort of illness. We have time. It's just two killings."

"And the missing women," Mariah said. "Whomever did this probably had something to do with their disappearance. They just haven't been found yet."

"I think we all know that's likely."

"I will do it," Sable blurted.

"What?" Mariah demanded.

"I will find the Jivina."

Van chuckled derisively. "And what are you, a hero now? What do you think you're going to do? Save the town? Get the girl? These people are our food, Sable. We are not here to be their champions."

Sable glared at him. "They are vulnerable. It's our responsibility to protect them."

"Since when? That's stupid. It isn't."

"It is our people who are attacking them. They have no way of knowing what they are up against. If we're going to stay here, we have to make it safe."

"This is pathetic."

"Sable is right," Mariah said. "We are stronger than the humans, and there is another Jivina preying on them. If we want to stay, we have to stop them."

"Whatever. I'm not interested in playing hero for a bunch of humans."

"Don't, then," Sable growled. "You're no one's hero."

"You think you're any better?"

"Yeah. I am, and I'll find who's doing this. I'll stop them."

"No," Mariah said. "When you find them, you will bring them to us. We will decide how to deal with them."

"This isn't Azil," Sable reminded her. "You aren't the elders anymore. This is the real world."

Adam frowned at him. "We don't know how strong they are. You might not be powerful enough to fight them."

"I have a good reason to. I think I can find the strength."

"Very noble, little brother," Van said with a sneer.

"I'm better than you."

Adam ignored them. "You are old enough to make your own decisions, Sable, but you will not put yourself at risk before we know what we are dealing with. When you find them, you will come to me. I will decide what to do about them."

"Yes, Father."

Chapter Eleven

The bodies of Susan Anders and Ellen Horne were discovered less than a week later, stuffed in a dumpster behind an abandoned warehouse. They might not have been found for many more weeks, months or even years if the building's owners hadn't decided it was finally time to clear out the several years' accumulation of garbage and debris that was beginning to attract vandals and small colonies of vermin.

The coroner was as stumped about these deaths as those of Mr. and Mrs. Kessell.

Susan and Ellen had been dead much longer. It was difficult to tell for how much longer, as their bodies were practically mummified. The mysterious cause of death was troubling, but not quite so troubling as the location of the bodies, which, to even the most remedial crime enthusiasts, suggested someone hadn't wanted them to be found. And that, of course, probably meant just one thing: foul play.

It was possible the women, drunk and unpredictable, had wandered that far toward the edge of town. It was possible that they had collapsed there after a night of drinking and some vagrant had found the bodies and stuffed them into the dumpster as a final burial. But what—or who—had actually killed them remained a mystery.

The press speculated wildly about it. If it had been foul play, this was an entirely unique form of murder of which even the most experienced and well-trained investigators had never heard. Perhaps it was some sort of cult ritual or poison. Or perhaps they'd been killed some other way, and the murderer had some sick fascination with old fashioned embalming techniques. Perhaps it was just some nut who wanted to see if they could make a mummy and had succeeded, if the responding officer's white-faced rambling could be believed.

If they had died from some mysterious illness, as the coroner might have shortsightedly implied at the time of the Kessell's death, it was the sort that struck without warning and killed almost immediately, for neither Susan and Ellen, nor the Kessells appeared to have been at all unwell before they'd suddenly died. Or perhaps it was a disease that displayed no outward signs or symptoms until the very last moment. Whatever it could be, it had most certainly never been seen or heard of before, at least by any local or state doctors, and it had—at least so far as they could tell—a one hundred percent death rate.

As could reasonably be expected, New Coventry was in a panic.

Most of the citizens hadn't left their house since the news broadcast. Even Josie didn't speak much as she picked up Aurora and Diana for school the next day. The streets were curiously deserted, especially for this time of morning. When they pulled in, the school parking lot was practically empty.

"Wow," Josie murmured quietly, as though speaking too loudly might upset the tense, suspenseful quiet of the campus. "It looks like everyone is too afraid to even come to school."

"Or they're just using it as an excuse to stay home," Diana said.

"Should we turn around?" Josie asked. "They probably wouldn't even count it as a truant day."

Aurora shrugged. "We're already here. We might as well go in."

"Anyway, if we're going to get sick, we're probably already sick," Diana added bluntly. "Going home or going in won't change a thing."

Josie looked a bit alarmed. "Do you think they were sick?"

"I don't know. It's the only one of the theories that makes any sense. I certainly don't believe there is a cult of ancient Egyptian shamans who are embalming innocent people to raise the spirit of some dead Pharaoh or something."

"It might not be a virus or anything," Aurora said. "Otherwise other people would probably have it, and there would be some trace of something wrong in their bodies."

"We don't know for sure other people don't have it," Diana argued. "And, anyway, the coroner is about as old as my great-grandfather. He's far past retirement by now. He's gone a bit off."

"Well, there's not much we can do about it but go about our lives. If we're going to get sick and dry up into mummies, I would rather not die cowering in my house and wishing I'd enjoyed my last days."

"I don't know if going to school when no one else is here qualifies as enjoying our last days," Josie remarked dryly.

"No. It probably doesn't."

"Well, I, for one, am not going to stay home everyday until they figure out what killed those people. It didn't work for the plague, and it probably isn't going to work with whatever this is. Anyway, if I don't end up dying of mummy plague, I will be very sorry that I neglected my studies and blew my chance at getting into a good college," Diana finished.

She had a good point. They trudged up the steps toward the building. They were the only ones.

"I don't know why they don't just cancel school anyway if no one is even going to show up," Josie said, looking around the empty halls.

Sable rounded a corner with a slightly confused expression. Aurora saw him before he noticed them. Her stomach erupted in butterflies. She hadn't seen him since the dance. When he caught sight of them, she couldn't read anything in his expression. He started toward them immediately.

"What's going on?" he demanded. "Where is everyone? There is school today, isn't there?"

"You didn't hear?" Josie asked.

"Hear what? What are you talking about?"

"The deaths."

He hesitated a beat. Aurora saw something change in his eyes. "Oh. Yes. I heard about those."

"The whole town is in a panic," Diana said disdainfully. "They think it's some sort of super flu or plague or something."

"It was only four people. That doesn't sound like a plague."

"I know. People here are a little sensitive," Josie told him.

"I can see that. So no one came to school?"

"Not many people," Aurora finally spoke up. "There were a few cars out in the lot."

"You guys aren't scared?"

"Well, we're scared," Josie admitted, "but Aurora thinks it isn't going to do any good staying in, and Diana thinks we'll be sorry if there's no plague and we let it interfere with getting into a good college."

"If it is some sort of virus, hiding out never did any good in the past. I doubt it would be any different now," Diana said. "Anyway, it doesn't sound like any illness I've ever heard of. It sounds like they were dehydrated or something."

"Or it could have been some sort of gas," Aurora put in thoughtfully.

"Or something they ate," Josie added.

"It might not be any sort of virus at all. Everyone's probably just worked up over nothing," Diana finished.

Sable's mouth twitched. "So what about school? Do you think it's actually going to happen?"

"We'll see," Aurora replied.

He fell into step beside them as the headed toward her locker. Jesse wasn't waiting there. The halls were quiet and echoing. It felt strangely appropriate. Sable wouldn't be walking beside them so casually if it had been a normal day.

The warning bell trilled. It sounded so loud they all winced.

"Well, at least something is still normal around here," Sable remarked sourly. He wasn't the type to appreciate clanging bells ordering him about. "Want to see how many teachers actually showed up?"

"I hope Mr. Ellis is gone and we have that crazy substitute with the blue hair," Josie said. "She sings all the lessons as AC/DC songs."

"That sounds stupid."

"It's awesome." Josie looked around as they reached Aurora's corridor. "Has anyone else seen too many horror movies? I keep expecting zombies to jump out at us or something."

"You're the only one, Jos," Aurora told her. "It's just a normal day in New Coventry. Everyone is acting like crazy people."

Sable didn't say anything as they reached Aurora's homeroom and peeked in. There was no one inside. There wasn't even a teacher. She turned to the others. "There's no one here. This is so surreal."

"What should we do?" Josie asked.

"Let's check another room," Diana suggested, frowning as if discovering the empty classroom was highly offensive. "They can't all be empty."

There was no one in Josie's classroom, either, and they did not encounter anyone in the halls. Sable sighed. "Come on. This is a waste of time. We can't keep just looking into classrooms until we find someone. Let's head to the cafeteria. Someone will know what's going on."

This proved to be more successful than prowling the halls. Thirty or forty students gathered together in the cafeteria, murmuring grimly to each other. The eerie mood of the nearly empty school permeated the air around them.

"You have got to be kidding me," Diana complained. "What is wrong with people?"

The tardy bell rang. It hardly caused anyone to even look up. There wasn't any class for which to be tardy. As soon as the bell quieted, Mr. Bell, the assistant principle, strode into the lunchroom. The students turned to look at him.

"If I could have your attention, please." There was no need for him to raise his voice; the words echoed through the room. He was highly annoyed. "So many of the teachers and students have called in today, normal class schedules have been suspended. We will be holding study hall here today, and I suggest you use the time to catch up on your studies."

A sophomore girl raised her hand. "Why not just send us home?"

Her suggestion was taken up by most of the students, bitterly disappointed that they hadn't thought to skip school like everyone else.

"It could be like a snow day," a senior boy added.

Mr. Bell frowned. "I'm afraid we have no choice but to remain open. Everyone in town might be acting like the next big plague has struck, but that doesn't mean life doesn't still go on. Everyone get out your books."

The students did as they were told. Mr. Bell was notoriously strict; he would not accept any arguments. Aurora was surprised when Sable joined her and her friends at an empty table, pulling out his assignments. He looked more like a normal high school boy in that moment than she'd ever seen him look.

There were a few teachers there, sitting around at the tables and talking quietly to each other. None of them seemed particularly happy with the situation. They probably wished that they'd just called in sick that day. Some of the students bent over their books, but most of them just sat around chatting in low voices to each other. No one bothered to scold them or order them back to work.

"This is ridiculous." Diana glared around the cafeteria disdainfully. "Even Zach stayed home today. I thought he was a bit more sensible than that."

"Well, everyone gets caught up in the hysteria sometimes," Aurora remarked, half-heartedly sorting through her outstanding assignments. "What have you got to do?"

"A paper in Earth Science," Diana slammed her book down on the table in front of her. "I might as well get it done. At least I won't have to worry about it later."

"I'm going to get started on my short story for English," Josie said. "Maybe I can write about a school that goes crazy and becomes infected by panic."

"Aurora, will you work on the exam review for English with me?" Sable asked abruptly.

"Sure." She ignored Josie and Diana, who exchanged a look before leaning quickly back over their books.

Sable moved to the other end of the table. Aurora smiled at her friends as she joined him. He watched her shuffle through her papers for the exam review sheets, but he didn't move to take out his own.

"Is this town always like this?"

"Kind of. They aren't always so ridiculous, but you should have seen what happened when there was an E Coli outbreak a couple years ago. No one shopped in the local stores for weeks. They had everything shipped in from other cities. Once one person gets into a panic it spreads around like a virus. It will blow over. It always does."

"Huh." He shuffled through his papers and found the exam review. It was already filled with small, neat print.

Aurora raised her eyebrows. "You've done it already?"

"Well, I took this class already."

"They let you take it again?"

"They didn't know, I guess. I like taking the easy way out sometimes." There was an almost guilty expression in his eyes. "I've pretty much got enough credit to graduate. I just haven't taken the certification test."

"Then why are you here?"

"I wanted to see what it was like to actually go to school. I haven't ever been to one. We moved around so much, I just sort of took care of it on my own."

"Your parents don't mind?"

"It's the same thing they did. They always lived sort of out in the country. They took care of their own education."

"I guess they must be very smart; they both became doctors."

"Yes. And my sister is an acupuncturist. She home-schooled, too."

"What about your brother?"

"Van...Well, he's not anything. I don't think he even bothered to get his certification, even though he did well enough. He just doesn't care about stuff like that."

"Do you want to be a doctor too when you grow up?"

"No. Definitely not."

"What then?"

"I never really thought about it."

"What about college?"

He shrugged noncommittally. "I guess I'll take classes online or something. I'm a year ahead, so I'm not too worried about it right now. I might even take a year off."

"To travel the world?"

"I've done enough traveling. Maybe I'll get a job or something."

"What kind of job?"

"I don't know. I like building things."

"What sorts of things?"

"Models. I like electronics and stuff. I like taking things apart to see how they work and then putting them back together."

"That's something you could do."

"I'm good at math and science and stuff. Maybe I want to study engineering or something."

"Sounds boring."

He laughed. "Maybe for someone who wants to be an adventurer."

"Not an adventurer," Aurora protested. "An archaeologist."

"They are pretty much the same thing."

"Only in books and movies. Otherwise, I think it's a lot of studying and searching for ancient civilizations without any results."

This didn't deter him. "You still want excitement."

"Maybe I do."

He broke eye contact to glance around the room, lingering a moment on Mr. Bell, who read a fat book and ignored the students completely.

"Aurora, how many new people have moved to do town recently?"

This change of topic surprised her so much she blinked at him for a few seconds.

"I mean, besides us," he prompted. "Do many new people move here? It seems like such an isolated place most of the time."

"It does, doesn't it? My aunt's new boyfriend Blaine just moved here about a year ago. He flips houses. I think he was planning to leave town when he finished the last house, but now he's thinking about staying around and taking on another project here. He says the real estate market is pretty good."

"Is he by himself?"

"Yeah. Well, his partner has been in town, but he doesn't live here."

"Are they the only ones?"

"The Landrys moved here last year. They bought an old inn and turned it into a bed and breakfast. Their daughter Ariel is over there." She nodded to a pretty girl with long, honey blonde hair who was smiling and talking with a friend a few tables over.

Sable turned to stare at Ariel with unexpectedly intensity. Something about the look in his eyes made Aurora's stomach churn uncomfortably. Then he turned back to her as though nothing odd had happened.

Aurora rushed to fill the strange silence. "Their family owns a few bed and breakfasts around New England. Their older kids run them. They bought the one here and are running it for Ariel until she graduates. Then she is supposed to take it over. At least, that's what I've heard about her."

"Is that what she wants to do?"

"Well, I don't know. I don't actually know her. She's a senior, and we

244

don't have any common classes. I only know what I've heard. People in small towns talk a lot. Just not always to each other."

"Do you talk about me?"

"Every now and again." The playful note in her voice surprised her.

"Oh, yeah? What do you say?"

"I can't tell you that. It would be breaking the town covenant. If you want to know, you'll just have to listen for the whispers on the wind."

"Or read the writing on the walls?"

"There is a particularly graphic cartoon of you on the wall in the ladies' locker room."

He was utterly shocked by this. "What?"

She laughed. "Come on. Girls don't do that."

"Well, neither do boys!"

"Yeah, right."

"It's totally true. At least, they haven't done it in any locker room I've ever been in."

"And how many locker rooms have you actually been in?"

"Well, just the one, but it's the only one that counts right now."

"That's not exactly a random sampling of locker rooms."

"It is. It just isn't a wide one." His eyes glittered in amusement. She felt a lighter mood settling over them. "Are there any other new people in town?"

"There was an older man who retired here a couple years ago, but he met a younger lady at the retirement community, and they went off in their RV together to travel the country. I can't think of anyone else."

He lapsed into silence.

"Do you know the answer to number six?" she asked abruptly, suddenly remembering what they were doing there in the first place.

"B."

She frowned. "Are you sure?"

"Yes."

"I thought it was C."

"It's B."

"I'm not sure I believe you."

He smiled at her. "Why wouldn't you? I wouldn't let you down, Aurora. I would tell you if I wasn't totally sure."

He looked so much different when he smiled. There wasn't anything cold about him then. "Thanks. Maybe I should check all of my answers against yours."

"You can just take my review. I don't need it." He slid the paper across the table toward her. "Do you think the rest of the students will be here tomorrow?"

"I hope so. This is weird, isn't it?"

"It's not so bad." He could be so strange sometimes, when he just stared at her with those unreadable eyes. "When you're done with that, do you want to work on Spanish?"

"Sure. Don't tell me you're good at that, too."

"I'm terrible. I was hoping you'd be able to help me since I helped you with English, which I can actually speak very well."

"It was only one question. I think I got the rest all right."

"It still seems pretty fair to me."

She returned his lopsided smile. "All right. But I have to warn you—my accent is terrible."

"Mine, too. This should be fun."

* * *

Ruby was curled on the couch in her pajamas when Aurora arrived home after school. "Aurora!" She made grabbing motions in the air as Aurora poked her head into the living room. "Come see."

Aurora joined her on the couch. "What is it?"

"The police chief is on the news talking about the deaths."

"Oh. Is there something new?"

"I hope so. The square was like a ghost town earlier. I was sure it would be busy even with everyone staying home, but the phone didn't ring once. I closed early."

"Where's Dad? Did he go to the shop today?"

"Oh, you know your dad. Mike Geller doesn't let little things like mummy plagues get between him and the engine of an old Mustang." Ruby gestured toward the television as the police chief addressed the very small crowd of people outside City Hall.

The reporters bombarded the police chief with questions. "Chief Warbello, have you discovered the cause of death?" "Is this some sort of virus?" "Will the CDC get involved?" "Is it safe to leave our homes?"

Chief Warbello was a stern, no-nonsense sort of man. He lifted his hands impatiently. "First, I would like to assure everyone that it is perfectly safe to leave your homes. A virus has been ruled out as the cause of the four recent deaths."

There were more questions, but he silenced them all with a sharp look.

"We have been in communication with other ME offices around the country and have discovered that there have been other cases of this nature and none have been determined to have been caused by a virus of any kind. The conclusions made in those cases are similar to the conclusions made by Dr. Carr. These appear to be cases of some sort of extreme dehydration, the cause of which we have yet to conclusively determine. Coroners in other counties confirm that only one or two of these cases were discovered. There is no reason, at this time, to believe there will be more deaths."

"Oh, thank god," Ruby breathed.

"I'm glad things are going to get back to normal around here."

"Well, it was a little fun."

"What? What are you talking about?"

"I did get to close the shop and spend all day catching up on my soaps."

"Oh, Ruby, that is not a good reason to wish for a widespread epidemic."

"I know, I know, but I really, really miss daytime television." Aurora opened her mouth to retort, but Ruby flapped her hands. "Shh. Shh. What is he talking about now?"

"I don't know. You were talking."

"Shh!"

"...I would like to take this opportunity to invite everyone to the annual

Spring Festival next week, which will still be held this year, despite the tragedies." Chief Warbello sounded stiff, as though he was reading a script. "It will be a time to celebrate life and honor the dead."

"I was wondering about that," Ruby admitted. "They ordered hundreds of flowers, and I had them all shipped in. I thought the shop was going to go bankrupt."

"Is that all you were worried about?"

"No! Not at all." Ruby's ears turned pink. "But I was a little worried about it."

"I'm glad the shop is saved. Some people lost their lives, but the shop was saved."

"Hey, I am not insensitive to the tragedy! It's just...well, anyway, I am glad they are still having the festival. After everything that's happened, the town needs something like that."

"Yeah. I think you're right about that."

Ruby clapped her hands together in excitement. "Let's get our hair done."

"What?"

"I feel like we dodged a bullet. I want to do something to celebrate life, like the chief said."

Aurora smiled. "Sure. I'd like that."

"I'll make an appointment for Friday afternoon after school. I'll even leave work early, and we can meet downtown."

"Okay. That sounds really good."

Ruby leapt off the couch. "I'll call Sherri right now. I'm sure she can fit us in." She paused in the doorway. "Should we get our nails done, too?"

"Of course we should."

"Maybe I should schedule pedicures, too."

"Why not?"

"And my eyebrows."

"Oh, yes, they are looking raggedy."

"Aurora Sky! Excuse me!"

"I hope you're planning to pay for this. My allowance doesn't cover mani-pedi-haircuts and eyebrow waxes."

Ruby laughed. "Of course! It's my treat. It's been a while since I've gotten to do girly things with my favorite niece."

Aurora smiled as Ruby disappeared into the kitchen. Her phone trilled on the couch cushion beside her. She sensed from the insistent tone of the ring that it was Josie. "Hey, Jos."

"Aurora!"

"You heard, then?"

"Heard what?"

"The police chief announced the deaths weren't caused by a virus, just dehydration. Isn't that why you called?"

"No. I don't typically talk about death in any serious fashion. That's good news, I guess."

"Yeah, well, I'm sure there's probably a little more to it. But he said there weren't any signs of any sort of virus. There have been other incidents around the country of other people dying like that. In those cases, it didn't turn out to be a mummy plague, either."

Josie snorted. "It figures the whole town would go crazy over something so silly. I knew it wasn't a virus all along."

Aurora rolled her eyes. "If you didn't call about that, what's up?"

"Seriously? What's up? What's up with you? What happened with Sable today? You totally ditched us to hang out with him all day!"

"I did not. We just have some of the same classes, and we were doing homework together. Actually, we have most of the same classes. I don't even know why. It turns out he doesn't even need to be in school. He could graduate any time he wants."

"Maybe he took those classes because you're in them."

"Oh, come on. That's stupid. How would he know what classes I was in? He didn't even know me before school."

"Yes, he did. You met him at the party."

"Barely. He probably didn't even remember my name after that. Anyway, it doesn't matter. Even if he did know me, he didn't take any classes just because I'm in them. We don't have most of them at the same time, so what would be the point? We just studied."

"No lovey-dovey moon eyes over your textbooks?" Josie sounded disappointed.

"No. There was none of that. I am sure you would have seen it if there was. I assume you were spying most of the time."

"Oh, we were. But you had your heads together most of the day. I suppose you didn't notice the bitch twins giving you the stink eye?"

Aurora hadn't. She was surprised; under normal circumstances, she had an internal bully homing beacon. She always knew when Sierra or the twins were within a hundred foot radius. "No. They were there?"

"Yes. You didn't even notice them. You were too busy making googly eyes at Sable."

"Oh, I was not."

"Please. Really, nothing happened?"

"Really."

"I still think he might like you."

"I wish I could tell," she admitted. "Sometimes I think he could, and other times he's so cold I just can't figure him out."

"That's what makes him so exciting, right"

"A little. So, are you going to the Spring Festival next week?"

"Oh, is that still going on?"

"Yes. Chief Warbello announced it on the news."

"Sweet! Yeah. Of course I'm going. I love the festival. I get to wear a sundress and eat things that are bad for me and listen to free live music. Oh, and shop. Yes. Lots of shopping."

Aurora laughed. "Ruby is taking me to the salon to get my hair and nails done."

"Fancy! Well, you do need to look good if you are going to catch sexy, sexy, mysterious Sable."

"It did cross my mind."

"So what are you going to wear?"

"Is that really all you can think about right now? We just escaped a town-wide pandemic, and it's more than a week away."

"Yeah, yeah. I'm horrible and shallow. So what are you going to wear?"

* * *

Sable scowled at the words on his computer screen. *"Authorities have discovered similar deaths in Maine, Vermont, Rhode Island, North Carolina, Massachusetts, and Connecticut..."* Yeah. Sable knew about the ones in Maine. And Connecticut. And Massachusetts. The Jaynes had never been to Rhode Island, North Carolina or Vermont.

The news articles hadn't mentioned New Hampshire or New York, but the Jaynes had been there, too, and Sable knew the authorities would find something there if they looked hard enough. He suspected Warbello had only dug far enough to assure himself and New Coventry that the deaths would not continue indefinitely. He was probably dead wrong.

He checked his hastily scribbled notes. The Landrys didn't own any inns in Rhode Island or North Carolina, but they had locations in Vermont and South Carolina. A search for suspicious deaths and mysterious illnesses in South Carolina turned up nothing more than food poisoning and unrelated outbreaks. Had there simply been no bodies?

Sable leaned back in his chair and pushed his hands through his hair. He sighed. It didn't matter. There were more of them. More Jivina. And they were here, in New Coventry. It could be the Landrys. Perhaps they'd been more careful in South Carolina. Perhaps they could control themselves—for a little while.

The other Jivina in New Coventry weren't controlling themselves now.

He scowled down at his notes. *Blaine Daniels.* He didn't know anything about him. Aurora hadn't told him much, but Daniels was close to her family. She would probably know something more. If she knew more...He put it out of his head for the moment. He had bigger things to worry about right now.

Blaine Daniels kept a low profile. Sable couldn't find anything about him on the internet. He didn't even have a Facebook page. He might be too busy for that sort of thing, or he might do his business under the table. He might be using a fake name. It didn't mean anything, really.

He sighed. It could be any of them. It could even be someone who'd been in town longer, someone who'd been able to control themselves until now. It wasn't a large town, but it was large enough that the search would be daunting. He'd have to start at the top.

He glanced back at his screen. *"Despite the recent tragedies, Chief Warbello and Mayor Alley have announced that the annual Spring Festival will still be held as planned next week. This year, it will be a celebration of life and honor for the dead..."*

Spring Festival. All these small towns had things like that, and everyone always looked at him funny if he didn't show up and pretend to show town spirit. No normal teenaged boy wanted to show spirit for anything except sports or video games or losing their virginity. His parents would insist he put on his human mask and parade around as though there was nothing strange or dangerous going on.

He squeezed his eyes shut. Unbidden, her face swam into his mind once more. She would probably be at the festival. She seemed like the sort of girl who liked things like that. She probably spread town spirit everywhere she went.

Maybe it wouldn't be all bad.

He looked down at the notes he'd made in study hall. The Landrys were new in town. They ran inns all other the country. They had a daughter, Ariel, who was around his age. Blaine Daniels was dating Aurora's aunt. He and his partner flipped houses all over the country. The Jaynes were new in town, had been all over the east coast and were definitely Jivina. Aurora hadn't given him that last one; he'd added his own commentary.

He didn't know where Daniels and his partner had been. He wondered if death followed them like it did the Jaynes. There were dots to connect somewhere. He just didn't know where to look. He wished life was more like television and movies. At least in them, the monsters could smell or sense each other. The Jivina had no such magic.

He leaned back in his chair. Aurora would know more. She would probably tell him anything. There was something so open and trusting about her, and it wasn't good. It was very, very bad, especially now. She shouldn't be anywhere near any of this, but she kept popping up everywhere—at school, downtown, at his house, in his head.

And if there was another Jivina close to her...

She wasn't safe if her aunt's boyfriend was one of them. She wasn't safe if her classmate was one of them. She wasn't safe with him or his family.

He shot to his feet to pace the room. He paused a moment to stare out his

252

window. It was dark, and millions of stars twinkled in the night sky. She loved the stars.

If she'd just stop popping up everywhere, it would make things so much easier.

Chapter Twelve

It wasn't quite warm enough for sundresses the Saturday of the annual Spring Festival, but Josie wasn't letting that stop her. She cooed over Aurora's and Ruby's hair and nails. Ruby was disappointed. She held out a foot with a tragic expression.

"I just wish we could show off our new toenails. We spent hours at the salon last night!"

Aurora rolled her eyes behind Ruby's back. She didn't care much about fancy toenails, and she'd only let the stylist trim her long, strawberry blonde waves, though Ruby had tried to convince her to try a new look. She didn't want a new look. She liked her look just fine.

"Then we went out for burgers at Archie's," Aurora told Josie, smiling. "It was the best."

"Did you tell her about your special time with--"

Aurora shushed Josie with a hiss. Ruby lifted her perfectly sculpted eyebrows. "Oh, are you really going to keep that from me after I just took you out for all that pampering?"

"There's nothing to tell. Josie is just making a big deal out of nothing."

"It not nothing!" Josie argued. "It's Sable Jayne."

"The new kid in town, huh?" Ruby's eyes glittered.

"Yes."

"He's cute."

"I know, right?" Josie gushed. "He's all aflutter over Aurora."

"What?" Ruby turned to her niece with a reproachful expression. "Is this true? Have you been keeping secrets from me, Aurora Sky?"

"No, it isn't true." She glared at Josie, but her friend ignored her and plunged on ahead.

"He rescued her from Jesse at the school dance."

"And then he ditched me without saying goodbye," Aurora reminded her sharply.

254

"And then he spent the whole day studying with her when the rest of the school didn't show up for classes."

"The whole day?"

"He needed help with Spanish," Aurora grumbled.

"I don't know that many boys who spend the entire day with someone they don't like," Josie told her.

"Well, I don't think he dislikes me. You're just blowing it all out of proportion."

"But you like him, right?" Ruby liked being one of the girls now and again. Aurora didn't mind. She was like a mother who didn't disapprove of things that were fun.

"Well..."

"Of course she does!" Josie replied for her.

"Josie! Can't you just keep my secrets for once?"

"You have to keep secrets from me?" Ruby looked hurt. "I don't tell your father or anything."

"I know. I trust you. It's just...embarrassing."

"No, it isn't. There's nothing embarrassing about liking a boy," Josie told her.

"You would know."

"Yes, I would. Quite well."

Ruby sighed wistfully. "It's been so long since I got to hear good gossip. Everyone my age is all grown up and settled down or coming out of awful marriages. They talk about PTA meetings and the other moms at soccer practices and good divorce lawyers. Not the sort of gossip that's any fun. This is much better. It almost makes me feel young again."

"Ruby, you are young."

"I'm not old, but I'm not so innocent as I once was."

"You have a super hot new boyfriend!" Josie told her. "Everyone is probably super jealous."

Ruby preened. "They probably are, aren't they? Blaine is a catch, even if he doesn't stick around anywhere for very long."

"Things can change," said Aurora. "He's already thinking about it."

"Don't distract me," Ruby accused. "I want to hear about this boy."

"There's nothing to tell. Josie has already told you everything. There's nothing going on."

"But there could be. Someday," Josie told Ruby.

Ruby smiled as she checked her watch. "We'd better head downtown if we're going to find parking. I suppose you two want to ride together?"

"I thought you would be riding with Blaine. Isn't he coming?" asked Aurora.

"He has a bit of work to do first. I'll meet him there."

"Do you want to ride with us?"

"No, no. You two girls go on. I might just walk. I could use the exercise. Besides, you don't need an old lady tagging along listening in on all your secrets. We would all look stupid."

Aurora scoffed. "No, we wouldn't."

Ruby made shooing gestures with her hands. "You two go on. See you there?"

"Yeah. Of course."

"We can get a hot dog or something later."

"Sure. Bye, Ruby!"

Aurora would have liked to walk, but Josie had flatly refused to walk anywhere since she'd gotten her car on her sixteenth birthday. Besides, Josie was wearing very impractical shoes.

"So, have you talked to Sable lately?"

"No," Aurora replied. "It's not like we're having text conversations every night or anything. Or ever, for that matter."

"Have you even exchanged numbers?"

"No. I've seen him at his house once or twice, but he doesn't really talk to me. He just sort of slinks around hoping not to be noticed."

"He talks to you at school."

"Sometimes. Not always. Sometimes he pretends he doesn't even know who I am. It's not really anything you're trying to make it out to be, Jos."

She sighed in disappointment. "Do you think he'll be at the festival?"

"I don't know. He seems like the sort of guy who avoids this sort of thing. But I don't really know him very well. I didn't think he would show up at the school dance, either. His weird behavior there was totally expected, though."

"It was?"

"Not the behavior you're thinking of, Josie. The part where he ditched me."

"You're forgetting the part where he danced with you. Only you."

"And then he left. I must not be a very good dancer. Maybe I ruined him for all other school dances forever."

"Ah, just give it time. Not the dancing part. You are hopeless there. The Aurora and Sable part. Sometimes these things are much better when they're drawn out."

"Not as much as you drag them out."

"Well, what would you do if he asked you out today?"

"What? I don't know. Say yes, I guess."

"It's not as easy as it sounds. Have you ever actually said yes to a date before?"

"No. I mostly just say no. To Jesse."

Josie laughed. "Well, you see? You don't know. It might be scarier than you think."

"Is that what your problem is? You're too scared to say yes?"

"I just think I'm not ready. I wouldn't know what to do with a boy if I actually had one."

"Well...I think I am."

"Really?"

"Not to go out with just any guy. But if Sable asked me...I would say yes. And see what happened." Aurora waved her hand dismissively. "Anyway, it's stupid. He's not going to do that."

"You never know. I was just making sure you're prepared if he does."

"Well, thanks. I guess."

The Spring Festival was already in full swing when they arrived, and Josie had to find a parking spot nearly as far from the town square as Aurora's house. The streets teemed with couples, families and groups of friends wandering around, talking and laughing over the music, which they could probably hear all the way across town.

"We should have just walked," Aurora remarked smugly.

"Come on. I know you like that sort of thing, but I didn't get this car for nothing. I had to work for it."

"You had to spend six months begging and pleading until you got it."

"That is harder than you think. Also, I had to get good grades and come home on time every weekend. Unlike you, I don't have 'a reasonable time' for my curfew."

Aurora laughed as they plunged into the thick crowd. The band started up a lively cover of Brown Eyed Girl. She liked them, even if they played mostly oldies songs she didn't know. The Willie Vinnies had been playing together for forty years, since they were in high school, and they usually played the local festivals and events.

"Do you see Diana?" Josie asked, straining to peer over the heads of the crowd.

"She and Zach came early. They wanted to get a good spot on the lawn."

The Willie Vinnies were set up in the large gazebo in the center of the square, surrounded by a large lawn that was already turning richly green in the early spring warmth. Currently, it was covered with a kaleidoscope of colors as people spread out on blankets and camp chairs to watch the band and visit with friends.

The local shops were wide open and turning a roaring trade as people wandered in and out. Street vendors set up along the perimeter of the lawn, peddling food, drinks and interesting merchandise. A few buskers were attempting to gather small crowds, but their lonely guitars and horns were completely drowned out by the rowdy Willie Vinnies. The buskers came every year, but none of them expected much more than a few dollars. Most of them just liked being seen by the crowd.

It took several minutes of winding through the maze on the lawn to find Diana and Zach, spread on a large blanket with Cera and Shane. Aurora and

Josie greeted them enthusiastically, happy to have a place to sit away from the throng. Diana grinned. "Hi, guys. Sit down."

"You got a great spot," Aurora said. They were close enough to see the band and the people who wandered around the square, but they weren't so close the music drowned out their conversation. Diana and Zach were very particular.

"We got here around eight," Diana admitted, looking a little embarrassed. "Zach wanted to get the best spot."

Aurora laughed. Zach did not look the least embarrassed by his strange habits. "There is no sense coming to these things if it's going to be uncomfortable. I like my space."

Aurora shivered a bit in her light jacket as a breeze swept across the lawn. "Anyone want to get some coffee?"

Josie hopped up. "I'll go with you."

Cera and Shane held up their cups in reply. Diana glanced at Zach. He shook his head. "You go on. We'll hold onto the blanket."

Josie clapped her hands together in excitement. "I want to see who's here."

"How will you be able to tell?" Diana asked. "There are so many people here. It's completely out of control."

"It's always like this and you say the same thing every year," Aurora told her. "You know you love it."

Diana rolled her eyes, but she allowed Josie to drag her along toward the coffee truck. There was a long line. It was still early, and the day hadn't quite warmed up with the sun. The band started up a lively cover of Johnny B Goode. Aurora tapped her foot to the beat. She liked this song. Her father liked it, and he was even known to sing it softly to himself as he messed around under the hood of old cars or went over the shop's books.

Josie and Diana gossiped about the people around them, as usual. Aurora tuned them out, looking around. She caught sight of Adam and Mariah Jayne sticking out of the crowd like two pillars of blinding light. Her stomach flipped excitedly, but she couldn't see any of their children around them. The doctors watched the band, holding hands and smiling at each other.

"The Jaynes are here."

Josie and Diana snapped their eyes to her, then looked around the crowd to find them. "Where?" Diana asked. Despite her skepticism, she seemed to like the Jaynes.

"Do you see Sable?" Josie craned her neck around.

"No. Just his parents."

Josie's shoulders sagged. "But that might mean he's around. Or will be around."

"I'm not going to let my happiness rely on whether or not he shows up," Aurora told her. "That's no way to be."

"I always let my happiness rely on who shows up."

"I know. And you have a miserable time complaining about how the boys you like aren't here."

Josie smiled. "Well, I am trying to get better."

Diana scoffed. "No, you aren't. Just Wednesday you were complaining about how James Rapier didn't show up in Chem class."

Josie laughed, and she didn't argue. They didn't see any of her crushes or Aurora's as they got their coffee and returned to the blanket to join their friends. Cera grinned at them. "Can you believe the scare this week? The whole town was acting like they'd just announced the second coming of the plague or something. It was so silly."

"Oh, come on," Josie told her, poking her playfully in the ribs. "You weren't in school either."

"Not because I thought I would get sick. I just wanted a free day off. Most of the teachers didn't even show up, so I didn't miss anything. You're the ones who were dumb enough to actually go."

Aurora smiled. "It turned out all right."

"Can you believe those deaths, though?" Josie said. "It's just crazy."

"Do you believe what the police say about it being some freak sickness or something?" Cera asked.

"What else could it be?" Shane put in. "I mean, I've never heard of any kind of virus that just dehydrates you until you're dead. Not like that, anyway."

"Maybe it was something they ate." It sounded stupid no matter how many times Josie said it. Aurora didn't think she'd given it much thought.

"I heard they think it could be some gas poisoning or something, but they don't know what sort of gas could have done it," Zach said.

"Maybe," Aurora murmured. "But Susan and Ellen died in such a weird place."

"Well, it's not like someone murdered them," Diana told her. "It's just too weird. No one's ever been murdered like that."

"Ugh," Josie said, scrunching up her nose. "Can we talk about something else? It's too creepy, thinking about them all dried up like mummies--"

"Stop, stop!" Shane ordered, holding up his hands. "We're supposed to be done talking about this. It's Spring Festival. We're supposed to be listening to music and cracking jokes and eating junk food and acting like nothing weird happened."

"You're right," Diana agreed. "Let's drop it. There's no sense speculating about it. It's not like we know more than the police, and when they know, they'll tell us."

Cera lifted a finger to point across the lawn. "Oh, look who's here."

She was pointing toward Sierra, who clung to Van's arm, smiling radiantly. Van didn't even look like he was having a terrible time, but Aurora never could read that glint in his strange dark eyes.

"Is she still going out with him?" Cera continued. "I thought she would have been sick of him by now."

"Please," Josie said. "He's wicked hot and totally mysterious. I would think he would get sick of her first. She probably likes showing him off like a pony."

They all laughed at this. It seemed to be precisely what Sierra was doing. She led him around the lawn as though they were on display, taking the long way to join Brooke and Claire on their blanket. The twins were nowhere to be found. Aurora guessed they were still holding a grudge against their friend. Sierra didn't look like this bothered her at all. In fact, she looked especially pretty today, which wasn't fair because there was a mean, smug edge to her smile.

"They deserve each other," Aurora muttered. "He's not any better than she is."

Cera looked at her in surprise. "Do you know him?"

"I've met him a couple times."

"Oh, yeah." Suddenly, Cera was grinning like the cat that caught the canary, and Aurora knew she hadn't forgotten anything. "I remember your little scene with his brother at the dance. Do you two have something going on?"

"No."

"Are you sure? Everyone's been talking about it. You know, how Sable Jayne swept in and stole you from Jesse Drake."

"Everyone is making a really big deal out of this."

"It was very dramatic. Like a scene in a movie," Josie told her.

"Great. That's just super. Everyone's talking about it. Nothing is going on! We just know each other. I suppose we're sort of...well, not really friends. We just know each other. We happen upon each other now and again."

"Uh, huh." There was a gleam in Cera's eyes. "It sounds a little... romantic."

"It isn't."

"Sure. So how much do you know about them?"

"The Jaynes? I guess I know as much as anyone else. They move around a lot. Sable has been home-schooled forever, but he decided he wanted to see what school is like. Van is...well, I don't think he does anything. Sable says he never did graduate from high school, but he could have." She cut off. She didn't think Sable would appreciate her revealing what he'd said in private conversations.

"Actually, you seem to know a lot more than anyone else knows," said Shane. "I have a couple classes with Sable, and I've never seen him talk to anyone more than he has to."

"Really? No one? He doesn't have any friends?"

"No. Just you."

"And he talks to you a lot," Josie reminded her.

Cera lifted her eyebrows. Aurora gave her a cold look, and she bit off anything she might have said. Despite her denials, Aurora's stomach fluttered. Was that true? She'd never seen Sable talk to anyone else for any length of time, but she wasn't with him all the time. He had opportunities for numerous conversations when she wasn't looking.

She wasn't the sort of girl who made assumptions. She didn't know how Sable felt about her. He might tolerate her, but that didn't mean he liked her. He'd never given her any sign that he was interested in anything more than those few conversations. In fact, half the time he acted as though he would rather not be having them. He was so hot and cold, sometimes she was almost sure he disliked her as much as he obviously disliked everyone else.

She realized her friends were waiting for an answer. "Don't read anything into it. We've just happened to run into each other a couple times. It's not like he seeks me out or anything."

Cera sighed dreamily. "I wish I could run into him now and again. He's so cute. He's like a character in a movie. Like a romantic, broody leading man or something." At Shane's swift sideways glance, she added, "I mean, not that I'm into guys like him or anything. I'm not into the quiet, broody type."

"Every girl is into the quiet, broody type," Josie muttered to Aurora, but she didn't say it loud enough for Shane to hear.

"You people are all so dramatic," Diana scolded them.

"Well, nothing interesting ever happens here," Josie complained. "We have to make our fun where we can, and sometimes that just includes reading dramatic romances and watching movies so we can fawn over the main characters for a little while."

Aurora rolled her eyes. "I think I prefer real life. I don't mind that it's not as exciting as books and movies."

"That's easy for you to say. We aren't all being pursued by the hottest boys in school."

"Stop," Aurora ordered. "It isn't like that. You're embarrassing me."

Josie didn't relent. "Please. It so totally is." At Aurora's sullen glare, she sighed. "But I will let you off the hook this one time because friends don't tease friends."

"But if something does happen," Cera put in, "we all want to know every single tiny detail."

"Of course you do."

"Nothing like this ever happens to us," Josie said sulkily to Cera.

"Not all of us are all sweet and pretty and innocent like Aurora."

Aurora leapt abruptly to her feet, but her angry retort died on her lips as they all looked up at her in dismay. "I have to find a restroom."

She spotted Sierra and Van wrapped in each other's arms nearby. She scoffed in disgust. They stared into each other's eyes, and if they were anyone other than two of the most horrible people she knew, she might think they genuinely liked each other. Considering the way Sierra treated her best friends and Van treated his brother, she wasn't sure if either one of them could genuinely like anyone.

The doctors Jayne were watching them, scowling. She had never seen either of them scowl. The expressions were so foreign on their faces she was taken aback. She'd come to see Mariah as the sort of woman who was always smiling, always serene and soothing. She wondered why they looked so annoyed with their son.

She knew Sierra was an evil witch, but parents usually liked her. She came from a good family, and she did well in school. Most people considered her a good catch for their sons. She didn't have any idea how old Van really was. Maybe he was older than she thought. Or, she thought, perhaps one of their patients had told them what Sierra was really like, and they didn't want someone like her anywhere near their son.

She turned away from the Jaynes and stopped dead in her tracks when she spotted Sable, craning his neck to look over the crowd. He didn't notice her. He relaxed suddenly and strode quickly to speak to his parents. They stopped scowling abruptly. As one, the Jaynes turned to walk toward Gwen and Harold Landry, who stood beside the bandstand, grinning and holding hands as they bobbed to the music.

Aurora watched curiously as Sable and his parents approached the Landrys, all smiles and charisma. The Landrys shook their hands warmly. Aurora couldn't tell what they were saying to each other, but the conversation seemed mundane and pleasant enough. Sable wasn't talking. His eyes darted between Gwen and Harold with an intensity that made no sense to her.

She felt like she was spying, but at least no one would notice in this crowd.

The Willie Vinnies started up a new song, and the Landrys excused themselves to dance, grinning apologetically. The Jaynes smiled at them, but the smiles slipped instantly as the Landrys turned away, leaving something strange in their faces. They looked uncertain and...disappointed. Whatever they had been expecting from the meeting, they hadn't gotten it.

Sable nodded grimly at his parents and disappeared into the crowd.

What is going on?

She would never ask him because then she would have to admit she'd been spying on him. She shook herself. The Jaynes might be acting a little strange, but no stranger than she was, skulking around and watching them from afar. She spun back toward the main street, hoping to catch sight of someone she knew or at least find someplace to hang out for a while before she faced her friends again.

She sighed in relief as she spotted Ruby's red-head beside Blaine by the coffee truck. They held hands and smiled around at the scene. Ruby grinned as Aurora approached them. Suddenly, she felt much better.

"Hey, Aurora," Blaine greeted warmly.

"Hi, Blaine. I thought you wouldn't be here until later."

He shrugged and looked down at Ruby. They exchanged a smile that made Aurora's heart ache a little. She wondered what it would be like to share a smile like that with someone.

"Yeah. I decided work could wait. I didn't want to miss my first Spring Festival. Ruby went on and on about it."

Ruby laughed. "Oh, admit it. You couldn't wait to see me."

He leaned down to press his lips to hers. "You got me."

When Ruby turned back to her niece, her eyes were bright with happiness. "Are you having a good time so far?"

"Yes." She suddenly felt foolish for letting her friends' teasing upset her.

"We always love the festivals," Ruby told her boyfriend. "We've been coming every year since Aurora was a baby. Rosa never missed them. I was afraid they'd cancel it with the scare. They outdid themselves this year, though. The mayor probably wanted to make sure everyone knows there's nothing to get worked up about."

Blaine's smile froze on his face, but the strange expression passed so quickly, Aurora was sure she had imagined it.

"Have you tried the hotdogs yet?" Ruby asked. "They're amazing as always."

"No, not yet. I thought you were going to wait for me."

"Oh, Blaine couldn't wait." Ruby rolled her eyes with a grin. "He said he was just simply starving."

He chuckled. "That was just a light snack. I could eat about three more. Come on. I'll buy you girls one."

Ruby laughed and clutched his arm. Aurora smiled at him. "Sure." She wasn't hungry, but she didn't mind an excuse to be away from Josie and the others, who were making a big deal out of nothing. If she was truly honest with herself, she was hoping to run into Sable. Maybe it wasn't exactly nothing.

Ruby seized Aurora's arm and leaned down to murmur in her ear. "So, have you seen that boy yet?"

"Yes. He's in the crowd somewhere. But, no matter what Josie says, he's not seeking me out or anything. I don't think he's noticed me at all."

"Well, give it time. I am sure he will notice you once he gets to know you."

Aurora sighed. Everyone always said stuff like that.

"How about the one who likes you?"

She hadn't even thought of Jesse. "No. I haven't seen him. I think he's avoiding me."

"Are you disappointed?"

"No. It's a relief, actually. It's been kind of nice being left alone." Perhaps Jesse had finally given up. She had made things pretty clear at the dance.

"Hotdogs!" Aurora hadn't realized they'd reached the stand until Blaine spun around with four hot dogs in his hands. Aurora took one. "Should we find someplace to sit down?"

"Is there any place?" Ruby looked around.

"I think we can find something, if we're clever." He grinned and led them toward an empty corner of a picnic bench. There was just enough room for the three of them.

As she turned, Aurora collided with someone in her path.

"Aurora? Are you all right?" Sable caught her arm to steady her. It was the same arm she'd been using to hold her hotdog.

She looked down at the pile of hotdog at her feet, then back up into his eyes. Her stomach flip-flopped.

Sable flushed pink with embarrassment. "Sorry. Are you okay?"

"Yeah. I'm okay. My hotdog isn't."

He bent down to pick up the remains and toss them into a nearby trash. "I'll get you a new one."

She laughed. "It's okay."

"No, I will."

"Who is this clumsy young man?" Blaine's eyes twinkled.

Aurora glanced at Sable, but she could not read his expression. "This is Sable. Sable, this is Blaine Daniels and my aunt Ruby."

She thought he would mutter an excuse and find a way to escape, but he didn't. He stuck out his hand. "Sable Jayne."

Ruby grinned. Aurora was afraid she would say something embarrassing, but Ruby no any such thing. She wasn't that kind of aunt; she was the good kind. "Nice to meet you Sable. We've met your parents. Welcome to New Coventry."

"Thanks." He didn't sound sullen at all. He was so polite she wasn't sure he was even the same person she knew.

"How do you know Aurora?" Blaine asked.

Aurora was amused that he was taking over the role of protective uncle while Mike was unavailable to perform his fatherly duties. Ruby was obviously too thrilled that her niece was actually talking to a boy to ask any intrusive questions.

"We're in class together," said Aurora because Sable seemed uncertain how to answer this question.

"Ah. I see. Nice to meet you, Sable."

"You, too." There was something odd about the way Sable looked at Blaine. Aurora was sure she was the only one who noticed. When had she become able to interpret his subtle, incomprehensible expressions?

Never. She'd never been able to. So she was probably just getting carried away.

"Your family just moved here, huh?" asked Blaine. "I just arrived a few

267

months ago myself. What do you think of it?"

Sable's eyes darted to Aurora for an ephemeral instant. "It's all right, I guess. It's about like most places I've lived."

"Well, you're still young. You can't appreciate things yet like you will when you get to be my age." He smiled. "I don't mean that to sound condescending. I just mean I have pissed away enough of my youth to know when I have something worth holding on to in my old age." He turned his smile on Ruby and wrapped an arm around her shoulders.

With Sable standing next to her, their affection was embarrassing. Aurora smiled tightly. Sable glanced at her again. This time, she had absolutely no delusions that she understood what that look meant. His face was perfectly unreadable.

"Why don't you join us, Sable?" Blaine asked. Aurora cringed inwardly. Boys like Sable did not sit around with random girls and their families—if Blaine could be considered family; under the circumstances, it was close enough.

"Okay."

Aurora glanced at him in surprise. She didn't suggest he reconsider, but she wasn't sure she wanted him there. There were definitely too many opportunities for someone to embarrass her.

Sable only had eyes for Blaine as they perched at the edge of the picnic table. He rarely showed interest in anything anyone had to say at anytime, but perhaps Blaine was just young and cool enough to warrant the attention of a teenaged boy.

Maybe he just admired him because he built things. Men seemed to like men who built things, in a gruff, grudging, manly sort of way. She thought they probably just liked being able to talk about guy things instead of trying to sound sensitive and enlightened for their women. She doubted Sable talked much about guy things, though. He rarely talked at all. The only man she'd ever seen him around was his brother.

Blaine cut off in the middle of a long-winded story about wainscoting and grinned at Sable. "I'm sorry. This must be incredibly boring for you. Ruby always listens when I talk about work, but I can tell when her eyes start to glaze over. It's been a while for me. What exactly do teenaged boys talk about, Sable?"

"What everyone else talks about, I guess. It's just usually grosser."

268

They laughed. "What year are you in?"

"I'm a senior. I homeschooled for most of my life, so I'm a year ahead."

"Ah. Any plans for after you graduate?"

Aurora tried to ignore Ruby's gleaming eyes from across the table. It was surreal sitting next to Sable, listening to her aunt's boyfriend question him about his plans for the future. She wasn't sure whether to laugh or to hide her face in her hands.

Sable took it in stride. "I'm not sure."

"Well, it's about time to start thinking about it, don't you think, even if you are a year ahead?"

"Yeah. I kind of like the idea of engineering." His eyes slid quickly to Aurora again, and she wondered if he really had thought about it.

Blaine raised his eyebrows. "Ah. The boring stuff."

"It's not boring." His voice was so even, Aurora was afraid he was offended. When she looked at him, though, he looked completely relaxed.

"Well, not to some," Blaine conceded. "Some people get really fired up about all that stuff. What sort of engineering are you thinking about?"

"Mechanical. I like figuring out how things work."

"I get it. I prefer to work with my hands. There's a lot of satisfaction. Even though I'm in construction, I recommend getting a college degree, no matter what it's in. There's no other way to get by these days. You can always do something else later. My degree's in business, and I couldn't care less about that stuff these days. I let other people do that for me."

"I think I will get a degree. I'm not sure what I want to do, but it seems like the only logical next step."

"So you're not planning to be a doctor like your parents?" Ruby finally entered the conversation, smiling at him.

"No. It's not really my thing."

Who was this guy? He smiled pleasantly, and he looked so normal, Aurora almost didn't recognize him.

"So you travel a lot for work?" he asked Blaine.

"Oh, yeah. Mostly New England. I'm from Massachusetts, so I like to stick close to home."

"Where have you lived?"

"Oh, quite a few places. Here and there and everywhere, it seems like."

The band started up an enthusiastic cover of an Elvis song, and Blaine's attention turned toward the stage. He tapped his foot along to the music.

He turned back to them with a grin. He'd completely forgotten the conversation. He glanced down at Ruby. "Looks like there are some people dancing. You guys want to join them?"

Ruby looked at Aurora with huge, sparkling eyes and nodded encouragingly. Aurora glanced at Sable. He looked completely impassive.

"You guys go ahead." Aurora smiled brightly to cover up the awkwardness of the moment.

"I owe Aurora a hotdog," Sable added.

"I guess it's just us, then. See you guys later!" Ruby waved over her shoulder as Blaine pulled her away, into the crowd in front of the stage.

For several moments, Sable watched after them with a thoughtful expression. Aurora suspected it would be impolite to ask what he was thinking. For now, he was still there, and she didn't want to go and spoil it by disturbing him. She tried to look as relaxed and comfortable in the silence as possible, looking out over the crowd as though she actually saw them.

Finally, Sable looked at her. "Come on. I'll get you a hotdog."

"No, thanks. I didn't really want one; I just didn't want to be impolite. We can just say we did. Ruby and Blaine will never know."

His mouth twitched as though he was going to smile. "Maybe later, then."

Her stomach flipped over. She smiled. "Sure."

"Your aunt and her boyfriend seem nice."

"They are nice. I like Blaine. He's cool."

"He's been seeing your aunt a lot?"

"Yeah. They've been spending a lot of time together."

"Do you know much about him?"

"What do you mean?"

"Never mind."

An awkward silence fell over them. For a moment, she thought Sable actually looked worried, but she couldn't imagine what about.

The strangeness didn't last. He looked at her, and she felt something crackle in the air as the expression in his eyes changed almost imperceptibly. The worried look was gone. He held her gaze steadily. She opened her mouth to say something, but she didn't know what she could say when he was looking at her as though he were seeing straight into her.

"Well, here you two are together again." Aurora couldn't think of a single voice in the world she wanted to hear less than the one that crashed through the strange, intense silence.

Sierra stood beside their table, smiling.

Aurora snapped her head up in surprise. Van lurked at Sierra's shoulder, peering at them with an amused glint in his eyes. Aurora braced herself for an attack even as she felt Sable slide closer to her on the bench so their legs nearly touched. She could almost feel the heat from his glower as he looked at his brother.

Sierra wasn't poised for attack. Her smile wasn't nasty. It was almost... sweet. Aurora had seen that sweet smile before, but Sierra had never directed it at her. This Sierra was a completely different person than the one she had come to know and hate. She didn't trust that smile. There was something lurking behind it. There always was when Sierra smiled like that.

"Well, this is cozy, isn't it?" Van said.

"It is, isn't it?" Sierra wrapped her arm around his waist, and he draped his around her shoulders in return. The edges of her smile sharpened. "Hey, I have an idea."

Aurora narrowed her eyes suspiciously. She chanced a glance at Sable. His face was blank, but his eyes glittered oddly. He met her gaze for the briefest second before he looked back at Van. She could feel the tension in his body.

"Why don't we all do something?" Sierra continued. "Together."

Aurora blinked stupidly at her. She opened and closed her mouth. She glanced at Sable again as though he might have some help to offer. He didn't meet her eyes.

"Yes, why don't we?" Van added.

"I don't know..." Aurora didn't like the wavering note in her voice.

"What's the matter, Aurora? You aren't afraid of us, are you?" His grin was wolfish. "We don't bite."

Something about the way he said this caused her to believe exactly the opposite.

"It's just a double date," he continued in a purr. "I'm sure my brother wants to."

Sable's mouth tightened into a thin line, but he didn't return Aurora's gaze. A muscle worked in his jaw. His eyes were on his brother, but she felt him move closer to her side until his thigh pressed into hers.

The air around the two brothers was oddly electric, as though a single spark might set them both aflame.

"Unless we misunderstood," Sierra drawled in a deceptively sweet voice. "I thought there was something going on between you two. Did I make a mistake?"

Sable's chin snapped up. "No." His voice was cold.

She was shocked, and if he were looking at her now, she wouldn't meet his eyes. When she finally chanced a glance back at him, he seemed to be having a silent, furious conversation with Van through their locked gazes.

"Sure. We'll go," Sable said.

"What?" Aurora knew she sounded stupid, but she didn't care.

His gaze flicked to her for a split second, and there was something so inarguable in his expression, she snapped her mouth shut against her own protests.

"Sounds fun," he said in a low voice that might have sounded serene if his jaw wasn't clenched so tight. That tone did not indicate that he thought it sounded fun. Obviously, there was something going on between the brothers that she didn't know about. She wondered how she'd suddenly gotten wrapped up in whatever battle of wills they were waging against each other.

How did she always end up in the wrong place at the wrong time? A date with Sable would have been nice—a double date with Sierra and Van sounded like a very unique and awkward form of psychological torture. She didn't have a lot of choice in the matter, not now that Sable had agreed on her behalf.

"How about tomorrow?" Sierra said, grinning like a shark that has come upon its favorite prey and decided to play with it for a while before actually eating it.

"To-tomorrow?" Aurora repeated, flushing slightly as she heard how ridiculous she sounded.

"Fine," Sable spoke up curtly.

Van grinned, his eyes glinting with some malicious amusement. "We could take a walk through the woods."

"No," Sable snapped so sharply Aurora looked at him in surprise.

Sierra was ever gracious. "How about we go to Lynchburg for the day? We could get lunch and walk around downtown."

Aurora stared incredulously at Sierra as though she was suddenly speaking a foreign language. Sable spoke through clenched teeth. "Fine."

Aurora realized her input was not necessary in this conversation.

"Great," Sierra said with exaggerated enthusiasm. "We'll pick you up at ten, Aurora. See you then." She flipped her hair and flicked her fingers in a wave.

Van gave Aurora a parting smile that set her skin crawling.

Sable looked at Aurora when they were alone once more. She couldn't tell what he was thinking. "I don't know what that was all about," she said. "I'm pretty sure this is some plot to embarrass me horribly or something. We don't have to go. In fact, we shouldn't go. I know you only agreed so you wouldn't embarrass me in front of Sierra."

"We can't back out now. It's too late."

"Sierra would never let me hear the end of it. But, if I know her, that might be better than what she has planned."

"We have to go. I won't let anything happen to you." There was something so serious in his voice she believed him instantly. "You should stay away from them."

"How? We're going out with them tomorrow. You said we have to."

His brow furrowed angrily. "Yes. We have to."

It wasn't as though one date was life or death; he didn't have to look so grave. "It doesn't—it doesn't have to be a date or anything. Not a real one," she stammered.

"Okay."

She felt awkward. What had she been hoping he would say? If she was finally going out with Sable, this was not how she imagined it. It would probably be so traumatic she would never be able to see him again without feeling the urge to run screaming. That thought was both horribly disappointing and slightly appealing.

His expression softened fractionally. "Don't worry about it, Aurora." He rose abruptly from his seat beside her. "I'll see you tomorrow."

With that, he strode away from her, disappearing as suddenly into the crowd as he'd first appeared. She dropped her head in her hands, groaning.

What was she thinking? She couldn't go through with this.

But Sable insisted. They had to. She realized, just then, that there was no way she was going to miss this, even if it did include Sierra and Van.

She sighed and rose to her feet. Her friends looked up at her with identical sheepish looks on their faces as she approached their blanket.

"Hey," Josie said tentatively. "We were just going to go look for you. Where have you been?"

"I ran into Ruby and Blaine and we got a hotdog."

Diana gave her a suspicious look. "They've been dancing for fifteen minutes. So where have you been?"

"Let me guess," Josie said, her eyes narrowed "With Sable Jayne."

"No, I—well, yes. But it's not what you think."

"Really?" Cera said. "Because I heard Sierra bragging to Callie and Cami that you two are going on a double date with her and Van."

"What?" Aurora demanded. "She—why would she say that?"

"So it's not true?" Josie knew Aurora would say no. Of course it wasn't true.

Aurora didn't say that. Her face flushed a deeper shade of red.

"It is true!" Josie was outraged.

"It's not what you think! Sable was just trying to be nice. Sierra was being nasty, probably trying to get him to reject me in front of them so she could rub it in my face. Sable was just trying to help—"

She closed her mouth abruptly as Jesse suddenly appeared beside their blanket, smiling shyly. Everyone turned to him with wary eyes, but he didn't

274

seem to have overheard any of their conversation. "Hi, Aurora."

She had had enough drama for the day. She was exhausted. "Hi, Jesse."

Her friends watched them as though they expected a bomb to drop at any moment. "Do you want to dance?"

Everyone looked at her. She didn't even feel bad for Jesse, not in this moment. "I'm not feeling very well right now, Jesse. I just want to sit here for a little while."

The last time he'd asked her to dance had gone so horribly wrong. Aurora was amazed he'd even tried again. "I get it." She'd never seen him look so shy. "Can I sit down with you?"

She opened her mouth to say something, but Josie cut across her. She swept a hand across the blanket in a welcoming gesture. "Sure!"

Aurora shot her an angry glare, but Josie looked completely unrepentant.

"You want to make sure Sable knows you're worth fighting for, right?" she whispered in Aurora's ear as Jesse took a seat on the edge of the blanket.

"That is not what I want, Josie."

"You're the one who keeps saying it's nothing. But if it is something, someone is going to need to sooth Jesse's broken heart."

She couldn't remember a time she had been so angry with Josie. She couldn't even muster a false smile for Jesse. Instead, she glanced away, directly into Sable's eyes. She was surprised he was still there. He watched her from across the lawn with narrowed eyes. Her breath quickened.

He took a step forward, as though something in her face had beckoned him.

Aurora held her breath. If he came it would create even more trouble for her. If he didn't, she would have to put up with Jesse all day. This was getting ridiculous. She just couldn't win.

Someone stopped Sable with a hand on his arm. He turned his head, but Aurora couldn't see the person to whom he was speaking. There was an earnest, deadly serious expression on his face. He glanced around the crowd with a small frown. Then his eyes met Aurora's again. He looked uncertain. It was the strangest expression she'd seen on his face yet.

She smiled at him and gave him a tiny wave. His mouth turned up just slightly in a returning smile. He nodded to her before he spun and strode away, back into the thick crowd.

"Aurora?"

She looked back at her friends. "Huh?"

Josie nudged her. "Pay attention. This is important stuff. We're taking bets on how long Sierra and Van will last."

Aurora smiled weakly. Her gaze flicked back to the place Sable had been, but he was long gone. "I'm not sure I want to take that bet.

Chapter Thirteen

Aurora had never been so nervous in her life. Her day would end in some horrible humiliation or pig's blood throwing incident. She just knew it. The fact that Sable would be there was only remotely soothing. At least he wouldn't let Van or Sierra do anything horrible to her, if he could help it. He'd never let anyone do anything horrible to her so far, anyway, and, if nothing else, she had someone on her side.

It didn't help that he was at least half the reason for her frazzled nerves.

She wore her nicest outfit. Even if it was some bizarre fake date that she didn't really understand, she wasn't going to give Sierra another reason to mess with her. She didn't want Sable to think she hadn't even bothered, even if they were perfectly clear that this wasn't a real date. She was going to hold her head high and try to enjoy herself as well as she possibly could under the circumstances. She would make a good show of it.

She did hope her favorite green sweater dress wouldn't end up drenched in blood. That would ruin even a fake date, for sure. Oh, Sierra was probably more original than that. She preferred mind games over violence, anyway. They suited her far better.

Chin up, Aurora told herself as she slung her handbag over her shoulder and hurried downstairs. *Don't let someone like Sierra Drew get the best of you. You can do this.*

Her dad was drinking coffee in his pajamas at the kitchen counter. She lifted her eyebrows as she poured herself a cup of the thick, strong black coffee. Mike liked his coffee strong. "Hey, Dad. I didn't expect to see you this morning. I thought you stayed with Julia last night."

He lifted his shoulders and glanced at her over the rim of his battered white mug. It had once read **Geller's Auto Repair**. It had been a gift from Rosalyn when he'd first opened the shop, years before Aurora had been born, and some of the letters had worn off. Now it just read **G l r Aut Rep r**. Mike had never been able to bring himself replace it. "Yeah, I did. I came home early. I have an appointment with a client in a few minutes."

"You should get dressed."

He waved his hand dismissively. "Corvette owners are always late. You look nice. Where are you off to this morning? You aren't normally up and dressed this early on a Saturday."

"Lynchburg."

"Oh? What for?"

She felt her cheeks heat. "I'm going with some...friends." It was funny, really. There wouldn't be a friend in sight, not today. In fact, she was pretty sure she could consider two of them enemies. And Sable...well, she didn't know what he was.

He didn't notice her blush. He smiled and rose to his feet to rinse out his cherished mug. "Well, don't stay out too late."

"I won't."

Mike was satisfied enough with this. He dropped a kiss on the top of her head as he hurried past to get ready for work. Aurora sighed. At least he hadn't asked for specifics. Even as laid-back as her dad was, she didn't think he would let her get away with going on a double date with Sierra Drew and the Jayne brothers, not without some explaining. She knew, whatever her answers would be, they probably wouldn't ease his mind.

The soft honk outside startled her. She sloshed coffee over the side of her mug. She frowned down at her watch. They were early. She thought she would have at least another ten minutes or so to prepare. She took a deep breath to steel her nerves. She squared her shoulders. She could do this.

She dumped her coffee hurriedly into the sink and raced to the door. She slowed as she opened it. She was going to stroll—no, saunter down the walk. As though she didn't have a care in the world. She wasn't nervous at all. This was a perfectly normal day.

It was all for nothing. The horn hadn't been from Sierra's shiny red Audi. It was Jesse, perched a little uncertainly against his motorcycle. Aurora blinked at him in surprise and paused halfway down the walk. "Jesse, what are you doing here?"

He strode toward her. "I wanted to see you." He ruffled the back of his shaggy blonde hair. "I'm sorry I've been such a jerk since the dance."

"It's okay." She sounded rushed. She needed to get rid of him before Sierra arrived with Sable and Van.

He smiled and gestured toward his motorcycle. "Do you want to go for a ride?"

"Uh...I can't."

Jesse's face fell. "Do you already have plans?"

"Yeah."

"Where are you going?"

She kept her face pleasant, but inside, she felt like screaming. "Just...to Lynchburg for the day."

"Oh. Is Josie coming to get you?"

"Ah...no."

"Then who are you going with?" There was a low, almost dangerous quality to his voice.

She opened her mouth to respond, but there was no need. At that exact moment, Sable's black sedan slid up to the house behind Jesse's bike. He was early. His timing couldn't be worse.

Sable climbed out of the car, slamming the door behind him. Jesse didn't speak as he watched the other boy stride up the walk toward them, but Aurora could feel the sudden tension in his body. It was palpable in the air.

"What are you doing here?" Jesse growled as Sable neared them.

"Picking up Aurora." There was nothing in his voice, but Aurora could sense the uncanny alertness in his entire body.

Jesse's eyes narrowed. "Is that so."

There was a slight shake in his voice. Aurora could see that he was angry—very, very angry. Sable must have sensed it, too. He moved past Jesse warily. Aurora was sure Jesse would strike him or stand in his way. Instead, he spun in place, his eyes glued to the other boy. Aurora could feel the chill radiating from Sable as he stood close at her side.

"Yes. What are you doing here?" The contemptuous in his tone was chilling. Aurora shivered.

Jesse's eyes flashed with anger as he looked at Aurora for the first time since Sable had appeared. "You're going out with him now?"

She stiffened. "No, I–"

"It's none of your business," Sable cut in coldly. "She's not your girlfriend. She can do whatever she wants. With whoever she wants."

This was not the right thing to say, and Aurora knew Sable knew that. She looked up at him sharply, and she was surprised by the rigid set of his jaw, the glint in his eyes. She tried to glare at him, but he was not paying her the slightest attention.

Jesse took a step toward Sable, his hands clenching into fists. Sable swept his arm back, shoving Aurora behind him, and stepped up to meet Jesse.

"I was here long before you," Jesse told him in a low snarl.

Sable didn't back down. Aurora didn't understand why he seemed so angry. "And you didn't get anywhere. So just leave her alone."

"Sable," Aurora snapped, her cheeks flushing with anger and embarrassment. She was right here, and she didn't appreciate being shoved to the back while they fought over her like she was a trophy. "Jesse, stop it. Please—just go."

Jesse did not move.

"You heard her," Sable said.

Jesse had no intention of turning away from the fight. Aurora's temper rose. She opened her mouth to snap at them both. The purr of Sierra's little red Audi broke the tense silence before she could say anything. Aurora had never been so happy to see the girl.

Of course, that meant Van was there, too. Aurora wasn't sure which side of the fight he would jump into, just for the hell of it. As she thought about him, he leaned out of the passenger side window, grinning. She couldn't see a hint of malice in his eyes, or perhaps she was just too far away.

"Well, look what we have here," he drawled. "This looks familiar." He turned his grin on Aurora, who felt her insides turn to ice despite the friendly twinkle in his eyes. "Aurora, did you invite another guy along? This is supposed to be a double date. You know what that means, right? It doesn't mean you get two dates. Are you messing my little brother around?"

Only Sierra was amused by this. "Jesse was just leaving," Sable said in a much calmer voice. His eyes stopped flashing. He almost relaxed. His side. He thought Van would be on his side. Or, at least, he was betting Jesse would think so and back off.

Jesse glared between Sable and Van for a moment before glancing once more at Aurora, as though she might suddenly realize the error of her choice. She didn't move, and after another tense moment, he spun and strode toward his bike, his shoulders stiff. He didn't even bother to wave goodbye. He jump-started his bike and peeled off, leaving a trail of black exhaust smoke in his wake.

As if this whole double date situation hadn't been bad enough.

Aurora felt Sable's hand on her back, and she glanced up into his eyes. His jaw was still rigid, but his gaze softened. He wouldn't let anything happen to her. She gave him a tiny smile and walked beside him to the little red car.

Sierra glanced over her shoulder at Aurora as she slid into the backseat beside Sable. She looked amused. "What was that all about, Aurora? Is Jesse still chasing you around? Is he ever going to get the message?"

It wasn't Sierra's words that shocked her; it was the complete and utter lack of malice in her tone. She sounded as though they were friends sharing a secret. Aurora stared at her a beat, then lifted her shoulders and turned to peer out the window. Beside her, Sable was silent, but his solid presence steadied her nerves. Her heart still thumped at his nearness.

Sierra was in a good mood. Aurora had never seen her smile genuinely before, not when they were in the vicinity of each other. The girl who kept up a continuous stream of good-natured gossip as she drove them toward Lynchburg was a completely different person than the girl Aurora had known nearly all her life. She seemed so normal and happy and...nice.

Aurora knew better than to trust her, but she was relieved she wouldn't have to spend the entire trip fending off snide comments and subtle insults. It was probably all prelude to the horrible disaster Aurora knew would come eventually. She glanced up at Sable, but he didn't seem to be listening as Sierra told a story about one of her father's work colleagues getting very drunk and mistaking her for her mother. He stared out the window. She could feel the tension in his muscles as though he was prepared for a strike.

Aurora would have laughed at the absurdity of the situation—of Sierra telling amusing stories to entertain her—but she couldn't drop her guard enough to see the humor. What was Sierra's game? What did she have planned? Whatever it was, there was no backing out now. She would play it out and see how it went. At least Sable would probably push her out of the way if the buckets of blood started flying. Maybe he would, anyway.

Van wasn't listening to his girlfriend's story. He cut in. "So, Aurora, how many other guys do you have hanging around?"

Sierra snapped her mouth shut abruptly. Aurora saw a flash of annoyance cross her beautiful face. Then her eyes darted to Van, and she schooled her features into a pleasant, patient expression. Sierra was horrible, but she wasn't truly scary. Van, on the other hand, freaked Aurora out. Was Sierra afraid of him, too?

Aurora didn't understand the dynamic between them. It just seemed... off. Aurora wondered if he was doing something to her—maybe he was nasty when she argued with him. Maybe he hurt her.

A shiver raced down her spine. She didn't like Sierra, but that didn't mean she wanted anything bad to happen to her. She didn't want anything bad to happen to anyone. Her fears were assuaged when Van turned to Sierra with an apologetic twist on his lips, and patted her knee. The tension in Sierra's shoulders relaxed instantly, and she smiled back at him.

That was even weirder. Did Van actually care that he'd irritated someone?

Aurora realized she hadn't said anything in response to Van's sudden question, and when it finally sunk in, she scowled and opened her mouth to retort hotly. Instead, Sable's low, calm drawl answered him. "Leave her alone, Van."

"Or what? You don't have to protect her all the time, Sable. She can stand up for herself. Can't you, Aurora?"

Yes, she could. "I don't have guys hanging around."

"Good thing," Van grinned. "I don't think my brother would like that."

"He doesn't have to worry about anything like that." Her voice trailed off, and her cheeks flushed. She could feel Sable's eyes on her. She steadfastly avoided his gaze.

"I thought we could go downtown," Sierra said cheerfully into the sudden awkward silence. "We could have some lunch and maybe go see a movie or something." She smiled at Aurora in the rear view mirror. "Or we could go check out some shops."

Van rolled his eyes. "Women. They always want to go shopping."

"Well, it's not everyday we get to go to the city." Sierra tossed her hair. "Don't you want to shop, Aurora?"

She tried to smile, but she suspected it came out as more of a tremulous grimace. "Whatever you guys want." She tried to catch Sable's eye, but he ignored her. For the hundredth time since Sierra had cornered them yesterday, Aurora wondered why he had even agreed to this.

He didn't offer any opinions, not that anyone expected him to.

Sierra and Van didn't seem to mind. They bickered good-naturedly, but it was a lost cause; Sierra was already steering the Audi downtown. Aurora tuned them out, glancing uncertainly at Sable. She didn't understand him at all. If he didn't like her, what was he doing with them? It wasn't as though he needed to protect her from Sierra and Van—well, he probably did, but if not for him, she never would have agreed to this ridiculous double date in the first place.

Maybe he just wanted to be with her.

Oh, please. She pushed that thought aside as quickly as it came. There was no sense reading too much into things. Sable might have reasons for doing what he did and behaving the way he did, but Aurora was pretty sure they had nothing to actually do with her. It was probably some guy thing, some battle of wills with his brother or something. They definitely had a strange relationship. That seemed a hell of a lot more likely than him having some crush on her.

Van suddenly laughed, and Aurora snapped back to reality. She'd heard Van laugh, but then it had been a sort of creepy chuckle. Just now, he was laughing like a normal person. It sounded so strange, so genuine and unexpected, that she wondered what she'd missed. Sierra threw him a smile, and when their eyes met, Aurora had the sudden realization that they might actually like each other. Could it be? She'd thought these two deserved each other—mostly for their awful personalities and mutual mean streaks, but perhaps she really didn't know anything about either of them.

Or, perhaps they were actually nice to each other and they saved the mean stuff for when they had someone else to do torment. Together. Today, it would probably be her.

Sierra steered the Audi into a parking spot downtown. The streets were packed with shoppers on this warm spring morning. When they stepped out of the car, Aurora felt a sudden urge to flee. How had she allowed herself to be taken so far from home, stranded here in Lynchburg with no way home but these people—these two enemies, one of whom she'd had since childhood and the other whom it had taken only moments to realize should be avoided at all costs.

Christian was at the college. If she could escape, she could call him. He would give her a hard time, and she knew Sierra was probably a sore subject with him, but he was family. He would come. He would keep her safe.

283

She was being ridiculous. It wasn't as though they'd kidnapped her. She'd come with them willingly enough, and she was determined not to panic. She was going to play it out and see exactly what they had planned for her. At least she was on her guard and...

And she met Sable's eyes as he rounded the car to walk beside her, and she remembered exactly why she was there. She gave him a tiny smile. He didn't exactly return it, but his expression changed almost imperceptibly. He might have been smiling on the inside. She didn't need to run to Christian. She was perfectly fine as long as Sable was beside her.

"Where do you want to have lunch?" Sierra asked.

"Sushi?" Van suggested.

Sable's voice was soft. "Aurora?"

They were all looking at her as though waiting for her to make the decision. Weird. "Sure. That sounds good."

"I know the perfect place." Sierra smiled brilliantly as she caught Van's hand and flounced ahead.

Beside her, Sable started walking. Aurora hurried to catch up with him. The perfect sushi place was the type with a conveyor belt moving around a row of seats along the bar. Aurora had only been to the place once. She'd liked it, but she didn't feel especially comfortable sandwiched between Sierra and Sable. She expected Sierra to kick her under the bar any moment or Sable to suddenly realize where he was, what he was doing and with whom he was doing it.

Sable grabbed a plate as it passed and asked in a perfectly normal voice, "Do you want to share with me?"

"Oh. Okay."

Lunch was companionable. Sierra was in high spirits through the whole affair, eager to try new things and share anything she liked with Van and Aurora. She even urged Sable to take a piece of fish from her plate, and Aurora was surprised when he did. They almost seemed like normal people, not the three people she thought least likely to ever be sitting around her, sharing their food.

She realized then that they were actually just people. Had she been thinking of them all this time as something else?

"Aurora, try this," Sierra said cheerfully, passing her plate to Aurora. "It's really good."

She hesitated, as she had each time Sierra had done this, each time suspecting she would suddenly sprout horns or something, even though she knew it was completely ridiculous. She hadn't yet, and she tentatively tasted the rolled up fish. It was good, as Sierra promised.

"Well?"

She glanced into Sierra's eager face and nodded. She almost smiled. "It is good."

"I knew you'd like it."

Van leaned over Sierra with a smirk. He held out a plate toward Aurora. "I didn't realize you were so adventurous, Aurora. Want to try mine?"

She eyed the plate of miniature squid piled on his plate. He looked amused, as though he expected she would wrinkle her nose or squeal in horror. The squid looked vile, but Van had been eating them the entire time, and she wasn't about to back down. "Okay."

Sable shifted beside her. "You don't have to try it if you don't want to, Aurora."

She rolled her eyes. She wasn't a coward. It probably wouldn't kill her. "I know that." She seized one of the larger squid between her chopsticks. She only hesitated for a split second before she shoved it into her mouth. She could feel the tentacles on her tongue. She pictured them suddenly squirming to life in her mouth.

They all watched her in interest. Van's eyes gleamed. Sierra smiled encouragingly. Sable just peered at her with those unreadable eyes.

She chewed the thing slowly, realizing it wasn't so bad. It tasted almost good, even though it felt disgusting in her mouth. She swallowed it and smirked back at Van. He laughed and winked at her. "That's our girl. I knew you were a brave one."

She smiled around at them. She was actually having a little fun.

Sierra paid for lunch, and when Aurora thanked her, she just smiled and waved her hand as though she did stuff like that everyday. They strolled downtown peering into all the shop windows. Ahead of Aurora, Sierra and Van held hands, talking to each other in light, intimate tones. She was thankful she and Sable were not expected to contribute anything to the conversation because she wasn't sure what she could possibly have to say to either of them. Sable didn't seem interested in saying anything at all to anyone, including her.

She heard Sierra and Van laughing and joking with each other. She idly wondered what they actually had to talk about, when this thing had happened and how they'd ended up together. They seemed quite good for each other, actually, if their attitudes today were any indication. Then again, it might all still be some elaborate prank.

Sable's hand brushed hers, just barely, as they walked side by side.

She was suddenly so aware of him she nearly forgot the odd couple plotting a few paces ahead of them. He didn't say anything to her. He didn't reach toward her. He was perfectly relaxed, which was very unfair, considering the swarm of butterflies that had suddenly taken flight in her stomach at the faintest contact. She'd touched him before. It seemed silly she should respond so strongly now.

It was different today. She was out of her element, on edge and prepared for the worst. Her heart thumped insistently in her chest. She hoped he couldn't hear. Her cheeks flushed, and she lowered her head so he couldn't see.

She was being ridiculous. She'd walked beside him before without coming undone. She could handle this.

"Oh, Aurora, look at this place," Sierra exclaimed, stopping in front of a window display of jewelry, hats and accessories. She caught Aurora's arm and drew her to stand beside her. "Want to go in?"

"Come on," Van complained. "Let's go to the paintball place and shoot each other."

Sierra rolled her eyes. "No way. Those things hurt, and you never hit anything properly anyway."

Van turned to his brother with an exasperated expression. "Sable, tell her to stop being such a girl."

"I will tell her no such thing."

Aurora looked at Sierra, and they shared a smile. Seconds after Sierra had turned back to Van with a smug expression Aurora realized what she'd just done. *Well, that was weird.* It was the first time they'd ever shared anything but insults. And raw fish. It was the first time before today she and Sierra had ever shared anything, anyway.

Van scoffed. "Whose side are you on, anyway?"

Sable lifted his shoulders. "Aurora's."

Sierra grinned broadly. "Perfect. Come on, Aurora." She didn't wait for agreement. She tugged Aurora into the shop. Sable followed, glancing at his brother, who gave a long-suffering sigh before sauntering in behind them.

It was a cheerful store, filled to bursting with scarves, hats, costume jewelry, and handbags. Sierra was quite enchanted by the place, and she flitted about, dragging Aurora around and cooing at the brightly colored merchandise. Sable and Van trailed behind them, but while Van looked completely bored, Sable just looked mildly apathetic. Nothing had seemed to bother him all day—not since his run-in with Jesse in front of her house.

"Oh, Van, look at these!" Sierra exclaimed, dropping Aurora's arm to drag Van toward a display of men's scarves. Van curled his lip in disgust, but Aurora could see the twinkle in his eyes. He didn't resist as Sierra pulled him toward the display, wrapping scarves around his neck until his hair stood up on end.

Aurora laughed. She reared back in surprise when she found Sable standing directly in front of her at a display of scarves and hats. He ran his fingers along the soft, silky fabric of an emerald-green scarf. "You should try this on." She stared at him. When she didn't move to lift it off the table, he picked it up and wound it around her neck. He studied her a moment, and she felt inexplicably short of breath. "It looks good on you. It makes your eyes—sort of sparkle."

She touched the material around her neck almost absently. Her fingers brushed his as he reached out to push her hair back over her shoulders and turn her toward a small, round mirror beside them. "It's nice."

She met his eyes above her reflection in the mirror, but she couldn't read his expression. Sierra's voice broke though their stare. "Aw, aren't they cute, Van?" She sighed dreamily. When Van just rolled his eyes, she elbowed him in the side.

"Yeah. Really cute. It's really sweet."

Sable stepped away from Aurora as though they'd been caught in some salacious act. He lifted his chin and looked absently around the store, avoiding her eyes.

"Aurora, you have to get that scarf. It's just gorgeous on you," Sierra told her. "I'm making Van get the navy blue one. It's looks so good with his

287

complexion, don't you think?"

It really did, and Aurora wondered how good Sable would look in that color. Van scoffed. "I'm a man. Men only wear scarves when it's cold out."

Sierra waved her hand dismissively. "They do so wear scarves. The fashionable ones, anyway."

"I don't need to be fashionable. I'm hot."

Aurora and Sierra burst into giggles at this. Sable turned his head to smirk at his brother. "Oh, just get the damn scarf. I'm sure no one will make fun of you."

Van narrowed his eyes. "I'm sure they wouldn't, little brother. Or they would be very sorry."

The girls continued giggling as Sable flashed his teeth at his brother. "Did you find anything?" Aurora asked Sierra.

"Oh, no, I have enough of this stuff. I just thought you might like to find something for yourself." She grinned. "And you did. You are getting it, aren't you?"

Aurora glanced down at the scarf, then up at Sable. His eyes sparkled with mirth. He gave her the smallest of smiles. "Yeah. I think I will."

The rest of the day was surprisingly pleasant, and, even as she stared out the window, watching Lynchburg faded away into New Coventry, Aurora was amazed she'd had such a good time. She hadn't even worried about some awful prank or horrible misfortune befalling her for the last couple hours. This was no time to drop her guard. They still had the ride back to drop her off in the middle of nowhere and convince her to skinny dip in a dirty pond while they stole her clothes.

Not that she would ever have done something so stupid, nor did she think Sierra would resort to such juvenile tricks. But, still. The day had just been too weird. Surely there was some ulterior motive behind Sierra's sweetness and Van's good humor. Surely Sierra, after all these years of mutual dislike, hadn't just decided to extend the hand of friendship because she and Van really thought there was something going on between she and Sable and wanted to make nice.

Because there wasn't, was there? There was nothing going on between she and Sable, no matter what sort of strange looks they shared or awkward, breathless moments passed between them. It was nothing at all.

When Sierra pulled up to Aurora's house, Aurora braced herself. This had to be the moment. Everything had gone too well. Something had to happen now because, if it didn't, Aurora might have to start rethinking everything she'd ever decided about Sierra and Van. Whatever terrible moment the really wonderful day had lead up to, it had to be now.

Sierra smiled. "It was really fun, Aurora. We should do it again sometime. Shouldn't we, Van?"

He smiled, too, but there was something wily in his eyes as he spun to glance at them over the back of the seat. "Yes, we should. Don't you agree, Sable?"

Sable's face was perfectly impassive. "Sure. Thanks for lunch, Sierra."

"Anytime. See you guys in school, okay?" Sierra winked at Aurora. "Make sure she gets in safe, okay, Sable?"

"Good night," Aurora said, and she actually felt like smiling. Whoever had taken over Sierra's body for the day, Aurora had kind of liked her. "Thanks for everything. See you at school."

She reached for the door handle, but Sable had beaten her to it. He pulled open her door and offered a hand to her. She blinked at in surprise, but she took it, and the world didn't make any more sense as she was standing hand and hand with him in front of her house than it had all day.

"Bye!" Sierra called, waving at them out the window before steering the car away from the house and down the street.

Aurora stared after them for a brief moment. She felt absently at her face and hair and arms, expecting something to be wrong with them. When she lifted her head, Sable was looking at her as though she'd gone insane. "What are you doing? Did you forget something?"

She relaxed and smiled sheepishly. "No, I just…I didn't actually expect to get through the day without Sierra doing something awful to me."

"I wouldn't have let her."

She looked up into his eyes. "I know you would have tried to stop her, but you don't know Sierra when she gets a mean streak. You really don't see anything wrong with me?"

His expression was suddenly serious. "No. Nothing."

"Wow. Well, that was actually…not bad, was it?"

"It was...okay."

She laughed, but his words cut a little. She'd had fun just being with him. She supposed he hadn't felt the same. "It was actually kind of fun."

He smiled as he walked her toward the door. "It was a little fun. It was pretty funny when you ate that squid. I thought you were going to spit it out at the sushi chef."

"Oh, I didn't look that disgusted, did I?"

"No. I just knew you were."

"How?"

"I could see it in your eyes."

"It wasn't that bad. Anyway, I like trying new things."

"And you didn't want to back down in front of Van and Sierra?"

"And I didn't want to back down in front of Van and Sierra. I learned a long time ago never to show weakness in front of that girl."

"You guys have a pretty bad history, huh?"

"Yeah, you could say that. You could also say that she's hated me since grade school and has made it her mission to make my life a living hell. So you can imagine my surprise at not being drenched in pig's blood or running naked down the highway in the dark right now."

He gave her that look again as though she'd gone nuts. "Has that sort of thing been going through your head all day?"

"I wanted to mentally prepare myself for any possibility. You never know. But she wasn't so bad today. If I didn't know what she can really be like, I might have actually liked her."

"She did seem different today. Maybe she's really trying to be nice?"

"I don't know. I've never seen her do that, so I don't know if she's capable of it. I am still not convinced something isn't going to go horribly wrong sometime in the near future."

"If it does, I'll be here to stop it. It was my fault you got caught up in it."

"Oh, I don't blame you," she told him, but his promise sent warmth curling through her body. "I'm sure Sierra would have found some other reason to mess with me." She smiled at him as they reached her front door. "Thanks for walking me up. You didn't have to."

"I wanted to. It's not like it's far." His expression became suddenly serious again. "Aurora. I don't want you to go around them without me."

"What?" She was completely confused. Moments ago, they'd been playful. Now he was back to his strange, intense, and mysterious self again.

"Van and Sierra. Just don't, okay?"

"Okay."

He stepped closer to her, gripping her shoulders. "I mean it, Aurora. I don't know what this was about today, but don't get comfortable with them. Promise me."

Her breath caught as he stared down at her, his eyes so dark, they were like bottomless pits. "I promise, Sable. Of course I'm not comfortable with them. They might not have done anything to me today, but that doesn't mean we're best friends now or anything. I'm not going anywhere near them if I don't have to."

He nodded, apparently satisfied with this, but he did not release her shoulders. He stared down at her. For a long moment, he didn't say anything. Then his gaze darted down, to her mouth. Her lips parted slightly as her breath quickened. For a brief, wild moment, he leaned forward, and she was sure he was going to kiss her.

He drew away abruptly and jerked his head in a nod. "Good. It's better that way. Good night, Aurora."

"Good night, Sable."

With that, he spun away and was gone without looking back. She sighed as she stepped inside the quiet, empty house.

At least she wasn't covered in leeches.

* * *

Aurora tried to slip through the crowd before classes unnoticed. She realized, when Josie and Diana found her outside of homeroom, glowering accusingly, that it had been a foolish idea. She didn't even know why she was avoiding her friends. She didn't know why she'd lied about catching a ride with her father that morning when the truth was, she'd just left early to walk to school and clear her head in the bright, warm spring air. She didn't know why she had tried to sneak into homeroom without talking to them when she knew quite well that there was absolutely no way they were going to let her get away with not telling them everything about the double date on Saturday.

She sighed and turned to face the music.

"Aurora!" Josie exclaimed, seizing her arm in a grip so tight she must have been expecting Aurora to bolt at any moment. "So what happened? I tried to call you last night but you didn't answer your phone."

Aurora hadn't answered any of Josie's dozen calls. She'd spent the morning sleeping in and the afternoon pretending to watch television on the couch as she replayed every moment she'd ever had with Sable over and over until she'd convinced herself that the moment she'd thought he was going to kiss her had just been her imagination. Or maybe it wasn't. She still didn't know.

"There was nothing to tell." It was mostly true. Nothing had happened except for Sierra's complete personality change and Van's sudden good-natured cheer, and the almost kiss with Sable... "We just hung out."

"Oh, come on." Even Diana didn't look convinced by this. "If it were anyone else, I might believe that, but you were with Sierra."

"And the Jayne brothers," Josie added.

"It's not like you *just hang out* with any of them on a regular basis."

"Or ever," Josie piped in. "So how was it?"

"It was...weird."

"Did they do something to you? Was Sierra--"

"No, no. Nothing happened. We just had lunch and walked around downtown Lynchburg for a couple hours."

"Thank goodness. For a moment, I was a little worried."

Aurora rolled her eyes.

"So how was Sierra?" Diana asked. "A total witch, as usual?"

Aurora felt she was betraying some base part of herself. "No. Actually, she was...kind of nice."

They both stared at her in shock.

"I'm sure it was probably just for show, though," she told them quickly. "She and Van seem to actually like each other. Maybe she didn't want him to see what she's really like."

"Weird," Diana muttered.

"How about Sable? Did anything happen? Was it like a real date?"

When she really thought about it, it had been a little like a real date, even if she was determined not to let herself read too much into it. She certainly didn't want Josie reading anything into it. "I'm not sure why he even agreed to it. He barely talked to me." She hoped her cheeks didn't redden as she remembered the moment in the shop when he'd wrapped the beautiful emerald green scarf around her neck. She'd thought about wearing it today, but the reality of wearing it might shatter the pretty fantasy of the day.

"We don't believe you," Diana told Aurora flatly. "He wouldn't have agreed to it if he didn't want to."

"We know something happened!" Josie added sulkily. "It did, and you are trying to keep it from us again!"

"Why would I do that?" Aurora was pleased that her voice sounded perfectly reasonable.

"I don't know! But you are, and it is totally unfair."

Aurora opened her mouth to reply. She snapped it shut as she caught sight of the Lawson twins passing by in the hall, their narrowed eyes searching the crowd of students as if homing in on someone upon which to rest their glare. She wasn't surprised when it turned out to be her. She lifted her chin against their hateful stares.

Then Sierra pushed past them as if they were no more interesting than two lost freshmen. She smiled as she hurried forward, brushing Josie aside to thread her arm through Aurora's like they were old friends. This didn't pass the twins by, but Sierra ignored them as they turned to whisper heatedly to each other. Nor did she pay any attention to Josie and Diana, who stood gaping at her.

Aurora was too surprised to do anything. Sierra was speaking before she'd made up her mind what she could possibly do. "Aurora, I had so much fun on our double date Saturday. We have to do it again. Van can't wait."

"Oh, I–" Aurora stammered, trying to ignore the heat from the twins' malignant stares. As if through a haze, she noticed Jesse leaning against a locker. She wondered how all her troubles could be in the same place at this one time to hear all of this. Not all her troubles, she admitted fairly, but enough of them. "Yeah. It was really fun."

If Sierra noticed the strain in her voice, she didn't let on. "I'm so glad you're dating my boyfriend's brother so we can hang out."

Her mouth opened in shock. "Since when? I thought you hated me."

Sierra tossed her hand and laughed. "Oh, come on. You're not going to hold a grudge, are you? I thought we were okay."

Aurora sighed.

"Things change, Aurora. Dating an older guy changes you. You forget about that stupid high school stuff, you know?"

Aurora doubted this was true. Van wasn't much older, and he certainly wasn't any more mature.

"Anyway, I have to be nice to Sable's girlfriend, don't I?"

Everyone was suddenly rapt with attention—as if they weren't already.

"I'm not his girlfriend."

"No? That's not how it seemed to me. You two were looking pretty snuggly."

Aurora knew Sierra probably knew the truth. She didn't know what the girl was playing at. Perhaps Aurora and her strange friendship with Sable had become an instrument of torture to use against the twins. Or Jesse. Or Josie or Diana. Or some other person who was hanging around listening to the ridiculous conversation. She might not look mean, and she might not be acting mean, but she had something up her sleeve.

"I think you misunderstood the situation—" And then Sable was there, as things that couldn't possibly get worse always got worse. He lifted an eyebrow as she trailed off. She looked up at him resignedly. "Hi, Sable."

Sierra grinned between them. "Hi, Sable. We were just talking about Saturday."

"Yes. I figured." His eyes met Aurora's. She couldn't tell if he was angry. His gaze measured the crowd around them. It lingered a moment on Jesse, who glared at him. Sable stiffened for the briefest moment before dismissing the other boy completely.

When his eyes met Aurora's again, she widened hers just a bit, hoping he could read the supplication in her expression. "Don't make such a big deal out of it," he told Sierra, as cool and untroubled as ever. He held Aurora's gaze as he added, "We were just hanging out."

She didn't expect his words to cut so deep, even if he was only agreeing with her. Something flickered in his eyes for a split second, but it was gone before she could identify it. Beside Aurora, Sierra just scoffed and rolled her eyes as though he was being such a boy. Then Sable spun and strode the other way with an unhurried gait, as though nothing out of the ordinary had happened.

"Wow, that was cold," Cami Lawson said in a low voice that nevertheless carried to everyone in the crowd. She smirked.

Aurora schooled her features into an unconcerned expression. "See? I told you there was nothing going on." She was amazed that her voice sounded so strong when her heart felt as though it had sunk into her knees.

Sierra's eyes were not on her. She looked directly at Jesse as she said, "It didn't look like that to me. It seems like Sable just wants to keep you two a secret for a while."

Jesse shoved off the wall and took a step toward them. "You don't know what you're talking about, Sierra. It sounds like you're just trying to stir up trouble again. You just picked a really weird way to do it this time."

Aurora felt Sierra's fingers clench around her arm. Sierra glared at Jesse's back as he stormed off.

Mercifully, the warning bell trilled.

Aurora exhaled heavily in relief. She peeled Sierra's fingers off her arm. "I have to get to class." She glanced at Josie and Diana. "See you guys later, okay?"

She started down the hall. Her friends snapped out of their shock and chased after her. "That was so mean!" Josie breathed.

"Which one?" Aurora asked wryly. "Sierra or Sable?"

"Both."

"I'm not sure if any of it was supposed to be mean or...what." She didn't know what mind games Sierra and the Jayne brothers were playing. She didn't have enough experience.

Josie and Diana weren't the only ones to have followed her. Cami and Callie were suddenly there, blocking her path like a beautiful, blonde-haired, blue-eyed wall. "You won't be on top forever, Aurora," Callie told her coldly. "Sierra will drop you just like she dropped us when something better comes along."

Josie's lip curled. "You're just being nasty because that something better was Aurora. How's it feel to not even be second rate to Sierra anymore?"

"Come on, Callie," Cami said, grabbing her sister's arm. "They're not worth even listening to. They don't even know what game they're playing."

They weren't wrong.

"Seriously, though, what did happen?" Josie asked. "That was kind of a weird thing for him to say."

"It wasn't weird. It was the truth. We were just hanging out. It wasn't a big deal. Sierra was just trying to make more out of it to get a rise out of Jesse or the twins or just to see what would happen or something." She stopped in front of her homeroom. "I really have to get to class, okay? I can't get another tardy or I'll be in detention. See you guys later."

"Sure." Josie was disappointed. Diana's small frown told Aurora she wasn't going to just forget about any of it.

She had enough problems without worrying whether her friends believed her. She paused outside English class later that day, dreading the moment she had to walk inside. She didn't know what would happen, but she knew she couldn't take another repeat of that morning.

She couldn't just stand outside looking weak and terrified, either. She straightened her shoulders and strode inside. Sierra was already there, and she smiled at Aurora as she passed. It wasn't a genuine smile like Aurora had seen on Saturday. There was something sharp and cold to it. She was back to her old self again, all right. Aurora wondered if Van had put her up to being nice the other day.

That, or the big disaster was still coming, and she'd just been softening Aurora up so she'd drop her guard.

No one said anything to her, but she felt her classmates' eyes as they murmured behind their hands. By now, news of the confrontation in the hallway had spread through school like wildfire. She'd heard about a hundred different versions, almost none of which that were close to what had really happened. Some of them involved Sable openly scorning her and others included descriptions of him kissing her in front of everyone and declaring his love while Jesse seethed nearby.

Not that she expected anything less. Perhaps it had been Sierra's intention all along. It wouldn't have been the first rumor she'd begun.

She ducked her face behind her textbook to hide her blush. She could handle a little gossip, but she didn't want to know what it would be like when Sable walked in. She didn't even have time to brace herself for it. When the class went quiet, she knew he was there.

She lowered her book, and she knew by the look in his eyes that he knew they'd all been talking about them. She was impressed with how perfectly cool and indifferent he looked. He obviously couldn't care less about what people were saying. She wished she could be more like him. She could never pull off that insolent slouch, not without looking like a complete fool.

He didn't meet her eyes, but he moved toward her. Her pulse leapt. She tried not to look like she was watching his every movement. As he passed, he met her gaze for only a split second before he turned abruptly and dropped into the empty desk beside her. Then he lifted his book to his face and pretended she and everyone else didn't even exist. He glowered at anyone who so much as glanced their way.

He might not have spoken a word to her, but no one else dared to either.

Chapter Fourteen

Sable bent over his knees, cradling his head in his hands. He looked up at his parents, who peered back at him expectantly. "I don't know. I'm not sure of anyone in this town."

"Whoever it is, they are hiding themselves well," Adam remarked.

"But we are certain there is another one of us," Mariah said.

"You know there is, Mother," Sable told her sharply. "We didn't kill those people. *Someone* did."

She pressed her fingers delicately to her temples. "I am not certain what is worse. At least if it was your brother, we would know how to deal with this."

"We are dealing with it," Sable snapped. "I am dealing with it."

"I know you are trying, Sable." Adam eyed him. "Though I am uncertain why you are so insistent about this."

"I think it's Blaine Daniels."

"Blaine Daniels. Interesting theory."

"He fits the profile."

"So do many others. The Landrys, for instance."

"I am not ruling anyone out. I've been researching the deaths that weren't—well, ours—and looking into the news reports around the places we know Daniels and the Landrys have been."

Mariah's mouth tightened in a grim line. "Any connections?"

"Yes, but not definite ones. I need to find out more. I need more to go on."

"We have spoken to the Landrys. They aren't as friendly as I expected, but we have been able to have a conversation or two. They have been in many places, but not all of them are connected to any deaths."

"Yes, the same goes for Daniels, but I haven't had a chance to talk enough with him yet. I need more time." There was a grim set to his jaw. "Daniels is seeing Ruby Geller."

"Aurora's aunt. Yes, I heard."

He tried not to shrink back from their sudden scrutiny.

"Does it bother you?" Mariah asked with deceptive calm.

"If he is one of us, he could be dangerous."

"To Aurora, you mean?"

"To anyone around him if he is Jivina and he loses control."

"What exactly do you want to do about it?" Adam asked.

Sable pushed his hands through his hair in frustration. "I can't do anything! I don't even know which one of them it is!"

"Then you need to find out," Mariah told him. "Not worry about Aurora."

He shot to his feet and paced in front of them.

"You know how we feel about human girls," Adam reminded him.

"You don't care when Van dates them."

"Oh, he isn't dating them," Mariah scoffed. "He's just playing around."

"Is that better?"

"No, but at least he doesn't get attached to them."

Sable barked out a humorless laugh. "No. Sometimes he just kills them."

"Sable!" The tinkling doorbell interrupted whatever his mother might have said. She sighed. "It's Aurora."

Sable glanced toward the door.

"Don't, Sable. Just leave it alone. You have work to do. You have to find out who is doing this." She looked him coldly in the eye. "Or you will never see her again, not even from the shadows."

His insides turned to ice. He kept his jaw rigid and his back stiff. He relented when she reached for the doorknob to meet Aurora at the door. "Mom." The soft, supplicating note in his voice horrified him.

She looked back at him. Her expression softened almost imperceptibly.

"Please don't change her anymore."

"Don't worry about Aurora, Sable. I won't hurt her. I won't do anything she doesn't want me to do." He scowled, but he pushed past her, into the hall. He did not miss the warning look in her eyes as she hurried to greet her patient warmly.

When Sable heard her voice, he froze.

"Hello, Dr. Jayne."

"How are you this afternoon, Aurora?"

She smiled as she walked into the foyer. Her eyes didn't hold Dr. Jayne's. They swept around the room, searching for something. Searching for someone. "Very well, thank you."

"Come in, please. Shall we get started?"

Sable flattened himself against the stairs, out of her line of sight. His mother would kill him if he disobeyed her again. He squeezed his eyes shut as she passed so close. The scent of flowers drifted to his hiding spot. He held his breath as if it might block her out. It didn't. It never did.

He was relieved when they entered Mariah's office, and her voice and scent faded behind the door. He had to stop this. He shouldn't even be thinking of her. He certainly couldn't be with her. It was as bad as Daniels being with Ruby, if he was one of them. It was certainly worse than Van and Sierra. At least Van didn't give a damn about his human girl.

For the first time in his life, being more like Van actually sounded appealing.

* * *

Sable slowed his car and shut off his lights as he rolled into Blaine Daniels' neighborhood. He was just in time to catch Daniels, dressed in expensive jeans and a black leather jacket, jogging down the walk toward the car idling on the curb out front of the house. Daniels tossed his curly hair, and a small smile crossed his rugged face. He looked happy. He looked...like a man in love.

Sable's his heart thumped as the older man climbed into his car and steered away from the house. He could guess exactly where he was heading. He kept a safe distance, only switching on his lights when he had followed the car ahead for a couple blocks.

His thumping heart sank as Daniels steered into Aurora's neighborhood. No. Aurora had been safe so far. The man had been around enough times, and she was fine. It didn't change the fact that, if he was one of them, Daniels was dangerous. He could snap at any moment, and if Aurora was there when it happened–

His breath constricted. He shoved the thoughts aside. *Find out who it is.*

Don't get distracted. Don't worry about her. That was easier said than done. He watched Daniels hop out of his car and hurry up the steps as though he couldn't wait another moment to be inside. He rapped eagerly on the front door.

Aurora pulled it open. She smiled at him. Her strawberry blonde hair glowed in the light of the room behind her. She didn't even hesitate to step aside and allow Daniels in, chatting amiably with him. She closed the door, shut herself off from Sable, and was trapped inside with a monster.

Maybe.

He was being ridiculous. There was no sense waxing poetic about a human girl, even if she was particularly pretty and seemed to be *everywhere.* He wasn't here for her. He was here to find the monster that was threatening the town and his life and everything he had worked for in New Coventry.

But what had been the point of that? The voice in his head was traitorous. He ignored it.

He looked back up at the house. The light in the room upstairs flipped on. He saw her move in front of the sheer curtains, a faint outline against the glow of the room. He was suddenly ashamed to be watching her pass back and forth in her room.

Then she was gone, and the light flipped off.

He let out a breath he hadn't realized he'd been holding. At least he wasn't spying on her like a Peeping Tom anymore. He wasn't here for her. He wasn't here for that.

When the front door opened again and Daniels emerged, dragging a laughing Ruby out by the hand, Sable groaned audibly in relief. The two giddy adults climbed into the car and Daniels pulled away from the curb.

Sable hesitated. He glanced up at the darkened window. For a moment, he wanted to stay so badly it felt like a weight had settled on his chest. If he was here, he could make sure nothing happened to her, that she was safe inside and no one could hurt her.

That wasn't what he was supposed to be doing. He was supposed to be hunting Jivina. It was the best he could do for her right now.

With that thought, he stamped on the accelerator, following Daniels from several car-lengths behind. New Coventry was a sleepy, safe town—or it had been before all the monsters had arrived. The man probably never considered anyone would be tailing him. He stopped the car downtown, in front of the small, brightly lit bar on the edge of the square. It wasn't one of the places Van hung around. It was nice and classy.

Daniels led Ruby inside. Sable waited. He was nodding off nearly two hours later when they emerged, still holding hands as though they couldn't bear to let go. He sat up quickly. They looked happy together. The way they snuck looks at each other and smiled made Sable inexplicably uncomfortable.

They looked like they were in love. He'd seen love before; his mother and father were as devoted to each other as they had been from the moment they met, but it was a comfortable, contented love. It wasn't like this—Blaine and Ruby practically shone with the newness of it. He'd seen Van and Evelyn in love, but then it had come with so much pain and heartbreak that it hadn't seemed worth it at the time. He hadn't understood why they'd let themselves fall so far.

He understood now. They hadn't been able to help it.

Daniels helped Ruby into the car. Sable sunk down in his seat in case they noticed or recognized him. He probably shouldn't have made himself known to Daniels so soon; it would be harder to tail a man who knew his face. He didn't follow right away as they steered back toward Daniels' neighborhood.

If he was one of them, could he really love this human woman? He'd been with her months now, and nothing had happened to her. She seemed as oblivious as everyone else to the cause of the mysterious deaths. Could Daniels really control it? Could he keep her safe?

But other people had died. If Daniels was a monster, perhaps he could keep from hurting the one he loved, but he couldn't control his urge to kill. She might even make it worse.

Sable sighed deeply, pushing his hands through his hair before backing out of his parking spot and catching up to Daniels' fading headlights. If this man couldn't control himself, how could Sable think he himself could? His mother was right. He had to stay away from human girls, even if his heart pounded and his palms sweated whenever they were nearby.

He was still brooding as Daniels and Ruby pulled up to the house and hurried up the walk, pausing a moment at the door to exchange a lingering kiss. In seconds they were inside. Sable could follow their movements through the house as the lights flipped on and off.

Finally, a light burned upstairs. Then it flipped off, and the house was dark.

He waited just a bit longer, until he was nodding off again, but nothing happened. No one came out. No lights flicked on.

Sable slowly steered the car away from the house, not even realizing he was driving through Aurora's neighborhood until he was looking up at that dark window again. The house was silent.

He yawned. There was no sense hanging around all night. She was all right. Daniels was somewhere else, and he probably wouldn't be returning to the house anytime room. Sable needed to sleep.

But when he was in his bed, laying on his back in the dark, he couldn't sleep. He stared at the ceiling instead and didn't bother trying not to think about her.

* * *

The gossip about Aurora and Sable had finally died down. She was relieved to walk down the halls without people whispering behind their hands as she passed. Sable hadn't said anything about it, and she was grateful for it. She didn't think she could handle the embarrassment. Somehow, he always seemed to be there when she needed him, and though he hardly spoke to her at all when he was around, his presence was an implied threat that had the effect of keeping even the most determine gossips from bothering her.

She avoided Sierra as often as possible, but the girl pretended as though she didn't get the message. She was acting like she and Aurora were old friends. It didn't stop the twins from grumbling behind Aurora's back, but at least they were easier to avoid than their former friend and partner in torture.

Today the halls were blessedly Sierra-free. Josie and Diana, though, knew exactly where to find her anytime they wanted. She wondered if she'd always been so predictable.

"Have you talked to Sable?" Josie demanded after only the most cursory greeting. Her eyes gleamed. Aurora might have hated all the gossip, but Josie loved it.

Aurora pinched the bridge of her nose. "No. I told you guys. Nothing is going on with Sable. I would tell you if there was."

"I don't think we believe you anymore," Josie said sulkily. "You've become all secretive and sneaky lately."

Aurora knew Josie would love to spend every waking moment analyzing every tiny detail of her interactions with Sable. She didn't think she could handle the false flashes of hope this would evoke. Or worse, the reality of her complete lack of anything resembling a relationship with him.

"Have you heard Josie is going out with Bryan Dymond?" Diana asked.

Aurora opened her mouth in shock. "What? Josie?"

Josie blushed. "Well...yeah."

"Since when? Why didn't you tell me?"

"Well, it just happened, and you've been so busy with your own stuff and boys and everything. I didn't think you were interested."

"I haven't been that busy!" This hurt her feelings. She hadn't been that bad of a friend lately, had she? "Of course I'm interested! So the Biology notes thing was just an excuse?"

"Yep. He even admitted it. Then he asked me out."

"And you said yes!" Aurora hugged her in delight. "I can't believe you didn't chicken out."

Her friend hugged her back, and all the hard feelings between them fell away. "Well, you went out with Sable. I thought I should just give it a shot."

"It wasn't a real date. I told you."

"Yeah, but you still did it. So I was inspired to be brave."

"I am so happy for you. So what's the deal? What's going on with you and Bryan?"

"Well, we just went to the movies and met for coffee a couple times."

"Anything else?"

"Well...we held hands. And I thought he was going to kiss me goodnight when we left the movies, but...he didn't."

"Well, there's plenty of time for that," Diana told her. "Sometimes it's good to take it slow. There's no need to get carried away."

Aurora and Josie rolled their eyes at each other. Josie threaded her arms through each of her friends' and steered them down the hall. "It's good to have you back, Aurora."

"I've been here all along. What are you guys talking about?"

"Please," Diana said. "You've been off in your own world. And it's like

304

your world revolves around the Jaynes."

"What? What do you mean?"

"Well, you've spent more time with Sable and Van than us lately, and you've been seeing Dr. Jayne every week."

"That is just ridiculous. I've spent tons more time with you guys than them."

"Yeah, but you don't tell us anything," Josie complained.

"Who's the one not telling anything? How many dates have you actually been on with Bryan?"

"Well, three if you count the time we studied together—which I did tell you about!"

"Excuse me, I have been on just one fake date ever, and I told you all about it before it even happened. You're saying I'm the one not telling things? I don't even have anything to tell!"

The girls stopped in the hallway, glaring at each other. Then they burst out laughing.

"Okay, okay," Diana said. "Maybe we've been a bit harsh."

"Yes, you have. I have enough problems with the twins making my life miserable. I need all the friends I can get. And Sierra does not count! I don't even know what her game is, but she definitely hasn't suddenly turned over a new leaf."

This shamed them both. Josie tightened her arm around Aurora's. "Sorry," Diana sighed.

Aurora smiled at them. It wasn't their fault; they hadn't been listening when she assured them nothing was going on, but she wasn't being entirely truthful, either. "It's okay."

The warning bell rang through the halls. The students around them surged forward toward their respective classrooms. "We'd better get to class," Josie said.

"I'll see you guys after school, okay?" Aurora said, glad they were at least back on friendlier terms.

"Yeah. Bye, Aurora!"

"Bye!"

She'd almost forgotten she was walking into the lion's den this period. She had to take a moment to steel her nerves as she headed into Mrs. Lima's classroom. It didn't help much. Her stomach flip-flopped. She didn't know if it was in dread or excitement. It was probably both.

No one said anything to her. Sierra just gave her a supercilious little wave as she took her seat near the back of the class. Sable arrived moments later. He moved toward Aurora immediately, taking the empty seat beside her. This was exactly the sort of behavior that confused her and caused all the gossip going around school about her, but she didn't mind. She smiled a tiny smile at the top of her desk as he settled in next to her.

She glanced over at him, but he was staring straight ahead. His face was as coldly unreadable as ever. This was the confusing part. Even when he was being nice, she could practically feel the chill radiating off his lean, relaxed body. At least she was used to this by now. She tried not to let his indifference bother her too much.

The bell rang, and the teacher popped into the classroom as though she had been hiding behind the door the entire time. She clapped her hands for attention, though most of the class continued to whisper amongst themselves. "Please continue annotating the text from last period. You should have everything you need, but if you don't, get it from a classmate. And don't forget your essays are due next week." She gave them all a stern look that fell short of intimidating anyone. "I'm sure you've all gotten a good head start and just have to work on the final draft?"

Wishful thinking, Aurora thought fleetingly as whatever Mrs. Lima was saying was drowned by the sound of shuffling papers and conversation.

Sable's low voice startled her. "Do you want to work together?"

She turned to him in surprise. He hadn't spoken to her all week, and she knew he didn't need any help—he'd probably already done this, too, and he was probably just recycling old essays. What was he even doing there?

"Have you done this already, too?"

He smiled. "Yeah, but you haven't. I can help. I mean, if you want."

She looked down at her text. It was tedious work, and she wouldn't mind a few hints. "Sure."

He spun his desk around so they were facing each other. For several moments, they didn't talk about anything but a story about a man and his dog, but Aurora found herself relying on his annotations rather than picking them

306

out herself. She realized quickly that having him there wasn't really helping her learn anything at all, but at least she would get the grade.

She couldn't concentrate. She didn't want to talk about a man and a dog. She wanted to talk about what had been happening all week, about the rumors and the way he'd been hanging around, silently protecting her from their busybody classmates. Of course, she had no idea how to start a conversation like that, and it probably wouldn't go well. Then things would just be awkward.

"How is your aunt?" he asked abruptly.

Aurora stared at him for a moment. "What?"

"Ruby? How is she doing? I was just wondering if she was still seeing Blaine."

"Why do you want to know?"

"I was just curious. I liked them. They seemed nice. I was just wondering how they were doing."

"They're good. They've been spending most nights together. I hardly ever see Ruby anymore."

"That's nice. I wonder what it would be like moving all over the place working on houses. I mean, I know what it's like moving all over the place. But making the choice to do it for a living."

"It sounds kind of neat. Blaine gets to work for himself and do what he loves to do. You aren't thinking about that kind of job, are you? I thought you were tired of moving all over the place."

"I am. It just seems like kind of a cool job. Never having to get up to go to work, living where you work, getting to work with your hands."

"Your parents live where they work."

"Yeah, but it's not the same."

For the first time, she thought she might understand what he was still doing in high school. Maybe he was just putting off deciding what to do with his future.

"So where has he lived before?"

Aurora snapped her eyes back to him. "What? Who? Blaine?"

"Yeah."

"I'm not sure of everywhere. He said he's from Massachusetts. He mostly sticks around New England." Her eyes slid away as she tried to remember. "I didn't really pay that much attention. Connecticut, I think. Vermont, maybe New Jersey and Maine. Definitely New York. I remember him talking about Manhattan. I think this is his first time in Virginia. Oh, and North Carolina."

"Do you know what cities?"

"No. Why would I? Why do you want to know, anyway?"

The lazy half-smile crossed his face again, and her pulse leapt. "I don't know. We just didn't get to finish our conversation the other day at the festival. I was curious."

When he didn't say anything else for a while, she turned back to the text, glancing at his notes to make sure she hadn't missed anything. She still couldn't concentrate. She lifted her head and narrowed her eyes at him. "Do you have a crush on my aunt or something?"

He laughed incredulously. "What? No!"

She leaned back in her chair and pinned him with an arch look. "Is there something about you I should know?"

His shoulders tensed. "Like what?"

"Do you have a crush on Blaine?"

His loud whoop of laughter drew the attention of most of the class. No one had ever heard him laugh like that before, not even Aurora. "No!"

"Okay." She didn't sound convinced.

"I just wanted to know. I wondered how to get into that kind of work."

"Oh. He and his partner were in college together. I guess Troy has some money or something, and they bought the house they were renting. Blaine flipped it for fun while they lived there, and then they sold it for a really good profit. They decided to start doing it for a living after that. Now they have other people who work on their houses for them all over the country."

"Really?" For some reason, he didn't sound that enthusiastic about it anymore.

"Yep. I guess you really just have to have enough money to buy your first house and be able to do the work if you want to get into that kind of thing."

"Huh. Where are the other people who work with them?"

"I don't know. Do you want me to ask them if they have a job opening?"

His laugh was different this time. It didn't quite reach his eyes. "No thanks. I just never met anyone who did that as a job before. I just wanted to know a little bit more about it."

When he fell silent again, bending over his paper, she studied him. She supposed him asking odd questions was better than sitting like a silent sentinel through the entire class, glowering at busybodies. She wondered if things would ever be normal with someone like Sable.

Probably not. It was half the reason she liked him.

She caught her teacher's eye over Sable's bent head and quickly turned back to her work. After several moments, she realized Sable was writing something. He wasn't making notes on his text; she had it in front of her and was doggedly trying not to simply copy. Instead, he was making ticks on a list of cities and states.

She watched him do this for quite some time. He sighed deeply as he stared down at the paper, muttering something under his breath. She wondered if he even realized she was there anymore.

Then he seemed to sense her attention and lifted his eyes to her. She glanced away, hoping he hadn't caught her staring at him. "Aurora."

His voice was so low, it sounded almost like a purr. She snapped her eyes back to him. "What?" She was embarrassed by the breathlessness in her voice.

There was no amusement in his eyes at all. They looked deadly serious. "I think you should stay away from Blaine."

She blinked stupidly at him for several seconds. "What?"

"I mean it, Aurora."

"But he's—what?"

If he intended to respond, the bell suddenly rang, interrupting him. He glanced up at the clock in faint surprise and shot out of his desk, quickly gathering his things.

"Sable!" she exclaimed. "What are you talking about?"

He had already started out of the room, but he stopped abruptly and spun back to her. There was something strange in his eyes again, and he stared down at her for several seconds before he cut his gaze away. "Just...forget it.

Forget I said anything."

With that, he spun and strode away, too quickly for her to catch up to him. She didn't even try. She blinked at his retreating back, uncertain how things had taken such a bizarre turn.

Then again, it was Sable. Bizarre turns were just a part of life with him.

Stay away from Blaine? What was wrong with Blaine? And honestly, whom else was he going to warn her away from? He'd been telling her to stay away from her own father next.

Sierra paused beside her on her way out the door. Aurora didn't believe her ingratiating smile for a single second. "Something wrong, Aurora?"

"No. Everything is fine. Thanks for asking, Sierra."

* * *

She was still looking for him when Josie and Diana found her prowling the parking lot after school. "Aurora, what are you doing?" Josie asked. "I thought we were meeting out front."

"Sorry. Have you seen Sable?"

They looked at her as though she'd gone insane. "What? No. Why?"

"I thought you said there was nothing going on," Diana added.

"I told you there isn't!" Aurora stamped her foot in exasperation.

"What's up, Aurora?" Josie asked cautiously.

She considered lying to them, but she'd done enough of that. She didn't have time to come up with a suitable half-truth. "He said something weird earlier. Something about Blaine."

Diana lifted her eyebrows. "About Blaine? What did he say?"

"He was asking a lot of questions. Then he told me I should stay away from him."

"What?" Josie's brow furrowed. "That's weird. Does he even know Blaine?"

"He just met him at the festival. I think, anyway. But if there's something wrong with Blaine, I don't want Ruby dating him."

"You think that's what he meant?"

"I don't know what he meant. That's why I'm looking for him! If there's something we don't know about Blaine that could hurt Ruby, I want to know what it is. I don't want her to get hurt. She's really into him."

"We haven't seen him," Josie told her.

Aurora sighed in frustration. "Thanks. I'll see you guys later, okay? I'm going to look for him."

She didn't wait for them to offer to help. She appreciated her friends, but she didn't really think either of them would be much help cornering Sable. She had enough trouble getting him to talk, and she was almost friends with him.

She didn't see his car in the parking lot, and by the time she'd walked its length, most of cars were gone. She scowled. She didn't know his phone number. He hadn't even given it to her when they had a date. She wondered if he even had a phone. She'd never seen him on it. She knew where he lived, of course, but she didn't feel comfortable enough to approach him at his own house.

Irritation thrummed through her as she wondered what she could do. She could just confront him. He'd been acting strange and giving odd warnings and making weird, cryptic remarks since the first time she'd met him. She deserved an explanation.

Was whatever he thought he knew about Blaine worth the humiliation and complete destruction of their tentative friendship? Ruby's happiness was on the line, but Sable had told her to forget it. If it were important enough, he would have told her in class. She thought he would, anyway. He probably didn't know anything. He'd probably heard some stupid rumor in town or something. People loved to talk in New Coventry, especially about other people.

She desperately wanted to know what he'd heard, even if it was stupid gossip.

There was nothing for it. He was gone, and she didn't even have a ride anymore. She'd have to walk, and there was no way she'd make it to Dinwiddie Hills that way. She headed toward the town square. She considered stopping into Mike's shop to borrow a car, but she changed her mind. She veered into the brightly lit *Ruby Rose*.

She saw Ruby right away, surrounded by bouquets of flowers. Her aunt's face lit up as she talked cheerfully with the young man standing at the counter who carried two dozen roses. Aurora had seen enough of the many types of men who came to flower shops to recognize them; he was in trouble. She smiled, but a curl of unease lanced through her belly at the sight of Ruby's flushed, happy face.

She looked like that a lot these days.

Ruby spotted Aurora as soon as the man walked away from the counter. A bell tinkled merrily as he closed the door. "Aurora!" She waved her niece over as though the visit was the highlight of her day. "What are you doing here?"

"I just wanted to stop by and see how you're doing."

Ruby lifted a skeptical eyebrow. "Uh, huh. What do you want?"

"That's not very charitable of you, Ruby."

"Sorry. You don't drop by much anymore. I just didn't know what to think about it."

"I just wanted to see what you were up to." Aurora couldn't believe how cool this lie sounded. Somewhere along the way, she'd turned into a good liar. "I haven't seen you at home as much lately. Are you seeing Blaine again tonight?"

Ruby rolled her eyes. "No. He has some business thing tonight, which probably just means he and Troy are going to drink beer and talk about the new house."

"Did they get it?" Something about this caused another ripple of unease.

"Well, they put in an offer. They haven't heard if it's been accepted or not—or I haven't, anyway. Maybe that's what Troy wants to tell him."

"Oh. Cool. Maybe we can have pizza again or something."

"You might be able to eat like that all the time and stay skinny, but I have to watch my weight."

Aurora scoffed. Ruby had never had to worry about her weight. She'd been the same size since high school.

"Is your dad going to be home?"

"I don't know. I haven't talked to him."

"Maybe we can make something."

"You cook?" Aurora teased.

"You always say that, but I always make something good, and you know it. If Mikey isn't coming home, we can make those veggie pitas that he hates. Find out, and I'll pick up the stuff on the way home."

"Okay. Sounds good. See you at the house?"

"Yeah. See you in a couple hours. Don't forget to text me about your dad."

"I won't." Aurora felt slightly better as she left the shop. Whatever Sable might have heard about Blaine, it could wait until tomorrow; Ruby was safe tonight.

But what could it be? Her mind turned over the horrifying possibilities as she walked. He could be married. He could have a whole bunch of wives in all different states. It had been known to happen. Blaine Daniels might not even be his real name. He could be planning to make Ruby his next illegitimate wife.

That was stupid. How would Sable have even found that out, anyway?

He could be married, though. To just one person. Even just one was bad enough.

Maybe he was an ex-con or fugitive or serial killer or something--

Serial killer? She was obviously overreacting. If Sable thought Blaine was a serial killer, she was sure he would have said something. He wouldn't have just let them keep going on spending all that time with him.

Or perhaps he would. She didn't really know. He might not care a single bit about her at all, not even enough to warn her that a serial killer was hanging around their house nearly every night of the week. Blaine wasn't a serial killer, she decided. He seemed all right, and she doubted he had spent time in prison; he just didn't seem like the type. Of course, she hadn't really met many ex-cons. Perhaps she had them all wrong.

She sighed and lifted her head. She hadn't been watching where she was going. Her feet were moving by memory. She gasped in surprise as she looked around her, spotting a flash of dark hair disappear toward the main road. This time, she knew it wasn't Van. She'd spent enough time with them now to know—perhaps it was his hair or the tilt of his head or the way he carried himself. It wasn't Van.

Her heart thumped, and she hurried to catch up to him. She wanted to shout out his name, but she suspected, if he knew she was behind him, he would find a way to disappear before she could reach him. He ducked down an alley. She wondered why he never seemed to use the main roads. She should have been searching for him in the darkest corners of the world, not the school parking lot.

She was within a few feet of him when she called his name, slightly breathless from the chase. "Sable!"

He stopped in his tracks. His shoulders stiffened before he even turned around. She waited with bated breath, but he didn't spin and race away from her. He came toward her with a tiny frown. "Aurora. What's up?"

She had him now, and though her mouth seemed suddenly remarkably dry, she wasn't going to waste time. "What's wrong with Blaine?"

"What?" He looked so shocked she began to doubt he'd said anything odd earlier. "What do you mean?" A shifty, wary expression crept into his eyes, though his face never changed.

"Why were you asking about him? Is there something wrong with him? Is there something you've found out that we should know?"

He looked at her as though she'd gone crazy. She half expected him to laugh in her face.

"Sable, he's dating my aunt. If there is something about him that could hurt her, I want to know about it."

He ruffled the back of his hair nervously. "I shouldn't have said that. I didn't mean it."

She did not believe the act for one second. She stomped her foot in consternation. "Sable! You've been acting weird. What's going on?"

His eyes widened slightly. Then they went completely blank. "Nothing's going on. It's nothing to do with you, Aurora."

She lifted her chin stubbornly. "If there's something wrong with Blaine, it has to do with me. Is he married or something?"

"What?"

"Did you find out something about him?"

"Why do you think that?"

"I saw you writing something down when we were talking about him, not to mention you were asking about him in the first place."

"It wasn't about him. It was nothing to do with him. I was just interested, is all."

"Right. Something weird is going on with you, Sable."

This seemed to thoroughly shock him. "What?"

"I don't get you. Sometimes you're nice and other times you're mean and telling me to stay away from you and other people. What's going on?"

It was as though a shutter had snapped down over his face.

She hitched her hands up on her hips. "Please, Sable. Tell me."

"I told you already. There's nothing going on."

"You said to stay away from him. Is he dangerous?"

His eyes glittered down at her. Then he looked away. "You don't know what you're talking about."

She stepped up closer to him, so close that she could feel his slightly shallow breath stir the fine hairs on her temple. He didn't move, but he wouldn't meet her gaze. "Is he? If he is, I have to warn Ruby."

"I don't know!" He lifted a hand to push through his hair, but she was too close, and he dropped his arm back down to his side. "I don't know anything about him. I just know what you told me about him."

"You're lying. I know you are. Something is weird about this. I can feel it."

His eyes snapped to hers, and her breath caught. "Don't worry, Aurora." His voice was so low he might have just breathed the words. "I won't let anything happen to you."

She held his gaze. Something deep inside her chest fluttered. Before she knew she was going to do it, she lifted herself on her tiptoes and pressed her lips to his.

He went completely rigid. He felt like immovable stone against her, and she suddenly realized what she was doing. She stepped back and felt heat spread across her face. She pressed her hands to the sides of her face. It was so hot she thought it might burn her.

"Oh, god. I'm sorry, I—I don't know what go into me. Just—can we just pretend that didn't happen?"

Sable's hand shot out to catch her wrist as she tried to back away. "No."

She turned her head away in embarrassment, but he grasped her flaming cheeks in his hands and drew her to face him. Then, without warning, he was kissing her as though he might die if he didn't, and she wrapped her arms around his neck, afraid he would pull away or disappear like a dream.

He kissed as though he was drawing out her soul. She felt dizzy and light-headed. Her knees weakened, and she clung to him, pressing her body flush against his for balance. His breath hitched in the back of his throat, and his arms moved from her face to her hair, down her arms and finally around her waist to hold her more firmly against his chest.

She always knew she was supposed to see stars or fireworks or something, but she didn't know kissing a boy like Sable would steal her breath and her senses. Suddenly, there was nothing in the entire world but him, and her body was floating away on some warm, intense dream of his mouth and his hands and the feel of his heart thumping wildly against hers.

She tried to draw a breath but found she couldn't, for his mouth was sealed so tightly to hers, she couldn't tell where her mouth ended and his began. Something was wrong, but it didn't matter because his lips and his tongue against hers felt so *right*, she didn't even care.

He shoved her away from him.

She stumbled, barely catching herself before she fell forward onto her flaming face. This time, when she gasped for air, her lungs filled and she wobbled slightly, pressing a hand to her spinning head.

Startled, she looked up at him. He spun quickly away from her.

Her breath caught. For a moment, she could have sworn his skin looked strange—red and puckered. But she still wasn't thinking clearly. The memory of his kiss still lingered on her lips. She waited for him to speak. When he did, her belly turned to ice.

"No." His voice sounded strange and garbled. He didn't sound like himself at all.

"I—Sable, are you all right?"

He didn't turn to face her. He drew his hood up over his hair, hunching his shoulders as if to protect himself from her. "Just go. Leave me alone, Aurora. I don't want you to come around me anymore."

He sounded more himself now, but his words were like a lance. She didn't know how to respond, for she was sure anything she would say would come out on a sob.

316

"Don't come around my house. Stay away from me. Stay away from my whole family. Just–go."

She couldn't move. She felt as though he'd reached inside her chest and twisted her insides.

She watched him walk quickly away, and even in the shattering that followed his words, she hoped he would suddenly change his mind, that he would turn back around and just–look at her again the way he had before she'd been stupid enough to kiss him.

He didn't even pause, and then he was gone.

She took a shuddering breath and swiped a tear from her eye. She turned back the way she'd come, and she prayed she'd make it home before the sobs began.

Chapter Fifteen

Aurora lifted her chin stubbornly, marching down the stairs. She lost her nerve when she reached the front door. She wasn't going, not after last night. She didn't care if it was cowardly. She was never going to the Jayne house again.

She was still brooding in the kitchen when Ruby arrived home. "Hey, Aurora. What are you doing here? I thought you had an appointment this afternoon."

She hesitated. "I don't think I want to go see Dr. Jayne anymore."

"Why not? I thought you liked going to see her."

"I just...well, I am feeling a lot better. I want to see how I will feel if I stop seeing her for a while."

"Are you sure that's it?" Ruby was awfully skeptical these days.

"Why else would it be?" She sounded perfectly calm. That was good.

"Did something happen between you and Sable?"

"What?" She didn't sound perfectly calm anymore, and she wouldn't meet Ruby's eyes. "No."

"Come on. Don't lie to your aunt."

"I don't want to talk about it."

"Okay. Well, if you change you mind..." She trailed off, her eyes narrowing as she studied Aurora more closely. "Honey, are you sure you're okay?"

"Yeah. I'm fine." Her smile felt brittle.

She wasn't fine. How could she be fine when she felt more hurt than she had in so long, she'd forgotten what real pain really felt like? She would give anything for that awful, yawning emptiness to come back. At least then, she'd had no idea what heartbreak felt like. She'd never have known how intensely her chest could ache with it.

Worse, she was humiliated. She couldn't believe she'd kissed him—she'd never kissed anyone before, not like that. She turned away from Ruby as her cheeks burned.

But, then, he'd kissed her, too, hadn't he? He'd kissed her like a dying man struggling to breathe.

He'd turned so mean he could have been a different person. Even his voice sounded different: low and scratchy and weird.

She took a deep breath, realizing Ruby was still looking at her. "I just don't want to go anymore."

"Okay." Ruby smiled gently. "If you say so. We won't make you if you really don't want to."

"Thanks. So, are you seeing Blaine tonight?" She was glad she sounded almost normal again.

"Since when are you so interested in my schedule?"

Aurora didn't allow her false smile to waver. "I was just curious. Do you have any plans?"

"No. I haven't talked to him tonight." She sighed happily. "I'm sure he'll call, though. He always calls." With that, she rose and started toward the stairs.

Aurora's heart thumped nervously. "Ruby?"

Her aunt turned back to her. "Yeah, honey?"

"How much do you really know about him?"

"What? Blaine? I don't know. I mean, a lot, I guess. We talk a lot, but I suppose I haven't known him that long."

"Do you know about...what he did when he was in all those other places?"

"What he did? You mean with his work?"

"No, I...I just..."

"What is it, Aurora? Did something happen? Did you hear something about Blaine?"

"No. No, I didn't. I just...I just want you to be careful. I'm starting to think you never really know anyone. Even if you have known them a long time. Especially if you haven't."

Ruby's smile was gone. "Did Sable do something to you, Aurora?"

"What? No! He didn't—no, it's not like that at all."

"Okay." But she didn't look entirely convinced. "If he did, though—"

"He didn't, Ruby. I promise. Boys are just—they can be really awful sometimes."

"Trust me. I know very well."

"You'll be careful, won't you?"

"Of course I will, Aurora. You will, too, right?"

"Yeah." She tried to return Ruby's smile, but her aunt was already turning back toward the stairs. She wanted to call her back, to warn her, but there was nothing to say. She didn't know anything about Blaine. She didn't even know if Sable knew something.

She would probably never know now, not after their last disastrous meeting.

Her stomach churned. She swallowed against the rising tears in her throat. The moment she heard Ruby's door close, she rushed up the stairs and threw herself down on her bed.

For a moment, Sable had kissed her like he'd wanted to—like it was the only thing he'd ever wanted. So what happened? What had made him turn on her as though kissing her was so vile, he couldn't even look at her?

What had she done wrong?

* * *

Aurora was quiet as she walked through the halls between Josie and Diana. Josie hesitated a moment before asking, "Did you find Sable last night?"

"No."

Josie and Diana exchanged a look. She ignored them because she couldn't bring herself to tell them, not while she still felt that ache in the pit of her stomach or the burning embarrassment over throwing herself at him. She lifted her chin and forced her face into a blank expression.

And then she saw him.

When he rounded the corner and caught her eye, Sable froze. He might have briefly considered turning back around and fleeing the way he came. Instead, he moved to the opposite side of the hallway and hurried past without making eye contact.

Aurora fought to keep her eyes forward. She felt tears burning in her throat, but she held her head high. She wasn't going to let anyone see her cry over Sable, least of all him. The effort to ignore him almost distracted her from the pain that gripped her chest when she saw the frigid look in his midnight blue eyes.

"Uh, what was that?" Diana demanded.

"What are you talking about?" Her voice came out slightly higher than normal.

"That was weird," Josie agreed, turning her head to look after Sable.

"Did something happen between you and Sable?"

"No." She knew they didn't believe her, but she didn't care. "It's just the way he is sometimes. It's the way he is a lot of the time."

"Since when?" Josie asked.

"I've seen him be like that with other people," Diana told her. "Never you."

"Well, apparently you two were wrong about us," Aurora said. "There's nothing going on. He wasn't interested in me at all."

Josie and Diana exchanged another look. Aurora's temper flared. "Are you sure nothing happened?" Josie asked carefully.

"I'm sure. I told you," Aurora snapped. "Just forget about it."

Diana sighed. "All right, all right. Sorry, Aurora."

"Uh, oh, Aurora," Josie said, her sulky expression brightening instantly.

Jesse leaned against Aurora's locker, watching her approach with his arms crossed over his chest like a teen idol. He smiled as they neared him. He never looked at anyone but Aurora. He was so different from Sable. Sable's eyes were so cold, she felt as though she were drenched in ice water, but Jesse's eyes sent warmth shooting straight from the top of her head to her toes.

"Hey, Aurora." His voice was soft velvet.

"Hey, Jesse."

Diana caught Josie's arm and dragged her away. Josie groaned, but she didn't resist.

Aurora waited as Jesse pushed his hand through his blonde hair. When he looked back up at her, his eyes glinted hopefully. "I heard you aren't really going out with Sable Jayne."

"I'm not. Far from it. We aren't even friends."

He didn't seem to notice how painful it was to say the words. "I'm sorry I... well, I'm sorry I got so upset. If you aren't going out with Jayne, will you go out with me on Saturday?"

He looked so hopeful. She couldn't believe he could still be so hopeful after all the times she'd turned him down. She opened her mouth to say no again, but her eyes drifted over his shoulder.

Sable paused outside his classroom to glance back at her. When he caught her eye, he turned away as though he hadn't seen her at all. She felt ice in her belly, and then she looked back at Jesse, and his expression was so warm, she changed her mind.

"Okay."

Jesse blinked in surprise. "What? Did you—"

"Okay. Yes. I'll go out with you Saturday."

Sable walked into his classroom. Aurora smiled at Jesse.

His face split into a grin. "You will?"

"Yes."

He reached for her, crushing her into his arms. "I knew you would give in eventually."

She laughed, but her stomach churned.

He pulled back, holding her out at arm's length. "You aren't going to change your mind, are you?"

"No. I'll go."

Jesse's eyes glittered. "Okay. I'm not going to ask why you said yes this time. I'm just going to hold you to it. I'll pick you up at seven."

Aurora stepped out of his arms. "Okay. See you then."

"See you then." He swaggered a little as he walked away.

She smiled, and she almost meant it. Josie rushed over to her. "What happened? He actually looks—happy for once."

Diana looked stern. "Did you just agree to go out with Jesse?"

"Yes."

"What? Why? Since when?"

"Why not? He's been chasing me long enough. Maybe once he goes out with me he'll realize I'm not as great as he thinks I am."

"I doubt that," Diana told her. "Aurora, what really happened with Sable? We know something did."

"It doesn't matter. It was nothing. I'm going to give Jesse a chance like Josie said."

Diana frowned at Josie, who was looking a bit too innocent. "Aurora, I'm not sure this is a good idea."

"Well, we'll find out this weekend. It's about time I went out on a real date instead of a weird fake double date with my mortal enemy and a guy who doesn't even like me."

Josie didn't look convinced. "Aurora...I'm not sure you should do this."

"What? Why? You've been the one telling me to go out with him for years. Now you're telling me not to?"

"Well, it's just...I'm not sure you're doing it for the right reasons. I think if you're going to give him a chance, you should give him an honest one."

Aurora's brow furrowed in irritation. "Who says it's not honest?"

"Come on. We've known you all our lives. You've never once even considered saying yes to Jesse."

"Seriously, Aurora. If something happened with Sable--"

"It didn't."

"But I thought there was something between you guys," Diana said.

Aurora looked away. Josie put a hand on her arm. "Aurora? Something did happen, didn't it? He was so--different just now. Before he was so nice to you--well, as nice as he was to anyone."

"Well, now he isn't."

Josie sighed. "Okay. You don't have to tell us if you don't want to. It's just...you can. When you're ready."

"Thanks, Josie, but Sable and I aren't even friends. We never were. Just let it go. I'm going out with Jesse this weekend."

"You shouldn't play with people's hearts like that."

"I'm not, Jos. I'm really...I'm really going to give him a chance this time. I'm seeing what happens. Anyway, it's doesn't seem like anyone else is ever going to ask me out. Jesse might be my only choice."

Josie and Diana exchanged a glance, but they didn't argue with her. She spun away from them and strode toward her classroom.

She could feel their eyes on her back. She spun back to them. "What?"

"Nothing!"

* * *

Aurora stood in front of the mirror in her bedroom, frowning thoughtfully at her reflection. Jesse was cute and sweet, and he had been devoted to her since they were small children. He deserved a real chance. He didn't deserve a date that spent the entire time thinking of another guy. She squared her shoulders and chose her favorite coral sundress.

She braided her hair into a long plait. Then she shook it out. She put on some mascara.

Ruby looked up at her as she hurried downstairs, setting down her wine glass in surprise. "Aurora Sky. You look great. Where are you headed?"

Aurora pushed her long hair behind her ear. "I have a date."

Her aunt's eyes lit up. "A date? Really? With who? Sable Jayne?"

She tried not to let her shoulders sag. "No. With Jesse Drake."

"Jesse Drake? The boy who's been after you for years?"

"Yeah."

"What happened?"

"What do you mean? Nothing happened."

"So you just changed your mind."

"Well, I thought it was time I had a real date, and Jesse's the only one asking."

Ruby smiled. "Okay. Well, at least he's cute. He's as cute as that Sable Jayne, anyway."

Jesse was as cute as Sable, but he wasn't...It didn't matter. She was going out with Jesse, not Sable. "Yeah. He is."

324

"So what are you two going to do?"

"I don't know. He's picking me up in a few minutes."

"Can I meet him?"

"Ruby, come on."

"I let you meet my date!"

"Yeah, but not until you went out a bunch of times. Give me a break."

Ruby laughed. "Okay, okay."

They both looked up as a motorcycle roared up the street, idling in front of the house.

"That's him."

"On a motorcycle? How very sexy and urban."

"Yeah. That's Jesse."

"You go on. I won't embarrass you."

Aurora smiled and scooped up her handbag. "Bye, Ruby!"

"I expect to hear all about it!" Ruby called as Aurora slammed the door, hurrying to meet Jesse.

He stood and pulled off his helmet, shaking out his shaggy, blonde hair. His face lit up as he watched her come toward him. His eyes were so bright, flawlessly blue. His white tee shirt stretched taut over his broad chest. He was gorgeous, and he looked at her as though there was nothing more he could ever want in the world.

She felt nothing. No racing heart or butterflies in her stomach.

It didn't matter. This was her first real date, and he was hot. She smiled back at him as he strode forward to meet her. "You look beautiful, Aurora."

She blushed under his warm, intense gaze. He'd always been so frank, so honest and obvious about how he felt about her. It was refreshing after the hot and cold treatment she'd been getting from Sable. "Thanks, Jesse."

"Here." He presented a pale, mint green helmet. "I thought you'd like the color."

She smiled and let him draw her closer to pull the helmet gently over her hair. "I do."

"Ready?"

"Yeah." She climbed onto the bike, wrapping her arms around his waist. He was so warm. "Where are we going?"

"How about Colletta's?"

Everyone in town would see them. Everyone would be talking about it. So what? Good. Maybe Sable would hear about it and have something to think about. She felt a stab of guilt. She wasn't going out with Jesse to get back at Sable. She was giving him a real chance, and he was so excited. He'd tried so hard for so long, she owed him that much.

"Sure. That sounds nice."

He smiled at her over his shoulder and kicked the bike into gear. She tightened her arms around his waist. They were downtown too quickly. She liked riding with him, even if her pulse didn't leap when she spread her palms across his sculpted abdomen. Even if she felt nothing as he leaned back against her.

Colletta's was packed and noisy when they arrived. She hesitated for a moment outside, but Jesse smiled at her and wrapped her fingers in his large, warm hand. She resisted the instinct to pull away from him. She ignored the turned heads and raised eyebrows as Jesse led her to an empty table in the back of the shop.

He was happy, and he wasn't trying to hide it. He grinned at her and reached across the table to brush his fingers so lightly over her hand she nearly shivered. "Aurora, I'm glad you decided to come out with me. I won't ask you why."

"Okay."

"People have been talking a lot about you and Sable Jayne."

She looked away. "It's just talk, Jesse."

"You didn't go on a date with him?"

"No. Not a real one. Sierra and her brother sort of bullied us into hanging out with them. It didn't mean anything. It was nothing."

"Good."

She was relieved when a young, blonde waitress paused beside their table. Her eyes lingered on Jesse longer than necessary. "What can I get you?"

Jesse smiled at Aurora, and the waitress turned to her unenthusiastically. "A mocha, please."

The waitress barely paused before she turned back to Jesse with a brilliant smile. "Black coffee."

She looked disappointed as he turned back to Aurora. She spun around, her long ponytail swinging behind her. Aurora watched after her a moment before looking back at Jesse with a shy smile. It was sort of nice to be the center of someone's attention. "This is nice."

"Yeah." His smile faded. He looked at her so seriously she couldn't hold his gaze. "I've been waiting to spend time with you for so long, Aurora."

"I know, Jesse"

"I did what you said."

"What? What did I say?"

"About school. I've been going to classes. I'm getting better grades. For you, Aurora."

"You shouldn't do it for me. You should do it for you."

"Does it matter why I'm doing it if I'm doing it?"

"I suppose it doesn't."

He gave her a lopsided smile. The waitress returned to the table with a sour expression. She plopped their drinks in front of them. "Anything else?"

Aurora smiled at her and shook her head, but Jesse ignored her completely. Aurora sipped her hot coffee quickly, wincing slightly when the liquid burned down her throat.

Jesse smiled. "Aurora, you have whipped cream on your nose."

She laughed as he reached forward and wiped it off with a gentle finger.

And then she saw him.

Sable sat across the room in a corner by himself. He held a book up to his face but she could feel his eyes as though they had branded her.

Her cheeks flamed, and she ignored him pointedly. She smiled at Jesse. "Thanks." She had known him forever, but she didn't know what to say when he looked at her with that glittering intensity in his blue eyes or with that sweet, lopsided smile. She felt awkward. "So, have you played any shows recently?"

"Yeah. Just a couple of coffee shops in Lynchburg, but nothing serious. I wish you could have seen some of them."

"Maybe—maybe sometime I will see one."

"We're really good, Aurora. We have a large following on social networks and regular fans who come see the shows."

"That's really great, Jesse."

"It doesn't mean much if I never get to see you there."

"Come on."

"I mean it. You know that, Aurora. You know how I feel about you."

She glanced away from him, unable to hold his intense gaze.

His hand covered hers. "Aurora?"

"I know, Jesse."

"Okay. That's good enough." She fidgeted nervously with her mug as he stared at her. "I really want you to see me play sometime."

"I have seen you play–" But she cut off because she realized she hadn't really ever seen him play. "No. I haven't, have I?"

"No. You could come by Sean's house some day and watch us practice."

"I'm not...I'm not so sure about that, Jesse."

His face fell.

"But I would like to see one of your shows."

"I would like that, too."

Her eyes wandered as she sipped her coffee. She fought not to seek Sable eyes. He probably hadn't noticed her at all, and, if he had, he was probably pretending she wasn't there. She spotted some of their classmates sitting together at tables over books and steaming mugs. Most of them were whispering behind their hands or staring openly at she and Jesse. She knew their date would be all over school by Monday morning if it wasn't already posted all over every social network on the Internet.

She ignored them. She was used to people talking about her by now.

As she turned back to Jesse, she caught Sable's eye. He was watching her over the top of his book. Then his eyes slid away so casually, she couldn't be sure she hadn't imagined his intent stare. Her stomach flipped uncomfortably.

Jesse caught the direction of her gaze. He turned in his chair, glancing over his shoulder. When he turned back to Aurora, he smiled as though seeing Sable there hadn't bothered him in the least. "You want to go somewhere else? Where less people are watching?"

She smiled gratefully. "Yeah. That would be good."

He tossed some money on the table then rose and offered his hand. She took it and forced herself not to glance in Sable's or anyone else's direction on their way out.

"Where are we going?" she asked as Jesse placed the helmet over her hair and fastened the strap under her chin.

"You'll see."

The ride was longer this time. Aurora closed her eyes, enjoying the soft, warm breeze that lifted her hair. She tightened her arms around his waist. When the bike started to slow, she opened her eyes, realizing he'd steered them to an overgrown park that overlooked Dinwiddie Hills. Her stomach lurched. She knew this place, though she'd never been there with a boy before.

It was well known for being the sort of place amorous teenagers could spend time together displaying their mutual affection.

Jesse parked the motorcycle under an overhanging tree and held his hand out to her. She bit her lip nervously, but she took his hand and allowed him to lead her away from the bike.

He'd been planning this. There was a blanket laid out by the tree with a large picnic basket in the very center.

"Sit," he said, but he sounded nervous, as though he thought she might refuse and demand he take her home.

Instead, she smiled and dropped down on the blanket beside the basket, watching him pull out small plastic containers of food. "This is really nice, Jesse."

"I am impressive and romantic, aren't I?"

She laughed. "Actually, yes. I am pleasantly surprised."

"Why? You didn't expect I would be? Don't you know me well enough by now?"

She should have expected it. This was Jesse. He'd always been sweet and romantic and so devoted to her, she wondered if he knew something about herself that she didn't. "You're right. I should have expected something like this."

He grinned. "But I bet you didn't know I can cook."

"No. I didn't know that at all."

"The truth is, I can't. My sister helped me with this."

"Well, it doesn't matter how it got here."

"Are you hungry?"

"Yes. As it happens, I am."

"Good." He piled a plate of chicken and salad for her. The chicken was still warm. She wondered how he'd managed to pull it off, but this was Jesse, and somehow, it didn't surprise her.

They ate in silence for several moments, enjoying the warm, peaceful evening. The sun had yet to completely fade below the horizon. She'd never seen him so content. There was something in his eyes that worried her, but she reminded herself that she was giving him a real chance.

He watched her eat with a smoldering look that made her slightly uncomfortable. He always looked at her that way, as though he could look at her forever and never feel compelled to look away, as though she was the most treasured thing in the world.

She couldn't hold his gaze. She leaned forward to hide her blush behind her hair.

Sable had looked at her like that seconds before he'd kissed her. He'd looked at her with such glittering intensity, her pulse raced and her knees went week.

When he'd pushed her away, everything came crashing down.

She glanced back up to meet Jesse's eyes. He wouldn't push her away. Somewhere, deep inside, she knew he would never let her go. She wished she wanted him. She didn't. Even this romantic picnic and his tender gazes did nothing to change it.

She would never have whom she really wanted. Jesse might be the best she could ever hope to have.

He smiled at her. She smiled back, and she tried really hard to mean it.

* * *

Sable glared across the crowded coffee shop at the door through which Aurora had just disappeared with Jesse. His body coiled to spring, but he fought down the urge to shoot to his feet and follow them.

He had other things to do.

It was better for her, anyway. He didn't like Drake, but at least he was human. He would never hurt Aurora, not even without meaning to.

His skin burned. He gritted his teeth against his agitation. He almost didn't notice Ariel Landry and the senior boy she was with gather their books and rise from their table. They didn't touch each other as they walked side by side toward the door, but they weren't fooling anyone. Sable had been watching them for several days. He was sure everyone in school knew they were more than study buddies.

Sable jammed his book into his backpack and hurried after them. It was impossible to remain unseen; he was almost getting used to the stares everywhere he went. Ariel and her date were too wrapped up in each other to notice him as they said their goodbyes.

Ariel gave the senior boy a secret smile as she climbed into her red Jeep. Sable didn't care about her date. He steered his car after hers, following at a careful distance. He didn't pay attention to where she was leading him, but he wasn't surprised when she turned into Dinwiddie Hills.

Sable had been to the overgrown park before, when he'd trolled New Coventry in search of his errant brother. He knew what people did there. If Ariel had come here, she wasn't coming alone.

It wasn't long before her date slid into the parking spot beside her Jeep. The young man glanced around before climbing into the Jeep's passenger side. Sable hoped the overhanging branches of the tree above his car would hide him as he leaned forward to get a better look into the Jeep.

The sun was just beginning to dip below the horizon.

He tensed. Ariel and the senior boy seemed just to be talking, but they hadn't come to a place like this to talk. He waited. Several moments later, Ariel leaned toward the boy beside her and pressed her lips to his. Sable sat forward in his seat.

Nothing happened. Her face was still pale and pretty. She still looked perfectly human.

He felt uncomfortable watching Ariel make out with her boyfriend, but he had to know. He had to be sure.

It was a long time before he was sure Ariel wasn't going to feed on him. If she was Jivina, she knew how to control it. He sighed and pushed his hands through his hair.

Why couldn't he?

He opened the door and swung out of the car. Ariel and her boyfriend weren't going anywhere anytime soon.

The light was fading to twilight, but he kept to the shadows of the low hanging trees.

He sensed her before he saw her. Something leapt in his chest. Then he heard Drake's voice, and he scowled, pressing back into the shadows beneath a neighboring tree.

"I'm so happy you finally decided to come out with me, Aurora."

His heat rose. He could barely see her through the canopy of trees. She smiled, but there was something desperately sad in that smile, something false. Perhaps he was imagining it. Perhaps it was only what he wanted to see.

"I'm having a nice time." Perhaps he was imagining the waver in her voice, too. "Thanks for this picnic. It was amazing."

"I'm a pretty amazing guy."

Sable scoffed and rolled his eyes, but Aurora laughed. "You're not what I expected."

"If you had, would you have gone out with me sooner?"

"Maybe it just needed to be the right time."

"Will there be a second date, then?"

Sable tensed. He shouldn't be listening to this. He should be focusing on Ariel and his investigation.

He couldn't move away.

"I don't know, Jesse."

"What do you mean? I thought we were having a nice time. I thought something was finally happening between us."

He sounded so crestfallen, Sable almost felt bad for him. He knew what it felt like to love someone he couldn't have.

"I just need to think about it."

"What else do I have to do, Aurora? I've waited for you for years. Almost all our lives. You know I love you."

"I do know that, Jesse. I'm just not sure if I'm ready."

Sable's shoulders relaxed. Jesse sighed. "Okay." He didn't sound happy.

She wasn't saying yes, but she wasn't saying no, either.

"I will wait for you, Aurora, but I won't wait forever."

"I know. Maybe you shouldn't wait."

It would be better if she were going out with Jesse. She would be untouchable then. His blood pounded in his head when he thought of her with the other boy. He gritted his teeth.

"I don't understand you," Drake growled. "Why would you even come out with me if you don't want to be with me?"

"Jesse, I just wanted to give you a chance. I thought you deserved that much."

"I did deserve that much, but is that really what you gave me? Did you ever even really consider bring with me?"

"I did." But there was that telling waver in her voice, and Sable knew she was lying.

"And what? You decided I'm not good enough after all?"

"That isn't it. You are good enough. It's just that..."

When she didn't finish, Jesse snapped, "What? You like someone else? Are you still hung up on Sable Jayne?"

Sable stiffened. He hadn't expected to be brought up in this conversation.

"I'm not hung up on anyone. It isn't anything like that."

"I don't believe you."

"You don't have to believe me."

"You're never going to say yes, are you, Aurora? Not for real."

"I said yes once, Jesse."

"Don't play with me!"

"I'm not playing with you. I promise I'm not."

"I've been putting up with this long enough. I can't do it anymore."

Sable tensed and leaned closer to peer through the leaves. Jesse dropped to his knees in front of Aurora and yanked her abruptly against him, pressing his mouth against hers. Sable started forward without thinking. Adrenaline shot through his body. He could feel his skin crawling as though bugs were squirming under the surface.

Aurora pushed Jesse away. He fell back on his heels. "Don't, Jesse."

Sable stopped dead. They couldn't see him like this. She couldn't see him like this. He scrambled back into the shadows, pressing his back against the tree trunk. He fought to catch his breath.

Jesse lowered his head in his hands. "I love you, Aurora."

"I'm sorry."

"I shouldn't have done that."

"Take me home please, Jesse."

"I really messed this up, didn't I?"

"It's all right. It's not your fault."

He wasn't listening. "I've been waiting all this time for you to give me a chance, and I screwed it up."

"It's okay."

He sighed deeply. "Come on. I'll take you home."

"Thanks."

Sable heard a car engine and hurried to watch Ariel's boyfriend backing up. He sighed in relief. The senior was all right. Ariel hadn't attacked him or fed upon him. Sable hadn't missed anything while he'd been listening to Aurora and her date. He shouldn't have let himself become so distracted.

He started toward his car as Ariel pulled out, but he stopped and turned back to watch Aurora climb onto the back of Jesse's motorcycle. She wasn't his problem tonight. She would have to take care of herself.

He followed Ariel to her house. The lights were already out, despite the relatively early hour. She was quiet as she let herself in, and in moments, a light flipped on in a room upstairs.

Sable sighed and leaned back against the headrest. It had been a complete waste of a night. Ariel Landry wasn't the monster for which he was hunting. He wasn't any closer to discovering who was behind the deaths.

And he couldn't get the conversation he'd overheard out of his head.

Chapter Sixteen

Aurora still hadn't gotten out of bed on Sunday morning. She could hear voices in the kitchen, and she knew Ruby would want to hear about her date. Her stomach growled, but she didn't move.

Her phone vibrated on the nightstand. She groaned, drawing the blanket up over her face. She waited for it to fall silent once more.

It rang again.

She huffed in aggravation and fumbled for it. She pulled it under the covers with her. Josie. She sighed and declined the call.

Josie called again.

She wasn't going to give up until Aurora answered. "Hi, Josie."

Josie didn't even scold her for ignoring her first two calls. "Have you seen the news?"

"What? No. I'm still in bed."

"At eleven o'clock? Does that mean the date went well?"

"No."

"You can tell me about it later."

This was unusual. Josie was usually concerned first and foremost with boys. "What's on the news?"

Josie's voice was oddly thick. "It's Sierra."

"Sierra? What about her?"

"She's dead."

"What?"

Josie sniffled.

"Are you sure?"

"Yes. It's just like Susan and Ellen and the Kessells. She was all dried up."

"Oh, my god."

"I'm coming over."

"Okay." Aurora sat up. Sierra was dead? She stumbled as she climbed out of bed and hurried down the stairs to flip on the news.

Ruby poked her head into the living room. "Aurora, are you up?" When Aurora looked up at her, she lifted her eyebrows. "What's wrong?"

Aurora gestured at the television. "One of my classmates."

"What?"

"She died."

"Oh, Aurora!" She hurried in to sit beside her niece, forgetting Blaine and Mike in the kitchen.

The news of Sierra's death was on every station. She'd been discovered in the woods by a hiker early that morning. The coroner was hesitant to admit the cause of death was the same as Susan Anders, Ellen Horne and the Kessells, but there was hardly any denying it.

This time, the police were sure something unusual had happened to Sierra before she died. This time, there were signs she had been with someone the night before, and they were looking for the last person who'd seen her alive.

Aurora's stomach roiled. What was happening?

"Sierra Drew?" Ruby asked in a hushed voice.

"Yeah." She'd just seen her. She'd just been avoiding her in the halls two days before. Though she'd died the same way as the others, Sierra's death felt different.

Sierra had been a part of her life. Sure, she hadn't always liked her; in fact, most of the time she'd almost hated her. Now she was dead. Aurora would never see her again.

She didn't know how she was supposed to feel. It was awful that anyone had died, but it felt nothing like losing her mom.

"That poor girl," Ruby murmured.

"Yeah. It's terrible."

"Her parents must be--" She passed a hand over her face. "I don't even want to think about it. It's just awful. Did she seem sick to you when you last saw her?"

"No. She was fine. The same as always."

Ruby sighed, and they lapsed into silence as they watched the report repeat over and over until they thought they knew every last tiny detail—except what had actually happened to her.

Josie barely knocked on the door before she burst in. Mike poked his head out of the kitchen in surprise. "We're in here, Josie," Aurora called.

She looked as though she'd been crying. She threw herself down next to Aurora and leaned against her shoulder. "Oh, Aurora, can you believe it? It's just awful, isn't it?

"No. I really can't believe it."

"I mean, we hated Sierra, but I didn't want her to die."

"I didn't hate her. I don't hate anybody."

Josie huffed. "Yeah, yeah. I know. You're perfect."

"What?"

"I'm sorry, Rora. I didn't mean it. I'm just—I'm all messed up."

"I know what you mean. I didn't want her dead, either. Especially not like this."

"Do you think it really is some kind of plague?"

"I hope not," Ruby whispered.

"No," said Aurora. "I don't. It can't be. I think it's something else."

"Do you think the guy she was with last night was Van?" Josie asked.

"Probably. Maybe, anyway. I don't know that much about Sierra. I don't know what sorts of things she was really capable of doing."

"We didn't really know her at all," Josie agreed, sniffling.

"What's is going on?" Ruby murmured finally.

None one could answer her. Josie reached over and snapped off the television. "Oh, how did your date with Jesse go last night?" She didn't sound as enthusiastic as usual. In fact, she seemed only to want to talk about something other than Sierra.

Suddenly, the disastrous date didn't seem to matter much anymore. "It wasn't great. It started out okay, but it got kind of weird in the end."

"So...it didn't turn out the way you were hoping."

"I was just hoping I would feel differently about him. I thought maybe if I gave him a real chance, maybe I would start to like him."

"But you didn't," Ruby guessed.

"No. I just don't feel that way about him. I don't think I ever will."

"Poor guy. Did you tell him?"

"Well, not exactly. Not in those words."

"What?" Josie demanded. "Are you just going to string him along?"

"No! I wouldn't do that. I wouldn't even know how. Anyway, I just didn't want to hurt his feelings."

"So what did you two do?"

"He took me to Colletta's."

"Oh, man, he didn't waste any time showing off, huh?"

Aurora pinched the bridge of her nose. "I know it's horrible, but at least no one will be talking about Jesse and me tomorrow. I shouldn't have said that. There is nothing good about what happened to Sierra. Anyway, then he took me to the top of Dinwiddie Hills."

"Is that still the place—?" Ruby cut off.

"Apparently," Aurora replied. Josie giggled.

"Aurora Sky!"

"Oh, it wasn't like that. We just had a picnic."

"A picnic? Really?"

"Yeah. It was...well, it was kind of nice."

"But you still didn't go for it, huh?"

"It wasn't the picnic that was the problem. I'm just not interested in him. I wish I were. I wish I could be."

"So what do you think is really going on with these deaths, if you don't think it's a plague?" Josie murmured abruptly.

Aurora sighed. "I have no idea. It's just so—weird and awful."

"Do you think everyone will be gone from school tomorrow?"

"I don't know. I think it's going to be really uncomfortable. Are you going this time?"

"Yeah. I want to see how it all shakes out."

"I feel bad for Cami and Callie," said Aurora.

"What? Why?"

"They've been best friends with Sierra since they were kids, but they've been fighting a lot lately. They probably feel really awful they didn't make peace with her before she died."

"I feel worse for Brooke. She's actually been Sierra's real friend. I don't know what she'll do without Sierra."

Aurora thought of Sable then. She wondered how Van and his family were taking the news. She'd thought Van and Sierra really had something. She wondered how he was doing. She wondered if he knew what had happened to her. She wondered if he had anything to do with it. A frisson of ice slithered down her spine.

Of course he didn't. How could he have? But then, nothing had happened until the Jaynes had arrived. No one had died until then. And Sable...he'd been acting so strange. Hadn't he warned her not to go near Van? Did he know something? Was Van...?

That was ridiculous. Of course Van didn't have anything to do with it. What could the Jaynes possibly know about the deaths?

"Aurora?"

She shook off the strange, uncomfortable thoughts. "Huh?"

"What were you thinking about?" Josie asked.

"Just...Sable."

"What? At a time like this, you're thinking about your crush? That sounds more like me than you."

"No, not like that. I was just wondering how his family is doing. How Van is doing. I wonder if his parents knew her and stuff."

"Do you think he brought her home to meet them?"

"I have no idea, but he seemed to really like her. I don't know if it was all for show, but it seemed like they were close. I'm sure he's upset. It couldn't just be easy to lose her like that."

Josie's eyes lit up. "You can ask Sable about it tomorrow. It would be a nice excuse to talk to him."

"I wouldn't exploit Sierra's death like that. It's horrible."

"You're right. I'm sorry. It is horrible. I shouldn't have said that."

"It was awful," Ruby agreed gently.

"Am I an awful person?"

"No," Aurora told her, patting her arm. "We're still just processing it all. I'm sure you will get it right soon enough."

"Maybe we shouldn't go to school tomorrow. If it really is some kind of virus or something, what do you think Sierra has in common with Susan and Ellen and the Kessells? How did they all catch it?"

"Janie, maybe? We have English class with her."

"Yeah, but then you and the rest of school would be sick, too, right?"

"Maybe."

"It could be contagious. What if it is going around school? What if we get it?"

"Josie, don't start getting paranoid. I don't think we'll get it. Janie hasn't died or anything, and she lived with her mom."

"Maybe she's immune."

"Okay." Ruby held up her hands. "I can't listen to this. It will just freak me out."

"I don't think it's a virus," Aurora insisted. "I don't think it's anything like that. The news reports say the police still don't know, and there isn't any evidence of any virus in the bodies here or in those other places they found the same kind of deaths."

Sable flashed into her mind again. He'd had a list of those places when he'd asked about Blaine.

She frowned. There was a lot more to the deaths than it seemed. She was sure. There was something going on that the police didn't know.

But perhaps Sable Jayne did.

* * *

Sable blinked at the sunlight streaming in through his window. He hadn't slept well. He sighed and stumbled out of bed.

There was a strange feeling in the house. He could hear the murmur of his parents' voices behind his father's office door. He knocked once, softly, and pushed inside the room. His parents sat side by side on the sofa. They glanced up at him with grim expressions. Evelyn nervously paced the room. She did not pause to acknowledge her brother.

"What's going on?"

"We have a problem," his father told him.

"What sort of problem?"

"The police were here."

"What?"

"Sierra is dead."

"Sierra?"

"Your brother's...girlfriend."

"I know who she is. She's dead?"

"Yes."

"I assume it was one of us?"

"Yes."

He pushed his hands through his hair with an agitated growl. "Damn it. Did he do this?"

"We don't know," Mariah said. "He isn't here."

"Of course he did this!" Evelyn snapped.

"Couldn't he just...couldn't he just try? For once?"

"We cannot be sure it was him," Mariah argued. "He is not responsible for the other four deaths. He was trying."

"And it's just coincidence the dead girl happens to be his girlfriend this time?" Evelyn asked tersely. "I can't believe you're still giving him the benefit of the doubt after all of this. You know what he's capable of. You know what he's done in the past."

Sable cursed. "I can't believe this."

"Sable!" Mariah snapped. "Just find him. Bring him home. We have to figure out what happened. If he did this, we need to know."

"If he did this," Adam added, "It's time to leave again."

"And if he didn't, even if he didn't...we might still think of leaving," Mariah murmured. "Too much has happened here."

Sable shook his head violently. "I will find him. But if he did this, you know what you have to do, Dad. You know. We can't leave again."

"Sable..." Mariah began.

"If you could keep control of him, this never would have happened!"

"Sable, do not speak to your mother that way."

"Why not? You could have stopped this! You could have stopped him. He is out of control, and you know it. You could have done something to make sure that girl didn't die. She didn't have to die!"

"This isn't helping anyone or anything. We need to find your brother. We will know what happened when we find him. There is still another one of us out there. We cannot be sure."

"It's a pretty big coincidence."

"Then we should go," Evelyn said. "The police already know he was involved with her. They are looking for him."

"And we don't need to draw attention to ourselves by disappearing right now!" Sable snapped at her.

"We will speak about staying or going when we speak with him," said Mariah.

"We cannot leave!"

"Just find your brother," Adam ordered. "And find the other Jivina. We have to understand the situation before we can make any decisions. Sable is right; it will look very bad for us if we disappear now, under this veil of suspicion. It will follow us wherever we go, and someone might start looking more closely into us."

Sable's shoulders relaxed in relief. "When I find him, if we find out he did this...you have to promise."

"What?"

"You know what I am talking about. You have to promise you will do something about him. We wouldn't have to keep running if you would just keep him under control. You can stop him."

Dead silence filled the room as they considered the magnitude of what

Sable was asking.

"We can't promise that, Sable," Mariah told him in a quiet voice.

"Why do you keep protecting him?"

"He is my son! He is your brother. You think I want to let him keep going on like this?"

"Their lives are on your hands. You've known what he is and what he is capable of all this time, and you keep letting it happen. This girl's death is on you!"

"That is not fair, Sable."

"Isn't it? How long have we been doing this? How much longer are we going to keep doing it?"

"Sable is right," Evelyn said. "Van is a problem. We can't keep letting him run wild. He's ruining all our lives."

Mariah held her husband's eyes as she spoke. "All right. If he did this, we will take care of it. He will not have the chance to do it again."

"And we can stay," Sable added.

Adam's jaw tightened. "We will speak of this when we have located your brother and identified the other Jivina."

Sable scowled. "You can't just send me out to do the family's dirty work and not give me anything in return. I am fighting for this life here. I want to know it isn't for nothing."

"I can't promise you anything, Sable. I don't know how this is going to shake out."

"Fine. I'll do it." He spun and stormed toward the door. Then he stopped. "But if you leave again, I won't go with you."

* * *

To Aurora's surprise, only a few students had stayed home on Monday. The ones who came were quiet and morose. Many of them were weeping openly. Even the people Sierra had spent years terrorizing were struck by her death. It was as though everyone had forgotten all the mean-spiritedness and the nasty insults now that she was dead.

Sierra's best friend, Brooke, wasn't in class, and Claire Ames told anyone who would listen that she hadn't left her room since she'd heard the news.

Callie and Cami Lawson didn't say anything to anyone. They spoke to each other in quiet voices and ignored anyone who tried to console them.

Aurora wondered how they were really feeling. They'd been close to Sierra since they were kids, but they had seemed to hate her as much as they loved her. Most people had hated Sierra a little, but no one was willing to admit it now. Instead, they whispered heatedly about what had happened to her.

Everyone was afraid that it would happen to them, too.

Something very strange was happening. Aurora waited for Sable to show up in school. He didn't. People talked about Van, speculating about whether he'd been with her before she died and if he had anything to do with her death. No one knew anything about Van. Even Aurora, who had spent time with him, knew nothing about him. She just knew Sable knew something that had made him afraid for her.

People said things. They said Sierra had spent her nights at the local bars, doing things she shouldn't, hanging around with older men. Aurora wasn't sure she believed this. There were always rumors around school and around town. If it was true, the police already knew.

She didn't think she really wanted to know what Sierra was doing. It sounded awful. Had she been so unhappy that she'd had to do terrible things just to feel alive or loved or—whatever it was she was getting out of it?

Where was Sable? She wanted to see him desperately, but it was worse than that because she was afraid he really did know what was happening. Or maybe he just didn't want to be hounded by his classmates asking him questions about his brother and Sierra.

Her nerves frayed as the day wore on and she didn't see him. She was going to find him. If he knew something about all this, she was going to find out what it was. He had been trying to get information from her about people in town, about Blaine, and if it had something to do with the deaths, he owed her an explanation.

She steeled her resolve. She didn't know how she would find him, and she wasn't even sure she wanted to know what he knew, but she had to find out. If it was just something awful about Blaine, Ruby needed to know about it. If it was about the deaths...

She shivered. She was probably making too much out of it. In any case, she was going to make him explain why he'd been asking all those questions. He was going to have to tell her why he'd been so strange about Van and Sierra.

He was going to talk to her instead of avoiding her.

Her friends found her after school. Diana had taken the news of Sierra's death well, but her expression was morose. Josie looked as though she'd been crying again. She threaded her arm through Aurora's. "Come on. I have to get out of this place. All anyone can talk about is how much they miss Sierra."

Aurora hesitated, and Diana frowned at the determined expression on her friend's face. "What's up, Aurora? Aren't you coming?"

"No. I want to go into do town. I have something I need to do."

"What?" Josie asked, looking a little hurt.

"I just need to talk to my dad."

"Okay." Diana stepped forward to hug her. "Just be careful, okay? We don't know what Sierra was really doing before she died. I don't want anything to happen to you."

Aurora smiled tightly. "I'll see you guys tomorrow."

She didn't worry about how she would find him. She was curiously confident that he would be lurking around downtown, as he often was. She didn't see him as she strode through the town square. She didn't let it dampen her determination.

She stopped in at Ruby Rose. The place was so crowded with people ordering flowers for the Drew family that Aurora had to fight her way to the counter. "Hey, Ruby."

Ruby's eyes looked red. She groaned in relief when she saw her niece. "Oh, Aurora, can you help me out here? The phone's just been ringing off the hook."

"Sure." It had been a long time since Aurora had helped out at the flower shop. She'd avoided it for the first year after her mother's death. She didn't have time to feel sad as she took order after order. She felt almost happy again, despite the awful circumstances.

Ruby sagged dramatically when the rush died down. "Oh, Aurora, thank goodness for you. Thanks for helping."

"It was no problem," Aurora said. "It was kind of fun."

Her aunt smiled weakly. "You know you always have a job here if you want it. I just thought...well."

"I might think about it."

"I feel so bad for Sierra's family. Did you know her very well?"

"Sierra? About as well as I would have liked, I guess."

"It's horrible. Just...someone so young. It was bad enough before. Now with this...I just don't understand what's going on."

"Me neither. I really don't." They were silent a moment. "How is Blaine?"

Ruby was grateful for the subject change. "He's been working a lot with Troy. You know, finishing up paperwork on the old house and closing on the new house. Even though they already have buyers on the old house, they're showing it a lot. It's good business. I know I shouldn't be happy at a time like this, but I think he's going to stay."

"It's becoming serious then." Aurora's smile wavered a bit. Something was seriously wrong in this town, and she wasn't entirely sure her aunt's new boyfriend didn't have something to do with it. Something wasn't right with Blaine or Sable. She was sure of it.

"Yeah. I think so."

"That's really great, Ruby. I'm glad you found someone you like so much."

Ruby studied her. "You know, you've been looking pretty down lately. Do you want to talk about it?"

"It's just...I feel bad for Jesse. The date really did not go well."

"It's hard to love someone who doesn't love you back." Ruby squeezed her arm. "But it would be crueler to string him along."

"I know."

"It will get better. For both of you. Sometimes it takes a while, but you will find the right person. You're still young. Look at me. It took decades."

She knew exactly what Ruby meant about loving someone who didn't feel the same. Could someone who didn't love her as she loved him possibly be the right person? She shook it off. It wasn't important now.

The phone trilled again. "I really want to talk, Aurora, but I have to take this."

"It's okay. I'll see you later at home." She waved at her aunt and stepped outside into the brilliant sunlight.

There was no flash of dark hair, no sign of the boy for whom she was looking. She had been so sure she would find him. He wasn't lurking around Colletta's or in the alley outside her father's shop. He wasn't anywhere.

She sighed and headed home, disappointed.

She lay in bed that night, unable to sleep. It was late, but Ruby was with Blaine, and her father was staying the night with Julia. She sighed deeply and threw the covers off. She needed some fresh air.

It was after midnight on a school night, but she didn't care. The clear night sky helped her think, and she needed to think. She wandered the streets around her house, her face lifted. The stars were brilliant tonight, glittering above her head without a cloud in the sky. She sighed contentedly. It felt right here, in the quiet, peaceful night, under the stars.

She was shocked when a shadow unfolded from under a tree. She recognized him immediately, even before he stepped out into the meager moonlight.

"Sable? Sable!"

He stopped dead in his tracks. He didn't even have to turn around. His shoulders hunched. "Just leave me alone, Aurora."

"No." She didn't even think about it. She raced forward and caught his arm.

For a moment, he just stared down at her hand. Then he shrugged it off. He didn't move.

"Please, just talk to me."

He spun abruptly, and the glitter in his eyes sent her heart racing.

She didn't wait for him to say anything more. "I know you know something about Sierra's death."

"What are you talking about?" His tone was low and strange. She knew it was stupid, that if she was wrong she was making a complete idiot of herself, but the odd note in his voice bolstered her confidence.

"You were asking questions about Blaine and about Ariel Landry. You were acting weird about Van and Sierra and you made me go on that date with you, and you told me to stay away from them, and now Sierra is dead. You had a list of places where other people were found dead the same way, and you were checking them off when you were asking me questions." She looked up into his face, and the cold, grim dread that crept across his features was answer enough. "What do you know? How did Sierra die? Did Van do something to her? Did he do something to the others?"

"You don't know what you're talking about. You sound crazy right now. How could he have done something? What could he have done?"

"I don't know. But I think you do. What's going on, Sable?"

He took a step back. "Just stay away from me, Aurora. I don't want to see you."

She followed him, stepping up so she was only inches away from him. "I think you do. I think you do want to see me, but there is something you're scared of. I want to know what it is. This isn't fair. I deserve to know."

"I'm not afraid of anything. I'm sorry if you thought there was something going on between us. There wasn't."

"And what about when you kissed me?"

"You kissed me."

"Yes, but then you kissed me. And you ran away. Why?"

"Because I didn't want to kiss you."

"Yes, you did. I could tell. And I think you're putting me off because you think what happened to Sierra might happen to me." He was so still, his body vibrated. "Is that why you told me not to see your mother anymore? Is your family dangerous?" She suspected she would regret her words in the morning. She knew none of them could possibly be true, but something spurred her on. They felt so eerily, terribly right.

There was something frightening in his eyes.

"What is it, Sable? What are you so afraid I'll find out?" She took another step, and she could feel his shallow breath stir the fine hairs on her forehead.

"You don't know anything," he said harshly. An intense chill radiated off his body. "This is ridiculous. I'm just not interested in you. Can't you just take a hint instead of turning it into some—whatever this is you're doing right now? Deal with it. I don't want you. I don't want you around me. Just stay away."

This hurt her, and she took a hitching breath, but there was something different in his eyes now. His words were as painful to say as they were to hear. She knew it. They weren't true. Somewhere inside her, she was sure. He was lying.

"I'm not going to do that. I'm not giving up on you, Sable. I'm going to find out what is haunting you. Why you keep moving around all the time and what your brother really is. Is he the reason you move around a lot? Does this happen a lot wherever you go? Do people die?" When he glared at her silently, she soldiered on. "I can find out, you know."

He spun his back to her, pushing his hands through her hair. She was prepared to grab him again, to cling on if he tried to flee. "Just leave me alone." He took one step, and she clutched his arm. He half turned his head. He took a shuddering breath. "It's too dangerous for you to be near me, Aurora. Stop this. It's for your own good. I don't want anything to happen to you."

He covered her hand with his, and his fingers clenched around hers. Then he pushed her hand away.

"What would you care if you didn't feel something for me?" She reached for him again, but he spun around, his eyes flaring in anger.

"Don't! Just go."

There was something different about him. The air around him was thick and heavy. It was dark, but his face looked different in the shadows, livid and deep red. Strange scars swirled over his skin. She gasped.

He spun back around. She had imagined the change. She must have.

"Just leave it alone, Aurora. I don't want anything to do with you."

She didn't move as he stormed away, disappearing into the shadows.

Her heart lurched. "Sable? What are you?"

He was already gone.

Chapter Seventeen

Sable didn't return to school all week. Aurora looked for him in the halls and lingered outside the front door, but he didn't come. She wondered if he was avoiding her or the rumors about his brother. Probably both. Everyone was talking about Sierra's death. The police were looking for Van, but no one seemed to have any idea where he'd gone. Unless the Jaynes were hiding him, he wasn't at home—or, at least, that's what Alexandra York, the daughter of the detective assigned to the case, told anyone who would listen.

Some people thought Van knew what had happened to Sierra. Others thought he was dead, too, and the police just hadn't found him yet. Aurora's blood ran cold at the idea, and she couldn't help thinking of Sable, worrying about him despite the awful things he'd said and the stupid things she'd said and...and how weird he'd looked the last time she'd seen him.

Obviously, she'd been imagining things. She was worked up about the deaths, and she had been mistaken. Either that...either that or something very, very strange was happening in New Coventry, and it had started when the Jaynes had arrived.

She held her breath as she walked into her English class. Sable wasn't there, but she hadn't really expected him. Sierra's absence was powerful. No one said much of anything. It was like standing at a dying person's bedside. Everyone spoke in whispers or just stared blankly forward without seeing anything. It was probably like this in every class she'd been in. Even Mrs. Lima was more subdued than usual.

At least she'd shown up. Many of the teachers had been replaced by substitutes.

Aurora didn't speak to anyone. She wished she could do something, but there wasn't much a high school girl could possibly do. Perhaps Sable was doing the very same thing. Perhaps he was just searching for answers now that his brother had disappeared, as well.

It struck her as she was standing outside the front doors. That's where he was. He was looking for his brother.

She jumped as Josie bumped her with the door. "Aurora? What are you doing?" Diana asked. "Are you okay?

Aurora spun to face her. "Yes. It's just...this Sierra thing. It's weird not seeing her in classes. It's like everyone's afraid to even say her name."

Josie heaved a deep sigh. "Yeah. It's so awful."

Diana's shrewd eyes didn't leave Aurora's face. "I haven't seen Sable around this week."

"I know."

"Do you really think Van...well, how do you think his family is taking it?" Josie asked.

"Van's missing. They're probably just worried about him," Diana told her.

Aurora voiced what'd she'd been thinking when the door had interrupted her thoughts. "They're probably looking for him." Her gaze focused on her friends. "I have to go."

"What?"

"I need to do something."

"Is there something you want to tell us, Aurora?" Diana asked suspiciously.

"What? No. It's just...I have to help Ruby at the shop. It's really busy with the memorial service tomorrow."

"Do you want a ride?" Josie asked gently.

"No. It's okay. Thanks, though. You guys go home. Just stay safe. We still don't know what's really going on here. I'll see you later, okay?" She didn't wait for them to say anything more. With a short wave, she hurried down the stairs and strode determinedly toward the town square.

She didn't stop at Ruby's shop right away. She knew her aunt was scrambling to complete the orders for Sierra's memorial service the next day. She could probably use some help, and it had been almost fun last time. Even after all these years, the shop reminded her and everyone else in town of her mother.

The last time she'd been surrounded by so many flowers was at her mother's funeral. She hated funerals.

She wasn't ready to go back, not yet.

Her father was finishing up with a customer when she arrived at Geller's Auto Repair. He looked surprised to see her again so soon since her last visit.

"Hey, kiddo," he said as he walked out the young couple, promising to have their car back as good as new in three days. "What are you doing here?"

"I want to borrow a car."

"A car? What for? I thought you hated driving."

"Yeah, but...well, with what's going on, I think it's better if I'm not walking around." She hated lying to anyone, especially her father and her best friends, but she didn't think anyone would like what she was really up to.

"Are you getting worked up with everyone else?"

"No, but...well, it's better to be safe."

"You're right. I was planning to stay at Julia's tonight, but maybe I should stay home."

"No, there's no need. I'm fine, Dad. Nothing's going to happen to me. I just thought it would be better to have a car for a while, that's all."

"Are you should you don't want me to stay home?"

"No. It's no big deal." She smiled. "It's not like I need protection. I'll be fine. Ruby will be home with me."

"All right. If you say so. Julia would kill me if I didn't make our date tonight. It's been so busy with work lately."

"Have a nice time with Julia, Dad. Don't worry about me. I'm fine."

He fished through his pockets for his key ring. "You can take the Civic. I just gave it a tune up."

Aurora rose on her tiptoes to kiss his cheek. "Thanks, Dad."

"Don't wreck it."

She laughed. "I won't."

"Do you need a ride to the house?"

"No, that's okay. I was planning to stop in at the shop and see if Ruby needs any help before the memorial tomorrow."

He smiled, as though this was the best news he'd heard in a long time. "That's great, Aurora. She could probably use it. She's busier than me these days."

"See you tomorrow."

"Sure. Be careful."

"I will. Bye, Dad."

Ruby looked desperately relieved to see her. "Oh, Aurora. I'm so glad you're here."

"Do you need help?"

"Yes. Thank you so much. With the memorial tomorrow, all the last minute shoppers are hoping for a miracle."

"I can answer the phones again."

"Actually, do you think you could help with the arrangements? Amy had to go home sick, and Ellie just can't keep up."

Aurora took a deep breath. She'd helped her mother with the arrangements years ago. It had been her favorite job at the shop. Ruby looked desperate, so she smiled and jumped in. It distracted her for a while, and she was thankful for the work. It felt good to be doing something.

"Are you going to the service?" Ruby asked, hurrying over to help finish up the flowers when the rush at the counter died down a little.

"Yes. It seems like the right thing to do. They cancelled school for it and everything."

"It's so sad. I'll be there to deliver flowers, but I can't imagine what her family is going through. They seem like such nice people."

Aurora wouldn't know. She only knew that Sierra hadn't been that nice, and she always thought her parents were either especially cruel or especially indulgent. She made a noncommittal noise as she handed Ruby a sprig of baby's breath.

"I heard they haven't found her boyfriend yet."

"No. Not yet."

"Do you think something happened to him, too?"

"I don't know."

Ruby lowered her voice and glanced around the shop. "I've been hearing things. Some people think he knows something so he's hiding out."

"What could he know? Sierra just got sick, right?"

"No one really knows. They think he might be able to explain what's happening. I heard some people out at the Boundary Stone saw her the night she died."

"What? At the bar?"

"Yeah. And it wasn't the first time. I heard she goes out there a lot."

"But she's underage. They just let her?"

"Pretty girls like Sierra usually find ways around stuff like that. I used to go to bars all the time when I was your age."

Aurora opened her mouth in shock. "What?"

"Come on, Aurora. I wasn't always well behaved. In fact, I was almost never well behaved. In case you forgot, I was a teen mom."

"But--"

"I know. I've grown up." Ruby smiled a wistfully. Then she gave Aurora a sharp look. "You don't do things like that, do you?"

"No way. So people saw her there?"

"A few people said they did. She was talking to a lot of people, as usual."

"Was Van there?"

"Yeah. They think he was there, too. Allie Weiss said it looked like they were arguing, and then he took off. Sierra left a little while after that."

"She left alone?"

"Allie thinks so. She was pretty sure. That's what she told the police."

"So there's no way to know who she was with. She might have met back up with Van or anyone else."

"It's all so terrible. I remember how reckless I was at that age. I'm always amazed nothing worse ever happened to me. Your friend Sable must be upset."

"I don't know. I haven't seen him in a while. He hasn't been at school. I'm sure he is, though."

"His parents must be worried sick if their son is really missing. He could be dead for all anyone knows. If he's got something to do with it, and they're hiding him..." Ruby shook her head. "I don't know which is worse."

Aurora reached over to straighten the arrangement of blue irises. "Yeah. I know what you mean."

* * *

It was late. She shouldn't be lurking outside the Jaynes' house. The old Aurora would never sit in the dark, watching a boy's house, even if she was worried about him and his family. The old Aurora would never have kissed Sable in the middle of the road or confronted him to begin with. The new Aurora did all sorts of things that would have shocked and horrified the old Aurora.

She wasn't sure which Aurora she would rather be.

She sighed and slid lower in the driver's seat. Lights burned faintly in the house. She wasn't sure if the light above on the third floor belonged to Sable, but her heart thumped as it blinked out. She waited, and when the black sedan pulled swiftly out of the drive, she ducked down, narrowly avoiding being spotted in his headlights.

She let him get a couple blocks ahead of her and steered slowly after him. She was right. He was looking for Van.

Or he was doing normal high school boy things. Like meeting a girl.

Her stomach lurched, but he didn't seem to be meeting anyone. She was surprised by the familiar direction he took. She'd seen his route nearly everyday since Josie had gotten her driver's license. He was driving toward her neighborhood.

He didn't stop anywhere, but he slowed as he passed by her house. The lights were off. Ruby and her Dad were out for the night, and the only other occupant was idling in a car a few houses away, shocked that Sable knew where she lived and was checking up on her.

Was that what he was doing?

She didn't know what he was doing, for he accelerated once more, steering out of her neighborhood. She knew this route, as well, though it took her a moment to realize why. He was driving toward Blaine's house.

He stopped the black sedan across the street and shut off the engine.

There was a light burning on the top floor. Aurora knew Blaine was upstairs with Ruby. What was Sable doing here? What did he think was going to happen? What was he trying to do? What did he think Blaine was going to do to her aunt?

Nothing did happen. After only half an hour Blaine's light flipped off.

Sable stayed for several moments longer. Aurora tried to catch a glimpse of his face, but a large tree obscured the streetlight above his car, making it difficult to see in the darkness. He'd been there before. He knew exactly where to park to remain unseen.

Finally, he started his engine and slid slowly away from Blaine's house without turning on his headlights. Aurora waited a beat and followed. Sable didn't take her anywhere this time. He drove aimlessly around town for an hour, finally slowing as he neared the Boundary Stone, the bar Sierra had visited the night she died.

He might have been looking for Van's car or he might...

Had he been there? Did he know exactly what had happened?

No. Of course he hadn't been there. He couldn't have been there. Whatever she suspected about Sable and his family, whatever she thought he might know, she knew he couldn't possibly have done anything to anyone. He couldn't have been there when Sierra or any of those people had died.

He stopped his car outside the Boundary Stone and stepped out. She caught her breath. He looked tired and worn. She wondered how long he'd been searching or doing whatever it was he was doing. She slunk down in her seat and watched him walk inside the bar.

It was only moments before he returned, scowling. He pushed his hands through his already disheveled hair. Van must not be inside. Or perhaps he was and there was nothing Sable could do to get him out.

For a brief, wild moment, Aurora reached for the door handle. To confront Sable or go inside to search for Van, she didn't know. The moment passed. Even the new Aurora knew it was stupid. She didn't want Sable to know she was following him. She didn't want to find Van. She didn't want to know what happened to Sierra, not intimately, anyway.

Instead, she followed Sable when he climbed back into his car. He led her back to her own neighborhood and parked across the street, in the shadows. He shut off the engine. He seemed intent on staying a while.

How often did he park outside her house in the dark?

She waited for him to get out of the car and approach the house, but he didn't. She remembered the night she'd first met him walking around her neighborhood. Had that been the first time he'd been wandering around her house? Had he known then what was happening? Had he been protecting her or...was he stalking her?

She reminded herself she'd been doing precisely the same thing, trailing him around town for the better part of two hours. Besides, why would he be? Perhaps he was watching for Blaine or perhaps he thought...

Perhaps he thought something was going to happen to her. Perhaps he was looking out for her.

She didn't know. It might just be a coincidence. She was more concerned, at the moment, with how she was going to get back into her house without being caught. She hoped he hadn't noticed her following him. Perhaps he was waiting to confront her and demand to know why she was still bothering him.

Maybe he'd known all along that she was there. Maybe that was why he'd gone to her house. Maybe he didn't care what happened to her at all. Of course he wasn't stalking her. Of course he wasn't lurking around her house, watching over her. He'd made it clear he wanted nothing to do with her.

She felt like a complete idiot. What was she doing? What had she even learned? All she knew was that he was checking out Blaine and had spent five minutes inside the Boundary Stone. He might have only been toying with her.

Her mind raced. Sable didn't move. She checked her watch. It was late. She couldn't stay in her car forever. If he were going to confront her, she would have to face him. She had, after all, been looking for him. She had questions, even if they might all be wild, ridiculous speculation.

Something wasn't right with Sable. She had to know what it was or she might go mad.

She sighed and restarted her engine. She didn't drive directly to her house. Instead, she circled the block, hoping he hadn't been paying attention to her car, hoping it was too dark for him to notice the car that pulled into her driveway was the same that had been parked just a few houses away only moments ago.

She held her breath as she stepped out of the car. She didn't turned back to look at him. She kept her back straight and waited for him to catch her or call to her as she strode up to the front door.

He didn't. He didn't even turn on the car. If she hadn't been following him all night, she wouldn't have even known he was there. It was dark and empty inside. Her heart raced as she thought of him out there. She could see him. She could talk to him. She hurried up the stairs and peeked out the window.

Sable was gone. She leaned her forehead against the cool windowsill. Was he worried about her? Was he afraid for her?

What was he afraid would happen to her?

* * *

She was still thinking of him at Sierra's memorial service the next day as she helped Ruby set up the flower arrangements around the chapel at the local Presbyterian Church. The church filled with mourners. Sierra's parents wept in the front pew before their daughter's closed coffin. Aurora avoided them.

She was sorry for their loss, but there was nothing to say that would make it any better.

Her gaze wandered from her work, searching in vain for Sable. She knew Van wouldn't be there. The police were still looking for him, and no one was even sure he was still alive.

Ruby let her go when Josie and Diana arrived. Aurora had never seen Josie look so subdued. She wasn't even wearing makeup. Her eyes looked red. Diana smiled weakly and led them to a seat near their classmates. No one said anything, and family's quiet sobbing echoed around the church.

Aurora looked around at the crowd. There were so many people there. Brooke Hadley wept openly on her boyfriend's shoulder. Aurora suddenly wondered how she would feel if it had been Josie or Diana. She wondered how they would feel if it had been her.

Her throat tightened. She remembered her mother's funeral. She couldn't remember the words anyone spoke or the consolations they'd given. She only remembered realizing this was the very last time she would ever be close to her mother again. By then, her mother had already been long gone.

She had smelled flowers. Hundreds of flowers. Just like now.

Sierra's few friends spoke about her. The twins talked about growing up with her. They didn't say anything about the nastiness or the fighting. They didn't say anything about bullying other students. They told stories of childhood hopes and dreams that Sierra would never be able to fulfill. They talked about everything she could and should have been. They talked about how she would have wanted them to go on and fulfill their own dreams. She would have wanted them to be happy.

That's what people always said. It seemed like the right thing to say.

Aurora wondered if that was true.

Brooke couldn't speak at all. She had truly loved Sierra. She'd been the only one spared Sierra's vicious tongue. She was the only one who had seen the sweet, generous and caring side of Sierra.

Except Aurora had seen it, too, once. She thought of the day she'd spent with Sierra and Van and Sable. She felt a tear slide down her cheek. She'd thought she could have been friends with Sierra that day, if not for all the awfulness that had come before. She'd wished it had been the first time she'd met her.

Beside her, Josie wept into a tissue. She'd never liked Sierra, but she couldn't sit amongst the people who had loved her without feeling the awful, heavy sadness that shrouded them all.

There was fear, too. A lot of fear. It was almost tangible.

She peered around the chapel, unable to watch Sierra's father stand on the podium at the front of the room, tears streaming down his cheeks as he spoke of his daughter in a husky voice. Her breath caught in her throat as she spotted a head of dark hair sitting alone in the back of the church. For a moment, she could not see his face, but she knew him. No one else felt like him. No one else sent her pulse racing just by being in the same room.

"What's wrong?" Diana murmured, feeling Aurora tense beside her.

"It's Sable. He's here."

Josie leaned closer to her. "Where? Is Van here?"

"No. Just him."

"Are you going to talk to him?"

"You can't just get up," Diana whispered.

"I know."

She tried to focus on the words from Sierra's friends and family and keep herself from looking over her shoulder at him. She didn't know what she would say to him. She couldn't ask him what was really happening, not here. She couldn't ask him why he'd been lurking outside her house.

He had told her to leave him alone. It didn't matter what he'd been doing outside her house. He didn't want anything to do with her.

But maybe she could just tell him she was sorry about his brother, whatever had happened to him. Maybe it would be enough.

She rose the moment the service concluded and spun toward him.

He was gone.

"I don't see him," Josie said.

"I don't either. I have to go."

"What?"

"I'm sorry, guys. I need to do something."

"Aurora!" Josie hissed after her.

Aurora ignored her. When she managed to push through the crowd, Sable's car was pulling out. She didn't stop to think about what she was doing. She climbed into her car and sped after him. She caught up to him at a red light and followed him aimlessly for several moments before he finally turned off toward the town square.

It was nearly empty with the memorial just ending. She pulled in beside his black sedan. She steeled her nerves and stepped out of the car.

He walked inside Colletta's, paying her no attention. Something so normal as getting coffee on a free morning seemed so strange for Sable. She hesitated. Had she been imagining everything? Was he really just a normal guy after all?"

No. Normal guys didn't ask weird questions and park outside people's houses, watching them from the shadows. Normal guys didn't look so odd and inhuman and frightening–

She'd imagined that part. She lifted her chin and strode inside Colletta's after him. She stopped directly behind him. She opened her mouth to speak, but he spun slowly on his heel to face her before she could. His eyes were like glacial pools.

"Aurora."

"I saw you at the service."

"What do you want?"

"You haven't been in school."

"So? What do you care?"

"You know I care." When he scowled at her, she smiled wanly at him.

"You're looking for Van, aren't you? I hope you find him. I really do."

His eyes narrowed, and he stepped past her, striding out of the shop without bothering to order his coffee. She hurried after him.

He stopped so abruptly at the door, she nearly collided with him. He turned back to her. "Don't follow me, Aurora."

"Why?" She stared up into his eyes, and there was something there, something behind the chill. She lowered her voice. "Are you afraid something will happen to me? Are you worried about me?"

He swallowed thickly and glanced away. "No. I don't care what happens to you."

She didn't move. An almost physical pain shot through her at the words. Then she saw his expression twist as though he'd felt it, too, in the split second before he spun away and strode out of the shop.

She raced after him and caught his arm. "That's a lie, Sable."

He threw off her grip, but he stepped toward her, so close she could feel his shallow breath stirring the fine hairs on her cheeks. "You have to stop this. You have to stay away from me."

"What if I do? Is that what you really want?"

His voice was hoarse as he replied, "Yes."

"I don't believe you."

He scowled for only the briefest moment before his face went completely blank. "She changed you. I should never have let her change you."

She opened her mouth in surprise. He was gone before she had a chance to catch up to him.

She watched him steer his car swiftly away and hurried after him.

* * *

Her phone trilled. She fumbled for it. "Hello?"

"Aurora, what happened you today? You left the funeral so suddenly, and you haven't been answering your calls."

"Sorry, Jos. I had to help Ruby at the shop."

Josie was silent. Aurora waited behind a red light, anxiously watching Sable's car ahead of her. She didn't care if he caught her this time. He'd been lying to her when he said he didn't care. She was sure. She'd seen something in his eyes. He cared more than he would like.

"Ruby was there. At the funeral," Josie said finally. Aurora remembered she was on the phone. "She didn't know where you went, either. What's going on? Why are you lying to us?"

"I'm not lying to you."

"Yes, you are. I know when you're lying. Why won't you just tell us what's going on? Is it something to do with Sable?"

"No. It's nothing."

"Come on, Aurora. I know something is wrong."

"I'm just...turned around about Sierra."

Josie sighed. "Yeah. I guess we all are. Aurora, are you sure you're okay? There's nothing weird going on?"

"No," she said, sliding her car under a low hanging tree across from Sable's house. "Nothing weird. Well, aside from the deaths. That's weird."

"Yeah. Okay. Well, I'll see you at school tomorrow?"

"Of course."

"Okay. Want me to pick you up?"

"It's okay. My dad insisted I take one of the cars. Just to be safe, you know?" When had she started telling so many lies? Why did she even feel like she needed to? Because she was outside Sable's house stalking him for the second night in a row. Because she knew it was crazy and stupid, and she didn't know what her friends would say about it, but they would certainly think something was very weird and wrong, indeed.

"Sure. I'll see you there, then."

"Yeah. Bye, Jos."

She didn't wait to hear Josie's reply. Sable's black sedan sped out of the gates toward town. Her heart pounded as she spun out after him. He wound through town, but this time he didn't stop at hers or Blaine's houses. He drove to the edge of town, to the woods that bordered New Coventry. It was a popular place for hiking during the day, but the darkness here was so thick now, she wondered what he could possibly be hoping to find.

She turned off her headlights as she slowed to pull into the small parking area outside Coventry Forest. If he knew she was behind him, he didn't turn to confront her. He flipped on a flashlight and plunged into the canopy of trees.

Aurora scrambled after him. She didn't have a flashlight, and she was afraid to pull out her cell phone to cast a meager light on the rough, bumpy path underfoot. She followed his bobbing light, stumbling slightly on roots and fallen branches.

It was stupid and dangerous to be trailing him along a barely-trodden path in almost complete darkness, but he was here for something. She intended to find out what it was.

He moved deeper into the woods. She was sure she would lose her way if he wandered from the path. He walked swiftly, and she had to jog to keep up, staying far enough away he couldn't hear her shallow breathing or the twigs snapping under her feet.

Then he stopped suddenly, and she reared back, leaning against a tree to catch her breath. He flashed his light ahead of him. Aurora leaned around the tree trunk to see what he was looking at.

Van lifted a hand to shield his eyes.

Aurora clapped a hand over her mouth to suppress a gasp.

"So you found me." Van's words were slurred. He leaned back over the bottle cradled between his knees.

"What are you doing out here?" Sable demanded.

"I didn't get to go to her funeral. Everyone is looking for me."

"That's because your girlfriend is dead!"

Van looked up at him. The haunted look in his eyes sent a chill down Aurora's spine. "I didn't do it. I didn't kill her. I actually liked this one."

Sable scoffed. "You liked her? You liked a human?"

His words were like a bucket of ice.

"Yes, I liked her! I didn't do this."

"Swear to me you didn't."

"I swear!"

"Then why haven't you come home?"

"You know they won't believe me."

"They have ways of finding out the truth, Van. You know that."

His eyes darted around like a hunted man's. His voice was low and hoarse. "Do you have any idea what that's like?"

"No." Sable sounded cold. "I haven't had to experience it. I don't kill people!"

"Neither did I! I didn't do this."

"You have to come home and let Mom and Dad handle this."

"You think the police will just let me go?"

"You didn't do anything, and they can't prove anyone did. They just want to know what happened. You just have to tell them you weren't with her that night."

Van shook his head and laughed with such bitterness, Aurora's stomach lurched. "I wasn't. It wasn't me who was with her."

"Who was it?"

"I don't know. Do you think I would be here if I knew? I would have hunted him down by now. I saw her the night she died. She dumped me. She said she'd met someone else."

"She didn't tell you who?"

"No! She said he was older and more mature. More serious. He had a career or something. She was tired of being with someone who has no *ambition*." He curled his lip, but then he took a hitching breath. "And then she left. If she was with that other guy, I don't know who he was."

"Blaine Daniels?"

"I don't know. Maybe. She didn't say."

Aurora's stomach sank into her knees.

"I have to take you home."

"No!" Van snarled. "I'm not going back there. Just leave me alone. You don't want me around, anyway."

"That isn't true."

"Oh, please. You hate me."

"You're my brother, Van. I don't hate you."

Van scoffed.

"I'm trying to save our family."

"Our family? Or your little human girlfriend?"

Sable's voice was so cold Aurora could feel the air around him chill. "I do not have a human girlfriend. You're the one who gets involved with humans. I'm just trying to stay."

"I know what you really want. What you're really doing this for."

Sable surged forward and yanked Van up by the collar. "Come on. You're coming home. We have to sort this out. We have to find out who's really doing this."

Van's lip curled, and then, in the meager light, he changed.

Aurora didn't make a sound. She couldn't move. Something seemed to be moving under the flesh of Van's face. It swirled and darkened to a livid red. His skin looked puckered and scarred, and his eyes glowed in the moonlight. He bared short, sharp teeth at his brother. His growl was animal as he leapt upon Sable.

She pressed against the tree trunk, rapt with horror. They spun in a circle, snarling and clawing at each other as though they might tear each other limb from limb.

When she saw Sable's face, she realized he'd changed, too. His eyes flashed fiery red, and his teeth looked as sharp as razors. He snapped them at Van and threw a punch into his face. His brother barely noticed the blow, but staggered slightly. He stumbled over a tree root.

Sable tossed Van down onto the forest floor and descended upon him. He seized Van's collar and lifted his face so their mouths were nearly touching. She couldn't see what he was doing, but the air around him shifted and glimmered. When he lifted his head once more, his face looked normal again, but Van wasn't struggling anymore. His eyes were closed, and he looked so perfectly human, Aurora was almost convinced she'd imagined the change, the livid, swirling scars and the sharp, ferine teeth.

Sable hoisted his brother over his shoulder and strode back along the path with long, unnaturally swift strides. Aurora had to run to keep up with the light. She didn't try to catch him. She didn't want him to catch her.

When he burst out into the parking area, Aurora waited for him to bundle his brother into the backseat of the sedan. She didn't emerge from the trees until his headlights had disappeared into the night. Her heart thumped and pounded as though it would leap from her chest.

She stumbled to her car, wiping the tears she hadn't realized were streaming down her face. She leaned over her steering wheel, gasping to catch her breath. Her mind spun and reeled from what she had seen, what she had heard. They'd called Sierra a human.

That meant they weren't human. They were something else, something dangerous and feral and murderous, and they knew exactly what had happened to Sierra and those others. Whatever had happened, Sable knew what it was. He could do it. Whatever he'd done to Van—was that it?

What are they? What did he do? Who else have they hurt?

"Oh, god," she whispered into her trembling hands. "He really is a monster."

Chapter Eighteen

Sable tossed Van at his father's feet. "What happened to him?" Mariah asked, dropping beside her unconscious son.

"What's going on?" Adam demanded.

"He's drunk, for one thing. For another, he wouldn't come home when I found him. I had to use force." Sable nudged his brother with his foot. "You wanted him; here he is."

"Where was he?" His mother gently brushed Van's disheveled hair from his eyes.

"Coventry Forest. Drinking alone. He's probably been there the entire time." He shoved his hands in his pockets. "He says he didn't do it."

Mariah looked up at him hopefully.

"He said Sierra dumped him for another guy. Someone older."

"Blaine Daniels?" Some of the tension left Adam's shoulders.

"I don't know. He didn't know. But whoever he is, he was the one who has been killing. I'm sure of it."

"You believe him now?"

"I still think you need to control him."

"I can't do that unless he is the one who has been killing."

"You can't do it?" Sable's eyes flashed angrily. "Of course you can do it. He didn't do it this time, but that doesn't mean he hasn't done it before and won't do it again. He is a danger to us all!"

"But he is innocent this time," Mariah insisted. "He really has been trying."

"Does that suddenly make up for everything he's done?"

"No," Adam said. "But it is a start."

Sable scowled and threw himself down on the couch to watch as Adam leaned over Van. He opened his mouth wide and breathed into Van's slack lips.

Van's eyes fluttered. Adam sat back on his heels as his son shot up abruptly, his eyes darting around at them. He leapt to his feet and rushed toward the door. Adam caught the back of his shirt and pushed him back down onto the floor.

"I didn't kill that girl!" Van snarled.

"Your brother has told us."

"He blames me for everything."

"I told them you didn't do it, you jerk," Sable snapped.

Van's eyes swiveled between his brother and parents. "It wasn't me. I swear. It was the other one."

"Blaine Daniels," Sable muttered.

"I told you I don't know. I don't know who she met, but she met someone. She dumped me, and she left. Whoever she was with wasn't me."

Mariah knelt beside Van. "Show me."

Van held up his hands. "Mom, please!"

"Show me! This is serious, Van. We have to know for sure it wasn't you."

Van's eyes slid to Sable's. Sable nodded. Van looked resentfully at his mother. "Go ahead."

Mariah bent over him. When she lifted her head, she nodded grimly at her husband. "It wasn't him."

"The other Jivina could know about us, even if we don't know who he is," Sable said. "He targeted Van's girlfriend."

Adam frowned. "That is possible."

"All the more reason to find him," Mariah added.

"The Landry's seem fine. Nothing shook out," Sable said.

"No, nor for us," Adam replied. "They're human. But nothing shook out with Blaine Daniels, either, did it?"

"He's the most likely suspect."

"We have to know for sure. We can't let him out of our sight if we can help it."

Sable scowled. "I have to live my life."

Adam looked sharply at his oldest son. "Van, you will help your brother. He can't do it alone. It's time to make yourself useful to this family."

Van's shoulders stiffened. "Fine. I'll do it."

"I would already have him if I hadn't been wasting so much time chasing down the Landrys," Sable said.

"It was necessary," Adam told him. "We had to eliminate them."

"We could have stopped whoever was doing this," Van snarled. "If you'd just did something instead of sitting back and giving orders."

"You could have just as easily. If you were helping your brother instead of messing around with human girls, we would have been able to stop this sooner. Our lives depend on finding the other Jivina. Your brother cannot be everywhere."

"I have to go back to school," Sable said. "I can't keep skipping. People are noticing."

Van rolled his eyes. "Why? What's the point of this? You've already gotten your credits. Just get your diploma and move on."

"We have to appear normal! I'm trying to be a normal person for once in my live."

"Sable, you are not normal," Mariah told him gently. "These deaths prove it. School can wait."

"For what? For when I'm Van's age and have no direction?"

She sighed. "All right. Van will help us discover the other Jivina."

Van opened his mouth to argue. His father interrupted him. "Or you will have to face the consequences of your actions. Now is the chance to redeem yourself."

Van paled. "Fine."

"You will have to speak to the police. They want to know what you know about the night Sierra died."

"I don't know anything!"

"You know something. Tell them what happened. You said she met someone else. Point them in their direction," Sable put in.

"It's not ideal," Mariah said. "If they find him before we do--"

"They won't. They know she was with someone, and we need them to stop looking at Van. Anything is better." Sable glanced at his brother. "But how are you going to explain why you've been holed up for so long?"

Adam was not concerned with this. "We perpetuate the misconception that what is happening here is a sickness. You will tell them how the human girl broke up with you, and when you found out she was dead, you were distraught and went into hiding, afraid you were sick, as well. You only came home when you were sure you would not infect anyone else."

Van scowled, but his mother held up her hand. "It does not matter what you like, Van. You will do this. You did nothing wrong, and it is the only reasonable explanation for your disappearance. They have no evidence this was murder. They will be looking to discover if the person who was with the girl that night saw some signs of illness or knows what potential contaminants she encountered. They will not persist in questioning you. We will make sure of it."

He curled his lip insolently. "Fine."

"The sooner the better," Adam added. "Get cleaned up. Get some sleep. We can't have you showing up at the police station smelling like the floor of a bar." Van glared at him, and Adam pointed toward the door. "Go."

Van turned and trudged grudgingly up the stairs to his room. Sable faced his father. "I found him. Now can we stay?"

"We won't go until this is cleared up," Adam promised. "We don't want that suspicion hanging over our family's head. But it isn't over, Sable. When we find the one who is doing this and we stop him, we will consider it."

"That's not good enough."

"It is all you will get for now. Go."

* * *

Today, Aurora was afraid he would actually be in school. Her eyes darted around the warm, sunny courtyard, searching for him. Her heart thumped. She tried to listen to her friends, who were finally talking about something other than Sierra and the deaths and the memorial service. She couldn't stop thinking about Sable and Van and what she'd heard between them.

They were monsters. They were the reason people were dying. They were killing them.

Or one of them was. It sounded as though neither of them had hurt Sierra, but perhaps they knew who did. How many of them were there? How many monsters? Was that what Sable had been trying to find out?

Was Blaine one of those—creatures? If he was, shouldn't they be able to spot each other? In books and films, the monsters always knew each other. Perhaps in the real world, they didn't.

What sort of real world had monsters in it, anyway? She wasn't sure what she'd seen. It had been dark, and the light had been odd. She might have just been seeing things.

She almost convinced herself of it, but then she would picture Sable's face again as he descended upon his brother.

Everything was different now. There were monsters in New Coventry, and the deaths weren't a virus. They were murder. Or something like it. And she couldn't tell anyone. She had to smile and talk with her friends and pretend she didn't know anything about any of this. She had to pretend Sable was a normal high school boy who was skipping school.

He wasn't normal. He was so far from normal, she wasn't even sure how much of him was human.

She understood now.

He had been trying to protect her. He had been pushing her away because he was afraid that what happened to Sierra would happen to her.

If she got close to him, it might.

No. He wouldn't hurt her. She knew he wouldn't. He'd spent too much time trying to protect her.

"Aurora?"

"Huh?" She snapped out of her daze, glancing at Josie.

"Are you with us? What's going on?"

She waved her hand and gave her friends a wan smile. She could pretend everything was normal. She had to. No one would believe her. If they did, they wouldn't understand. Sable had been protecting her. Now she would protect him. "Nothing."

"It looks like something is going on."

"I'm all right. I was just lost in thought."

"Things in this town are getting really weird," Diana remarked. "Everyone is going a little crazy."

"Did you hear about Van Jayne?" Cera asked.

"What? What about him?" Aurora demanded.

"The police finally found him. Well, he turned himself in, anyway. He said he and Sierra broke up the night she died. He wasn't the one who was with her that night."

That wasn't news. She'd heard it all already. Sable and his parents must have forced him to talk. In his state, she doubted Van would have done any such thing voluntarily. "Do they believe him? Are they holding him?"

"For what? He didn't do anything, even if he was with her. He said he didn't come forward before because he was in hiding in case he was infected with whatever killed Sierra and anyone else got sick because of him."

This was a lie. Sierra hadn't been sick. She'd been killed, and he knew it. Sable knew it, too. Despite what Van had said to his brother, he might have been responsible. If he wasn't...

If he wasn't, it could be anyone. A chill raced down her spine.

"I wonder if Sable will be in school today, now that his brother's cleared," Josie murmured.

Aurora doubted it. He was probably still sneaking around town looking for—whatever it was for which he was searching. She hoped he wouldn't be there almost as powerfully as she longed to see him. Now that she knew the truth, what could she even say to him?

"I'm glad they found Van," Diana said. "His family was probably worried sick about him, afraid he was hurt or dead, as well."

The Jaynes had been worried sick, but not about his health. "Yeah. They probably were."

"Are you sure there isn't anything you aren't telling us?" Josie asked suddenly. "I know something isn't right with you."

"Josie, don't be insensitive," Diana scolded. "People respond to grief and death differently than others. Leave Aurora alone. What happened to Sierra hits close to home."

Aurora thought of Sierra. She felt bad for Van. He had cared for her. She was sure of that. Even if he had hurt her, she knew he hadn't meant to. He might be a monster, but he obviously had feelings like any human. Perhaps they were human most of the time, and that side of them that was monstrous—she didn't know, but she was sure they could care about others.

"Aurora? Did we lose you again?" Josie nudged her.

"I'm here. Let's go inside. Class is about to start." They didn't look convinced, but they fell into step with her as she strode toward the front doors. Suddenly, she remembered something. "Josie, how are things going with Bryan?"

Josie was surprised. "I didn't think you remembered. You haven't said anything about it."

"I didn't. I'm sorry. Things have been so weird I keep forgetting to ask. So, anything new?"

"It's going okay." She smiled, and the conversation seemed so light, so normal, it felt oddly inappropriate. "We haven't moved past hand holding. He's shyer than I am."

Aurora laughed. "That's saying a lot."

"I know. It's kind of nice, though. We've been spending a lot of time together just talking. We like a lot of the same movies and music and stuff."

"It's nice to move slow," Diana told her. "It's better to know each other quite well before you make mistakes like...well, like the kind Sierra made that cost her life."

The light mood darkened instantly. They walked inside in silence. Aurora craned her neck, hoping to catch sight of Sable. She didn't see him in the halls.

"Don't look now," Josie whispered in that voice that she used that usually meant look right over there, nudging her in the ribs.

Her stomach flipped in excitement, but when she did look, she spotted Jesse, not Sable. He smiled at her, but he didn't move toward her. She returned his smile and ducked her head, disappointed. Sable wasn't there.

She didn't pay attention in class. She drew strange, swirling patterns in her notebook. *Sharp teeth. Red, scarred skin. Use mouths to*—She didn't know what Sable had done to his brother. *Feed? Super strength.* She wasn't entirely sure about the super-strength part, but Sable had lifted Van as though he'd weighed little more than a sack of potatoes. He'd moved fast, too.

She frowned down at the list she'd penned without realizing what she was writing. What were they? Vampires? Maybe, but they weren't like any vampires she'd ever seen in movies.

Vampires aren't real. She didn't know what sort of monster they were, but they weren't any sort she'd ever heard of before. She pulled out her cell phone and typed in monsters. There were so many. There were boogeymen, werewolves, demons, psychics, zombies and yetis. None of them were right. None of them did what she had seen Sable and Van do.

None of them were *real.* Did people really not know there were creatures like the Jaynes out there?

She typed in *vampire.* She frowned. No. They weren't vampires; of that, she was sure. They didn't drink blood. They walked in daylight. They didn't *sparkle.*

So, what were they?

A shadow fell over her. She looked up in surprise. Mr. Collin s, her World Cultures teacher, stood over her with a stern expression on his face. He held out his hand. "Aurora. Phone."

She sighed and handed it over.

He wasn't in English class. It still felt strange without Sierra there, but Aurora was grateful no one paid her any attention. She stared down at her notes again as she slid into her seat, but they didn't make any more sense to her now than they had before.

The bell rang, startling her.

And then Sable walked in.

She felt a thrill of fear and something else as she stared at him. He didn't meet her gaze. Some of their classmates whispered behind their hands, but he ignored them. He strode past Aurora without looking at her and sat in the back of the classroom.

Her heart thudded frantically in her chest. She hadn't seen him since he'd become...whatever he became when he wasn't human. She fought the urge to look over her shoulder. By the end of class, her entire body vibrated with tension.

When the bell rang, he was out of the classroom so fast she'd barely shot out of her seat before he'd disappeared out the door. She knew why he'd run. She knew exactly from whom he was running. She squared her shoulders. It didn't matter. She would catch him after school.

As soon as the last bell rang, she raced out of class. She didn't bother waiting for Josie or Diana. She was just in time to see him climb into his black car, parked on the edge of the lot. She veered toward her father's Civic and peeled out after him. She didn't bother keeping a careful distance. If he knew she was following him, all the better. He might stop sooner.

She didn't know where he was leading her this time. She didn't care. She had nothing to lose now. She was going to find out the truth.

He pulled off in a part of Coventry Forest without any paths or parking areas. He stopped his car on the side of the road. Her blood ran cold as she realized where they were.

It was where they'd found Sierra.

What was he doing here?

It was yet another question she intended to ask him as soon as she caught him. She threw her car into park and vaulted out after him. She hopped the guardrail and plunged into the trees. She didn't try to quiet her footsteps, and twigs snapped under her feet.

Sable stopped, his shoulders tensing, and spun around. When he saw her, his eyes flashed in anger. He strode toward her. Fear surged in her belly. She stood her ground.

"What the hell are you doing here?"

"Following you."

"Why? I told you to stop following me."

"I saw you last night with your brother."

Instantly, the color drained from him face. "What are you talking about?" His voice shook.

"I saw what happened. I saw you."

"You were following me?"

"Yes."

His mouth twisted into a snarl. "Stop following me! I told you I don't want you. Why are you still hanging around me?"

The words stung. "I knew there was something strange about you. I just didn't know you were...not human."

He stared down at her. There was no anger in his eyes now. He just looked...frightened.

"It's okay, Sable. You don't have to lie. I know what you are. I know you're some sort of...monster."

It was the wrong thing to call him. His face twisted and he spun away from her. "Leave me alone, Aurora!"

She stepped forward and caught his arm. "No. I didn't mean it the way it sounded. I didn't mean it—like that. I know you aren't human. I know you can turn into something else. Is this why you've been so cold to me? Are you afraid what happened to Sierra will happen to me?"

He didn't turn to her. "Are you still on about that? I told you there is nothing between us."

"But you lied. And now I know why. I know you drive by my house at night. Are you watching over me?"

His shoulders tensed, but she clung onto his arm. He could have thrown her off. He could have moved away so quickly, she'd never catch him again.

"I don't care what you are. I think you want to keep me safe."

"You don't know anything! You aren't safe with me."

"I think I am. I don't think you would ever hurt me."

Sable spun to face her. "I don't want to. I don't want to hurt you, but that doesn't mean I wouldn't."

She stepped closer to him. "I think you would protect me."

"Why are you doing this? Why won't you just leave me alone?"

"Because I know that isn't what you really want. I know you feel something for me." She lifted a hand to do touch his cheek. It felt like fire beneath her fingers.

Every muscle in his body tensed. He stared raptly down at her.

"I know what you are, Sable. I know you're something else. Something dangerous. And I don't care."

"You should care!"

"I don't. It doesn't change how I feel."

He scowled, but she rose on her tiptoes and leaned forward, pressing her lips to his. His body quivered with tension, then he lifted his hands to her face, and he pulled her flushed against him, kissing her back urgently.

She felt his skin moving under her fingers, and she knew he was changing.

He shoved her away from him and spun his back to her. "Go!"

She didn't move. "I already know what you are. I know what you look like." She touched his arm, and he recoiled as though she'd burned him. "Let me see you."

"Don't touch me." His voice sounded low and garbled.

"Do you want to hurt me right now, Sable?"

"No! I don't want to. You have to go before I do!"

"I don't think you will. I think you can control it."

"Why can't you just leave me alone?"

"Because I love you." She smiled, for the answer was so simple, and it felt so perfectly right.

He stiffened and turned so she could see only his livid, scarred red cheekbone. "You don't."

"Don't tell me how I feel. I know how I feel."

"How can you love me when you know what I am?"

"It doesn't change who you are. It just changes what you are."

He breathed deeply, his fists clenched. He seemed to be trying to calm himself down.

"I think you feel the same way about me."

"You don't know anything." There was no fight in his voice.

"I know it's someone like you that's killing all those people, but I don't think it's you. And I don't think it's your family. I think you're trying to help."

He exhaled in a heavy sigh, and when he turned back to her, he looked like himself again.

"You see? You didn't hurt me. And now you're all right. You can control it."

"I don't know for how long. I don't know if I could control it forever."

"That's your worst fear, isn't it? Killing someone on accident."

He looked away. "You shouldn't be here."

"You can't keep putting me off like this, Sable. I know the truth now. I know everything."

When he met her eyes, ice curled in her belly. "I could make you forget."

"It's what your mother has been doing to me, isn't it? What you did to Van when you found him? Your mother made me better."

"She changed you!"

"I wanted to be changed."

"I didn't want her to change you! I wanted you the way you were!"

"I'm still me. I'm just...better. I'm not scared anymore. And I'm not scared of you."

"She shouldn't have done it. It was a mistake. You should be scared of me."

"I'm not. And I'm not leaving."

He pushed his hands through his hair. "I could kill you, Aurora." His voice broke.

"But you don't want to."

"No! I don't want to hurt you. I would never want to hurt you."

"Then give this a chance. Give us a chance."

"I can't do that!"

"Why? You want to. I know you do. I can see it in your eyes. I've always seen it. I just didn't know what it was."

He sighed and shook his head.

"I trust you." She lifted her hand to do touch his face. He closed his eyes. "Let me be with you."

He jerked his head away from her. "No."

"If it's because you don't want me, then I'll leave you alone. Tell me the truth, Sable. Do you?"

He didn't answer. He gritted his teeth.

She stepped toward him and gripped his arms, drawing him closer to her. He leaned forward, resting his forehead against hers. She could feel his harsh, shallow breath on her cheeks. "You can't say it, can you?" she whispered. "You can't tell me you don't feel something for me."

"It's isn't about that, Aurora. It doesn't matter how I feel."

"It does matter. That's all that matters. It doesn't matter to me what you are. I'll take you no matter what."

He opened his eyes and leaned back to meet her gaze. "I don't frighten you? Aren't you afraid I could hurt you? Kill you? You've seen what we can do."

"I'm not afraid. I know you'll keep me safe." She gazed up at him. "Have you ever?"

"Ever what?"

"Ever killed anyone?"

He hesitated. "Yes."

"When?"

He swallowed thickly. "Don't make me talk about it."

"I told you, Sable. I trust you. I don't think you will do the same to me."

His hands clenched around her arms. "I don't trust myself, Aurora!"

"You can be careful. You stopped yourself before. You can do it again."

He shook his head.

"Just try." She leaned forward and kissed him. He didn't bother to resist. He pulled her up against him. She could feel the change, and she felt light headed. His body went rigid, but then he relaxed and kissed her earnestly. She sighed and wrapped her arms around his neck.

Then she pulled back, and she was shocked at the first glimpse of his face so close to hers. The pattern of swirls on his red skin was tribal. His features were the same, but his eyes were dark crimson, and his teeth were short and razor sharp.

He stared down at her, bracing himself as though he expected her to recoil from him or shout in fear. She reached up and brushed her fingertips across his cheek. She smiled, and then she watched as his face cleared and smoothed and he looked perfectly normal again. "See? I knew you could do it."

He took a deep breath, and then he smiled, tightening his arms around her. He leaned down to press his forehead against hers. His fingers tangled lightly in her hair. Aurora closed her eyes, reveling in his touch, in the warmth and strength of his arms around her.

"What are we going to do? My parents forbid me from seeing human girls."

"But you want to be with me."

"Yes." His voice sounded hoarse. "Since the moment I saw you."

She smiled and looked up into his eyes. He leaned down to kiss her, and this time nothing happened. When he pulled away, he looked the same as always, but the heat in his eyes was so intense she felt warmth spread through her entire body. "We can keep it a secret."

"I don't know, Aurora. It could be dangerous."

"Could you just go on, then, like nothing happened? Just forget about this?"

"No."

"Neither can I. So let's try."

"If my parents catch us...I don't know what they will do."

"Sable." She reached up to cup his face in her hands. "I'm willing to risk it. I'm not going to be afraid of what might happen."

He closed his eyes for a brief moment. "I don't want anything to happen to you, Aurora. I can't risk you."

"Let me decide what I'm willing to risk."

He pressed her closer to him, resting his cheek against the top of her head. "You would risk your life just to be with me?"

"I suppose I am. So let me. You can't stop me, you know. If anything happens it will be my fault, not yours. I know what I'm doing."

"Aurora..."

"Sable. You want to be with me, don't you?"

"I do, but--"

"Then we'll be careful." She lifted her head to look at him. "Just say yes."

He peered at her a long moment. Then he smiled. "All right. Yes. But we can't tell anyone."

"I can deal with that." He leaned toward her once more. Her phone trilled, startling them both. She fished it from her pocket. "It's my dad."

Sable stepped away from her. "Go ahead. You should get it."

She smiled at him and answered the call. "Hi, Dad."

"Hey, kiddo. Where are you?"

"I'm just driving around."

"It's getting late."

She lifted her eyebrows in surprise. "Are you worried about me?"

"I'm your dad. Aren't I supposed to? Are you heading home? Do you want me to pick something up for dinner?"

"Sure. Sounds good."

"I'll stop at Archie's. Head home. I'll see you soon."

"Okay. Bye, Dad." She sighed as she slipped her phone back in her pocket. "I have to go."

"Okay."

She moved closer to him. "Promise you won't change your mind?"

"I know you won't let me." He leaned down to kiss her.

"See you at school tomorrow?"

"Yes. I'll be there."

She stepped away from him. "See you tomorrow.

He caught her arm as she started away, and when she turned back to look at him, his expression was so serious, she was afraid for a split second. "Just think about it, okay? It's all right if you change your mind."

"I won't. Good night, Sable."

"Good night."

* * *

It was harder to pretend she wasn't happy than to pretend nothing was wrong. She smoothed her expression and squared her shoulders as she strode toward the school to meet Josie and Diana. When she caught up to them, they looked her over silently for a long moment. She realized she wasn't doing a very good job.

"What?" Her cheeks flushed.

"What's going on now?" Diana asked.

"What do you mean?"

"Well, yesterday you were all weird and lost in space, and now you look like a totally different person."

Aurora rolled her eyes to cover her unease. "Nothing's going on. I just feel better today."

"Okay."

Josie lifted an eyebrow, but she remarked lightly, "You look nice."

"Thanks."

"I guess it's because Sable's back in school now?"

Aurora smiled genuinely. "Maybe." She wished she could tell them. She was dying to tell them, to tell someone, but she knew she couldn't say a word.

"Are you sure nothing happened?" Diana persisted.

"I'm sure. Nothing happened. I just woke up today, and I felt better. I wasn't thinking so much about all the death and the horrible stuff."

They didn't look completely convinced.

She tried not to look for Sable as they walked inside, but she'd been doing it everyday since he'd arrived in New Coventry. No one would know the difference. She didn't see him.

"Did you see the news last night?" Josie asked as Aurora pulled books from her locker. "The police have finally ruled Sierra's death a freak accident."

"A freak accident?" Diana scoffed.

"Well, they didn't say that. They said it was an unidentified illness or something."

Aurora sighed in relief, but they didn't notice.

"They're saying that because they have no idea what really happened," Diana said.

"Some people are talking about leaving town."

"What people?" Aurora asked.

"My parents talked about it."

"What? Josie, you can't leave!" Diana exclaimed.

"I know; I know. I talked them out of it, but they've been trying to get me to stay home from school."

"Really?" Aurora turned to her in surprise.

"They're just scared. They'll come to their senses. They're just getting caught up in the craziness."

"I don't think we have to worry about getting sick," Aurora told her. "I think it's something else."

"You say that with a lot of confidence," Diana remarked.

Aurora slammed her locker shut. "I just...have a feeling, I guess."

"You are really weird these days, Rora," Josie said.

She laughed. "Things are weird, Jos. I'm just trying to adjust."

They started toward her homeroom. Her stomach flipped. He was nearby. She glanced around and caught Sable eyes as he passed in the middle of a thick crowd of students. He lowered his head, but he held her gaze from under his lashes. His mouth turned up just slightly at the corners. Then he looked away.

The warning bell trilled. Aurora wiped the smile from her face. "I'd better go. See you guys at lunch?"

"Bye, Rora."

She tried to concentrate in class, but it was a lost cause. She was relieved when the bell rang for lunch. Sable leaned against the lockers, waiting for her as she stepped out of her classroom. She ducked her head to hide the smile that split her face. He tilted his head and disappeared around a corner.

Aurora followed him, finding him waiting under a stairwell, leaning against the wall. She smiled as she hurried toward him. She couldn't read his expression. He watched her coldly as she approached. She took a deep breath as she reached him. "Hey."

"Hey."

For a moment, he didn't say anything. She chewed her lip nervously. Then he smiled. He glanced around to ensure no one was watching and reached for her hand, tugging her into his arms. She smiled against his chest.

"Can I see you later?" he asked.

"Yeah. Of course."

"Meet me after school."

"Sure."

"At Coventry Forest? Where I found Van?"

She lifted her head to smile up at him. "Okay."

"You'll be there?"

She laughed. "Yes, I'll be there."

"Good." He smiled and stepped away from her. He gave her hand a final squeeze. "Bye."

"Bye." She fell back against the wall with a happy sigh, listening to his footsteps on the stairs above.

Josie and Diana looked up at her as she dropped into their usual table beside them. Josie lifted her eyebrows. "Where have you been?"

Aurora smiled. "I just got caught up."

* * *

She was anxious to race to her car after classes, but her friends caught up to her. "Where are you off to?" Diana asked suspiciously.

Aurora smiled, but she felt as though the butterflies in her stomach might fly right out of her throat. "Just heading downtown."

"Want company?"

"I thought I'd stop in and see how Ruby's doing. I've been helping around the shop a lot lately."

Josie narrowed her eyes. "If I didn't know better, I'd think you were sneaking around having some secret relationship."

"Come on. Me?"

"Well, you never know. People do things that don't make sense all the time."

She hoped they didn't sense her uneasiness. "Well, I'm not. I would tell you. It's just nice to be in the shop again, and Ruby pays me."

They sighed. "Okay. I guess we'll see you later, then."

"Yeah. Bye!" She practically ran to her car, too anxious to see Sable to play it cool. His car was already there when she pulled into the small parking area around Coventry Forest. The last time she had been there...the last time she had discovered the truth.

She vaulted out of the car and hurried over to him. He wasn't in his car. She didn't find him in the trees on the edge of the dirt lot. She stepped onto the path and let the trees swallow her. "Sable?"

He wasn't in the clearing where she'd spied on him as he spoke to his brother. Her heart thumped. She heard a twig snap. She spun around.

He stood directly behind her. She caught her breath. He didn't speak. He caught her face in his hands and kissed her breathless. She sighed when he pulled away and leaned into his chest. "Hi."

He chuckled low in his throat. "Hi."

"I couldn't wait to see you. You ignored me in English class. It was terrible."

"I'm sorry. You know why I did that."

"Yes. It's not any different than usual, anyway. I'm used to you pretending I don't exist."

His eyes slid away guiltily. "I always knew you existed, Aurora. I was always aware of you. I knew right where you were all the time."

"Yeah? Are you some kind of stalker, or something?"

"Not in the way you're thinking. I was worried about you. I'm still worried about you. My brother..."

"He's very dangerous, isn't he? That day in the alley with him and Jesse...if you hadn't come along, I might be dead too, wouldn't I?"

"Yes. Very possibly. Van isn't evil. He's just...he can't control himself. I think he wants to be good, but he just doesn't know how."

"He's killed before?"

"Many times."

"Is that why you're always having to move around?"

"Usually. Sometimes...Well, once or twice, it's been me." His voice was low and sad.

"Do you have to kill?"

"No. We can feed without killing. Sometimes we can feed to help people."

"Like your mom and dad. That's why everyone thinks they can work miracles. They can. They can take the bad things?"

He smiled as he twisted a lock of her hair around his finger. "You're quick."

"Well, when I realized what you are, I realized what might have been happening to me when your mom hypnotized me."

His fingers stilled. "I didn't want her to do that, Aurora."

"I know. You warned me away. Many times."

"I didn't want her to change you. I liked you the way you were."

She held his eyes. "Are you disappointed that I'm different?"

"No. Not disappointed. You're still you."

"I never would have had the courage to come to you if she hadn't changed me."

"Maybe it would have been better."

She lifted an eyebrow. "Really?"

"You'd be safer now."

"Would I really be? I'd be safer with you just lurking around outside my house?"

He laughed uneasily. "Well..."

"If it wasn't Van, who was it? Are there more like you in New Coventry? More...what is it that you are?"

He led her to sit beside him on a fallen tree trunk, wrapping his arm around her shoulders. "Jivina."

"Jivina? What is that? It sounds like some kind of vampire or something, and you—well, the way you feed."

He scoffed. "Vampires. They aren't real. They're just romantic notions. We're nothing like them."

"Nothing?"

"No. Well, not really. And there are others. There are many others."

"Have you met any of them?"

"We came from a village where only Jivina lived."

Aurora was surprised. "Really? Where?"

"Romania."

"You're Romanian?"

"No. My family just lived there for a while. It was a safe place for us. We could live without fear of being discovered."

"So who is it? The other Jivina?"

"I don't know. I'm not sure. We've been trying to figure it out. My family didn't kill those people. So someone else did. One of us."

"Blaine?"

"You're paying more attention than I thought."

"I catch on quick. You were asking weird questions about him and checking a list of the places where other people have died the same way. Then I found out what you are and thought you must suspect Blaine of being one of you. You're trying to help us? The town, I mean. You're watching over us?"

He lifted his shoulders. "In a manner of speaking. We know it's one of us, and we have to find them and stop them."

"Why? Why do you have to do it?"

"The humans--" He cut off and looked down at her face, but she wasn't offended. "They don't know we exist. They can't. And so they don't know what they're looking for. We have to stop whomever is killing. It's our responsibility. If anyone else figured out what we are, they would hunt us all down and kill us, even if were aren't the ones who did it."

The idea sent a chill down her spine. "I understand."

"If it is Blaine, Aurora, he's dangerous."

"Is Ruby in danger?"

"I don't know. I honestly don't. I don't know if he is able to control himself. He must be. If he is the one doing the killing, he's been controlling himself with her all this time. He either isn't feeding on her or he is feeding little by little."

"If he does that...will it eventually kill her?"

He looked at her sharply. "No. Not unless he takes too much. We feed on the essence of humans. It is continuously replenished."

"He could be doing that." She looked up at him. "Will you need to do that to me?"

"I wouldn't do that to you."

"Your mom did it, and it made me better. It wasn't so bad."

He shook his head violently. "I won't."

"How do you feed?"

"A little at a time."

"On who?"

"People. Just...random people. When I get the chance."

"They don't remember?"

"No. I never take much. Just enough to stay healthy."

"So you just grab people in alleys?"

He looked embarrassed. "Sometimes in the bathrooms at school."

"Ew. I don't want to think about how that would work."

"I try not to think about it, either. I do what I have to do to live."

"How about teachers?"

"Anyone. It doesn't matter, as long as I'm sure I won't be caught. They never remember, and I would never hurt anyone."

She thought about it. "You can do it to me if you have to. I mean, if you can't find anyone else. From what I remember of it, it felt kind of nice."

"No. I won't. I will never do that to you."

"I'm just letting you know it's all right. If Blaine is the one, maybe he can feed on Ruby without hurting her."

"Maybe he can, but he is still out killing people. He killed a high school girl."

"You're sure Van didn't do it?"

"Yes. I'm sure. We have ways of finding out. He isn't the one."

"That's quite a coincidence that the other Jivina went after his girlfriend."

"I know. I thought so, too."

"Do you think that means he knows about you?"

"I considered it. It also sounds like Sierra put herself in a dangerous position."

"That doesn't mean she deserved it."

"No. I don't think she did. But it is a coincidence. Jivina can't usually sense each other. It's possible some can, but my family has to see them change to know for sure. Or feed on them."

"So we just have to wait until Blaine does something—if he does something?"

"Yes. Pretty much," he replied unhappily.

"That's not very efficient."

"We're doing the best we can. We're all watching him. We will see where he goes and if he hurts someone."

"Even if he isn't hurting Ruby, if he is the one—you have to stop him."

"We're going to, Aurora. I promise you."

"He seemed like such a nice guy."

"He might be a nice guy. It's just..." He looked down at her seriously. "We're monsters, Aurora. I have killed myself. Sometimes...we just can't control it."

"I don't think you're a monster," she snapped. "Tell me about...about the Jivina."

He didn't say anything for a long moment. Finally, "Most of us feed on human energy. Some of us...well, they prefer the fluids."

"Blood."

"Amongst other things. My family doesn't feed like that."

"But you eat normal food."

"Yes. We still require sustenance. We just...need more. When we feed or become excited, we change. If you touch me when I've changed, my skin can burn you."

"You haven't burned me."

"I could, if you held on too long."

She ignored this. "Are you hungry all the time?"

He looked away. "Yes. It's like a slow burn. But we can benefit people by feeding, just like my mom and dad do."

"How do they do it?"

"They can take memories or negative feelings just as easily as good ones. We can take disease or pain."

"But it doesn't affect you?"

"No. We don't get sick like humans."

"Do you live forever?"

He laughed. "No. I told you; vampire stories aren't real. We can walk in the sunlight; we don't sparkle or drink animal blood. We aren't invincible, and we don't have super-strength."

"But I saw you carry Van like that the other night."

"We get stronger when we've fed."

"Why are your teeth so sharp?"

"Like I said, some of us feed on...more than energy."

She lifted a hand to touch his cheek. "Is this your real face? Or are you really...the other way?"

He smiled wanly. "This is my real face. The other is also my real face. I have two faces."

"When you're with other Jivina, do you have the other face?"

"No. We all look like humans unless we've fed. I suppose a long time ago we all looked like Jivina, but we've adapted. Or we've always looked liked this. I'm not sure. No one really knows."

She nodded, and she lapsed into silence.

He tensed slightly beside her. "Well? Are you frightened?"

"A little, maybe. I'm more frightened of Blaine if he's one of you."

"Aurora, I need you to understand. If you change your mind about...us, it won't hurt my feelings. I'll understand."

"Sable, don't."

"Listen, I need you to know what I am, and what I am capable of."

She looked up at his serious face, and her stomach flip-flopped. "Okay."

His voice was low and strained. He didn't look into Aurora's face. "When I was six, I accidentally killed a girl who lived down the street. I didn't know she wasn't like an adult. She couldn't lose as much of her life force before she died."

"Oh, Sable, I'm so sorry. It must have been horrible."

"It was horrible. It was the worst I've ever felt in my life."

"But it happened again?"

"Yes. It happened when I was thirteen. It was a boy this time. He was a few years older than me. I thought he could handle it, but I couldn't control myself." He sucked in a deep breath through his teeth. "Then when I was fifteen, it was a girl I...was friends with."

"Like me?" Her voice was hushed.

He looked down at her now. "It's possible, Aurora. It's possible something like that could happen. I could lose control of myself again."

"But you were feeding on them at the time, weren't you? You weren't just hanging out and lost control of yourself, right?"

"Well...yes."

"So you're right. You shouldn't feed off me. As long as you don't, you probably won't kill me, right?"

He sighed. "Well, no, probably not."

"That's why your parents wouldn't want us together, isn't it? They are afraid you will lose control."

"Yes. That and they don't approve of mixing species."

"We're the same species."

"No, Aurora. It might look that way, but we're not."

"Could we reproduce?"

He looked horrified. "What?"

She laughed. "Oh, relax. I'm not asking you to. I'm just asking if a Jivina and a human could reproduce."

He still looked unconvinced, but he nodded slowly. "Yes. I'm sure they could. I do know some Jivina who have been with humans. This isn't the first time this has ever happened. There are a lot more of you than there are of us. The dating pool is pretty narrow."

She smiled. "So you're not exactly a different species."

"I'm not sure about that. Anyway, my parents would want me to be with another Jivina. It's safer for everyone. My sister married a Jivina."

"He isn't here?"

"No. He's in Azil. Our village. They're estranged. They're estranged most of the time. She will go back to him when she is over whatever fight they're in this time."

For a moment, neither of them said anything. Aurora folded Sable's hand between hers, and he smiled, clenching his fingers around hers. Finally, she asked, "So what are we going to do about Blaine?"

"You are not going to do anything, Aurora. I am going to figure out if he is the one and stop him."

"But how, Sable? You haven't gotten far, and I'm close to him. At least my aunt is. I can get you close enough to check him out."

"How?"

"I can get you near him. Like at the festival. That was what that was all about, wasn't it? Getting close to Blaine."

He looked slightly ashamed at this. "That wasn't all it was about. I wanted to be close to you, too. It was just...convenient."

"It's okay, Sable. I understand. I can get you more time with him. You could come over for dinner or something. I could talk Ruby into inviting him."

He looked extremely uneasy. "I don't know--"

"Oh, don't be ridiculous. It's not like you're meeting my parents or something. It's an investigation. You can just come over as my study partner or something."

"But I would be meeting your parents. Sort of."

"Yes, but not—you know—that way."

"Actually, that's not a bad idea. But I'm not really ready..."

"I know. I haven't told anyone about us. I won't tell them we're...well, whatever we are."

"Together."

"Yes. That." She smiled. "I won't mention that at all."

"All right. It's a good idea."

"I'll talk to Ruby. I'll let you know when."

"What are you going to tell your parents about me?"

"I'll just tell them you're coming over to study for English." She grinned. "I'll tell them I have a crush on you so they have to be cool."

He laughed. "You tell your family stuff like that?"

"Sure. My aunt, anyway. My dad wouldn't even notice."

"How will you get Blaine there?"

"Ruby will make it happen. I'll just tell her you thought he was interesting and it would make me feel more comfortable having him around to entertain you. She's always looking for an excuse to invite him over, anyway. She would never even consider I wasn't telling the whole truth."

"Okay. If you can make it happen, I'm in."

"Good."

As though this had ended the conversation, he tilted her chin up and leaned down to kiss her. She sighed and wrapped her arms around his neck. For a long moment, they didn't say anything more to each other. Then he pulled back and sighed. "I'd better go. I'm supposed to be trying to catch Blaine."

"I understand."

He rose and offered her his hand, pulling her to her feet. He kept her hand in his as he led her to her car. "I'll see you soon," he told her, and then he pulled her in for another kiss.

He didn't pull away for a long moment. He peered down at her with such intense heat, her chest fluttered. She smiled up at him when he didn't move away. "You'd better go."

"Yeah." Finally, he stepped back. "Good night."

"Good night, Sable." She climbed into his car and waved at him, watching him walk to his black sedan. She sighed happily and drove away, still breathless from his kisses.

Chapter Nineteen

"Have you started seeing Dr. Jayne again?" Diana asked suddenly as they strode toward Aurora's homeroom.

Aurora lifted her eyebrows. "No. Why do you ask?"

"Because you haven't stopped smiling in days," Josie told her. "Something must have happened to change your attitude."

"I just feel like things are going to be okay. How's Bryan?" she asked.

Josie sighed dreamily. "Things are going really well. Last night...well, we had our first kiss."

"What? Why didn't you tell me?"

"Well, you've been so busy lately."

"I'm never too busy to hear about my best friend's love life—now that you have one. Where is he, anyway? I never see him around school."

"He's usually late, but I get to see him in Government in the afternoon. It's nice. We get to cuddle in the back of the class when Mr. Ferrera isn't looking."

Aurora laughed, picturing how Sable would react if she tried to cuddle with him in the back of English class. Diana rolled her eyes. "That is not the place to cuddle. If you're going to do that, you should do it in the privacy of your own home. Or a car."

"A car?" Josie repeated, giggling.

"Oh, my god, Diana. What do you do with Zach in cars?"

Diana lifted her nose imperiously in the air. "I do not kiss and tell. It's not dignified."

The other two girls grinned at each other. "I wish you had a boyfriend, Aurora," Josie said. "We could triple date."

Aurora smiled, but she didn't reply.

"You could invite Jesse. You know, just for the date?" Josie asked hopefully.

"Oh, I don't think that would be such a good idea. I don't think Jesse is going to hang around waiting for me anymore. I think he got the hint the last time."

"I did notice he hasn't been around much lately. What do you think he's been up to?"

"I have no idea."

"You don't seem too upset about it," Diana said.

"Well, you know how I feel about Jesse. I don't want to date him. I wish we could just be friends, but we can't. Too much has happened for that. Maybe he'll find someone else."

"Maybe you could ask Sable to go," Josie suggested.

"What?"

"Well, he went on that double date with you."

"That was with his brother. It wasn't for me. Anyway, I think he's got enough on his mind with his brother's girlfriend...well, you know. But we should all get together. No boys. Just the three of us. Like old times. It's been too long."

Josie beamed. "We could go into Lynchburg and go shopping or something."

"Yeah. That sounds really nice. I miss you guys."

"We miss you, too, Rora." Josie linked her arm through Aurora's. "Things have been so weird, it felt like we were losing you."

"No. I'm here."

Sable barreled past them without looking at them. His hand brushed Aurora's.

"How rude is he?" Diana complained.

"And to think, we were considering him for our triple date," Josie said, shaking her head.

Aurora laughed and tucked the small square of paper he'd passed her into her pocket. "I guess we'll have to find someone else."

    * * *

Ruby Rose was much quieter when she arrived that afternoon. Ruby looked up from her computer as Aurora entered. She smiled. "Hi, Aurora."

"Hey. It's a lot less chaotic in here today."

"Yes. It's gotten much calmer around here. I know it's a terrible thing to say, but all the—stuff that's been going on has been really good for business. I could use the break, though."

"How about dinner?"

"Oh, yes, I'm starved. How about Archie's?"

"I thought...well, actually I kind of have a study date with Sable Jayne."

Ruby perked up. "Oh, a date? With Sable, huh? So things are better between you two?"

"It's just a study date. It's not really a date. We're working on an assignment in English class. I thought maybe we could make a night of it."

"And how does he feel about this? Is he aware of your evil machinations?"

Aurora laughed. "Well, I thought maybe we could make it a little more casual. Invite Blaine over? Sable got along well with him."

"You want my boyfriend to be your buffer so you can reel in a cute boy?"

"That's about it, yeah."

She laughed. "I love it. Perfect idea. I could make something nice." When Aurora shook her head, she reconsidered. "We could order pizza. I'll let Blaine know to play it cool. You want to impress him, but you don't want him to know you're trying to impress him."

"You're good at this. I knew I could count on you."

"When is it happening?"

"Tomorrow."

"Okay. I think I can make it happen. I'll call Blaine. He's been spending a lot of time with Troy, but I think he will do this for me."

Aurora's smile faded as she remembered Troy. She'd put him so completely out of her mind, she'd forgotten all about him. If Blaine was the Jivina...did Troy know? She was anxious to tell Sable about him. He might think it was important.

She plastered the smile back on her face. "Thanks, Ruby. I owe you one."

"Yes, you do. If things work out with Sable, just remember who helped you out. I accept gifts." She looked around the room, smiling wanly. "Just not flowers, okay?"

* * *

Aurora stumbled through the trees toward the clearing. It was dark. She didn't see him right away, but when his figure unfolded from the shadows, she grinned and threw herself into his arms. "I got your note," she told him when he seemed satisfied he'd kissed her thoroughly enough.

"I wanted to see you."

"I have good news."

"Yeah?"

"I convinced my aunt to invite Blaine over."

"What did you tell her?"

"I told her I'm trying to impress you but wanted him around to make it seem more casual and fun."

"She bought that?"

"Oh, yeah. Girls do stuff like that all the time."

"So you're going to pretend to secretly like me while I'm pretending not to like you back?"

"You can pretend to like me back if you want. It will make my aunt happy to think things are going well."

He laughed. "Okay. I will pretend to secretly like you back and be too afraid to tell you."

"Perfect. It should make for a fun and awkward evening." He wrapped his fingers around hers and led her to sit beside him. "Have you learned anything else about...the deaths?"

"No."

"Oh! Did I tell you before? Blaine has a partner. He's in town. His name's Troy Hallow. He finances all the houses they flip. He travels all over, but he's been here for a few weeks. Have you seen him?"

"No. I've seen Blaine with your aunt, mostly. Are you sure he's still here?"

"Ruby said they've been hanging around a lot, but..." Her stomach lurched. "I suppose he could be gone and Blaine's just lying. If Blaine's Jivina, do you think he is, too?"

"It's possible, but I doubt it. He probably doesn't even know."

"They've been friends a really long time. Maybe he does know."

"It doesn't really matter. Do you know much about him?"

"No. Not much. Just that he's the money guy. He was staying at the Coventry Inn, I think."

"I should look into him, at least." He sighed. "I'm sorry. I want to spend time with you, but I should go. This could be important. The sooner we find the Jivina, the sooner we can get to normal."

"I understand. It's okay. I know this is important. If you can fix this—well, maybe we can just have a normal relationship."

"I'm not sure that will ever be possible, Aurora."

"Well, we're almost adults. You don't have to stay with your parents all the time, do you? It's not some Jivina thing?"

"No."

"So, see: it's not the end of the world. We'll be all right. So go on. I'm looking forward to not having to be afraid anymore."

He pulled her close to kiss her on the forehead. "If I stop whoever is doing this, are you sure you won't still be scared?"

"Not of you. I will never be afraid of you."

He pulled her to her feet to walk her back to her car. "I'll see you in class tomorrow?"

"Yeah. Plan to be at my house tomorrow night. I'll let you know if anything changes."

"Okay." He pressed his lips against hers. "I'm sorry I have to leave so soon. I'll see you tomorrow."

"Good night."

* * *

"Aurora!" Ruby called up the stairs. "Are you ready yet?"

"Yes!" She hurried down to meet her aunt at the foot of the stairs.

Ruby goggled at her in horror. "Are you going to wear that?"

"What?" Aurora looked down at her tee shirt and sweat pants. "What are you talking about?"

"I know you want to keep it casual, but come on, Aurora. Put in a little effort. You don't want him to think you don't care at all, do you?"

Aurora laughed. "Okay. You're probably right. I was trying too hard not to try too hard."

"Go up and put on something nice. Your best jeans."

She rolled her eyes.

"Or your second best jeans, at least. And pull your hair down. You look much prettier."

Aurora hurried back upstairs. Sable wouldn't care what she was wearing. This would be awkward enough without worrying about how she looked. Sable wasn't coming to see her; he was coming to investigate Blaine.

She really wasn't looking forward to what he might find out. She tried not to think too hard about what would happen if Blaine was the one for whom the Jaynes were looking: the one who was killing. She shuddered as she searched through her wardrobe for something to wear.

Sable. He was coming. Butterflies fluttered in her stomach. He ignored her in school, or appeared to, but there were secret, careful brushes of his hand and small, private smiles when he passed her in the hall. She sighed and fell back on her bed. It would be hard to be with him tonight and pretend, but they were always pretending.

A knock on the front door startled her. "Hey, babe," Ruby exclaimed happily from downstairs.

Aurora shot up. Her dreamy mood faded instantly. Her heart thumped nervously. She hadn't seen Blaine since she'd found out the truth about what Sable was—the truth about what Blaine might be, what he might have done.

She hoped Sable was wrong about him. She hoped it wasn't Blaine because she knew Ruby loved him. Ruby deserved something good. She didn't deserve a monster in human skin.

But wasn't that what Sable was, too? She wondered for the first time if Ruby knew. Aurora had figured it out. Surely her aunt would have noticed something was strange if her boyfriend was a monster?

She doubted Ruby knew anything. If she'd discovered something so big, so significant, would she still have those stars in her eyes when she talked about Blaine? She was never good at hiding her feelings. Aurora was sure it would have been obvious.

But, then, Aurora had never been good at hiding her feelings, either. Not until she'd started lying with every second breath she took.

She hurried down the stairs. "Hey, Blaine."

He grinned at her. "Feeling a little nervous?"

"It's just a study date."

He laughed. "Uh, huh. Don't worry. I'll be totally cool. I'm glad you girls invited me over to be part of this high school girl subterfuge. I never did understand girls. I thought it might give me a little insight."

Ruby patted his shoulder. "I don't think it will, sweetie. The machinations of women are not meant to be understood by men. It would ruin the mystique."

Blaine rolled his eyes. "If you say so. I think I know enough about you that the mystique has been ruined already."

This didn't offend Ruby. She laughed and rose up on her tiptoes to kiss him.

"Where's Mike?" Blaine asked.

"Oh, I thought it would be too much pressure on the kid," Ruby explained. "He's with Julia."

"Not going to put him through that yet, huh?"

"Which one?" Aurora said.

"Yeah. Exactly. I guess I'll have to do the dad duty, then." He grinned at Aurora.

She smiled back. "Take it easy on him, okay?" Ruby ordered. "He's not her boyfriend yet. We don't want to scare him off or tip him that anything's up tonight. Don't put too much pressure on him."

Blaine waved his hand. "Nah. He seems like a nice kid. If he has any sense, he'll be on his best behavior trying to win you over, Aurora."

The doorbell rang though the house. Aurora jumped.

"Get it together, girl. Be cool!" Ruby shoved her toward the door.

Aurora waved them away impatiently. Blaine winked as he pulled Ruby toward the kitchen. "Don't spy!" she warned, waggling her finger at them before striding with dignity to the door.

She could still hear Ruby giggling as she pulled open the door. When she saw Sable, her pulse leapt. "Hey."

His mouth turned up in that smile he reserved only for her. "Hi, Aurora."

"Come in."

He didn't move. Instead, he peered inside.

"They're in the kitchen," she whispered.

Sable grinned and stepped inside, pressing his lips quickly against hers. She smiled and tilted her head toward the kitchen. He brushed his hand lightly against hers as he preceded her into the room.

"Hey, Sable," Blaine greeted heartily as they entered the kitchen, striding forward to pump the young man's hand. "Nice to see you again."

"You, too." He nodded politely to Ruby. Aurora was impressed with his nonchalance. He was much better at deception than she was.

"So you two are working on some English paper?" Ruby asked him.

"Yeah. Aurora is helping me with our term paper."

She rolled her eyes. She seemed to remember him helping her.

"Are you hungry? We ordered some pizza."

"Uh, yeah. That sounds good."

"Great." Ruby grinned at Aurora. "Why don't you two go up and get some work done. We'll call you when it gets here."

"Thanks, Ruby."

As soon as the door closed behind them, Sable drew Aurora into his arms, kissing her earnestly. She sighed dreamily as he pulled away. "I know I shouldn't do that. We're supposed to be pretending we aren't together."

She smiled. "That's what makes it so much fun." He laughed, and she rose up on her tiptoes to kiss him. "Want to do some homework?"

"No. I already did the term paper."

"Well, I didn't."

"That's your problem." He pulled her back toward him. She laughed and pushed him away. "Okay, okay. We can study."

They didn't get very far. She couldn't concentrate on her term paper while Sable stood behind her, toying with her long hair and making comments over her shoulder.

"I don't think you quite grasp the theme of the story here."

She spun in her chair to glare at him. "Are you going to be helpful at all?"

"I am being helpful. I pointed out that you're doing it all wrong."

"Oh, thank you very much. That's very nice. Could you maybe point out how to do it right?"

"That's not a lot of fun." He brushed her hair over her shoulder and bent down to press his lips to her neck.

She shivered. "Did you find out anything about Blaine's partner, Troy?"

"Yeah. I went to the Coventry Inn, but he's already checked out."

"He must have already left town. He did have somewhere else to go. I suppose it's not like he would have checked in with us to say goodbye. I'm sorry to send you on a wild goose chase."

He shrugged and bent down to kiss her. "I've been on a wild goose chase since I got to town. It's just as helpful to eliminate suspects. Less people to follow around."

The doorbell rang again. Aurora jumped. Sable tightened his hands on her shoulders. When she looked up at him, he kissed her.

"Hey, guys!" Ruby called up the stairs. "Pizza's here!"

Aurora rose. Sable wrapped an arm around her waist and drew her up against him. "You are not being very good tonight."

He laughed. "I'm sorry. What do you expect? I'm a teenaged boy alone with my girlfriend in her bedroom. It's nice, by the way. I like the stars."

"My mom put them up before she died." For once, the words didn't feel like a knife in her belly.

He tightened his arms around her. "I'm sorry."

"Thanks. Come on. Let's get pizza. Now's your chance to interrogate your suspect."

"You'd think you don't want to be alone with me."

She laughed and leaned up to kiss him. "Of course I do. But I think you enjoy the fact that we could get caught any moment."

"Maybe a little. I mostly just like kissing you, though." He took her hand and led her to the door. As soon as she reached for the handle, he released her and took a step back. "Okay. Let's go."

Ruby and Blaine waited in the kitchen. Aurora was glad Sable was in on the set-up; their wide grins were entirely too suspicious. "Get any work done?" Ruby asked with false nonchalance.

"Yeah. A little, but Sable seems more interested in telling me what's wrong than telling me what's right."

He laughed. "You'll never learn anything if I just give you the answers."

Ruby's eyes twinkled as they sat down to eat. Aurora glanced at Blaine. "So where has Troy been? I haven't seen him around in a while."

"He had some business with another one of our houses in South Carolina. The contractor had some issues with the inspector. He left a week or so ago."

"Have you closed on either of the houses yet?"

"We're still in negotiations. The buyers asked for some extras right before the paperwork went through, and we're trying to find a middle ground."

"Have you bought the new house?"

"Still in talks. They want more than the house is worth, and it won't be worth our money if we don't get a good price. We'll work it out. They want to sell it; they're just playing hard-ball because they want to see how much they can get out of us."

"Do you ever think about keeping the houses your flip?" Sable asked.

"Oh, yeah. All the time, but I like my freedom. I don't like to get tied down to one place."

Ruby rolled her eyes. "He doesn't want to commit to staying anywhere."

He laughed and wrapped an arm around her shoulders. "I'm changing my mind about that. I have a pretty compelling reason to stick around these days."

Aurora glanced at Sable as Blaine leaned over to kiss Ruby. His face was blank, but she knew he was uneasy. She felt the same way. Her aunt loved Blaine. Perhaps she had from the beginning. If Blaine was the monster...

could he possibly love a human?

Could Sable?

She glanced at him again, but he wasn't looking at her. "Do you like New Coventry?"

Blaine grinned. "I love it here. If I were going to stay anywhere, it would be a place like this. I've been all over the country. I've worked in the Midwest a few times—Illinois and Michigan, but I was born in Massachusetts, so I mostly prefer to stick around New England. I was last in Connecticut flipping a house in Waterbury. I like working on houses with history. They have the most problems, but they have the most potential and rake in the most when they're flipped. People are willing to pay a lot these days for restored historical homes."

"There are a lot of those here," Aurora remarked.

"Yeah. The houses around here are beautiful. They have a lot of history and character. The architecture from the eighteenth and nineteenth centuries is very sound. I've even done some work for some of the cities in Massachusetts, restoring historical monuments."

"That sounds awesome."

"It's a lot of fun. It's a lot of work, but it's worth it to see the end result."

Aurora glanced at Sable, but she couldn't read anything from his neutral expression. "This is your favorite of all the places you've been? Have you ever thought of sticking around anywhere else?" he asked Blaine.

Blaine shook his head. "Not really. I enjoyed working in Maine, but it's kind of boring. I really loved home, near Boston, but I prefer not to live the big city life. It's too noisy. New Coventry has been...very welcoming. And there are several benefits to being here." He winked at Ruby, and she smiled at him. "It's the first place I felt like I might fit in."

"Have you ever been to Rhode Island?" Sable blurted.

If Blaine thought the question was odd, there was no indication in his face. "No. Not Rhode Island. Troy wanted to work on a house there a few years ago, but I had another job. He got another contractor. Have you been there?"

"Yes. We lived there for a few months." Aurora suspected he was lying. "It was pretty quiet."

"Yeah. Boring." Blaine smiled. "I prefer to have a little fun when I'm working. My work is pretty time-consuming, but I like to have a nice place to take time off when I need a break."

Ruby smiled as they finished their pizza. "Shouldn't you two get back to work?"

"Yes," Aurora said. "We still have that essay to write."

Sable rose to help clear the dishes. Ruby winked at Aurora behind his back. "Why don't you let me do that, Sable? You guys just go on."

"Sure. Thanks for dinner," he said politely as Aurora led him back upstairs. He frowned as he sat down on her bed. "You know, this is not what I expected your room to look like while I was sitting in my car looking up at it."

She laughed and sat down beside him, gesturing around at the simple photographs of her family and friends sitting on the nightstand and the desk beside her computer. Other than the stars overhead, she had few decorations. "Why?"

"I don't know. I guess I don't know what a girl's bedroom usually looks like."

"Depends on the girl. Josie has movie and band posters all over her room. Diana has paintings her mom does. I used to have some paintings and other things, but after my mom died, I took them down."

"Why?"

"I don't really know. They reminded me of her or something. One day, I just needed to take them down. Until I met your mom, I was sort of...empty inside. I felt like my room should be empty, too, I guess. Maybe I should put some stuff back up. It never really mattered much to me, but I could never get rid of the stars."

"Now that I expected."

"You expected glow stars over my bed?"

"No. But something like it, I guess. A telescope and planetarium ceiling or something."

She laughed, but then she looked at him seriously. "So what do you think? About Blaine?"

"I don't know. It's...well, it has to be him. I've eliminated everyone else. It's not the Landrys. They've all been pretty well accounted for."

"You thought it was them? That's why you were asking me about Ariel."

"Yes."

"I kind of thought maybe you just liked her."

"No. I like you. Blaine hasn't been to all the places there have been Jivina killings. And he's been to some places where nothing has happened."

"Well, what about your family? Did something happen in all the places you've been?"

His expression was grim. "Yes. Or we would have stayed."

"Maybe the killings aren't all him. If there are more of you—whole villages, it could be someone else. That doesn't mean it's not him."

"I thought of that."

"So we're no closer?"

"We're closer. I mean, it has to be him. We just have to keep watching him."

"But he could be all right, couldn't he? I mean, you are."

"I'm not sure where to draw the distinction, Aurora. I have not always been good. My family is not always good."

"But you don't want to kill, and you're trying to help now."

"Yes."

"So you're the good guys now."

He didn't look convinced. "If he's the other Jivina in town, Aurora, he's not good. Five people are dead. One of us did it."

She covered her face with her hands. "Yeah. I suppose you're right. I just wish...I really don't want it to be him, Sable. Ruby..."

"I know. I'm sorry." He wrapped his arms around her.

"So she could really be in danger."

"Even if he did kill those people, it doesn't mean he'll hurt her."

"But you said accidents happen."

"Yeah, but..."

"He's still a killer."

"Is that what you think of me, Aurora?"

"What? No! No, Sable. I didn't mean you." She reached up to press her hand to his cheek. "I didn't mean it like that. I don't think that about you at all. I'm just worried about Ruby. I don't think anything we could say will get her away from him. And it's not like we can tell her the truth."

"I know. I'll make sure she's all right."

"Thank you," she whispered.

He looked down at his watch. "I'd better get going. I don't want anyone to figure out where I am."

"Well, you're investigating, aren't you?"

He smiled. "Yeah. A bit. I don't think anyone would believe I didn't really just come because I wanted to see you."

She tilted her face up to him as he kissed her. "I'll walk you out."

"What are you going to tell your aunt about...how things went?"

"I'll tell her your obsession with me is embarrassing, and I had to turn you down."

He rolled his eyes. "Please. As if you'd turn me down."

Aurora laughed. "I'll tell her we studied and nothing happened." He kissed her again, and when he pulled away, she frowned at him. "Including you helping me with my term paper."

"I thought you were supposed to be helping me."

"If they only knew the truth."

He grinned. "Walk me out."

Ruby and Blaine were curled up on the couch when they descended the stairs. "Leaving so soon? Ruby asked.

"Yeah. I have to get home," Sable told her.

"I hope you two got some work done."

"Yeah. A little bit. Thanks for dinner."

"Oh, sure. You should come over again."

"Maybe I will. I'll see you guys. Aurora, I'll see you in class."

"Okay. Good night." She closed the door and turned to lean back against it with a sigh.

Ruby lifted her eyebrows. "So? How did it go?"

"It went all right."

"Any hanky panky?"

"What? Ruby!" Her aunt laughed. "We just worked on our papers."

"He seems to really like you."

She shrugged. "Maybe."

"So we did good?" Ruby looked hopeful.

"Yeah. You guys did good. Thanks for tonight." She leaned into the living room. "Thanks, Blaine!"

He waved a hand. "Anytime. You just make sure that boy is nice to you."

"I will. I'm going to get ready for bed."

"Okay."

"Thanks again."

"I had just better be the first one to know if something happens with you and that boy," Ruby insisted.

"I promise."

* * *

Sable stopped dead as he stepped outside Aurora's house. "What are you doing here?"

A slow, malicious grin spread over Van's face. "I could ask you the same thing. I thought you were expressly forbidden from seeing that human girl, and here you are, having dinner with her family."

Sable narrowed his eyes. "I was not having dinner with her family. I was having dinner with Blaine Daniels. In case you've forgotten, I'm still trying to figure out who killed your human girlfriend."

A muscle jerked in Van's jaw. "Don't talk about Sierra."

"Then don't make more out of this than there is."

""More than there is? So you're just investigating Daniels?"

"Just like Mom and Dad said."

"Uh, huh." He grinned as he leaned back against the hood of Sable's car. The glint in his eye sent a frisson of ice down Sable's spine. "So, you found out something?"

"I am sure he's the one, but he has a partner that comes around sometimes. He's not in town now. Get in the car. We shouldn't talk out here."

"I'll meet you at home. Mom and Dad will want to know what you... discovered tonight."

"Fine. See you at home then."

Van was already waiting in their father's office when Sable arrived. He wondered fleetingly how he'd gotten there so quickly.

Adam rose to meet him. "Van tells us you have learned something about Daniels."

"I talked to him. I found out he's been in a few of the places we've mapped but not all of them. He has a business partner who does the same work. They travel around to different towns and states working on houses."

"And his partner?"

"He's been in the general area of some of the deaths. I couldn't get specific dates, but it's a big coincidence."

"It could just be a coincidence. Of it's possible one or both of them are the Jivina we're looking for."

"I still don't have any way to know for sure."

"Where is this partner?"

"His name is Troy Hallow. He's not in town. He checked out of his hotel a few days ago."

Mariah sighed. "So we are still no closer."

"We are closer."

"I think my little brother is concerned about Daniels being so close to the Gellers, aren't you, Sable?"

Sable gave him a sharp look. "I'm worried about him being close to anyone in town. If he's killing innocent people, he's dangerous to everyone around him."

Adam frowned. "Yes. He is. But there is still no evidence it's him. We

410

can't do anything about it until we know for sure."

"Why not?" Van demanded. "What's the worst that can happen? If he's Jivina, he'll fight back. If not, no harm done. He won't remember a thing."

"It will be difficult to get close to him," Mariah murmured. "I have tried. And it does seem rather extreme."

"It might be the only way," Adam replied. "It's not a bad idea. We have been spinning our wheels for weeks."

"What if he isn't the one and you accidentally kill him?"

"I can stop myself, Sable. I am not a child. I do not lose control."

"It's the only way to be sure," Van added.

"I can find out for sure," Sable argued. "I just need a little more time."

"What do you care? If he's not the Jivina, he's just a human. Are you friends with him or something?"

"No."

"Then what's the problem? It's the easiest way to find out if he's the one who killed Sierra."

Sable sighed. "Yeah. You're right. All of this is a waste of time. The fastest way to discover the truth is to draw him out. We just have to get him alone."

"He is difficult to stumble upon," Mariah told him.

"But he spends most of his time working alone."

"It is best not to waste any more time with this. We have eliminated nearly everyone else. We have to know for sure." Adam looked at Sable. "Where is he now?"

"He's at the Gellers. I think he is spending the night."

"Okay. I will take care of it."

"But--"

"No," Adam cut in. "I am the head of this family. I will take care of this. Stay away from the Gellers, Sable. They do not need you. You can only be trouble to them."

Sable bristled, but there was nothing to say. He spun on his heel out of the room.

* * *

Ruby looked up at Aurora. "You look nice this morning. Any particular reason?"

"Come on, Ruby."

"Or any particular person you're trying to impress? You know, I think Sable likes you. He has sort of a dreamy look whenever he looks at you."

"Do you think so?"

"I know that look, honey." She sighed happily. "Blaine gets it sometimes."

"What's the suitcase for?" Aurora asked suddenly.

Ruby glanced down at the red flowered case beside the kitchen island. She smiled. "Blaine is taking me away for the weekend."

Her stomach sank. "What?"

"We're going to the country. He's rented a cabin and we're just going to... well, enjoy each other's company."

"Are you sure that's a good idea?"

"What do you mean?"

"I just...ah..." She cut off, wringing her hands. She couldn't tell Ruby the truth, of course. She couldn't reveal Sable's secret or ruin Ruby's relationship without knowing for sure. She didn't know if Blaine was Jivina at all, and, even then, he still might not be the killer. "Just...Just be careful okay, Ruby? I don't want anything to happen to you."

Ruby laughed. "Are you worried Blaine might do something to me? I'm sure you have nothing to worry about. Even if he did have wicked designs, I told lots of people where I was going and who I'll be with. Everyone will know it was him."

Her amusement sent unease curling through Aurora's belly. She tried to smile. "Yeah. I'm just being silly."

Ruby rose to wrap her into a hug. "I know all these deaths—especially your classmate—have made things hard. It's hard to trust anyone. I understand why you would be worried about me. I promise I'll check in, and if Blaine tries anything weird, I will hit him with the heaviest thing I can find."

Aurora laughed, but she wasn't amused. If Blaine was what Sable thought he was, she doubted it would do much good. "Sure. Have a good time"

"I will have my cell if you need me. But...well, if would be nice if you didn't need me. I'm looking forward to just spending some quality alone time with my boyfriend. I've never met anyone like him, Aurora. He makes me so happy. I feel like I can be myself, and he'll love me no matter what." She took a sip from her mug and glanced back up at Aurora. Her eyes looked far away and wistful. "I think he might be the one."

Aurora's throat felt tight. "Really? How do you know? How can you be sure?"

"Well, I'm not an expert, lord knows. But I think when you find the right guy he'll be the one who will take you as you are. He will always make you better, and you will make him better. He'll make you feel safe and loved and happy just knowing he's around. When you meet him, you'll know." She smiled a little sheepishly. "I got a little carried away, huh? It's just...I don't want to jinx it or anything, and I know it's soon and I know I might just be letting my imagination get the best of me, but—I think it's possible he might be planning to propose to me this weekend."

"To what—to propose!"

Ruby grinned conspiratorially. "Uh, huh. I mean, he does spontaneous stuff like this sometimes, but this time I just get the feeling it's different. But don't tell anyone. I would be embarrassed if he isn't planning anything like that. I might be getting ahead of myself."

"If he asks...what will you say?"

"I'll say yes, of course! I love Blaine. I would give anything to spend the rest of my life with him."

Aurora shifted uneasily. "Are you sure you know everything about him?"

"No. Of course I don't know everything about him. No one ever really knows everything about anyone. But I know the important stuff. I know how he was raised. I know what he does. I know what he's like."

"What if...what if he has some secret or something?"

"Like what?"

"What if he...well, I mean, what if he has wives in other states or something?"

"Come on." Ruby rolled her eyes. "You need to stop watching so many crime documentaries."

"Well, he moves around so much, and he hasn't really committed to sticking around. I just don't want you to jump into something when you've only known him for a few months."

Her aunt squeezed her arm. "I know it's dangerous to jump into things, and Blaine does like his freedom. Getting engaged doesn't mean you can't spend more time getting to know each other and figuring out your next steps together. You don't have to worry about me, Aurora."

"Yeah. You're right. I'm sorry. I didn't mean to be a naysayer. I know you're really happy."

Ruby waved her hand. "It's okay. I know you're just looking out for me."

"I am. I want you to be careful."

She hugged her again. "I will. Don't worry about me. You'd better get to school. You're going to be late."

"Oh!" Aurora scooped up her backpack. "Yeah." She wrapped her arms around her aunt and squeezed her tightly, as though it might be the last time. "Be careful. Have fun. I'll see you when you get back."

"I'll check in."

"Good. Have a good weekend."

"I will. Good luck with Sable. If he doesn't ask you out today, he's an idiot."

* * *

"Hey, Aurora," Josie greeted. "What's up? You look upset."

Aurora blinked at her. "No, no. I'm fine. Ruby is going away for the weekend with Blaine."

"So?" Diana lifted her eyebrows.

"Just...Nothing. I'm just worried about her."

"Why?" Josie demanded. "She's going away with a totally hot guy who is totally into her."

"I'm just not sure we know much about him. He moves around a lot. He could be some kind of...well, I have no idea. He could just be more than he seems."

Her friends looked at her as though she'd gone insane. "What is going on with you?" Diana asked. "You're acting totally weird about this."

414

"I'm just worried about my aunt, that's all. I guess I also...well, I guess I don't want her to leave."

"Leave?"

"Well, Blaine's job takes him away a lot. What if she decides to travel around with him?"

"Oh, that would be good for her," Josie said, smiling. "Don't be selfish, Rora."

She laughed half-heartedly. "Yeah. Right. I shouldn't be selfish." Her eyes strayed over Diana's shoulder.

Sable leaned against a tree several yards away. She caught his eye.

"I've got to go," she said suddenly. "I need to grab my math book from my locker. I forgot to bring it home last night, and I need to finish an assignment."

"Uh...okay," Josie said.

"I'll catch up with you guys at lunch, okay?"

"Sure. See you in a while."

"Bye!" She spun away from them, keeping a careful distance as she followed Sable inside to a stairwell where they wouldn't be overheard. "Hey."

His expression was grim. He didn't smile when he saw her. "Hi."

"Ruby's going away for the weekend with Blaine."

He stiffened. "What?"

"She thinks he's going to propose, and I'm worried about her."

Sable reached for her. "It's okay, Aurora. Calm down."

"But she's going to be alone with him--"

"She's been alone with him before, and he's never done anything to her. I don't think he's going to hurt her."

"But what if he loses control or something--"

"Aurora." His voice was low and stern. She relaxed into his arms. "We still not even sure it's him. You have to calm down."

"Okay. Okay."

"My dad has a plan."

"What is it?"

He hesitated. "We have ways of finding out things...about people."

"You mean..."

"The way my mom did to you."

"Right. So you're going to do that to him?"

"It's the only way to know for sure. If he's one of us, he will change and we will know. If he isn't, we won't hurt him. He'll be fine, and he won't remember a thing."

"What if your dad kills him on accident?"

"My mom didn't kill you, did she?"

"No. Of course not. She made me better."

"It's going to be fine. Don't worry about Ruby. Don't worry about anything anymore, okay? I'm going to protect you. I'll make sure you and your family are safe."

She sighed as he drew her closer and rested her cheek against his chest.

"We need to be more careful," he said suddenly, and the top of her head bumped his chin as she looked up at him.

"What?"

He glanced around them as though afraid someone was watching. Then he ducked his head to kiss her. "I think Van suspects something."

"About us?" She took a step away from him.

"Yeah."

"What does he care? He was the one dating Sierra."

"I know, but...well, my mother has forbidden me from seeing you."

"Me specifically?" This was unexpectedly hurtful.

"Yes."

"Why?"

"She doesn't want me to get involved with humans at all. I think she...I think she knows how I feel about you. She doesn't want me to put you at risk."

"But you aren't."

416

Sable sighed and pulled her back against his chest. "Yes, Aurora, I probably am. But I can't help it." The warning bell rang, and he leaned back to look at her. "Don't worry about Ruby or Blaine anymore. No matter what, we will sort it out."

"Okay. I'll see you soon." She took a step away from him and started toward her homeroom.

"Aurora, wait. " She turned back to him. "I want to see you tonight."

"I thought you wanted to be more careful."

"More careful doesn't mean I can't see you. I think I know how to hide from my brother by now."

"Okay."

"Meet you at the forest?"

"Yeah. I'll see you there."

* * *

It was still light out when Aurora vaulted out of her car at Coventry Forest. Her heart beat rapidly. She'd only just seen him in class, but she couldn't wait to be close to Sable. Even the roiling anxiety in her belly was nothing compared to her excitement.

She shouldn't feel that way. She should be worried about Ruby and what could happen.

But he'd promised he'd take care of Ruby. He promised his family was going to make sure she would be all right. Besides, she was sure Blaine loved Ruby. Even if he were a killer, he'd never hurt her aunt.

Sable leaned against a tree trunk as she emerged into the clearing. When he saw her, he surged toward her, wrapping her into his arms. "I brought you coffee," he said against her hair.

"You did?"

"Mocha, right? It's your favorite?"

"You are surprisingly sweet for someone who was so mean when I first met you."

"I wasn't mean. I was just...keeping my distance. I was trying to protect you."

She sipped her coffee happily. "Thank you."

Sable leaned down to kiss her. "I missed you."

"You just saw me this morning. And in class."

"I know, but I want to see you all the time."

"Me, too."

He took her hand and led her into the trees. She didn't worry that they would lose their path; Sable could always find his way. He guided her to sit on a large, fallen tree branch. "Aurora, I don't want you to worry about any of this anymore."

"I'm trying not to. It's just...it's scary."

"I know. I'm sorry."

"It's not your fault. You don't scare me."

"But if we'd never come—"

"If you'd never come, I wouldn't have met you, and this other Jivina would be running wild killing anyone they wanted without anyone to know what was happening or to be able to stop them."

"They're doing that anyway."

"Do you think he knows about you?"

"No. I don't think so. But if he does..."

"Maybe that's why he's taking Ruby out of town?"

"No. If he does know about us, he has no reason to take her away. She has nothing to do with my family or me. I doubt he'd worry much about me, anyway. I haven't presented a threat to him."

"You are a threat to him."

"No, I'm not. But my father is. I doubt he could know what we've planned."

She leaned against him. "I don't want to talk about it anymore."

"Did you finish your term paper?" he asked cheerfully.

She laughed. "Yes. No thanks to you."

"Hey, I helped."

"Sure you did."

"I am a perfect boyfriend. Aside from having to keep our relationship

418

completely secret, I bring you coffee and help you with your homework and keep you safe from evil murderers."

She laughed. "Are you my boyfriend?"

He lifted an eyebrow. "Am I missing something? What else would I be?"

"I don't know. I hadn't really thought about it. I was just happy to be with you."

He leaned down to kiss her. "Me, too. I wish we didn't have to sneak around. You deserve better."

"It's not so bad, but I don't know if I could do it forever. Will we have to?"

"I'm not sure. I hope not, but it's possible."

She sighed. "It's okay, I guess. I would rather that than not have you at all."

Sable wrapped his arms around her. "Are you going to be alone tonight?"

She looked up at him in surprise. "Are you thinking of coming over?"

He laughed. "Don't be so dirty-minded. I just want to make sure you're going to be okay."

"My dad usually stays at Julia's on Friday nights. She's his girlfriend."

"Maybe I could find a way to get out of the house. I could bring over some burgers or something."

"Do you think that's safe?"

"Yeah. It should be. My parents are used to me being out all the time, usually doing things for the family. They won't ask any questions."

"Yeah. Okay. That would be fun."

"I should probably get home and tell them about Blaine. They will want to know we have to wait on our plan."

"I wish someone could watch over Ruby, but I don't know where they are going, and it's a little creepy to spy on a romantic getaway."

He laughed as he rose to his feet, drawing her up beside him. "I will call you and let you know when I'm coming."

"Okay."

They didn't say anything as they walked hand in hand out of the trees toward their cars.

Adam and Mariah were waiting for them.

"See," Van said, smirking. "I told you he was sneaking around with her."

Sable pushed Aurora behind him. She could feel the tension in his body. "What's going on?" he demanded, but his voice wavered slightly.

"Sable, Aurora, get in the car," Adam ordered. "I think we need to talk."

"She isn't going anywhere with you. Leave her alone."

Mariah frowned. "Sable, you know we can't do that. You know what's at stake."

"She doesn't know anything."

"She knows everything," Van said.

Sable glared at him. "You son of a bitch. You've been following me around."

"I asked him to," Mariah told him. "I was concerned that something was going on. I am sorry to discover I was right." She looked at Aurora. Her expression was curiously gentle. "Aurora, we aren't going to hurt you. We just want to talk about this."

Aurora gripped Sable's arm. Her throat felt tight. Her heart pounded wildly in her chest. He spread his arms in front her as though he could hide her from his parents. "You can't do this," he said.

"Sable, don't force your father's hand."

"It's all right, Sable," Aurora murmured. "It's okay. I'll go with them."

He half-turned his head, keeping his eyes on his family. "No! Aurora, no."

She ignored him. She stepped around him to face his parents. Sable gripped her hand, but she didn't let him pull her away. "I don't think they'll hurt me. They never have before." She looked at Mariah. "I trust you. I'll go."

Van grinned. Adam turned curtly toward a large, white Cadillac. Mariah's expression was terribly serious as she gestured Aurora and Sable into the backseat. "Come."

   * * *

Aurora tried not to appear as nervous as she felt as she sat beside Sable

420

on the couch in Mariah's office. She could feel Sable's tension. She wanted to reach for him, but she didn't want to make things worse than they already were.

"How long has this been going on?" asked Mariah.

"Nothing is going on," Sable replied coldly.

"Don't lie. We know what is happening here, Sable. We brought you here to talk. We need to know what is happening so we can deal with it."

"About a week," Aurora piped in.

Van rolled his eyes. "It's been going on much longer than that."

"No," Sable said, glaring at him. "It hasn't. I tried to stay away from Aurora, Mom, but–" His expression softened when he looked at Aurora. His eyes hardened again as he looked back at his mother. "I love her."

Van scoffed. "You love her. A human."

Sable shot to his feet. "What about you? What about Sierra?"

"Sierra is dead! That's what happens to humans when they become involved with us. They die." He lifted a finger to point at Aurora. "She will die, too, if you aren't careful."

"Van!" Mariah warned.

"Thank you for your loyalty, Van," Adam said.

"Some loyalty," Sable spat. "Van, you son of a bitch."

His father ignored him. "Van, please leave us alone. We need to speak with Sable and Aurora privately."

Van scowled, but he held up his hands. "Fine. I'm going." He paused at the door to smirk over his shoulder at his brother, and then he was gone.

Aurora felt better as Sable sat back down beside her, gripping her hand tightly.

"This is very serious," Mariah told them. "You have been lying to us, Sable."

"I have not been lying to you. I have been doing everything you asked. All I ever do is what you ask."

"And yet here you both are."

"Aurora and I...it just happened."

"She obviously knows about us."

"She knows. She saw Van and me...when I found him and brought him home."

"How could you be so careless?" Adam demanded angrily.

"It's not his fault," Aurora told them. "I was following him."

Mariah lifted her eyebrows. "Why?"

"I thought...I thought something might be weird. But, mostly, I just wanted to see him."

Mariah passed a hand over her face. She paced in front of them. "You know about our family. And the deaths."

"I know it wasn't you," Aurora said earnestly. "I'm not scared of you."

Mariah shook her head. "Sable..."

"We can trust her," Sable insisted.

"We can't afford to trust anyone!"

"She isn't going to tell anyone. We just want...we just want to be together."

"That is not possible," Adam said.

"Why?" Aurora burst out. "Sable isn't going to hurt me! He's careful with me."

"It isn't just about that, Aurora. You could be in danger from us, but you could be far more dangerous to us."

"No, I—I would never tell anyone."

"There is no way to know for sure what could happen. I'm sorry, Sable. You know what we have to do."

Sable leapt to his feet. "No! No! I won't let you do this."

Adam strode forward and seized his son's arm, dragging him away from Aurora. He struggled, but Adam was much stronger.

Aurora shrank against the back of the sofa as she though she might escape them. "I don't understand. What are you going to do?"

"Aurora—" Sable growled. "Mom, don't."

Mariah stepped toward Aurora. She held out her hand.

"Don't." Aurora didn't know what she would do, but Sable's fear sent a chill down her spine. "Please. Don't do anything to me."

"Mom, please!" Sable exclaimed. His eyes looked strange and glassy and nearly black. "Don't."

Aurora trembled as she looked at him. "Sable." Her voice broke.

"No!" he shouted, but he could not break his father's hold on him.

Aurora rose to her feet. A single tear trickled down her cheek. Mariah looked sad as she peered down at her. "I'm sorry, Aurora. I am so, so sorry."

"Are you going to kill me?" she whispered.

Mariah reached out to stroke her hair. The gesture was curiously tender. Aurora's tears fell more rapidly. "Of course not, my dear. I would never kill you."

And then she changed, and it was more terrifying than Aurora could have imagined. She had seen it before on Sable and Van, but somehow, Mariah's beautiful face shifting and swirling and turning livid red was horrifying. "Sable!"

"No! Aurora!" Adam wrestled him out of the office and slammed the door in his face.

It was the last thing she saw before Mariah leaned toward her, and she saw nothing more.

Chapter Twenty

Aurora opened her eyes. She was surprised to see Dr. Jayne's lovely face smiling serenely down at her. She looked around the office. Her body felt so light. She smiled back at the woman contently. "Did I fall asleep?"

"You were relaxing for a while. How do you feel?"

Aurora stretched languidly. "Good."

"That is excellent, Aurora. I think your sessions have been very successful. How would you feel about taking some time on your own to assess your progress?"

"Are you dumping me?"

Dr. Jayne laughed. "No, of course not. It is the next step in your treatment. There comes a time in therapy when the patient needs to try to stand on their own. The idea of therapy is to get better, not to have to be in therapy forever."

"Okay. That sounds good." She followed as Dr. Jayne rose. "Thanks for everything, Dr. Jayne."

"Of course, dear."

Aurora saw Dr. Jayne's son, Sable, watching her from the stairs with an odd expression. She smiled vaguely at him and turned away. She followed Dr. Jayne to the door.

"Have a wonderful weekend, Aurora."

"Thank you. You, too." She was surprised to see her father's Civic outside. She didn't remember driving there. For the briefest moment, she wondered why she had it. She hated cars.

Of course. She had borrowed it to make it to her appointment.

She climbed in and steered out of the Jayne's driveway without a second glance.

* * *

Sable shook with anger as he watched Aurora leave with blank, glassy eyes. He heard Van's footsteps on the stairs behind him. He didn't turn around.

He gritted his teeth.

"Aw, my poor little brother. Your girlfriend's forgotten all about you. Are you going to cry?"

Sable spun on him so suddenly Van didn't even fight back as his little brother shoved him back against the wall. "Why did you do that?" Sable snarled. "Why did you tell them? You took her away from me! Do you hate me that much?"

Van's eyes flared. He shoved Sable back against the railing. "Why should you get what you want? I have never gotten what I want."

"What happened to you? What happened to you to make you like this? Are you so unhappy you have to destroy everyone else's life, too?"

"You know the danger of dating a human. I learned the hard way. I thought I could make it work. I thought I could pretend it didn't mean anything, and that I wouldn't hurt her. But if someone else hadn't done it, I would have. You know I would have. And you would have hurt Aurora. You might even have killed her. We are monsters, Sable. We cannot love. We aren't heroes. That girl didn't deserve that. She deserves a chance. Do her a favor. Stay away from her. Forget her."

Van released his brother and turned to stride up the stairs. Sable watched him angrily, but he wasn't entirely sure Van was wrong this time.

His mother appeared at the foot of the stairs. "She's gone, Sable. I'm sorry. It had to be done."

Sable glared down at her. He couldn't even look at her face.

"Stay away from Aurora. She is safe now."

"How is she safe?" he snarled. "She doesn't even know she has a reason to be afraid!"

"That is exactly as it should be. Your father and I will handle this from now on. You just remember what happened. Leave her alone. Next time, your father will be the one to take care of things." She paused to let the words sink in. "You know how that will turn out. You are lucky he was lenient this time. Don't give him a reason to change his mind."

Sable's insides turned to ice. He spun away from her and stormed up the stairs. He could hear his mother sigh sadly as he slammed the door.

* * *

Aurora smiled at Josie. "Good morning," she trilled cheerfully.

Josie eyed her suspiciously. "What's up with you this morning?"

"What are you talking about?"

"Nothing. You just look...I don't know. Weird."

Aurora laughed. "I'm not weird. I'm great. I haven't felt this good in a while, except..." She frowned suddenly.

Josie lifted an eyebrow. "What?"

"Except I feel like I've forgotten something."

"Like what?"

"I don't know. I checked the curling iron and the coffee maker and looked to make sure I had all my assignments before I left. Maybe I was supposed to tell Ruby something when she got back to do town. It's probably nothing. I just feel like that sometimes." She pushed the thought away and grinned. "So, did you see Bryan this weekend?"

Josie's cheeks colored. "Yeah. We went out to the lake with his parents."

"Oh, you're meeting the parents now?" Her smile froze. She shook off the strange, nagging feeling in the back of her mind.

"Well, we have been going out for a few weeks."

"Has it been that long?"

"Yeah."

"Wow. Your first real boyfriend."

Josie giggled and spun the car toward Dinwiddie Hills. "Yeah. It's going really well."

"I'm happy for you."

"I think I might be ready to...you know."

Aurora looked at her in surprise. "Already? I thought you were going to take it slow."

"I am! I just...really like him."

"Don't be too hasty. You don't want to do something you'll regret."

"I know. I won't. I just...like to think about it."

"Well, thinking about it is totally okay."

426

They laughed as Josie stopped the car to pick up Diana, who was waiting on the street for them. She moved toward the passenger seat and paused, surprised to see Aurora. She climbed into the back. "You're back to riding with us, are you?"

Aurora blinked in confusion. "Yeah." She looked between the two of them. "What?"

"Nothing. It's just nice to see you," Diana told her.

"You, too." Aurora stared out the window, her brow slightly furrowed.

Josie grinned. "Are you looking for Sable?"

Aurora looked at her. "No. Why would I be?"

"Uh..." Josie and Diana exchanged a glance in the rear view mirror. "Okay. Did something happen?"

"What do you mean?"

"I didn't realize you'd given that up."

"I guess...I didn't realize it either. Not until it was gone. There's no sense in wanting something you can't have."

Aurora threaded her arms through her two friends' when they stepped out of the car and headed toward the school. "You know, we should go on a triple date," she declared.

They both looked at her incredulously. "What?"

"Maybe I could ask Jesse."

"What?" Diana repeated. "But I thought your date went terribly last time."

"Right," she said slowly. "It did. But...maybe he deserves another chance. He tried very hard."

"Is he even still asking you out?" Josie asked doubtfully.

She took slightly longer to think this through. "No. He isn't. Maybe you're right. It didn't go well last time. I think he might have finally stopped chasing me."

"Are you sure you're okay?"

Aurora gave them a baffled smile. "Why wouldn't I be okay?"

"You're just...acting even weirder than usual. You don't seem quite like yourself," Diana told her.

"What are you talking about? I feel exactly like myself."

They didn't say anything as they walked inside the building toward Aurora's locker. She smiled dreamily as she gathered her books. They were still staring at her with concern as she turned back to them.

"Guys, what's the matter with you? I'm fine. I'm great."

They didn't look convinced. Sable Jayne strode toward them, his midnight blue eyes boring intensely into hers. His fingers brushed lightly against the back of her hand as he passed. She gave him a polite, cursory smile and looked back at her friends as the warning bell rang.

"I'd better get to class," she chirped. "I'll see you guys at lunch."

Josie and Diana glanced after Sable. "What was that?" Josie demanded.

"What was what?" Aurora asked, mystified.

"With Sable just now."

"I didn't notice anything."

"Okay. If you say so." Diana tugged on Josie's arm. "Come on. We don't want to be late."

It was the best day she could remember having in a long time. It was terribly sad that that awful virus had killed Sierra Drew, but it was nice to go an entire day without being teased or tormented by her and the twins. She didn't have to be on her guard in English class. Instead, she absently doodled in her notebook, drawing strange spiraling patterns in the margins.

She looked up as Sable Jayne passed directly beside her desk. He was being weird today. She shrugged it off and looked back down at the strange doodles. She cocked her head to the side. For a split second, they made her feel strange and desperate and sad.

The feeling was gone so quickly, she was sure she'd imagined it. She snapped the notebook shut and smiled vaguely as the bell rang to begin the class.

* * *

Sable scowled as he watched her walk toward the parking lot between her two friends. She didn't even notice him as they passed. He narrowed his eyes. She looked all right. She looked the same as she always did, but something was wrong. Something was missing. When Mariah had taken him from her, she'd taken something else away, too.

He pushed his hands through his hair. He cursed under his breath.

She was the innocent, naïve girl he'd met under the stars behind his parents' house. She was the slightly broken, tragic, lonely girl who had awakened some part of him that he hadn't even realized was there. She was Aurora, the Aurora she'd been before his mother had changed her.

But she wasn't his Aurora. His Aurora was gone.

His mother had given him the old Aurora back, but he couldn't have her. He couldn't touch her or talk to her. She didn't even know him anymore.

He turned away from her to stride toward his car.

Van was waiting for him, leaning against the driver's side door. "How about a ride home, little brother?"

"What the hell are you doing here?"

"Oh, just hanging around. Mom wanted to make sure you didn't relapse or do anything stupid."

"Are you serious? You're babysitting me now?"

"This is serious business. I have to make sure you don't try to talk to her. You know what will happen if you do."

Sable scowled. "Has Dad found Daniels yet?"

"No. He won't tell me anything he has planned." For a moment, he looked almost normal. "I think we've messed this one up. It's probably about time we got out of town."

"No."

"What's the problem? You were hanging around for your girl, right? And now she's gone. She doesn't even notice you anymore, does she? She doesn't love you anymore. What's the point in staying here? What's the point in protecting this town? It's not our problem. Dad's probably planning to just pack up and let the other Jivina keep it. It's nothing to any of us anymore."

Sable didn't reply to this.

Van smirked. "Don't worry about that ride. I've got my car." He flicked his fingers in a dismissive wave and walked away.

Sable glared after him, but he was right.

* * *

He stared up at her window. The light was on in her bedroom. He could see her moving around. She pushed aside the curtain, peering around at the darkness below. Sable retreated further into the shadows. For a moment, she looked as though she expected to find something—someone—below.

Her eyes slid over him. Her brow furrowed in confusion. He took a shuddering breath, and hope blossomed in his chest.

She didn't see him. She stepped back, dropping the curtain. Sable closed his eyes, gritting his teeth against the surge of desperation in his gut.

"Remember," he whispered. "Please, Aurora. Remember me. I'm here."

The light flipped off in her bedroom.

* * *

The news of another mysterious death no longer shocked the town. This time, the victim was a young college freshman who'd been visiting her family over the weekend. Her parents hadn't even realized she'd been missing until her body had been discovered in Coventry Forest late Monday evening.

Aurora fumbled for her ringing phone on the nightstand. She wasn't surprised to see the number on the caller ID. "Hey, Josie."

"Did you hear?"

"Of course. It's all over the news."

"Are you going to school?"

"I don't know. It's...so scary. What if whatever's killing these people is contagious?"

"I thought you were positive it wasn't."

"When? What?"

"You seemed to think there was some...weird secret or something behind it all."

"I did? I don't remember. I was probably just...my mind's been reeling from the deaths. I suppose we might as well go to school. If it is contagious, we can't hide out from it forever. It sounds like this girl was only here a couple days, and there hasn't been any other deaths since Sierra's. It's hard to believe she could have caught something Sierra had that no one else seems to have gotten."

430

"Right. That's good logical thinking."

"Yeah, except there is nothing logical about people who have all dried up like mummies and die alone in an alley or the woods somewhere."

"Aurora!"

"Sorry. That was pretty horrible. I shouldn't have said that."

"Pick you up in a bit?"

"Yeah. I'll be ready. Come get me."

When Josie pulled up to the house, Aurora was sitting at the kitchen island, staring into space. She jumped as Josie burst inside. "Aurora! What are you doing?"

She snapped back to attention. "Huh?"

"I've been outside honking for five minutes."

"You were?"

"Yes! Didn't you hear me?"

"No. I guess I'm...Josie, I just have that feeling I've forgotten something again. I was trying to figure out what it was."

Josie peered at her closely. "Aurora, are you sure you're okay? Have you thought of going back to see Dr. Jayne?"

"Huh? No. I'm not seeing her anymore. She said I should take some time to see how the therapy is working for me before I see her again."

"That's weird. I don't know any therapists who let people go early."

"Dr. Jayne is very different."

"It seems like maybe..." She trailed off as Aurora looked up at her.

"What?"

"Nothing. I'm sure it's fine. I'm just glad you're okay. For a minute, I was freaked out something had happened to you."

"I'm sorry. I didn't mean to scare you." Aurora rose and scooped up her backpack. She stopped abruptly. "It feels like I'm forgetting something about the deaths."

"What?" Josie squawked. "What do you mean?"

"Like...like I am supposed to know something about them."

"What would you know about them?"

"Nothing. At least not now. I don't know if I knew anything before." She smiled. "It must not have been important, if I've forgotten it."

"So, have you..." Josie began cautiously. "Have you talked to Sable lately?"

Aurora looked at her in surprise. "No. I've seen him in English class, I guess, but I haven't talked to him or anything. It's not like we're friends."

"Since when? I thought you guys had gotten...sort of close."

"No. Not really."

"But...you don't like him anymore?"

"No."

"But you really liked him before."

"Well, I guess I just lost interest. I don't know when it happened. It just happened."

"Okay. Sorry I brought it up." Josie was silent as they walked outside to her car. She glanced sidelong at Aurora. "Are you sure nothing happened? If something happened, you can talk about it. You don't have to be embarrassed if he rejected you or something."

"Why would you think he rejected me? We never even talked about anything. Nothing ever went anywhere with him. You know I wouldn't have asked him out or anything. That's not my style. Besides, I tell you guys everything. I think you would have known."

"If you say so."

Aurora stared out the window as Josie headed for Diana's house. "I wonder if everyone will stay home from school again today. I bet they will. We should just ditch and go into Lynchburg for the day."

Josie looked at her in shock. "Seriously?"

"Well, it'll be like a free ditch day. No one got in trouble the last couple times. Why not? It would be fun."

"Yeah," Josie murmured doubtfully. "It would be fun, but I doubt Diana will go for it. You know how she is."

Aurora chuckled. "Yeah. I know how she is. It was a good idea, anyway."

* * *

Sable watched Aurora skip toward the school between her two friends. She was smiling, and her long, strawberry blonde hair swung out behind her. She laughed as she passed him without even turning in his direction. Pain lanced through his chest.

He sucked in a deep breath and followed her. "It would have been fun to ditch out and drive to Lynchburg," she said cheerfully as she pulled her books from her locker. "But we really should go this weekend. It's been so long since we've hung out!"

"Yeah," Diana said with false enthusiasm, as though something about Aurora concerned her. "It sounds fun."

"We can have a girl's trip. I want to buy a new swimsuit," Aurora went on. "It's almost summer. I'm looking forward to summer."

"I wouldn't mind buying a few more pairs of shoes," Josie replied brightly. "I love shoes."

"Oh, and we should go have sushi. I love sushi. I think there's a good place in Lynchburg. Saturday?"

Sable took a shuddering breath.

"Okay," Diana agreed. "It's a date, then."

"I'll see you guys at lunch." She waved and spun toward her homeroom.

He rushed forward and caught her arm. "Aurora."

She looked up at him in surprise. "Sable? What are you doing?"

"Just...nothing." He stared down into her face. There was nothing in her jade green eyes. He sucked in a breath. "What did she do to you?"

"What are you talking about?" she demanded, tugging her arm out of his grasp. The bell rang. "I need to get to class."

She spun away, but he caught her again and tugged her back toward him. "Aurora—"

Her expression was exasperated. Once she'd looked at him with longing in her eyes. She'd looked at him with love. Now, she looked at him as though he were nothing more than a vaguely irritating insect.

And then her brow furrowed in confusion, and she cocked her head at him.

"Aurora?" he asked hopefully.

"I feel like I'm forgetting something."

Hope leapt in his chest. "You do?"

"Yeah. Just..." Her expression cleared. "Did you have something you wanted to say, Sable? We're going to be late for class." When he just looked at her blankly, she rolled her eyes. "I'll see you later in English, okay?"

He didn't let go of her arm. "Wait, please--"

"What's wrong?" Suddenly, her eyes brightened, widening as they searched his face. "Sable, I--"

The tardy bell rang. She shook her head as if to clear it.

"We're late for class. Let me go, okay?"

Sable stepped away from her. He exhaled in deep disappointment. He'd thought, for a moment, that she'd started to remember.

She didn't now. She waved at him dismissively as she ducked into her homeroom.

Sable wiped a hand across his face, not surprised when it came back wet. He spun away, striding straight outside to his car.

* * *

There were no patients' cars parked outside the house. He stormed into his mother's office, slamming the door against the wall without bothering to knock. She rose from behind her desk in surprise. "Sable? Why aren't you in school?"

"I want her back."

"What?"

"Aurora. I want her back. Make her the way she was before."

"Sable, you know I can't do that. What I did was for your own good. And hers."

He pushed his hands through his hair in agitation. "You can't do this to me. Mom, please, give her back to me."

His mother rounded her desk to lay a hand on his shoulder. "Sable, it is for her own good. She is not safe with us. And we are not safe with a human who knows what we are. You know you cannot be with her. It's better that she forgets you. And all of this."

434

"Mom, I—"

"I know you think you love her now, Sable. You may truly love her. But it will pass. You will forget her in time."

"No, Mom. I won't."

"I do not want to see my children in pain. But I also have to do what is best for them. I am sorry, darling. I cannot give her back. She is safer this way."

He spun away from her gentle, sympathetic eyes. He took a deep breath and swiped at the hot, angry tears that streaked down his cheeks.

His father walked into the room. "Oh, Sable. You're here. Good."

Sable didn't look up at him.

"What's going on, Adam?"

"There has been another death."

Mariah sighed. "You see what happens when we are not focused on our priorities."

"There is a problem."

"What problem?" Sable demanded, finally looking up into his father's face.

"The girl disappeared over the weekend. She was found late last night, but she was already dead by then."

"What are you saying?"

"Blaine Daniels was out of town, wasn't he?"

"It wasn't him," Sable said, squeezing his eyes shut. "It was someone else."

"Yes."

"Who?"

Adam exhaled heavily. "It could be anyone."

Sable cursed. "I can't believe this. We've looked at everyone! Who else is there?"

"We missed something. Somehow, we missed something."

"Damn it! I thought we had figured this out! I thought...I thought things were going to be okay."

"Maybe it's time we go," Mariah said.

"No! I am not leaving."

"Sable, you cannot be with her," Adam growled. "Perhaps it would be best if we left here so you won't have to see her anymore."

"I'm not going anywhere," Sable told him coldly. "Leave if you want, but I'm staying."

"You will do as you are told!"

"I'm not a child anymore, Dad. I can make my own decisions."

"Then prove it! We have another Jivina on the loose, and they have not stopped killing. We haven't gotten any closer to discovering who they are! Find them. And I will consider remaining in New Coventry."

Sable looked up at his mother with glittering eyes. She didn't meet his gaze.

"But we will not give you back that human girl. No good can come of it. Forget her." With that, Adam spun and strode toward the door.

"Dad!"

"I mean it, Sable. She is dead to you. If I have to make you forget her, I will."

Sable recoiled as though his father had struck him. "No," he breathed.

"Then prove you can be a man and take care of this. Go."

* * *

"Thanks for the ride, Josie! I'll call you guys later."

"Okay," Josie replied, smiling wanly as Aurora climbed out of the car.

"Don't forget about Saturday," Aurora ordered imperiously.

"We won't."

Aurora waved cheerfully and hurried inside. She smiled when she saw her aunt sitting at the kitchen island. "Hey, Aurora," Ruby greeted grimly. "You heard about Liz Hannigan?"

"Yeah. I'm surprised you're not at the shop. I suppose you'll need some help."

Her aunt nodded wearily. "I couldn't face another day of it. I took the afternoon off. That poor girl."

"I haven't seen you since you got back," Aurora said, trying to lighten the mood. "How was your trip?"

"Oh, it was great."

"So did he..." She left the question hanging.

"No. I shouldn't have gotten my hopes up. But I didn't let it ruin my time. We stayed in a beautiful resort, got massages and facials."

Aurora laughed. "Blaine got a facial?"

"Well, he is a very modern guy. He works with his hands, but he likes to feel pretty sometimes. So, did anything happen with Sable?"

"Huh? No. He just came over and studied."

"But...I thought maybe there was something happening there. I definitely saw some sparks."

"I don't really know what you mean. We just studied."

"Okay." Ruby stared at her a moment in concern. "Are you okay?"

"Why do people keep asking me that? I'm fine. Everything's great."

"Okay. Well...I know better than to push a teenage girl when she doesn't want to talk."

Aurora jumped when Ruby's cell phone vibrated beside her.

"Oh, that's just Blaine," Ruby said, glancing at the message.

"I guess the weekend wasn't enough, huh?"

Ruby laughed. "I guess not. He's taking me out for dinner. Then we'll probably have a quiet night in."

"That sounds nice. Is Dad staying with Julia tonight?"

"You know him. If not for us, he would have already moved out."

"It wouldn't be so bad."

"We could just live here together, and he could go live there," Ruby said, smiling. "We'd just be two girls, having a nice time. What do you think?"

"It sounds pretty much the way it is already."

Ruby laughed. "Yeah, that's true. Well, I'd better get ready." She pointed at Aurora with mock sternness. "And you had better do your homework, young lady."

Aurora rolled her eyes. "Is that what you call two girls having a nice time?"

"Well, if I'm going to be the boss of you, I thought I would get a head start."

Aurora laughed and followed her up the stairs, veering off into her own room. She turned on her radio and unpacked her backpack, but she didn't open her books. She lay back on her bed and closed her eyes for a moment.

Two men were fighting in the trees. They looked strange. She saw short, sharp teeth and livid, scarred red skin. Not men. They weren't men. They were monsters.

Someone was kissing her. Her head spun, and her chest fluttered. She was happy. She'd never been so happy in her life. She was in love. She knew, in that moment, as his lips pressed against hers, that she loved him.

She awoke with a gasp, looking around in disorientation. Tendrils of dreams drifted away. She squeezed her eyes shut to cling onto them, but they were already gone.

She pressed her hand to her chest. It ached as though something had been torn from her, something she needed to know, needed desperately to remember.

It was gone. There was nothing to cling to. She threw her legs over the side of the bed. Night had just begun to fall, but she couldn't sleep now. The house was empty. Ruby must have gone while she'd been asleep. Her father might not have even come home.

The evening air was warm and clear. The sun was still too bright for the stars to appear. She frowned as she stared up at the dark blue sky. It was wrong. There were no stars. It was too early for--

For what?

She didn't know. She trudged to the park nearby and sat on a bench. She waited. She didn't know for what she was waiting. She closed her eyes.

Sable Jayne.

That was it. She had been dreaming of Sable Jayne. But why would she dream of him? She hadn't thought about him in—when had she last thought of him? She couldn't remember thinking of him at all.

She sighed and leaned back against the stiff, wooden seat.

438

Night fell, and the stars shone above, but nothing happened.

* *

Sable's phone vibrated on the seat beside him. He glanced down at it and scowled. He flipped it open. "What do you want, Van?"

Van didn't sound smug or amused. He was deadly serious. "The police came by to ask me more questions."

"What did you do this time?"

"Nothing. They are still asking about Sierra."

"What did they say?"

"They asked if I knew a guy in his late thirties with short, light hair. Average looking."

"Why?"

"They said some witnesses came forward and described a guy they saw Sierra with a few days before she died." He sounded angry.

"Oh."

"He might also have been at the bar on Friday night. He might have been talking to the new dead girl, Lisa or whatever her name is."

"So that's our guy."

"Yeah. It must be. He's a person of interest. The police are looking for him to ask him some questions. They want to know if he noticed anything unusual about the girls before they died, but no one seems to know his name."

"They don't think being seen with both dead girls is a coincidence?"

"I'm sure they do, but what can they do about it? They don't suspect murder."

"Right. So no one knows his name?"

"I'm at the bar right now. A couple people said they saw him with Daniels a few times, but he keeps to himself most of the time. He pays cash for everything."

Sable caught his breath. "It's his partner. Troy Hallow."

"Yeah, I'd already caught onto that."

"Why didn't you just say so?" Sable snapped.

"I knew you'd get there."

Sable cursed. "He is supposed to be gone."

"Well, apparently, he's back. Or at least he was back when the girl died."

"But why? Daniels wasn't even around."

"How the hell should I know? I haven't had a chance to ask him."

"This is getting ridiculous. What's the point of being a monster if we can't even identify each other?"

Van chuckled humorlessly. "He isn't at the bar."

"Great. Meet me at the Coventry Inn. If he's back, he might have checked back in."

"I'll see you there in a few minutes."

* * *

Aurora stared up at the sky. Her mother had loved the stars. She loved the stars, too, but there was something wrong about them tonight. There was nothing left in them. There was nothing to see but twinkling dots in the sky. Had they gone blind?

There was something she should remember about them. Something was missing. There was something missing inside her. There was hole. She knew it now with such sudden certainty that her chest tightened painfully.

She couldn't breath. Tears streamed down her cheeks. She closed her eyes.

She felt arms around her. Strong, warm arms. For a moment, the sensation was so real, so intense and physical it might have been a real memory. Then the sensation passed, and the same feeling of terrible loss washed over her. She exhaled in a quiet sob.

Her mother...she'd loved the stars. She was gone.

But, no. It was something else. Something that gnawed at the back of her mind.

Aurora sunk down in the middle of the sidewalk, wrapping her arms around her legs. She lowered her head and wept into her knees.

* * *

440

Ruby hummed cheerfully as she stepped into the house. "Aurora? Are you here?"

Aurora wasn't in her room. Perhaps she'd met up with Josie and Diana. Or maybe she was secretly seeing that Sable Jayne and just didn't want to talk about it. She smiled at the idea. Not her Aurora Sky. Aurora wasn't the type to keep secrets. She simply wasn't good at it.

She hurried to her room to pack a change of clothes. The shop would be bustling in the morning with the recent death. She should go in early after taking the afternoon off.

The door banged open downstairs. "Blaine? What's wrong? I thought you were going to meet me at your place."

His dark eyes were wide and wild. "We have to get out of here."

"What?"

"We have to leave."

She cocked her head at him in confusion. "I'm just packing a change of clothes. I thought you wanted to stay in at your place tonight."

He strode toward her and gripped her shoulders. She'd never seen him look so desperate. "No, I mean we have to leave New Coventry. Now."

"We just did. We spent the whole weekend away. I have to run the shop--"

"That's not what I mean! I have to get you out of here. You're in danger."

"Blaine, I don't know what's going on," she said as he tugged her toward the door. "Just talk to me! I can't just leave."

He ignored her. He was extremely strong. She struggled. "Ruby, come on!"

"Blaine! Stop and just tell me what's going on!"

"I can't explain! We just have to go!"

"But my family and the shop--"

"There's no time for that! You're all in danger." He stopped suddenly. "Where's Aurora?"

Ruby's eyes widened. "Aurora? Is she in danger, too?"

"I don't know."

Fear curled around her belly. "I don't know where she is. She must have gone out."

Blaine cursed. "Then we have to leave her. Come on. I have to get you somewhere safe."

"Blaine Daniels, I am not going anywhere with you! If I am in danger, you had better explain yourself, and I am not leaving without Aurora!"

His expression was grim. "It might already be too late."

"Blaine, I don't understand. What happened to you? Are you drunk or on drugs or something?"

He wasn't listening. He stiffened the air like a dog catching a scent. "Oh, no." His voice was a whisper.

"What? What is it?"

She jumped at the sudden pounding on the door.

"Don't answer it!"

"But, Blaine—"

"Don't!"

She looked at him as though he was a dangerous animal. "This is ridiculous." She started toward the door, but he tugged her back toward him. She glared at him. The door banged open. Ruby looked toward it in surprise. "Troy?"

"Hello, Ruby," he greeted cheerfully. He grinned at Blaine. "Hello, partner."

* * *

Van was already waiting outside the Coventry Inn when Sable pulled up, vaulting out of the car. "Have you been inside?"

"I was waiting for you." Van looked strange. His body vibrated with tension. "I didn't want to risk—doing something stupid."

Sable understood completely.

The front desk clerk was a young, pretty girl in her late twenties. She smiled at them as they approached her. "Hi," she greeted brightly. "How can I help you?"

"We're looking for Troy Hallow," Sable told her before Van could say anything.

She tilted her head at them. "I'm sorry, Mr. Hallow isn't here."

"Where is he?" Van asked through gritted teeth.

She studied him warily. Sable smiled at her, though he felt his body might snap with tension. "Has he checked back into his room recently?"

"No. I haven't seen him since he checked out a week or so ago." She furrowed her brow and leaned over to whisper, "Is this about those girls who died?"

"What?" Van asked.

"I just heard that description on the news of the guy they're looking for. It sounded like Mr. Hallow."

"We're not looking for him for that," Sable assured her. "He's just an old friend. We wanted to catch up."

She smiled back at him. "Well, I'm sure he had nothing to do with those deaths. He seems like a really nice guy. If he came back into town, he hasn't come back here. If the police are looking for him, though, I guess he might already be gone again. I'm sorry I couldn't be more help." She leaned toward them to speak quietly. "I don't know him that well, but do you think he knows something about how those girls who died?"

"I thought those deaths were accidents," Sable said in a low voice.

"Accidents? Six people found in weird places all dried up like that? It sounds like some kind of vampire or something."

"Vampires aren't real," Sable and Van replied in unison.

She looked disappointed. "You two aren't any fun at all."

"Thanks for the information," Sable told her. He jerked his head at Van. They stopped to face each other in the parking lot.

"That was a waste of time."

"If he isn't here, where is he?"

"How the hell should I know? He's probably out at the bar trolling for his next victim."

"Yeah. Actually, that's not a bad idea. Let's go." Sable paused to turn back to his brother. "Just because we're working together doesn't mean we're good. I just want you to know that."

"Whatever. I want to find the person who killed Sierra. I don't care about you."

"Good. Let's go."

* * *

Blaine stepped in front of Ruby. His shoulders tensed. "What are you doing here?"

Ruby smiled bemusedly. "Hey, Troy. I wasn't expecting you."

"No. But I see my partner was."

Ruby laid a hand on Blaine's shoulder. "What's going on?"

Blaine ignored her. "Troy, you need to leave."

Troy's smile didn't waver. "What's the matter? I thought we were friends. I thought we shared everything."

Blaine narrowed his eyes. "Not her."

"Are you telling me you care about this human?" Troy laughed.

"Blaine, what's going on?" Ruby whispered in alarm.

"Ruby," Blaine said quietly. "Run. Out the back."

She didn't have to be told twice. She bolted toward the backdoor. Troy lunged for her, but Blaine threw himself at his partner with a snarl. They stumbled back against the wall. Troy was the stronger of the two. He seized Blaine by the throat and bent his head toward him.

Ruby couldn't see what Troy was doing, but when he stepped away from his partner, Blaine's eyes looked glazed and empty. "Ruby." His voice was strange and hollow.

She turned toward him uncertainly. Something was wrong. He looked wrong. She turned to run, but he strode forward so quickly, his arms were clamped around her before she got a few feet into the kitchen. He looked down at her, but she knew he wasn't really seeing her. There was something feral and hungry in his eyes. They glowed red.

She opened her mouth to scream. He bent down and pressed his mouth to hers. She struggled for only a moment, shoving at his shoulders. Her head spun. Sharp pain seized her entire body but only for a moment. Then she felt light, like she was floating languidly away, drifting out of her body.

She slackened in Blaine's arms.

The last thing she heard was Troy's laughter.

Blaine pulled away. His eyes cleared. He looked down at the body in his arms. It was nearly unrecognizable, but her long, red hair was unmistakable. Horror shot through him. "No. Ruby! No!"

He dropped her and stumbled back.

Troy was waiting for him. He clapped a hand to his shoulder. "How did that feel, brother?" His voice was a purr. "It felt good, didn't it? Letting it all go, doing what you're meant to do?"

Blaine spun on him. His eyes were huge and dark. They glistened with furious tears. " You made me do that! How could you make me do that? I loved her! She was mine!"

Troy's lip curled. "She was human. And now she is exactly what humans are meant to be." He looked down at the dried, crumbling husk that had once been the woman Blaine loved. "Leftovers." Blaine rushed at him, wrapping his hands around his neck. Troy laughed and caught his arms, patting him on the back. "Now, now. You know why you had to do it, brother."

"No! I didn't want to."

"You did want to. You were just pretending you didn't." Troy leaned back to look at him. "Come with me. Forget this town. Forget the human woman. She's gone. Let's go back to where we belong."

"No! You did this!" His face changed. He bared his teeth. He lunged at Troy.

Troy shoved him away with little effort. "Don't be ridiculous. You did this, Blaine. It was you. You killed her. *Ruby.* You killed your girlfriend because you are a monster, and you cannot be with humans. You will always hurt them in the end. Always."

"No! I could have controlled it—you made me! I didn't want to."

"Stop acting so weak!" Troy's face changed in an instant. His red eyes bore into Blaine's. "We're brothers! We are the same. You and that woman were not the same. And now she is dead. Come back to your people. Stop acting like a child. Now that she's gone, it's time to give up this charade and come home."

Blaine spun away from him, pushing his hands though his shaggy blonde hair. He turned back to Troy. His voice sounded weary and resigned. "You shouldn't have done this."

445

"I had to prove a point."

The back door opened. Aurora trudged inside, looking downcast. She stopped dead in her tracks when she saw her aunt. Her eyes widened. "Ruby? Ruby!" She rushed toward her, dropping to her knees beside the body.

"Aurora," Troy purred. "I was hoping I'd get to see you before I left."

Her head snapped up to look at him. Stricken tears streamed down her cheeks.

She knew his face—the monster's face. She'd seen it before. Oh, she'd seen it, and somehow she'd forgotten. How had she forgotten?

She scrambled back from Ruby's body. "You did this," she whispered in horror. "You're monsters. I remember. I know what you are. You killed her!"

"Aurora--" Blaine said.

Troy was still smiling. He held out his hand. "Don't, Blaine. Don't treat her as anything more than she is." He was upon her in seconds, lifting her up by the collar. "Now don't you go anywhere, Aurora."

Blaine caught his arm. "Don't! She's just a child!"

"Are you protecting her? After everything? I assure you, she isn't a child." He dragged a sharp fingernail across Aurora's neck. She trembled. "And her essence is so pure and innocent. She hasn't been tainted by the trials of life yet."

Aurora struggled to break free, but he was so strong. "No!" Blaine growled. "You've gone far enough." He yanked Aurora away from Troy, shoving her behind him.

Troy's eyes flashed red. "Be very careful, Blaine. Think about what you're doing." He gestured toward Aurora with utter disgust. "For this human! For this human girl who means nothing!"

"I'm not going to let you kill her." He reached behind him and shoved at Aurora. "Run, Aurora!"

Troy flew at him, forgetting Aurora completely. "You weak, pathetic child!" He yanked Blaine toward him and pressed his mouth to his.

Aurora didn't move. She wasn't seeing Blaine or Troy any longer. Memories flashed in her mind of the night Sable had done the same to Van, the night Mariah had bent over her just the same and took everything away.

She remembered. She remembered everything. She gasped for breath.

She snapped back to the scene before her. Blaine's body had grown slack in Troy's arms.

She stumbled back, but Troy lifted his head to look at her. He tossed Blaine negligently aside and stalked toward her. "Alone at last," he said in a low, garbled voice. His eyes were wild and feral, and his sharp teeth bared in a smile. "I'm going to enjoy this. I've been thinking about it since the moment I saw you."

She threw up her hands, but he caught her in his arms. She struggled, and he let her. He seemed to be enjoying her fear. He laughed. She reached up a hand to claw at his cheek, but his skin burned the tips of her fingers. She remembered what Sable had said. She called out for him in her desperation, as though he might hear her.

And then he was there, or someone who looked like him was there.

It was Van. He burst into the house and grabbed Troy, his teeth sharpened as he opened his mouth in a snarl. His face swirled and burned and changed. Aurora remembered everything.

Troy was too surprised to fight back. Van had descended upon him before he had a chance to fight.

"Aurora. Aurora!"

She looked up into Sable's face. He caught her in his arms and dragged her away from his brother and his prey. "Are you all right? Did he hurt you?"

"No, he—Sable." Her voice broke. She clung to him, sobbing into his chest. "Sable." She looked up at him, catching his face abruptly in her hands. She pressed her lips to his, tightening her arms around his neck as though she might never let him go.

"You remember."

"I remember."

"All of it?"

"Most of it."

Van looked human again when he met them in the kitchen. His expression was grim, but his eyes glowed with some wild, unidentifiable triumph. "He's dead. They're all dead. What the hell are we going to do now, Sable?"

447

Aurora stepped back to look up at Van. "Ruby?"

"She's gone. I'm sorry."

Aurora's knees went out. Sable caught her before she fell. "Ruby."

"Aurora, we have to get out of here."

She didn't hear him. She looked up at him with wide, stricken eyes. "What am I going to tell my dad? His sister...Oh, god. I should have remembered. If I had just remembered! I could have warned her before—"

"Aurora, stop. This is not your fault."

"We don't have time for this. We have to get out of here!" Van growled. "Now. Mom and Dad will know what to do."

In the look that passed between them, Sable knew all the anger and the animosity between them had passed.

"You know they aren't going to be happy," Van said. "Aurora...they might do it again."

She lifted her chin. "I won't let them."

He chuckled humorlessly. "I don't think you're going to have much of a choice."

She looked at Sable. There was something awful in his face. He looked so terribly sad, she felt her heart wrench. "I remembered once. I'll remember again. I'm not going to let them take you from me."

He kissed the top of her head. She could feel the desperation as he gripped her arms. "Come on," Van said. "We need to sort this out before anyone finds the three dead bodies in your house."

"They're really dead?"

"I'm so sorry, Aurora," Sable told her.

"I know Ruby's—I mean them. Troy and Blaine. Can you kill each other that way?"

"It's the same for us as humans," Van replied. "They are dead. I made sure."

She let out a hysterical laugh. "Man, my dad is going to be so mad if he gets home before we clean this up."

Chapter Twenty-One

Mariah and Adam stared at them in silence. Aurora looked up at Sable's stiff back as he stood protectively in front of her. "So you found them," Adam said finally.

"Yes," Van replied.

Sable crossed his arms over his chest.

"And they are dead."

"Yes."

"But now we have three dead bodies in Aurora's house we have to dispose of," Adam continued.

"Yes."

They peered at each other in silence a moment. Mariah looked down at Aurora. Sable tensed. His mother did not move any closer. "Aurora, I am sorry about your aunt."

Aurora took a hitching breath. "Thank you." She wiped the tears from her cheeks. "What are we going to do?"

"You are not going to do anything," Sable told her. "We will take care of it."

"But it's my house—"

"This is not your fight, Aurora," Adam said.

"It is my fight! They came after me! They killed my aunt! I'm in this, and you can't take it away from me again."

Mariah looked at her youngest son. "She has recovered her memory?"

"Yes."

"All of it?"

"I remember," Aurora told her defiantly. "And I know what you did. You tried to make me forget. You tried to take Sable away. It didn't work."

Adam and Mariah exchanged a glance. "You were feeding off her regularly," Adam said. "Perhaps she has become resistant to you."

"If you try again, I will remember again," Aurora said. "You can't take it from me."

Mariah nodded reluctantly. "Yes. I believe you might actually be right. That is unfortunate."

Sable tensed. "What are you going to do?"

Adam looked at his son. There was a terrible sadness in his eyes. "She is not resistant to me."

"No," Aurora said, gripping Sable's hand. "Please. Don't do it again. It was horrible. I felt like there was nothing inside me--"

"That's not important right now!" Van snapped. "We have to figure out what to do with the bodies. We do not have unlimited time."

"Yes. You are right," Adam agreed. "We have to get them out of the house. The last thing we want is for Aurora to have to explain them."

"That seems so...so horrible," Aurora whispered. "So disrespectful."

"Would you prefer to explain how they got there?"

"No."

Sable tightened his fingers around hers.

"Van, Sable, you need to get the bodies out of there. Take them somewhere they won't be found for a while."

"No. I will go with Van," Mariah put in. "Sable should stay with Aurora."

Her husband scowled. "I will not have my wife dragging dead bodies around town."

She rolled her eyes. "It wouldn't be the first time. Don't do anything to them until I come home. We need to talk about this."

"Fine." He turned to Sable and Aurora. "Enjoy the time you have left."

With that, he turned and strode from the room. Mariah jerked her head at Van. He followed her out, glancing back at his brother with a strange, unreadable expression.

When they were alone, Aurora looked up at Sable with wide, terrified eyes.

"Come with me." He held his hand out to her. She took it without hesitation and followed him in silence to his bedroom. She barely registered the band posters on the walls or the comic books scattered around the room.

She didn't care what it looked like. She was with him now. It would be the very last time.

He reached for her, wrapping her into his arms. He wiped the tears from her eyes. "Is he going to erase my memory again?"

"No," he said vehemently. "I won't let him. I will take you away from here first."

"We can't just run away."

"But we could be together."

"I want to be with you, Sable, but...my aunt just died. I am all my father has left now. I can't just leave him here alone, never knowing what happened to me."

"We could come back. You could explain."

"No. Sable. We can't just run."

"But they will take us away from each other again!" He pressed her fiercely against his chest. "I don't want to lose you again. I was...Aurora, it was awful watching you in school, knowing what we were to each other and seeing nothing in your eyes when you looked at me."

She tightened her arms around his waist. "If he does...I remembered once. I can remember again. You have to promise to make me remember."

He tried to smile. "I'll do everything I can to make you remember."

"Can I fight it? Can I do something to hold onto my memory?"

"No."

"But...but this last time, I felt it. I knew something was missing. I didn't know it was you, not even when I looked at you."

"Never?" His eyes were oddly glassy.

"Maybe—maybe for a second. When you stopped me outside class, for just a second, I thought—and then I dreamed about you."

"You did?"

"I felt like something had been torn out of me. But tonight, tonight I *knew*."

His smile was so sad, she felt as though the earth might shatter at any moment. "I'm sorry, Aurora. I'm sorry it's like this."

"It's not your fault, Sable. You didn't choose to be what you are, and I can't help how I feel about you."

"I would give anything to be human," he whispered, leaning his forehead against hers.

"Would you? But you're different. You're something special."

"If I were normal, we wouldn't have all these dead bodies lying around."

"No, Sable. If you were normal, I would be dead because it wasn't you who killed them, and you wouldn't have been able to stop the ones who did. You saved me. And Van helped you. I have to say, I did not see that coming."

He laughed half-heartedly. "Actually, neither did I. I think he was more interested in avenging Sierra. I think he really cared for her."

"Why did they let him have her, and they won't let us be together?"

"I don't think they thought it meant anything. And she didn't know anything about us."

"It's not fair."

He pulled her down to sit beside him on the bed. He wrapped an arm around her shoulders. As one, they fell back to lay side by side against his pillows. He leaned over to kiss the top of her head. "I know."

For a long time, they didn't speak. When he kissed her, she closed her eyes and tried to pretend it wouldn't be the last time. She could feel the desperation in his touch.

"I won't let them take you away from me, Aurora," he whispered fiercely. "I will fight it. I will fight for you. Even if you do forget me, I will keep coming back for you until you fall in love with me again. I don't care how many times I have to do it."

"What if—what if they make you leave?"

"No. It's over now. We stopped Troy and Blaine. No one will ever know what we are."

She laid her head against his chest. "As long as you don't have to leave... eventually I will get my memories back. I'll know." She rose up on her elbow to look down at him. "Maybe we could have a safe word or something."

"What? A safe word? Are you sure that means what you think it means?"

She ignored him. "Like, if I forget you, you can say something so I'll know what I've forgotten."

"Okay. Like what?"

"Something they won't know to take. Something that has nothing to do with us. They didn't take my other memories. Just you. Wait!" Her eyes lit up.

"What?"

She fumbled her phone from her pocket. She lay back down beside him and held the camera above their heads. "Smile." She snapped a photo. "Now I'll know what it is I've forgotten. When it gets awful and empty and feels like I'm being torn apart from the inside, I'll be able to find you again."

"Don't let him see it."

"I won't." She tucked it back into her back pocket, threading her fingers through his. "You just have to remind me it's there."

"And I'll remind you that you like it when I do this." He leaned over her and kissed her neck. She giggled. He cut her off, pressing his mouth against hers. She wrapped her arms around him and clung to him as he rolled on top of her.

"Just kiss me," she whispered against his lips. "You don't have to say anything. Just kiss me, and I think that will be enough. Even when I'd forgotten, I hadn't forgotten how this felt. I never stopped remembering it."

He drew back enough to look into her eyes. "Yeah?"

"I'll never forget."

He didn't say anything more for a long time. She could taste salt on his lips as she lost herself in his kisses. She could feel tears on their cheeks. She didn't know whose they were. It didn't matter.

It might have been hours or mere moments. Sable stiffened above her as they heard voices murmuring outside the door. "Aurora, it's time. He's going to do it. I know he is." He lowered his head to kiss her. She felt his lips tremble against hers. "The picture, Aurora. Don't worry. I won't let you go. We'll be all right."

She buried her face in his chest as she clung to him. "Sable."

"Don't be scared. They won't hurt you."

"Yes, they will," she whispered. She looked up at him. Fresh tears streamed from the corners of her eyes into her long, strawberry blonde hair. "It hurts when you're gone."

He cupped her cheek in his hand, brushing her tears away with the pad of his thumb. "I'll remind you. I swear I will."

Adam rapped his knuckles once against the door. "Sable."

"We have to go," Sable told her, and now she reached up to wipe a tear from his cheek. "If he has to come in for us, it will be worse." They didn't let go of each other's hands as they walked to the door. Adam was already gone. Sable nodded encouragingly at Aurora. "We'll be all right. Come on. He's waiting for us."

Van wasn't in Adam's office when they walked in side by side. Mariah looked at them gravely. "It is done. I am sorry, Aurora, but your aunt will be found in due course. I am sorry we could not give her the respect she deserves."

She felt Sable's hand tightened around hers.

Mariah's expression softened. "I am sorry for this as well, Sable, Aurora. You know what we must do."

"Please don't do it again," Aurora pleaded one last time. "It hurt so badly the last time."

Mariah lowered her head, and Adam spoke for her. "I am truly sorry, child, but we must do this."

"I promise I won't tell anyone."

"It is not simply a matter of you revealing our secret, Aurora. It is a matter of life and death."

She took an involuntary step backward. Sable moved in front of her. "Dad, please--"

Adam did not shove him aside or reach for Aurora. He seized Sable by the collar and yanked him forward. Aurora's body turned to ice. Adam's face changed, and the air around them shifted.

Then Aurora understood. She tried to rush forward, but Mariah caught her in her arms, pressing her into a hug. She could feel the older woman shaking. "No. No! Stop! Please! Don't do this! Please! Dr. Jayne, you can't let him do this--"

"I'm so sorry, Aurora," Mariah murmured in her ear. "I'm so sorry."

454

Aurora sobbed into her shoulder. Her knees gave out. Mariah dropped to the floor with her as Adam released his son. Sable staggered backward like a drunken man. He spun toward his mother and Aurora on the floor, but the blank, glassy expression did not change.

"Sable, go to your room and get some sleep," Adam ordered in a low, gentle voice.

Sable nodded absently. "Sable," Aurora moaned. He did not even turn to look back at her as he marched mechanically out of the room. He was gone. They had taken him from her before, but he had remembered. He had known all along. Now there would be no one to remind her.

Mariah caressed her cheek so tenderly Aurora let out an anguished sob. "Aurora, dear, don't fight it. You know there is no sense in it. It is for the best."

Adam kneeled beside her. "I will attempt to make it painless."

She looked into his burning red face. There was no fear any longer. There was something so much worse, much more terrible than fear. She took a hitching breath as he leaned toward her. She tried to move away from him, but Mariah's curiously soothing arms held her firmly.

Pain surged through her body. It wasn't physical pain. The loss of her mother, of Ruby, and now of Sable was like an invisible, gaping wound in her chest. She held onto it, clung to the pain as long as she could. She tried to remember it. She could remember this pain. It wouldn't go away. It would stay forever. She would *make* it stay forever.

And then she felt nothing at all.

Chapter Twenty-Two

Aurora stared blankly down at her soggy cereal. She swirled the spoon around. She didn't even look up at her father as he walked into the room She hardly registered the redness around his eyes. "Aurora."

She snapped out of her fugue. "What's up, Dad?" She focused on his face. "What's wrong?"

"It's...it's your aunt."

"What?" She shot to her feet. "What about her?"

"She--" He cut off, passed a hand across his forehead. "I'm sorry, Aurora. I don't know how to tell you...She's dead."

"What? When? How?"

"It was another...another illness."

"Like the others?" Her voice was barely audible.

"Yes. She and Blaine and Troy. They found them all together."

"Oh, god." She rushed forward and wrapped her arms around him. He hugged her tightly. "I'm sorry, Dad. I don't...how did this happen?"

"I don't know." He took a hitching breath. "My big sister."

"Dad..." He leaned back to look at her. Her heart wrenched. She hadn't seen him look so sad since...since her mother. It wasn't fair. He shouldn't have to do this twice. Not so soon. "Does Chris know?"

"Not yet."

"I'll call him."

"No. I think I should be the one. You shouldn't have to do that."

She swiped at the tears streaming down her cheeks. Suddenly, they felt horribly familiar. The night the policeman had shown up at their house with the terrible news about her mother seemed just days ago. Her stomach ached, and her head spun wildly. She stumbled out of her dad's arms to sit back down on the stool. She moaned softly and pressed her hands to her head.

"Rory? Are you okay?"

"It's just--" She choked off with a sob.

"Why don't you go upstairs and lie down? I'll call Chris." He stared off into space for a moment. "I have to...I have to make plans for the funeral."

"Who will make the flower arrangements?" She'd asked the same question when her mother had died.

Her father didn't have an answer. He hadn't had an answer the last time, either. She trudged up the stairs and collapsed on her bed. She fumbled for her phone and dialed a number. By the time Josie answered, she was crying too hard to speak.

"Aurora?" Josie sounded shocked. "What's wrong?"

"Ruby," she managed to croak. "Dead."

"What? Oh my god! Aurora, do you want me to come over?"

She had to think very hard about this. She wanted someone. Josie wasn't the right one. She needed someone else. Ruby. It must be Ruby, but she couldn't have Ruby because Ruby was gone forever, and she would never have her again. She would never see her smile or share secrets or smell flowers...

"Yeah," she said finally.

"Okay. I'll call Diana. We'll be right over."

"Thanks, Josie."

They were there in record time, charging up to her room to find her lying on her bed, staring up at the fading stars on her ceiling. She swiveled her eyes to look at them as they entered, but she did not move. Her stomach ached so badly, she though she might be sick if she did.

"Oh, Rora!" Josie exclaimed, hurrying to her side.

Aurora pushed herself up, gritting her teeth against the nausea. They wrapped their arms around her, and she sobbed into their shoulders.

"I can't believe it," Diana murmured, stroking her hair gently.

"How did it happen?" Josie asked.

"Like...like the others. Like Sierra."

"Oh, my god. What is happening?" Diana sounded as though she was struggling not to cry.

"I don't know. I hope...I know it's horrible, but I hope it doesn't happen to me and my dad, too."

"Aurora, the police are certain it is not a contagious disease," Diana assured her firmly. "It's something else."

"But it just doesn't make sense," Aurora whispered. "I wonder...I mean, could someone do this?"

"What do you mean?"

"I mean...could it be something else? Could there be someone who's done something to them?"

"Like murder?" Josie asked incredulously.

"Well...yes."

"I don't...I don't think so, Aurora. If it is, it's nothing like anyone has ever seen before," Diana said. "The police are sure it's not a person."

"But what if...it's just so strange," Aurora whispered, pressing her hand to her forehead.

"Oh, Aurora, I am so sorry!" Josie burst out. "I'm so sorry it was Ruby!"

"And Blaine," she said absently. "He was with her. He and Troy. It's so sad. They were so happy. She liked him so much. They were probably going to get married, and–god, my dad has to tell Chris. I don't even know if he knows what's been going on here. He hasn't come back since before the first deaths. He's never even had a dad, and now he doesn't have a mom."

"Aurora," Diana said in alarm. Aurora went on, ignoring her.

"I know. I know how it feels to lose your mom. You never...you never ever get over it. I wish he didn't have to--" She cut off with a sob.

"When is the funeral?" Josie whispered.

"I don't know. We just found out. My dad will have to plan it. At least...at least he's done it before. I don't think it will make it any easier."

Diana wrapped her into a hug. "I'm so sorry, Aurora."

"Do you need anything?" Josie asked. "Chocolate? Ice cream? Cheetos?"

Aurora laughed through her tears and leaned back to look at her incredulously. "Cheetos? No thanks. Just..." Her stomach clenched painfully. "I feel like...like nothing is ever going to be right again."

"It is, Aurora," Diana said fiercely. "You have to believe that. It was okay after your mom died, right?"

"I...I thought it was, for a while. Then...something happened. I don't even know what it was. Something awful. Everything is all wrong now. I'm all wrong."

They exchanged a worried glance. "It's going to be okay, Aurora," Josie told her, patting her back. "It won't feel like this forever."

She took a hitching breath. "I hope not. It feels like everything is just... gone. Empty. Like there's a hole in me. I think it started even before Ruby, and I can't figure out why."

* * *

Sable rose to pace the room. He'd been shiftless for days. His parents, dressed in black for the funeral, exchanged a worried look. "Another funeral," Adam said darkly. "I hate these things."

"Try to be respectful," Mariah told him. "You know why we have to go."

"Hopefully it will be the last, at least under these circumstances."

She squeezed his arm. "Yes, I hope so too." She glanced at her son. "Are you all right, Sable?"

His eyes looked strange and empty. He wasn't seeing her at all. "Why wouldn't I be? I didn't know them or anything. I don't know why I have to go."

"We have to keep up appearances."

"At least it's over," he muttered to himself.

"Yes, Sable." His father laid a hand on his shoulder. "It's over."

"Where is your brother?" Mariah asked.

"He doesn't care about the funeral. He isn't coming."

Mariah sighed. She sat down on the sofa to await her daughter and sister. They arrived moments later. Elise glanced at her nephew. "How are you, Sable?"

"Why does everyone keep asking me that? I'm fine. Let's just go and get this over with."

Sable was silent on the ride to the church. He was silent through the service as Ruby Geller's friends and family stood up beside the closed coffin to make tearful speeches about her life and her kindness and her vivacity. He wasn't listening. He didn't know her at all. He'd seen her once or twice, but he couldn't remember a thing about her besides her long, red hair and a strong, almost achingly familiar scent of flowers.

His eyes strayed to her family. He knew her niece. Aurora. He'd seen her in school. They might even have a class together. She sat beside an older boy who was stiff beside her, his jaw set to hold back the tears he didn't want anyone to see. She was weeping into her hands. Her long, strawberry blonde hair fell around her face like a veil. Her pain was almost tangible. Something twisted in his gut.

He tried to look away from her, but something held him rapt. He felt ill. He took a shuddering breath. His chest ached so abruptly and so terribly the pain stole his breath. It was as though someone had reached in and torn out a piece of him. He gritted his teeth.

He hadn't even known the victims. He hardly knew their family. The lost, empty, listless feeling made no sense. "Her family is very sad," he said almost to himself.

His mother glanced at him with something like alarm on her face. "Yes. She had a son. And now he is an orphan. Family is important. It is a terrible loss to the Gellers."

Sable nodded slowly. His eyes slid back to Aurora. She lifted her head as the service ended. He'd hardly heard a word of it. He watched her rise to her feet. She looked so pale. Her eyes were red-rimmed, and she swiped at them, but he didn't know why. The tears didn't seem to be stopping. Fleetingly, he wondered if they would ever stop. He wished they would.

She was beautiful. He didn't remember ever noticing it before, but she looked so fragile and tragic and so lost, and he thought he had never seen anyone as beautiful. He blinked in confusion. Why had he thought that? He looked away from her, frowning, and shot to his feet.

"Sable?" Adam asked in a quiet voice. "Is something wrong?"

Unexpected rage surge up in his belly. He glared at his father. "Yes. It's a funeral. Three people are dead. There are a lot of things that are wrong." He turned away from his parents and strode toward the doors.

He paused just inside them and looked over his shoulder at Aurora Geller. She was trying to smile bravely through her tears at the line of people offering comfort and condolences. He could see her desperation to escape, to be alone. For the briefest moment, he thought he should turn around and go to her, to offer some sort of—something. Comfort, commiseration—what did he have to offer her?

And why would he want to? He turned back and walked out into the bright sunlight. It shouldn't have been sunny, not on a day like this. He sighed and pressed his hand to his aching chest.

Something wasn't right. Something was very, very wrong.

* * *

Aurora sobbed into her pillow. It had been days since the funeral, but the awful, empty feeling in her chest hadn't gone. She didn't know if she would ever be whole again. Without Ruby, it felt as though a part of her had been ripped away. She'd never realized how deeply she'd needed her aunt until she was gone. Ruby was the only mother Aurora had since she'd lost Rosalyn.

It was so tragic, so senseless. Ruby had just found Blaine. She'd struggled for so long. She'd tried so hard. Aurora had seen her go through so much pain and heartache, and she'd finally been happy. She'd been so happy the last time Aurora had seen her planning a date with Blaine.

She'd been so in love. She should have gotten her chance to be happy, to be with him.

Aurora missed her. She missed her so terribly the silence in the house was like an open wound. She'd always smelled like flowers. At first, it had hurt Aurora. Her mother had smelled like flowers, but then there was Ruby, so full of life and hope, and now no one smelled like flowers anymore.

She took a hitching breath. It just wasn't fair. She should have had a mother. She should have had an aunt. She should have had—whatever it was that had been torn out of her.

She fumbled for the well-thumbed scrapbook in her desk drawer. When her mother had died, Ruby had painstakingly gathered every photo of Rosa and their family she could find into the book. Aurora couldn't look at it for years after her mother's death, but then it had become her deepest comfort when she started to fear she'd even forget her mother's face.

Don't forget. Remember.

She sighed deeply as she flipped open the scrapbook. Ruby had pressed a blood red rose into the first page. She brushed her fingers over the old, dried petals. Ruby Rose. She took a hitching breath and brushed away her tears before they could stain the delicate flower.

Her mother had been so beautiful when she'd been young. She'd always been beautiful. She looked carefree in the old pictures of she and Aurora's father and Ruby. They all looked so happy. Her father had loved them both so much. She could see it on his face, even in the old, fading photographs.

Blaine had looked at Ruby the way her dad had looked at her mom. It was so eerily familiar.

She sobbed over the photos, reaching out to touch her mother's and Ruby's tiny, unmoving faces. The smooth feel of the cellophane made her heart ache. Ruby had been there when her mother couldn't be. Now there was no one. Her father was trying, but he was a broken man. He'd lost his wife and his only sister. Julia was caring for him now.

They hadn't added any photos to the book, and the empty pages in the back sent a surge of fresh tears into her throat. She would have to be the one to add them now. She didn't even know if she had any photos of Ruby. The last time they'd hung out together was...For a moment, she couldn't remember. It was as though the last few weeks were a strange, spiraling blur. Then she remembered. It was the night before the festival. They'd shopped and gotten their nails done and giggled about boys as though Ruby were her best friend.

Ruby insisted on photographing the entire affair. Ruby loved photos. She had a pile of half-finished scrapbooks in her bedroom and in the back of the shop...who would run the shop now? Aurora knew she could never do it. It had been painful enough to answer phones after her mother had died. She couldn't bear the thought of stepping in there ever again. She couldn't bear the smell of flowers. At the funeral, she felt as though she might suffocate from it.

She snapped the book shut and fumbled for her phone on her nightstand. She opened the photos. They'd been having so much fun that night. She couldn't remember a time she'd felt happier. She'd been so excited to see...

Who had she wanted to see? It hardly mattered now. She couldn't remember seeing anyone the day of the festival.

There weren't any photos of Ruby in her phone. She stared in shock at a photo of herself and Sable Jayne, lying side by side. They were smiling, but there was something so awfully sad in their eyes she gasped.

She tossed the phone away as though it had burned her. Was she going insane? She didn't remember the photo. She hardly remembered anything about Sable at all, except that he was in her English class, and she'd had a fleeting crush on him that hadn't gone anywhere.

When had they taken this?

She scrambled over the side of the bed to pick up the phone. She wasn't even sure the photo would still be there when she looked at it again.

It was there.

She studied it. She didn't recognize the place, but they were lying—on a bed? When had she laid on a bed with Sable Jayne? She looked at the time stamp.

It was just a week ago. But, how could that be? She stared at it. A week ago, she had been...where had she been? She couldn't remember. She remembered looking up at the sky. She remembered stars that had seemed dull and dead and blind.

She didn't remember this photo.

"What's going on?" she whispered. If this had happened, why didn't she remember it?

* * *

Sable lay over the hood of his car, staring unblinkingly up at the stars. There was something up there he needed to find. He sighed deeply. The stars looked different tonight. They looked wrong. There was something missing. Nothing up there made sense.

He heard footsteps on the walk behind him. He didn't bother to glance over at his visitor. He knew it was Van. He knew the timbre of his brother's breath and the weight of his step. He didn't speak to him. For a long moment, Van stood silently beside him.

Sable didn't trouble himself to ask what his brother wanted. He didn't care. Van didn't matter. He was a broken, empty man. He couldn't help Sable. He couldn't help himself.

When Van finally spoke, his voice was uncannily quiet in the darkness, but his words carried to Sable as though he'd shouted.

"They took her away from you."

Sable blinked and sat up to look at him. "What?"

There was no mocking tone in Van's voice. "You forgot her. They made you forget."

"What are you talking about?"

"Aurora."

"Aurora?" He remembered her. He remembered watching her at the funeral. He remembered the strange, painful emptiness he'd felt as he'd looked at her. She'd been so sad, and she'd been so pretty.

He didn't remember anything else.

"They made you forget," Van repeated.

He looked so grave. Sable couldn't see any malice or cruelty in his eyes. Van drew his phone from his pocket and handed it to him.

Sable stared down at the screen in shock. He saw a photo of himself standing beside Aurora in the woods. They were holding hands.

"There's more."

Sable was looking down at her as though she was the answer to everything in the world, as though he'd never wanted anything more in his life. He was kissing her, holding her so tightly against him, there was hardly a breath between their bodies.

Sable's head snapped up. He narrowed his eyes. "How did you get these?"

"I was watching you. When you were with her. They didn't know I had them, or they would have made me erase them."

Sable didn't need to ask about whom he was talking. He knew, and suddenly, everything made sense. "Aurora. She and I?"

"You loved her. She loved you. You forgot, but that doesn't mean it didn't happen. That doesn't mean it isn't true."

"What do you care? Why are you even telling me this?"

Van sighed. He glanced up at the sky. "Despite what you think," he said without looking at his younger brother, "I don't hate you. I shouldn't have told them about you two. It was my fault they found out. It was my fault they took her away. I didn't have the right to do that."

Van was apologizing. Sable didn't remember what Van had done, but he understood. He stared at his brother. Van wouldn't meet his eyes.

Van reached over and snatched his phone back. He strode away.

Sable stared up at the sky. *Aurora Sky*. He didn't remember their time together, but something about the yawning emptiness in his chest and the stars and her name felt right. He spun toward the house and stormed into his mother's office.

She looked up at him in surprise. "Sable?"

"You took her from me." His voice was low and controlled, but his eyes flashed with barely contained fury.

Mariah's mouth tightened. "I don't know what you're talking about."

"Yes, you do. Aurora. You took her from me. You made me forget her. You made her forget me, too, didn't you? You shouldn't have done that."

She took a hitching breath. "You remember?"

"Not yet. I knew something was missing, and now I know what you've taken. I'll remember, and when I do, you won't be able to do it to me again." He turned on his heel and strode toward the door.

"Sable."

There was something indefinably tender in her voice. He turned to look at her.

"Your father won't like it. You know that."

"I don't care, Mom."

Her expression was deadly serious. "Are you sure about this, Sable?"

He met her gaze with absolute certainty. "Yes."

* *

She didn't know what to do. She didn't say much as she walked toward the school with Josie and Diana, and, for once, they didn't ask if she was all right. They already knew. She wasn't all right. She was even less all right than she'd been before she'd found the photo on her phone.

How could she have forgotten it? It had just happened. What had made her forget? She didn't remember being near anyone who could have given her drugs or alcohol. She'd been alone, as far as she remembered.

But she hadn't been alone. She'd been with him. She'd been happy, and she'd been desperately sad.

It was a beautiful, sunny day. It should have been stormy and cold and miserable.

Josie and Diana spoke in hushed voices beside her as though any loud noise would spook her. She didn't mind. She didn't want to join the conversation. She hadn't been to school since the police had discovered Ruby's body. She was missing nearly a week's worth of assignments. She would probably regret it, but she didn't care now.

Everything was spiraling out of control. Christian was a mess. He hadn't returned to school since he'd gotten the news, and Mike was afraid he would flunk the semester. Chris didn't seem to care any more than Aurora did about school. Mike could talk little sense into either of them. He'd been relieved when Aurora had finally returned to school that morning.

Her thoughts were a confused jumble. She couldn't hold one down for longer than a few moments. She didn't understand how she could have forgotten something so significant as what she had seen in her own face in that photo with Sable Jayne.

And then he was suddenly standing in front of her outside the school. She gasped, for the intensity in his eyes was so bafflingly familiar. "Hey," Sable said.

Aurora took a deep breath. "Hey."

"We'll just...ah...catch up with you later, Aurora," Diana said, grabbing Josie's arm to drag her away.

Aurora didn't care that they were whispering feverishly all the way into the building. She didn't glance away from him. "Sable, do you remember--"

"You remember?" he cut in suddenly. His eyes glittered eagerly.

"No, but I have this picture." She drew her phone from her pocket. She'd hardly been able to look away from it since she'd found it. "I don't remember taking it. Do you?"

He held up his own phone. He had them, too. She'd been with him somewhere—in the woods. She'd been holding his hand. She'd been kissing him. She didn't remember a single moment.

She looked up at him in shock. "But I—but I don't--I don't understand."

"It happened, Aurora. We just forgot it."

"No. There's no way I could have forgotten."

He peered down at her, as though trying to find the answer to some mystery in her face. "There is a way. I promise you, there is a way. We were together, Aurora."

"But—when?"

"Very recently."

"My picture is only a week old."

"These aren't much older."

"But—do you remember?"

"No. But it doesn't matter."

He wrapped an arm around her waist and pulled her against him. She opened her mouth in surprise. He bent down and pressed his lips to hers. She didn't even notice the noise around them as their classmates exclaimed in surprise.

Suddenly, the world stopped spinning out of control. Everything narrowed to a single point in the universe. She was in the only right place that was left.

She was with Sable Jayne.

He pulled away and looked down into her face. "It doesn't matter if we've forgotten it. It's not too late. We can start again."

She closed her eyes as he brushed a hand through her long hair. When she opened them again, he was looking down at her with a strange emotion she couldn't identify but which she was suddenly absolutely certain she'd seen in his eyes before.

"If I loved you once," he said, "I will love you again. We'll start again. If we forget again, we'll do it over and over, and eventually, no one will be able to make us forget."

"I have no idea what you're talking about." But she didn't really care as he dipped his head to kiss her again.

"It's okay. It doesn't matter. We're together now. As long as we can be. And then, we'll be together again. We won't let them tear us apart."

"Who?" she whispered. "Who's tearing us apart?"

He didn't answer her. He wrapped her into his arms and rested his chin on the top of her head. She sighed contentedly as the persistent pain in her chest slowly loosened. She could feel his heart thumping against her cheek.

"No. Don't tell me. I don't care. It doesn't matter as long we're together."

"It won't be easy, Aurora. We'll have to be careful. We might have to fight for each other."

She lifted her shoulders. She smiled. "That's okay. I don't remember what happened, but I get the feeling it was worth fighting for."

"So do I."

THE END

ABOUT THE AUTHOR

Stella Drexler is the author of several science fiction and fantasy novels, instruction manuals, essays, articles, and shopping lists. She lives in Dallas, Texas and enjoys doing things that are fun. For more about Stella and her ill-advised adventures, visit her blog Books, Monkeys and Cheeky Dreams at www.stelladrexler.wordpress.com

More books by Stella:

Nightmare Island Book One: False Awakening

Nightmare Island Book Two: Dream Walker

Rebel Grey

Angel of the Abyss

Hex Breaker

CHANT

Little Agnes and the Ghosts of Kelpie Wharf

Divine Disorder: The Unmaking of Everything